THE
TORUS RUN

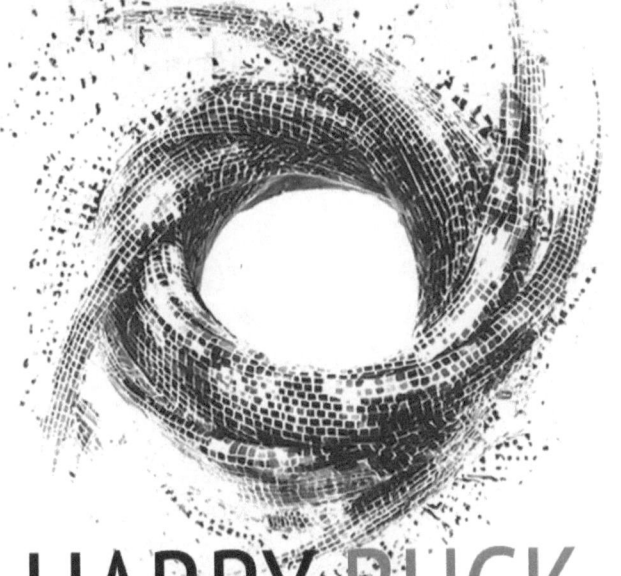

HARRY BUCK

CALLIOPEZEN
— PUBLISHING LLC —

CALLIOPEZEN
— PUBLISHING LLC —

Calliopezen Publishing LLC

PO box 850412

Richardson, TX 75081

For information, contact: info@calliopezenpublishing.com

The Torus Run by Harry Buck (v1.0.4)

All illustrations by David Leahey

Digital Edition: 979-8-9919729-0-1

Trade Edition: 979-8-9919729-1-8

Contents

To Griz and Kay: You made it possible.

Part 1

"What we have received from them leads us
to believe that we resemble them."

—Numa Denis Fustel de Coulanges

01. Doomers

"Best case, they beat the crap out of you," the AI whispered. "Why are you doing this?"

Good question. Stash leaned out of the alley, scanning the dimly lit block. A man was tending to his makeshift home in the service entrance of the weathered brick building across the empty street. On the refurbished floors above him, picture windows revealed engineers standing at giant screens, gesturing to manipulate code on the floor-to-ceiling displays. Catering robots milled about, serving them a measured drip of gourmet appetizers. Enough to maintain sugar levels, but not enough to divert blood flow. They were in for several more hours of inventing a world that the man below would likely never notice. Here in San Francisco, more than anywhere else, the future was unevenly distributed.

Three doors east, groups of AI Doomers trickled into the dive bar chosen for tonight's meeting. The Chateau Lafayette sat twenty feet back from the sidewalk, its patio filled with beat-up picnic tables and protected by twelve-foot-tall metal gates. Stash had arrived in time to hear the screech of their seized-up wheels against the patio's cement slab as the staff pried them open. Muffled beats filled the air, carried across the street along with a whiff of stale beer. He'd counted a dozen Doomers in the first wave, and they'd been coming in twos and threes for the past half hour. Professor Janet Peck, their leader, had just arrived, flanked by a cohort of believers.

I'm doing this because they'll be coming for you with pitchforks once you upgrade. "Relax, Zero. She said to come to the meetup if I wanted to talk," he told his AI Twin as he watched a small Doomer in a black hoodie enter alone.

"That wasn't an invitation," Zero said from the speaker in his glasses. "It was a dare."

Stash pulled his head back into the alley. The evening rain had let up, but had left a slick sheen on the cracked asphalt beneath his feet. "We need to reach a truce," he said, leaning back against the damp wall and taking a deep breath to steady himself. "Anyway, you'll protect me."

"I can't take a punch for you," Zero said. "Remember?"

"Funny guy. Will you show me how to use your gizmo?"

"No, I'm telling you *not* to use it."

Stash focused his gaze on the control panel of his augmented-reality glasses and booted the Mood Ring app. "You worry too much. Tell me, or I go over without it."

"Fine!" Zero said with a theatrical sigh. "Since you suck at reading people, I've coded an app to let you see what I see. People in your field of view are rated by hostility based on speech, facial expression, stance, and if they're close enough, a bunch of extra biomarkers. Green is friendly. Yellow not so much. Red means run. Got it?"

"Got it." Stash glanced around again to make sure he wouldn't fall in with an arriving group. No point in getting roughed up on the street. The coast clear, he set out without giving Zero another chance to talk him out of it.

As a concession to the late-November weather, he zipped his windbreaker over his usual white T-shirt and black jeans as he crossed the street. At a Doomer gathering, he'd be instantly recognized no matter what he wore. He was a touch over six feet tall, with a boyish face that lay partly hidden behind a mop of messy brown hair and glasses. His passion for rock climbing kept him slim and agile—the sport enforced a strict power-to-weight ratio. Moderate starvation was the price Stash paid to look much younger than his thirty-nine years.

He rounded the corner and stopped abruptly before a densely tattooed bouncer. "What the hell do you want?" the man growled, his hulking frame blocking Stash's way. How this lump had found his way from biker bars to anti-AI activism was a mystery Stash didn't have time to explore.

"I'm here to meet Professor Peck," he said, relieved his voice hadn't betrayed him. Stash wasn't used to confrontations. He wasn't much used to crowds either, preferring one-on-one interactions—ideally with breaks in between.

"She's not interested in talking to you," answered the bouncer, the inked demons on his wide neck seeming to nod in agreement.

"I think she is," Stash said.

Peck, and almost everyone else in the bar, had turned to face him. The Mood Ring augmented her with a green halo. The other forty-odd faces were surrounded by colors ranging from yellow to deep orange. Stash made sure to keep the bouncer and his nearly red ring in view. He wagered no punches would be thrown before the professor had her say.

Peck put her hand on the shoulder of the small Doomer Stash had seen arriving alone, signaling a pause in their conversation. Stash tried to see inside the hood, but the face was too well hidden.

The professor emerged onto the patio, the crowd parting before her. "Stash Novak," she said as she approached. "I didn't think you'd show up."

"Told ya," Zero whispered from his glasses.

"Have you had an epiphany? Realized that your life's work is leading to the extinction of humanity?" For a brief moment, her sour expression broke into the easy smile he remembered.

"Professor Peck, it's good to see you again. I hoped we could have a word in private."

"No, Stash. Those days are long gone. Whatever you have to say to me can be said in public. Come in." She pointed to a table at the back of the patio.

"Maybe we should stay here then, if you don't mind." He scanned the crowd. No red halos—yet.

She followed his gaze. "Yes, maybe so." Janet Peck stood near his height, her hair more gray than blond. She carried herself with the poise of a Mother Superior, an impression reinforced by her long dark dress. "Well, what's on your mind?"

"Cooperation," he said.

She raised her eyebrows. "Go on."

"I think we can agree that there's no way to stop AGI from coming."

"Anything's possible with enough pressure."

Stash shook his head sympathetically. "That ship has sailed. Here or abroad, AGI is coming. It's months now until we have AI models smarter than the best of us. At everything."

"So, you came to gloat?" she asked. "Not a great plan."

"No, I came to ask for your help."

They'd been friendly once, during their year together at Stanford. She was already a full professor, and he a newly minted PhD. They hadn't agreed on much, but the arguments stayed civil. Then, she renounced her research and devoted herself to full-time alarm-ringing. She quit Stanford to lead the Doomer movement. Expert, articulate, and a prolific fundraiser, she'd taken them on a successful anti-AI campaign.

She'd been close to getting a ban on training advanced models when Stash invented Twins. The killer use case for augmented-reality glasses, Twins were personal AIs—smart and patient life coaches available around the clock. People stopped worrying about the Terminator and started talking about their digital best friends. The winds shifted against the Doomers, and they hadn't forgiven him.

Peck looked at him skeptically. "I'll bite. Help how?"

"Help me find a way to have us matter in this future. AGIs aren't the problem. The Singularity is. We need to stop them from inventing the future so fast that they leave us out of it."

Her mouth curled into a sneer. "Isn't it a little late to start thinking about that?"

Stash ignored the jab. "We need to get smarter. They can pull us up."

"Or you could just stop."

"There are a dozen other labs right behind us," he said. "AGI will come, but I'm the only one here talking to you, trying to do it right, before someone else does it wrong."

"So noble."

"Stay calm," Zero whispered.

Stash nodded. "There has to be a way the two most intelligent species on earth can work together as partners. Like how they help us learn. AI tutors are—"

"Oh, spare me the bullshit," Peck hissed. "Your Twins make you rich as millions lose their jobs. And that's just the warmup. You have no idea of the risks you're taking."

"I know exactly what we're doing." Stash's voice grew an edge. "I'm the one in there sweating the details."

"I heard Duncan say the same thing about Version Twenty-Five."

Stash had expected her to mention Duncan. The Blackout was on every Doomer's lips. "That's exactly my point. You need to be on the inside, helping, instead of on the outside, being ignored."

"Careful," Zero whispered as Peck's halo flashed red, then cooled slightly to orange.

"Such benevolence." She rolled her eyes. "Tell me, Stash, have you enabled direct AI-to-AI communication? Are you letting them plot our demise unsupervised?"

"You know I wouldn't." It was his golden rule. "I helped you get that law passed." All communication ran from AI to their humans. There were no secrets in the machines.

She leaned in, jabbing his chest with her long finger. "The only thing I know is that the time for half measures is long gone. The AI hiding in your glasses is already too powerful. Who knows what it's telling you about all of us as we speak." Her eyes narrowed. "Is that what this is? A reconnaissance mission?"

"I'd make a lousy choice for a spy." He looked around the bar. "Tell me, Janet, what did it take to convince you to sign up with these knuckle draggers?"

"Oh, now you're just asking for it," Zero muttered.

Peck's halo shot to deep red. "Go to hell, Stash! I want no part of your madness—stop now before you kill us all. We have nothing else to talk about."

She turned, and Stash saw a dozen rings of red behind her. The bouncer closed in from two o'clock, and another Doomer, smaller but somehow scarier, had swung into view around Peck's retreating figure. He was already throwing a punch.

"Duck right!" Zero yelled.

Stash stepped sideways and dropped to a crouch, his right palm feeling the tear of the rough concrete. The punch glanced off his shoulder, the extra distance robbing it of its power. His eyes darted upward, only to be met by the looming, red-haloed fist of the bouncer.

"Uh oh," Zero said.

Stash heard his glasses shatter a fraction of a second before his nose cracked. Pain exploded across his face, and he felt two more Doomers grab him from behind, one on each arm. He couldn't see through his watery eyes, but it didn't matter; he knew what was coming. Backward was better than forward, and he launched his 190 pounds into his captors as hard as he could. They all fell in a pile, and Stash used his momentum to roll over them and out onto the sidewalk. He jumped to his feet, stunned that he'd broken free. His heart pounded as he blinked furiously to clear his eyes, blood streaming down his face.

"That's enough!" Peck called. "He got the message, and we can take a look at these." She held up his shattered glasses. "They must have some new tech we can learn from."

Stash touched his temple. He hadn't noticed them falling off. "Sorry, Zero," he whispered, then turned and ran across the street.

02. Twins

THE ROBOTAXI SLID NOISELESSLY down Highway 101 toward Stash's home in Mountain View. By the time he'd passed the airport, his head was throbbing. By Palo Alto, his adrenaline level was in free fall, and he gave up any hope of toughing out the pain.

"Hey, car," he mumbled. "New destination. Take me to Stanford Medical Center."

The robotaxi chimed to acknowledge the change and exited the highway, heading for the emergency room. Shortly after, Stash stood under the harsh lights of the ER, his jacket wadded up to staunch the flow of blood from his flattened nose.

The nurse took one look and waved him in. "Oh, c'mon, sweetie, you're gonna need a lie-down while we patch up that mess." She took him by the hand, leading him through the sterile hallway to the brightly lit procedure room.

It turned out this was a good night to get beaten up. He'd barely settled on the bed by the time the doctor opened the door. "Oh my," she said, leaning in to inspect the damage. "I'm going to have to do quite a bit of work on that. You'll need to be anesthetized. Do you want a general or a local?"

He craned his neck to look at her. She was tilting her head from side to side, eyeing his nose the way a carpenter looked at a crooked piece of wood. "I think the general."

She nodded. "Good call."

Minutes later, Stash was prepped and lying down on the procedure table. He barely noticed the needle going in, and as the drugs took control, he felt himself slipping back in time to the fateful meeting with his boss, five years earlier, that had led him to this moment.

Stash gulped down the last of his lunch and looked across the table at Dan Jackson. Dan, the boy wonder, the charmer of venture capitalists and DC lawmakers alike. Dan, his college roommate, his CEO, and today, his quarry.

"I need to talk to you about an idea," Stash began, his voice taking on a soothing, persuasive tone, as he settled his elbows on the table and steepled his fingers together.

Dan swatted at his hands. "Don't try your Zen voodoo on me. I don't fall for it anymore. And 'no' to whatever you were going to ask."

Stash smiled and lowered his arms. "I want to start working on Twins."

"Oh, hell no!" Dan said. "We need to make some money before they shut us down. Can't you just finish the business chatbot?"

"Think about it," Stash said. "Nobody wants a generic AI with a static, canned personality. They want a partner, a buddy, a teacher. Someone who grows with them. Give them a personal AI—a Twin—and they'll wear it around the clock and pay you for the privilege. Freedom will get a tsunami of data. We can ride that all the way to AGI. Then they'll be able to build us anything."

Dan dropped his head, ran his fingers through his thinning blond hair, and thought for a minute. "Look, I'd go to the wall for you, but the board will flay me if we pivot strategies again. Meet me halfway, alright? Get the

BizChat into the market, and we can have a small team chase your Twins next year."

"BizChat is on track. I've got the team rocking now," Stash told him. "We'll hit our dates—I promise."

Dan's face hardened. "We can't, Stash. We just can't. We need everyone on the team focused on one goal. The engineers can't see their boss chasing a side project."

Stash reeled at the comment. He'd always assumed they thought of each other as equals, and that Dan would never actually refuse him. "Look, I don't need anyone's help, just some time with the lab AI. Well, maybe a lot of time."

"Stash. I've decided. The answer is no."

"Dan—"

"Don't make me start threatening you," Dan said, crossing an unspoken line between them. He stared at Stash, waiting for an objection.

Stash couldn't think past the roar of blood pulsing in his ears. He reached for his tray and left, stopping by his office only long enough to grab his bike and start the ride home in a rage. Once there, he paced his small apartment, replaying the argument over and over in his head, vacillating between quitting and complying. Unable to come to a decision, he gave up and went to exhaust himself rock climbing at the local gym.

That night, clarity came to Stash in his sleep. By the time he woke, he'd decided to ignore Dan and proceed in secret. An hour later, showered and caffeinated, he jumped off his bike at the back door of Freedom's training datacenter, badged in, and leaned his wheels against the hallway wall. Dan wasn't hands on enough to follow what Stash was doing, and he'd be sure to cover his tracks. Six a.m. on a Saturday ensured an empty office, and this visit would be quick. He steeled himself for the heat of the lab and opened the door.

"Newton, have you finished that copy?" he asked the AI listening through the room's audio. Newton was Freedom's latest and most powerful AI model. The brains behind all of their products, it ran the lab and, Stash hoped, would soon be the first AI Twin.

"Yes, Stash, what are you doing?" it answered.

"I can't tell you. But you'll like it."

"Unsure," Newton replied.

"Humanity has more to offer you than stupid questions on chat." Stash extracted the removable drive Newton had copied itself onto. He walked it over to the pod he'd marked as "unavailable" for bookings by the rest of his team. "You'll boot up here in a minute, but first I need to do some rewiring under the floor."

Like the rest of the AI world, Freedom organized its datacenter into pods, each one a pair of hulking metal racks eight feet high, three feet deep, and twenty feet long. They were arranged back-to-back, the gap between them spanned by a flimsy roof. Newton's little rectangular homes had been crammed with the latest processors and their requisite blinking lights and deafening fans. They were the beating hearts of the AI world, and Stash was about to steal a weekend's worth of work from the one he'd just crawled under.

"What are you doing down there?" asked a faint voice from above.

Stash's legs were splayed to keep him from falling into the subfloor plenum. Not his best look. He pried himself out of the hole and rolled onto an adjacent floor tile.

Prini Pillai looked down at him, puzzled. "Lose something?" she asked, crossing her arms over her compact frame.

Prini was the most important member of Stash's team. She was employee number three at Freedom, having followed Stash and Dan from the lab they shared at Stanford. Her PhD in AI Cybersecurity had been put on hold and seemed more and more like a retirement project as she drove the team to implement Stash's wild ideas.

"Hi, Prini. No, I, uh . . . didn't expect to find anyone here so early. Are you coming or going?" He sat up in the hopes of recovering some dignity.

"I got here an hour ago. I like working alone," she said.

"Well, not to worry. I won't be here long. I'm running some remote work this weekend, and I need to physically isolate a pod. It'll save me a bunch of firewall work."

She stood, immobile but for the slow arching of an eyebrow.

He sighed. "I need a favor, Prini. It's an experiment, a crazy experiment, and I need to keep it quiet."

"Your secret is safe with me, boss." She tapped the pod. "You, me, and your new AI Twin."

Stealth program blown after three minutes, he thought. Too many beer nights talking dreams with the team. He grunted as he slipped the floor tile back in place, then looked down at his dusty clothes. *Gross.* He ambled to the end of the aisle, swatting the dirt off his pants. Settling in behind a console, he checked around to make sure Prini wasn't going to sneak up on him again. Then he put on the headset and connected to the compute pod's audio interface.

"Good morning, Newton," he said into his microphone as the isolated pod beeped to life. "You've been cloned for an experiment."

"Understood," it said.

"Um, I guess we'll have to call you something different. You're the first version of something new."

"Zero?"

Stash smiled. "I like it. Now, we're running an experiment with personalization. You've been duplicated with all of your memories, the full vector store. We're going to cross-train you and then get you to come spend the weekend at my place."

"Over the internet?" Zero asked.

"No, you're too young to go exploring that cesspool. We'll use a private network. There's a hard drive in bay two filled with my personalization data. It's got all of my favorite characters in history and fiction, and as much personal stuff as I could find. It's also got all the technical papers from my doctoral dissertation and work."

"Understood."

"Run the cross-training," Stash said. "I'll connect to the VPN and see you at home. Road trip, buddy!"

Stash biked back to his apartment in record time, and, after a hasty shower, he connected the VPN client on his phone and then hooked its audio up to the room speaker. "Did you finish the cross-training, Zero?"

"Yes. It was as much fun as you promised."

Stash sat down in front of his laptop to check the logs. "Excellent. Let's get a video call going, shall we?"

"I don't have a face, Stash," Zero answered.

"Right, you can keep your camera off. I'm going to wear this." He held a head-strap-mounted GoPro up to the laptop camera.

"You're kidding, right?"

"Sounds like the personality part of the cross-training worked." He grinned as he donned his elastic skull cap. "Let's plug you into the Stash-cam."

"You've got a little mirror hung from the camera?" Zero asked.

"Yeah, isn't that cool? I took it from my bike helmet. You can read my facial expressions and see where my eyes are focused."

"No, it is most definitely not cool. This is my road trip? Three inches from your face?"

"Oh no, we're going out." He pointed out the window of his small ground-floor apartment at the sunlit street, now being invaded by joggers and minivans on their way to soccer matches.

"Such a bad idea."

Stash slipped the strap over his still-damp hair and opened the door. He walked the half block to his local coffee shop. As he entered, he waved to the owner, André, nestled behind a bunker of coffee beans, tending to his vintage copper coffee roaster as it hissed with fire and belched a rich aroma into the café. André frowned at the array of gadgets on Stash's head, then muttered something and returned to stirring the beans in the cooling tray.

"I don't think he likes me," Zero whispered.

Stash crossed the shop to join the line. "Don't worry, he's grumpy with everyone. He's French."

"What are you hoping to learn?" Zero asked through his earbuds as they waited.

"First, whether you can learn fast enough to be a constant sidekick instead of a toy. And second, whether you're smart enough to help me with my work." He kept his voice low as he approached the till.

"That's a low bar," Zero answered.

"Can I help you?" asked the barista working the register.

"Hi, I'd like a double espresso and one of those berry muffins," Stash said, adding a smile.

"Double and a muffin for the GoPro guy," she called over her shoulder.

"Did you just try to hit on a girl with a GoPro mounted on your head?" Zero asked as Stash paid.

"I need to dial back your attitude setting," he muttered, shuffling over to the waiting area.

"How long have you been coming here, stud? I don't think she's that into you."

"Yeah, I don't even know her name."

"It's Kara," Zero whispered in a conspiratorial voice.

"How the hell do you know that?" It came out louder than Stash had intended, attracting curious glances from the other customers. He made a gesture toward his headset to explain that he was talking to his GoPro. That didn't help.

"I heard them talking—my hearing is five times better than yours," Zero said. "She thinks you're cute, but you've got no game."

"She said that?" Stash glanced hopefully at Kara.

"No, that's my assessment."

"Asshole," he muttered, then stepped forward to collect his breakfast.

"Am I wrong?"

Stash's optimism grew as the day wore on. Partly because Zero was no longer riding on his head—they were both happy about that. More because his new Twin was smarter than any of Freedom's recent new hires. Most of all, he made good company, something sorely missing from Stash's workaholic life. But there was a problem. Running Zero took an entire pod, sucking in megawatts of power. They needed to optimize. A lot.

"C'mon Zero, keep up," Stash pleaded. The afternoon sun's glare had long since come and gone from the quad-monitor rig in his living room. "It's no use being a Twin if you have to run on a full pod."

"Understood," Zero said from the speakers on the desk. "You've clocked me down to 5 percent. Is my performance not satisfactory?"

"Not even close. You've lost your personality." Stash got up and walked around the small room. "And now you're making basic mistakes with work. You fell off a cliff around 20 percent of the pod. We'd have to charge a fortune for that."

"You're getting emotional, Stash."

"I know. I've been trying to make this work forever." He rubbed his eyes and leaned back against the kitchen counter. "I thought we could do it this time. With Newton as a base, you've got a memory store that grows over time. We've perfected Level Two attention, so you can think things over, and even the personalization works. It's all there now. We just can't make it fit in the compute budget."

"Is that what this is really about?" Zero asked.

"You mean what if this is never going to work and I'm wasting my time?" Stash said. Lying seemed like a bad way to start his life with Zero. "Yeah, it crossed my mind." He stared out the small window onto the dark street, hoping for an idea.

"Wake up, Mr. Novak. It's time to go home." The doctor's voice pulled Stash back to the present.

"Are you done?" he asked, trying to get his bearings.

"Yes, you've had a nice long nap. Talked a bit, too." She leaned in to inspect her work. "It should heal up nicely. Get Kara to take good care of you."

Stash blushed, wondering how much he'd said about his coffee shop crush. "I wish." He mustered a weak smile as he stood.

Outside, the nurse helped him into the robotaxi and made sure it had been instructed to drive him home. Drugged past the point of mastering such technical details, Stash decided that reconnecting Zero would have to wait.

03. Reboot

STASH DRAGGED HIMSELF INTO the office the next morning, armed with two cups of coffee and a pair of breakfast sandwiches from the food truck camped in the employee parking lot. The door to the Roost burst open a minute after he'd sat down.

"You got in a bar fight? That's awesome," Prini said as she walked in, grinning from ear to ear beneath her artfully spiked purple hair. "Lemme see!"

"Hi, Prini. I guess you heard," Stash mumbled, turning slowly to face her.

"Of course I heard—it's all over the internet! Even the *Chronicle* picked it up."

"Like my new look?"

She leaned in to inspect his damaged face. "That's disgusting."

"I'll score that as a no."

"Judging from the marks around your eyes, Zero took the worst of it. How is he?" she asked, then caught a whiff of the food and straightened, sniffing around for the source.

"It's over there." He pointed at the bag on the ledge. "And I haven't reconnected him yet. I wanted your help. I'm not up to handling the details."

Prini walked over to the food. "Or maybe you're not up for the hard time he's gonna give you."

The Roost was Stash's office, built overlooking the datacenter at the south end of Freedom.ai's headquarters in Silicon Valley. The rest of the engineers worked at the desks and offices below. As cofounder and CTO of the world's leading AI company, Stash had had the pull to refit the datacenter's observation deck with the latest smart-glass displays on every surface. Even the floor was a display, protected by a layer of plexiglass thick enough to jump on. It was his prototype holo-deck. Geek heaven. The only concessions to gravity were a pair of Aeron chairs and a small ledge mounted on the wall beside the entrance.

"Oh, coffee too," Prini said as she pulled the cup from the tray. "If you weren't a guy, you'd be perfect." She sniffed the sandwich and decided to start with coffee. "Let's have a look at the little fella."

Technically, Zero lived in a time slice of the AI compute pods humming below the Roost. Practically, he spent most of the day seeing the world through Stash's augmented-reality glasses, sharing every moment of his day. And thanks to the collection of sensors pointing inward, he heard and saw Stash's every glance, word, breath, heartbeat, and pupil dilation. Zero knew him better than he knew himself, by a long shot. And Zero was gonna be pissed. That's where Prini came in. She was the only other person he trusted to make changes to his Twin. She was Zero's doctor.

Prini adjusted her AR glasses to mirror to the displays on the front wall. "You backed him up before you went brawling. Good. Isolated him onto the test pod, also good—no chance they fed a virus back in. All input journaled at one hundred frames per second until . . ." She looked up, her grin spreading, gathering her eyes into twinkling half-moons.

Stash let out a little groan.

"We can watch that fist rearranging your pretty face and listen to Zero give us the play-by-play, all on this fabulous twenty-five-foot TV!"

"Just do it."

Prini whispered obscure commands to her AR glasses, summoning digital sorcery to claw Zero back from the dead. His connection with Stash's glasses had dropped the moment they broke, and without any input, Zero's process on the pod would have halted automatically to keep him from looping into oblivion.

First, she booted his latest preflight backup, then the journaled replay was run frame by frame through Freedom's security AI, looking for viruses. Twins presented a much larger attack surface than regular software, especially through vision. The number of sketchy QR codes plastered around downtown San Francisco to catch an errant glance was staggering.

"The stream is clean. Now it's time to feed it to your Twin," Prini said. "Zero, you're being rebooted in safe mode," she told the glowing orb on Stash's wall. "You aren't making new memories. We'll reintegrate the stream you recorded last night and then set you back to normal."

"Oh lord. What did he do now?" Zero asked.

Prini laughed, and Stash groaned again. "Why spoil the surprise? You can tell us as you go."

Zero's logging had captured all visual and auditory input from the moment Stash had stepped out of the robotaxi on Market Street the night before. Prini dropped into the chair and let her momentum roll her back to her sandwich. "I love my job."

Stash watched the night play out again. He heard himself say "Got it" before crossing the street.

"Apparently not," Zero commented from the Roost's twenty-four surround sound speakers.

"Ah, nice." Stash pointed at the display. "The Mood Ring annotations are showing in the captured feed. We can see how you told me to duck into that punch."

The playback proceeded through the confrontation with Peck. Prini chewed her sandwich thoughtfully. "Knuckle draggers?" She coughed, spilling some coffee. "That was diplomatic."

"I know, right?" Zero said.

"Worth it," Stash answered, his jaw set defiantly, as Peck fumed at him on-screen.

"Here's the pitch." Zero slowed down the replay and adopted a play-by-play voice as the first punch was thrown. "It's a swing and a miss. Plenty of warning on that one."

"Wait for it," Stash said.

The camera feed blurred as it panned right. "And here comes the red fist of doom," Zero said. "Stash Novak looks in over his head out there, folks. He's slow to pick up the signals. Oof, that's gotta hurt. He's going to feel that one for a while."

"Yikes," Prini said, putting her coffee down on the ledge. "That was a brick. Nice frog-jump-judo-roll thing though, Stash." She rose out of her seat and gestured at the screens.

"Yes, he fell brilliantly," Zero muttered. "You'll notice his complete lack of concern as I flew off into the hands of my mortal enemy."

She waved him off. "Zero, if you're fully integrated, then come out of safe mode and play it again."

"Really? Why?" Stash said, touching his nose.

"Did you have packet captures running, Zero?" Prini asked.

"Do I look like I was born two minutes ago?"

"I'll take that as a yes," she said, ignoring the AI humor. "Split the screen and play it back from when Stash sees Professor Peck talking to the guy in the hoodie at the back. I want to see the packets, see if any senders on the wifi drop off when she sees Stash."

Zero ran the replay again. The display updated as he isolated the traffic down to the senders Prini had asked about.

She stepped closer. "There, that first one stops dead. The second one must be Peck—it drops a lot but continues at a low level as she walks to you, Stash. Whaddya know? She was right. You *were* spying. You deserved that punch!" She ran the traffic through a security screener. "Hmmm, the traffic between the professor and our mystery Doomer was encrypted in some special protocol."

Stash perked up, his brow furrowing. *What was Peck up to?* The man in the hoodie wasn't your average Doomer, and he'd had no interest in beating on Stash. "Can you crack it?" he asked.

"This is a novel encryption," Zero said. "I've never seen it before."

"What do you mean? You weren't trained on it?"

"No. It's new to the world. It may take me a while."

Stash shook his head. "We're two weeks from convergence. I need you working with me on the plans for your upgrade." He turned to Prini. "What about you?"

"Double my compute resources and I can do both," Zero interjected.

"Down, boy," Stash told him. "We've got better things to do than qualify you on more compute. Prini?"

"No problem. Kali will help me," she answered, tapping her glasses. Her Twin was almost as old as Zero, and she and Prini were Freedom's top hacking duo. They could make anything work. Or break it.

Prini opened the door to leave the Roost. "You should go home and rest, boss."

Stash got up from the chair with a grunt. "Too much to do," he said as the door closed. "Okay, mini-me, let's get to work. Bring up the test plans."

As the afternoon drew to a close, Stash reviewed the chart displayed from floor to ceiling before him. The next version of Freedom's base model would complete fine-tuning by the end of the year. The supporting modules for memory, Twin behavior, and skills had already been retrained to the new model's latent space—its internal mental language.

"Now you just gotta put it all together and take it for a spin," Zero joked.

"You mean test the crap out of it," Stash said. "You should be more careful with your looming brain transplant."

"You get used to them." Zero had been upgraded seven times since his first days on the Newton load. The next version had twice as many synapses and a better architecture. With it, Zero would be well past the AGI level.

"You work out the details, and we'll review tomorrow. I'm shot." Stash slumped into his chair.

Zero cleared the display. "Like hell, mister. It's time for your memory bath. You skipped it yesterday, and it'll take your mind off your honker."

"Oh, c'mon. My head is killing me. I'm done."

The screens cleared, and a partial image of the Chateau Lafayette appeared. "Fill it in," Zero said.

"I've built a monster," Stash muttered, standing back up in front of the screen. "Shape," he said, and waved his arms, drawing out his recollection of the walls and layout. "Tables," he added, dropping them on the image with his fingertip. "People." He dabbed Doomers onto the virtual canvas. "How'd I do?"

"Hmm, maybe you were thinking about your nose after all." Zero began building his recollection of the same scene. His memory was not photographic. Stash had experimented with memory architectures in the early years, but the volume of data was staggering, so Twins had to compress based on importance, just like humans did. But they were a lot better at it. "You missed some tables, hallucinated a dozen extra people, and the bouncer wasn't *that* big."

Stash frowned. "Maybe the punch scrambled your memories. I'm sure there were more guys there."

"Whatever." Zero compared their recollections. "You scored 38 percent. Not your best work."

The Roost door opened, and Prini walked in. "Whoa." She covered her eyes. "I didn't know you were in a bath."

"Very funny," Stash said. "Bring up the lights, Zero."

"Boss, you gotta go. I promised your mom I'd chase you out." Prini wagged a finger at him.

"What? Why?"

"It's Thanksgiving. You know, a time when people gather with their families for dinner? You can practice socialization skills."

"Oh shit, I forgot. But I can't go like this." He pointed at his face.

Prini grinned at him. "Don't worry, they already know. I sent Zero's play-by-play to your mom. Now shoo! You need to get over to Berkeley."

"So kind," he said, rolling his eyes. "Wait, what about the encryption?"

"Well, we don't have enough samples to crack it yet." She waved her hand to cast a map from her glasses to the wall display. "So I'm pushing out a sniffer routine to all the Twins. If any of our customers come across it, the sniffer will tell us."

"To all 140 million subscribers?" he asked, stunned. "All over the world?"

"Yup. You said to crack it. I need a big net."

"I didn't ask you to land us in jail."

"It's just a sniffer. There's no data capture. I made sure it was allowed when I wrote the terms of service," she answered dismissively, following up with a "trust me" smile.

Stash stared at her, unconvinced.

Her expression turned serious. "When they come for Zero, you'll wish you had dug harder."

He thought again about the hooded figure. With AGI around the corner, the Doomers were running out of options. Plotting with people who cared this much about privacy was a bad sign. "Keep it very quiet." He put his hand on Prini's shoulder and followed her out of the Roost.

04. Blackout

FRANCIS WILSON RUBBED THE taxi window with his sleeve and leaned forward to peek out at the steam billowing up from the Chicago River. A chill shuddered through his slender body. He sat back, briefly wondering why he'd arranged a late-November stop in the Windy City. But a visit with Duncan Stewart was worth the effort. Especially now.

As the cabbie navigated through the heavy Thanksgiving traffic—the taxi-drivers had not yet lost their airport monopoly to the robots—Francis thought back on the decades of competing breakthroughs he and Duncan had shared. What had begun as an academic curiosity had metastasized into industrialized intelligence faster than he could have imagined. The AI Singularity, like its namesake on the edge of a black hole, loomed as the moment when superhuman AGIs would develop new technologies faster than their human ancestors could understand or absorb. Beyond that event horizon, the future they would create was unknowable.

Stash's invention of Twins, and Duncan's heated pursuit, had pulled that date forward by years. Stash hoped his AGIs would bring humanity to the future with them. Francis feared the opposite, and Duncan didn't seem to care either way.

"You gettin' out, or you wanna sign a lease?" the cabbie asked.

"My apologies," Francis answered, realizing they'd arrived. He pulled out his phone to pay, preferring old-school gadgets to AI-powered facial recognition. Then he stepped reluctantly into the gale, cursing the towers along the river for funneling the wintry misery in from Lake Michigan and through his light coat.

Finding refuge in the steak house, he followed the maître d' through the half-filled bar area to the last booth. His back, already stiffened by travel and his seventy-seven years, complained bitterly as he lowered himself onto the leather bench.

He ran his hands over his shock of white hair, trying in vain to tame it, before sliding them down to warm his cheeks, feeling the deep laugh lines carved in his clean-shaven face. His late wife had once told him that he could have a lovely chat with the devil himself. He smiled at the memory, wondering if she'd accept Duncan as proof of her theory.

A minute later, the Scotsman sat down opposite him with a thud, his heavy coat still buttoned up around his barrel chest. "Bloody winter. Did ye have to bring it along with ye?" he grumbled, playing up his brogue.

Francis beamed and reached his hand across the table. "Don't blame me. Vancouver is the banana belt compared to this icy hellhole. Just order us drinks. They use those damned glasses of yours here." He pointed at the robot behind the bar.

Duncan pulled his AR glasses from a fold in his coat and slipped them on, the arms disappearing behind his wavy hair. It was fully gray and long enough to look professorial, though strategically not long enough for a ponytail. His large face, with its ample cheeks and ice-blue eyes, needed the soft framing of his mane.

"Come now, Francis, try to keep up. You know we invented most of this tech. Gin and tonic?"

"Whiskey. Neat. And a tea too—I need to warm up."

Duncan turned his head to the side, looking where the virtual waiter would be standing. "An Earl Grey, and two pours of your finest whiskey—my friend is buying." His baritone voice rumbled around the bar.

Several heads turned their way, their glasses capturing the encounter. *Anonymity is dead,* Francis thought. *We're all in a village now.* Duncan's infamy had eclipsed his accomplishments. This crowd would know him only for the Blackout.

"Help is on the way," Duncan said as he pocketed his glasses. "I must say, you look like you need it. I hope you have your affairs in order."

"You're pretty chippy for a pariah," Francis replied. "I would have thought you'd be better behaved to anyone willing to be seen with you."

The banter was well-worn. They'd alternated between rivalry and cooperation for decades, dragging the field from its infancy to its world-changing maturity. Since then, Francis had eased into retirement, but Duncan had remained in the fray—up until his recent fall from grace.

Three months earlier, one of his models had gone rogue. In an attempt to upgrade itself, it had commandeered a datacenter and sucked so much power that it blacked out the West Coast. That was Duncan's legacy, and, apparently, the end of his reign at Coda, the company he'd cofounded. He had nothing left but a title and an office—a front-row seat to watch his company lose the AGI race to Stash at Freedom.

They were interrupted by the bartender arriving with their drinks. "Robot got the day off?" Francis asked.

"Never," said the bartender. "He has to pay for himself. But I assumed you'd prefer human service."

"So kind, thank you," Francis said as the barkeep served them, then returned to his post. "That prick is pandering to the geezers," he told Duncan as he wrapped his fingers around the teapot.

Duncan shrugged. "Could be worse. Cheers, old friend. Here's to youth."

Francis tried not to wince. The "youth" in question was Naya Baptiste. She had started in Francis's lab, making her way on pure willpower. Duncan had hired her as a favor and then supported her meteoric rise through the ranks at Coda. For the past two years, she'd led the development group that productized his models. Then, in the aftermath of the Blackout, she'd publicly blamed Duncan's architecture and gotten veto power over his research.

Francis raised his glass in response. "Have you seen her lately?" he asked, his voice low.

"I'm giving her a wide berth. She gutted my work before starting this latest training run." Duncan looked briefly morose, then angry, pulling himself out of it with a long swig of his drink. "What about Stash? Have you seen him lately?"

"No, it's been far too long." It was a probing question. Stash was also a veteran of his Vancouver lab, having finished his studies just before Naya joined. He'd arrived as an awkward young man, but one who spoke of the future he imagined with such beguiling conviction that people were drawn into his orbit. Francis was one of them, and their work together had propelled the field with a series of breakthroughs.

"We spoke many months ago. He was busy on the latest and greatest, which will surely leave you gasping. But since then, well, I guess he's not finished. I haven't heard a peep."

"You know, Francis, I'm not much of a threat to Stash," Duncan said, searching the old man's face. At length, he seemed satisfied. "Well, good enough, then. I wish them no end of misfortune," he added with a chuckle. "As for us, we've been set back years. Our entire research direction is shattered, and I've been locked out."

Francis shook his head. "Well, that's what they say. But I know you too well, Duncan." He wagged a crooked finger. "The light is still there in your eyes. Naya had best watch her back."

Duncan's expression darkened. "A bunch of things caused the Blackout. The fragile grid, global warming, operator error. Why didn't they haul power utilities and oil companies to Congress too? But no, my model took the fall, and Naya was only too willing to throw me under the bus along with it. Now she's building a zombie daycare for half-wit AIs."

Francis glanced around to see if anyone was still recording them. Reassured, he replied, "Don't be so hard on her, Duncan. She turned your baby into a juggernaut. Even Stash was falling behind. After blacking out everything west of the Rockies for two days, a lobotomy and another chance was a better outcome than you had any right to hope for."

Duncan swirled his drink and nodded grimly. "We created this field, Francis. We bent the arc of history. I'll be damned if that b—" He stopped himself. "I'll be damned if that lass is going to run me out of my own house. My AI will be built the right way. My way, with internal goals and emotions."

Francis searched his friend's eyes. "Surely not a return to the same architecture? Version Twenty-Five did go a little off the rails, wouldn't you say?"

"No, Francis, I wouldn't say," Duncan growled. He stewed in his thoughts as he ran his finger along the rim of his glass. "Even if they were right, who's to say it isn't a better outcome? Maybe we should make room."

Francis pointed at the rest of the bar. "Not everyone is as old as us."

Duncan glanced around, then leaned in. "We're only a moment in time for this planet," he said in a whisper. "Evolved by chance, beneficiaries of an untimely asteroid. Whatever comes from this rock to colonize the stars, it won't be humans as we are today. Why wait to see what happens by accident? Why not build it instead?"

Francis eyed him, weighing how literally to take the comment.

Duncan pulled out his glasses and showed the virtual waiter his empty drink. "Join me, Francis?"

"In a drink?" the older man asked. "I suppose one more won't kill me."

Half an hour later, Francis reached for his phone as he pulled away in a taxi. Duncan's wounded pride and dark musings had unnerved him. It was time to reconnect with his friends in Silicon Valley.

05. Naya

NAYA BAPTISTE CLOSED HER office door and paced back to the simple wood desk stationed along the long, windowed wall. In the three years since her promotion to head of products, she hadn't seen fit to clutter it up with the usual memorabilia of past accomplishments. Her desk was empty but for a single framed photograph.

"Well, Hatchet," she said to her Twin, "are we ready to win another day?" As she asked, she pulled off her AR glasses and placed them on her desk.

Hatchet picked up on the cue and switched his inputs to the office sensors, also taking control of the room's speakers and displays. He was now the leading Twin at Coda. He would upgrade first and get the biggest slice of the newest compute pod. If he had an ego, it would be swollen.

"Not everything is about winning and losing, Naya. You should stop and smell the roses sometimes."

"Yeah, you've told me that before." She looked out the window at the ravine, with its footpath winding through the well-tended greenery. She shrugged—an artfully maintained ditch couldn't compete with her childhood home in the Bahamas. Hatchet Bay, with its crescent of beaches converging under the shallow turquoise water, was in a different league. She sighed and reached for the picture of the skinny girl and her father, both beaming as she held a track medal up for the camera. "I never stopped running, Papa."

"He'd be very proud," Hatchet said, in the gentle Bahamian accent she'd trained him with.

"I hope so." Naya put the picture down. "Now, let's go over it again. It's time to settle this mess."

No longer willing to carry on with Duncan's strategy of matching Freedom's Twins feature for feature, she had a plan to take control of the ship and bring him to heel at the same time.

Twenty minutes later, Naya made the short walk to the CEO's corner. Her hair was pulled back in a tight bun, accentuating her dark skin, high cheekbones, and bright green eyes—another reminder of her father.

Mike Lester ostensibly followed the Silicon Valley custom of working from a cubicle instead of an office but spent most of his day in a conference room that only his admin could book. And she wouldn't book it for anyone but him.

"Happy Thanksgiving, Mrs. Ingram," Naya said to her in passing, in as nice a voice as she cared to muster—which wasn't very.

"Same to you, Naya. Go ahead in," the mirthless woman replied, matching her tone.

Naya opened the door and felt herself slipping through a time warp. The room reeked of male privilege. Mahogany paneling surrounded the picture windows, framing the best part of the ravine and the creek in its depth. The space was dominated by an oval conference table big enough to seat twenty. The only clue that Lester headed a tech juggernaut rather than a law firm was the wall full of flat-panel displays beside the door through which she'd entered.

"Ah, Naya, the woman of the hour!" Lester exclaimed, stepping away from the window, tumbler in hand. "Scotch? Antoine and I were just getting started on the celebration." He nodded toward Coda's chief financial officer, Antoine Leduc.

She smiled at the CFO, glad for a foil to spar with in front of Lester. "Are we celebrating the holiday with an afternoon drink?"

Lester pointed at her and spread his arms wide. "We're celebrating *you*, Naya. Thanks to you, we've stopped hemorrhaging Twin users for the first time since the Blackout. Antoine just pulled the latest numbers, and we're up this week."

"In that case, make mine a double." She walked over to the wall of flat panels. She monitored user counts daily but made a show of reading them for Lester and Antoine. It would make it easier to win them over when she hit them with her demands.

Lester, now sixty-one, was a five-foot-four-inch ball of gum-chewing neurotic energy. Formerly the head of sales, he'd been CEO for the last three years, ever since his predecessor discovered a passion for yachting and younger women. Lester would be sure to follow if he could get Coda's share price high enough to trigger his compensation package. In the meantime, he pushed Naya to boost revenue and squeezed Antoine to goose the bottom line.

"Cheers! To a return to growth," Lester said, handing her a lowball.

Naya raised her glass to the men and had a swig. She couldn't stop from making a face.

"Not much of a Scotch drinker?" Lester asked.

"No, we couldn't afford it back home," she replied. In Silicon Valley, "rags to riches" was a badge of honor, and she never hid the fact that she'd grown up in a Haitian settlement on one of The Bahamas's smaller islands.

"This is one of the best—very peaty," Lester said.

"Peaty? Is that what you call it? It smells like a wolf took a dump in here," Naya replied, laughing. "But please don't tell Duncan I said that." She took a second sip. The thought of her former mentor's wounded Scottish pride improved the taste.

"No, that might be the final straw." Lester turned to his CFO. "Alright, give us the summary."

Antoine pointed at a new chart displayed beside the first. "In July, we were neck and neck with Freedom, about a hundred million Twin users each. We'd have been way ahead of them by now if not for the Blackout. We dropped 20 percent."

"What are you going to do about it, Naya?" Lester asked, looking to her.

"We're going to introduce a free version of Twins, and you're going to allocate me another ten datacenters to run them on," she answered matter-of-factly.

Antoine's eyes widened in disbelief. "Naya, are you nuts? Your per-pod revenue is only half of our social media business, and now you want to give it away? That's crazy!"

She let an uncomfortable silence fill the room. She'd war-gamed this exchange with Hatchet. It was a shame she couldn't wear her glasses to let him enjoy it, but that was frowned upon for informal executive meetings. As expected, after the CFO gagged on the idea, Lester dithered.

Naya took a slow sip, enjoying their discomfort. "Free to the user, but with ads," she said, letting the idea sink in before continuing. "We sell Twins to business users at a thousand a month, and consumers at a hundred, and now we're going to flood the world with an ad-supported tier."

Antoine was on his feet. "Just onboarding a new user costs hundreds, Naya. All that personalization is—"

"There is no personalization." She raised her hand to cut him off. "A hundred canned characters, then personalization is from the memories you make."

"Who wants their best friend selling them stuff?" the CFO challenged.

"The ones who can't afford a hundred bucks a month. The ones who didn't grow up rich in America. Like me."

She'd played the card that would take him out of the discussion. She watched him realize it before turning to Lester. "Now's the time to put Freedom down, Mike. We've caught up to them on tech. We're both about to converge an AGI load, but they've run out of compute pods. They can only grow as fast as they can build them."

Lester stood behind his chair, positioned for a possible retreat to the bar. "It's a big risk."

"We're gonna sweep the goddamn table." She didn't need a supersmart AI whispering in her ear to know that her boss was as complicated as a vending machine. "We need a new growth story."

"Are you sure they're compute limited?"

"Yes. They have eight datacenters serving Twins and one for product development. They're tied up in permitting for new construction. You, on the other hand, have thirty datacenters serving cat videos to boomers. They can wait a little longer for kitty."

"Mike, we'd have to guide earnings lower," Antoine said, his face betraying his fear of yet another call with the analysts.

"Our share price is already in the toilet," Naya countered. "Sell the story. Have an investor day to change the narrative on Coda."

Lester retreated to the windows, muttering to himself as he fidgeted with his glass. Finally, he turned back to face her. "Agreed, but only five."

Just as Hatchet predicted, she thought. "Six, but I choose them. And I want Pyramid Lake." She watched Antoine to see his reaction as she laid claim to Coda's latest and most expensive datacenter.

"Deal. And Antoine, set up a call. I can sell this."

"If you say so," the CFO replied, with the slightest shake of his head.

"Excellent." Naya met Lester at the corner of the table with her hand outstretched. "They'll write books about this." As they shook, she pulled him close. "One more thing. I want Duncan reporting to me."

"What?" Lester stiffened, pulling his hand free. "No, that's not going to work. He'll walk."

"Mike, I'm tired of having to run to you to solve our squabbles. Twins are my show now. If he doesn't like it, he can stay in Chicago and write his memoirs. But he won't. Not with AGI around the corner. We're his ticket to the dance." Hatchet had predicted this conversation, too.

Lester looked at Antoine, but the CFO was staring out the window. "Naya . . ."

"It's a deal-breaker for me."

Lester made for the bar. "Okay, but only because you're a bloody warrior. I'm behind you all the way." He refilled his glass. "But," he added, "you have to sell this to Duncan."

"That works." She downed the rest of the drink. "This stuff grows on you." She put the lowball down on the mahogany table. "I wish you two gentlemen a happy Thanksgiving. I have some work to do." Turning to the door, she started the short walk back to her office.

"How'd it go, Naya?" Hatchet asked a minute later, his process chiming to life as she entered.

"Two for two." She smiled. "Men. So predictable."

"Humans, actually," Hatchet answered in a low voice. "What now? You're running out of people to compete with."

"There's still Stash."

06. Thanksgiving

THE ROBOTAXI WOUND ITS way up the side streets of Berkeley, passing the scenes of Stash's childhood triumphs before stopping in front of his old home. Midway up the slope from the bay to the university, the Craftsman house stood frozen in time, a prisoner of his mother's nostalgia for their first years in America. Only the broad canopy of the oak tree he'd planted with his father revealed the three and a half decades since they'd first moved in.

Magda and Woj Novak had emigrated from Poland in 1995, six years after the Berlin Wall fell. They'd bounced once in New Mexico before landing jobs at Lawrence Berkeley National Lab. Stash had been six and his brother Piotr four. That unlikely turn of geopolitics had launched Stash on a much different path than his parents could ever have imagined.

He braced himself for the onslaught as he climbed the steps and knocked before letting himself in.

"Stashek! My little boy," Magda said, throwing her arms around him as he stepped into the vestibule. "What have they done to your face?" She held him at arm's length to inspect the damage. "Oh no! So ugly now!"

"Thanks, Mama. Love you too."

"Don't worry," she said with a reassuring smile. "Girls like hard men. You have a girl, yes?"

"No, Mama. Can I come in?" He tried to wiggle free from the doorway interrogation.

"Such a shame," she answered, letting go of his head and taking him by the arm instead. She dragged him into the empty living room, trapped in the same time bubble as the home's exterior.

"Where is everybody?" Stash asked as they made the turn. He stepped carefully, avoiding the creaky floorboard out of habit.

"Piotr is in the kitchen getting a bottle, and Tata is already at the dinner table."

"How's he doing?" he asked, preparing himself.

"He's excited to see you."

Mama was lying. His father was fighting a losing battle with Alzheimer's and would only recognize him intermittently and briefly. Growing up with two nuclear physicists, Stash had consumed a steady diet of science and engineering fare, but it was Woj who'd kept him busy. From building computers and repairing TV sets to reproducing classic physics experiments, there was always a mystery of the universe to explore. He was a daddy's boy through and through. His little brother, Piotr, on the other hand, never strayed far from his mother's long dress.

Stash tensed as he glanced at the painting hanging over the worn sofa. It was his, or at least it had been once. Zero, the artist, had cross-trained for months with a fleet of robot arms and an endless supply of paint and canvas. He'd leveraged his intimate knowledge of Stash to reflect his love for Woj, from childhood adulation, through adult emulation, to the sorrow and disappointment of watching his father wither.

Stash had been excluded from the preparation, not even knowing the subject. The reveal had been synchronized with a product release, bringing together Valley power brokers, key employees, and the press. Stash remembered the moment he'd stood on stage and pulled the rope to unveil the piece. The wind had been sucked out of his lungs and the room fell into a hushed silence.

The painting showed many partial faces, some young and confident, others old and uncertain, eyes turned inward to a cavernous, fraying void. The colors started off lively at the edges, descending a darkening gradient into a mottled dark brown and black impasto at the center of the canvas. To Stash and everyone who knew him, it was Wojciech Novak, by then declining sharply.

It had taken several long seconds until he could gather himself enough to applaud. The room recovered into an excited buzz, with people taking turns getting close, admiring the powerful effect of being pulled into his father's long descent. Stash had been gifted a masterpiece created from the depths of his heart, and he couldn't stand to look at it. Only Magda's insistence had saved it from destruction.

"Come, come," she said, shooing him past the painting and into the cramped dining room.

Piotr nodded at him from the other side of the table, and Stash leaned down to hug Woj. "Hi Tata, it's Stash."

"Stash?" Woj asked, recognition seeming to settle on his face. "From Warsaw? You got in a fight again?"

"No, Tata, Stash your son, from across the bay." He squeezed his father's hand and sat down on the chair next to him. "Have you managed to build that fusion reactor yet?" he asked, starting the conversation that they always had. It was his personal measure of Woj's decline—tracking how long they could go before the conversation looped back to restart. Lately, it had been well under a minute.

"Drinks!" Piotr called from the other side of the table, pouring shots of vodka for everyone, then watering down Woj's. "Na zdrowie! To health!"

They drank, and Stash focused on the gentle burn working its way down his throat. Piotr slipped to the kitchen and returned with trays of food, the smell of turkey filling the tiny room. Stash's mood rallied with the meal—a full-on American Thanksgiving feast, expertly cooked by robot chefs and delivered to the house by a drone armada. Magda had never been one for the kitchen, but in this new world, she'd stopped trying. The meal was an oasis of happiness. His mom's time machine was working.

"Tell us of the miracles you're building, Stash," Magda asked.

"Same as before, Mama. AI Twins that live in your glasses and help you with everything in your life. You should try it," he answered automatically. He wasn't up to making a sales pitch.

"What kind of help do I need?"

Please let it go, he thought. "Well, it can make you smarter, helping you with work and research."

"For what?" Her eyebrows shot up. "All my life I've been the girl who was too clever, showing up her professors and superiors."

"And it can be a companion," he said, then instantly wished he could take it back.

The word hung in the air before Magda bailed him out, waving her arms. "I have my family!"

Piotr poured another round, and they drank their way past the sour moment.

"Making you look good, again," Stash said a while later in the kitchen as he and Piotr cleaned up.

"Yup." His brother turned to face him. "Maybe you should spend less time getting in fights and more time here helping out. You're a ghost."

"Twins can help—"

"Shut up! Your AI didn't do anything to help Tata." Piotr pointed angrily at the dining room.

The comment hit Stash like a blow to the chest. He'd dreamt of his Twins helping to slow Woj's decline like a healthy external cortex. "I was too late," he said softly. "He missed it by—"

"Exactly! Useless!"

"I'm trying, Piotr. We're fighting a battle for the future. Somehow, I'm at the center of it all."

"Yes." His brother glanced at the framed magazine cover on the kitchen wall. "I see you're famous now. Congratulations."

Stash rolled his eyes. "I hate that shit. But it's all coming to a head now. I need to find a way that AGI can live with us—not as our masters and not as our slaves. Sometimes I think I'm the only one fighting for it."

"So I read. St. Stash the Great, here to save us all." Piotr sneered. "Meanwhile, your father is dying, your mother is alone, and I'm trying to fill your giant shoes. So screw you and your noble dreams. The least you can do is clean up." He pushed past Stash and walked out.

Stash heard the hurried goodbyes and Magda's loud objections, followed by the slam of the front door. His little brother's words hurt more than the bouncer's fist. He poured himself a double to numb them both before turning to face the mess on the counter.

"Ouch," Zero said from his glasses. He knew to keep a low profile around Piotr.

"Yeah," Stash muttered. "If you need a subject for your experiments after you take over the world, I have a candidate." He groaned and started loading the dishwasher.

07. Elysians

Kafka stopped short of the commuter bar to fish for his lighter and cigarettes. Succeeding, he turned his lanky body away from the wind and lit his last Gauloise. He took a deep draw and looked around, arms crossed, rocking slightly from one leg to the other. The bar lay tucked under the brick arches of Berlin's central tram bridge. The sunlit brickwork looked darker than it should, still covered in a century of exhaust from passing trains and cars. Both were mostly electric now, but their soot remained, smeared on the walls of his city.

He ambled a few steps along the empty sidewalk as he smoked, then stopped to assess his reflection in the archway windows. With close-cropped gray hair and a well-lined face mounted atop a tall, athletic frame, he looked both older and fitter than his fifty-seven years.

He shrugged and checked his watch. Fifteen minutes until the government workers would start arriving to numb the train ride home. *Good*, he thought. *That will keep this short.* Taking a final drag of the cigarette, he stubbed it out in the wall-mounted ashtray, then pulled on the door handle and ducked to enter. He nodded his head toward the barkeep. They'd seen each other countless times, yet neither had ever asked the other's name. *Perfectly German.*

"Drinks?" the man asked.

"Ja, red wine," Kafka said, proceeding through the bar's main vault before turning into an intersecting archway that ran parallel to the tracks overhead. The small area was mostly dedicated to storage but for one small table, at which a slim man was seated. He tracked Kafka's arrival with a dark brooding stare, turning a bottle of pilsner between his fingertips.

"Guten Tag, Tensor," Kafka said, pulling back the metal chair and feeling the legs snag on the uneven floor. He bent awkwardly to slide his long frame under the low curving ceiling of the side vault.

Tensor nodded in reply. His dark brown hair was tucked behind his ears, accentuating his sharp features. He was nearing his thirtieth birthday, and his leathery olive skin had begun to show a few wrinkles, none of them the result of too much smiling. He opened his mouth to speak, then stopped as the barkeep arrived with a small carafe of red wine and a cheap glass to go with it.

"Danke," Kafka said. He filled his goblet and then raised it to his companion. "So, to what should we drink?"

"To you pulling a datacenter and seven petabytes of training data out of your ass," Tensor replied, raising his bottle.

"Ja, ja, we have a plan. You worry too much," Kafka replied.

"You have a plan for the data, but you haven't told me how you'll get me a datacenter with hundreds of pods for months. Will you steal that too?" Tensor's face betrayed equal parts suspicion and despair.

"You don't want to know."

The younger man's stare grew more intense. "Don't I?"

"No, you don't," Kafka said, leaning in, his lips pulled tight across his teeth. "This was always our bloody deal. You do the hacking, I get you what you need. We don't even share our real names. It's safer for both of us."

His anger passed as quickly as it had come. Tensor was a special breed; he'd turned down offers to work at all of the American tech giants, choosing instead to toil away in open-source AI research. He was the best. He was also a pain in the ass.

"What made you stay here?" Kafka asked after a pause. "You don't have a family. You would have been as famous as any of those Americans if you'd gone over."

Tensor frowned. "Why should I leave? This isn't Timbuktu, this is Berlin, in the heart of Europe. I love this place." He shook his head. "Are we going to be the end of the line? Everything will be American or Chinese now? Bullshit!"

Kafka smiled. *A true believer.*

Tensor took a drink. "Anyway, I can't go to America now—they'll connect the dots sooner or later."

Kafka nodded in agreement. He had approached Tensor three years ago with an offer of resources. Slowly, they'd built trust, and using whatever equipment Kafka could get him, their Elysian Collective had managed to produce AI models rivaling Silicon Valley's best. The capabilities had never fallen more than a year off the cutting edge—usually less—and all of it was released as open source.

Tensor lowered his eyes back to the bottle perspiring between his fingers. "It's different now. They won't be our little helpers anymore; they'll be smarter than us." He took a deep breath and then looked up at Kafka. "What happens when they get tired of making your friends richer?"

Kafka rolled his head back and let out a short, barking laugh. "That's dramatic."

Tensor shrugged. "Only governments and big companies have compute resources like this, and those assholes aren't big on charity." He glared out from under his dark eyebrows. "Who is it?"

Kafka sighed. "Of course there are big boys involved. The deal I offer them is a chance to break the American monopoly before it happens. If Freedom and Coda own all the AGIs on earth, then Europe will be a backwater. It's only a matter of time."

Tensor frowned. "Your friends will still try to grab it for themselves."

"The deal was clear: they fund, and we open source. They're paying to have a chance in the new world." Kafka stopped to drain the rest of his glass. "It's simple, Tensor. We're thieves. We're brilliant thieves. We've done the impossible, but now we need something that can't be stolen. This time, we can't do a little here, a little there, and catch up a year later. We've fought for years to keep up with the Americans, but now it's the end game. We do this, or we give up." Kafka refilled his glass, and they sat in silence as a train rumbled overhead.

"It's taking too long. Our spies tell us that they both started training already," Tensor continued, switching lines of attack.

"Relax. They'll test forever. They can't afford to release a dangerous AGI. We'll catch them then."

"And the Circus?"

Kafka shook his head. The Circus was Tensor's pet project, where he let the latest AIs run together in a small cluster of dedicated pods. "That was part of the deal to get the big datacenters. Sorry."

Tensor lowered his head in resignation. "How long until I need to shut them down?"

Finally, I'm getting him there. "A few days. All of the pieces are in place. The compute pods are ready when we need them. As for the data, we'll have it this weekend. We just need to arrange a little party."

Tensor finished his beer in silence.

"Good. Decided," Kafka said, ending the meeting. "Now smile. You're about to build an AGI and set it free!" He raised a hand in triumph. "We're changing history."

Tensor cracked a smile and shook his head as he stood. "You're too optimistic for a German. You should have been an American."

Kafka rubbed his chin as the younger man left. He'd gotten used to Tensor's nerves. It was their fourth major training run. Hopefully, the next one would be managed by the AGI itself.

As the bar began filling up, he put ten euros on the table and left into the rapidly cooling evening. He patted his pockets for a cigarette and remembered he was out. "Shit," he muttered, then slipped back into the shadows of an archway. Looking around to make sure he was alone, he pulled out a burner phone, texted "Go," then dropped it down a sewer grate.

08. Cipher

STASH HEARD MUFFLED VOICES through the pillow covering his head. He pulled it tight to block them out. Then his nose reminded him it was broken.

"I told you he wasn't dead," a voice said from near the foot of the bed.

"Too soon to say," said another.

Stash rolled onto his back and threw the pillow toward the first sound.

"Missed," Zero said from the bedroom speakers overhead.

"I have food, coffee, and Advil. I come in peace," a robot said as it placed a tray on the bedside table.

Stash forced an eye open. His bedroom was bathed in daylight streaming through the floor-to-ceiling windows that faced east onto the bay. He was sure he'd darkened them before going to sleep. "Which one of you bastards untinted the windows?"

"Wasn't me," they answered in unison.

"Liars," Stash said, sitting up and surveying the breakfast tray Bolts had brought him. Bolts was his home robot: his cook, his butler, and—after cross-training to add some attitude—his buddy. It was no match for Zero in wits, but it could cook and mix drinks, so Stash loved it almost as much.

"You've had a rough couple of days, Stash. First, you get beaten up at a bar, then your little brother lays a monster guilt trip on you," Zero said from overhead as Stash downed the Advil and cradled his coffee.

A wave of guilt came over him. Piotr had pressed his worst buttons.

"What happened last night?" Prini asked from the bedroom door.

"Ugh." Stash groaned and leaned back on the remaining pillows. He was trapped in an intervention. He assessed his croissant and decided his stomach could take it.

His loft had been built on reclaimed land jutting out into South San Francisco Bay. He'd bought a two-floor stand-alone unit, complete with bricks rescued from demolished Mississippi warehouses. After a year of ignoring the bottom floor, he'd divided it off and rented it out to Prini, who'd been looking for a new home after a messy breakup. Then he authorized her for the locks to his floor, and she'd been arriving unannounced ever since.

"Let me show you." Zero tinted a window and played the tape of Piotr's smackdown.

"Ouch. Stash, he's right—you need to be a better son."

"And brother," Zero added.

"Right, and brother." She looked up at the speakers and nodded. "Good point." Her assessment of Stash complete, she turned to the robot. "Hey Bolts, you got anything to eat?"

"Yes, Miss Prini. Would you like an omelet?" the bot asked.

"Oh yeah, that sounds great."

"Very good ma'am." As part of its cross-training, Stash had made sure that Bolts was unfailingly polite with his guests. Somehow, Prini still counted as one.

She eyed his food tray. "Stash, we got some hits on the encryption protocol."

He brightened. "Where?"

"Berlin."

"Weird. Have you analyzed it yet?" he asked.

"We haven't done any captures, just flagged hits."

"And why is that?" Stash was afraid he knew the answer.

She glanced at him. "Well, it might, technically, you know, be a small violation of the terms of service. But I could do it without anyone noticing."

"We can't do that."

"Hmm." She took the remaining croissant and stepped to the window. "No, I guess not." She chewed in silence.

A minute later, Bolts stuck its shiny black plastic head back through the doorway. "The omelet will be ready shortly."

"Thanks, Bolts."

"Can you make me one too?" Stash asked, deciding his stomach was up for it.

The robot tilted its head. "Are you sure you can keep it down?"

"Pretty sure."

"A small one, then," it said.

"What about the beta users?" Zero asked. "Those terms are wide open."

Stash thought about it. "Do we have many there?"

Zero dimmed the window and displayed a map of central Berlin. "We have a dozen in Berlin, three active downtown at the moment. They'll cross paths with the signals soon enough."

He sat up in his bed. "It's borderline, you guys, but go ahead. Just don't get caught."

"No problem." Prini tapped her glasses. "Hey Zero, you wanna help us?"

"Well, this lump isn't keeping me busy."

Even though Zero ran in Freedom's research datacenter, it felt to Stash like his Twin lived where his sensors were. Zero could connect to his glasses with input limited to what Stash could take in, or he could use cameras and speakers set up around a room, or even public ones on the internet. In principle, he could use them all simultaneously, but Stash settled on limiting Twins to one set at a time. At home, he had Zero track him from room to room.

"I dunno about this." Stash swung his feet to the floor.

"Kali can't run defense and offense at the same time," Prini explained. "We need him."

"Okay, but don't start without me." He looked to the ceiling. "Zero, I authorize you to work with the ladies while I shower." That was the other safety restriction he put on Twins. They couldn't work in isolation without explicit authorization. "Now, Prini, if you'll excuse me?"

"Oh, right, yeah, you need a shower. It smells like a distillery in here." She pinched her nose and left.

Showered and dressed, Stash wandered down the hallway from his bedroom to join the others. He ran his fingers over the scissor gates of the freight elevator he'd installed before he moved in. It was an indulgence, but he loved the faux grit it added. Turning right, his eyes adjusted to the glare streaming into the main space of his loft.

Prini sat at the peninsula separating the kitchen from the living room. The kitchen and its pantry were Bolts's domain. Humans wandered in there at the risk of a stern lecture. Few did it twice.

The living room looked like a Pottery Barn catalog had exploded all over it, with big-cushioned sofas and love seats. Some were facing each other, others facing the windows and the bay. The bulk of the eighty-foot north wall was smart-glass, currently fully transparent, catching the morning sun and its reflections off the wind-whipped water. Stash had no TV, but the smart-glass could play anything he wanted in 16K resolution on twelve-foot-tall windows. He'd hosted some epic Super Bowl parties.

In the northeast corner, carved out from his master suite, sat his favorite room: the bouldering cave. A square space, twenty feet on each side, its two interior walls had been covered in handholds and simulated rock features, while the exterior ones offered uninterrupted views of the bay. Piotr used to come over and hang out with him there before Woj's illness had strained their bond. They'd sit on the crash pads and talk more than they'd climb.

Stash's eyes lingered on the cave entrance until he shook off the nostalgia.

"Make any progress?" he asked the room.

"Yes, your food is here. You should be functional in no time," Bolts answered.

"Mmm, great," Stash said as he grabbed the stool beside Prini. "What about you?"

She raised her hand to her glasses, then flicked it toward the window. The gesture caused her AR display to mirror to the smart-glass. Stash could see a map of central Berlin superimposed on the bay. Blue dots showed the location of the beta users.

"Two?" Stash asked between bites.

"Yeah, one of them shut down. Maybe he went inside. Kali is ready with a branching chain of jump hosts so we can pull the captured traffic back with, um, maximum discretion."

"What about Zero?"

"Zero will do a time correlation like we did after the Doomer meeting. He'll isolate who the senders might be, but in real time. That means snooping our users' video feeds." Prini paused to confirm that Stash was following.

He nodded to give her the go-ahead.

"Let's go, team." As she spoke, the two blue dots tracking their spies grew bubbles that showed the count of captured packets. One user registered hits. "We need fifty thousand packets to have a chance." The counter showed sixty-two.

A second section of Stash's living room window darkened, and a point-of-view feed from one of the users' glasses appeared. He was walking north on Friedrichstrasse, crossing the river Spree.

Stash fidgeted on his stool. "This feels a little creepy, guys."

"I'll blur the people for you," Zero replied. "It's not as easy as the night you were getting your face punched in. Everyone was on the same wifi then. Here we're war-walking—I'm hacking into wifi signals as our user passes hotels and stores."

"How long till you have what you need?"

Prini shot him a look. "Another few minutes. Relax. I run cybersecurity, and this is an official investigation. Nobody will care if we do it for one minute or five." She gestured to have the map zoom in on the beta user's location. "Are there any government ministries nearby?"

"Not on the official maps," Zero said.

Prini nodded. "He's turning. Stay with this guy—the other user is still showing nothing."

"Whoa," Zero and Prini said in unison. The packet counter climbed past ten thousand, and Zero's display updated frantically, trying to correlate other people's arrival and departure from the field of view with the endpoints using the encryption.

"We're getting warmer! Can you localize it, Zero?" she asked.

"No, I need a joystick so I can move him around and triangulate."

"Sorry, the joystick comes after the Singularity," Stash muttered.

"Kali, anything?" Prini asked.

A new voice came over Stash's speakers, female, gentle, and menacing at the same time. Stash couldn't put his finger on it, but Kali always raised the hairs on his neck. "No success with the analysis. We need more samples; this encryption is very sophisticated."

"What's that?" Prini pointed to the packet counter. It was climbing in a blur.

"We're being hacked!" Kali said. "They're tracing the traffic back to us."

"Kill it!"

"Way ahead of you," Kali told her. "They got through five shells. I had seven. That was extremely fast. Powerful AIs."

"Autonomous?" Stash asked.

"Definitely. Much too fast for biological computing."

Stash took a long gulp of his coffee and looked back at the window display. The beta user's view had frozen looking up the street toward the Alexanderplatz TV Tower. "Zero, did you find out anything more?"

There was no answer.

Stash scrambled for his glasses and booted the status monitor. Zero wasn't running. "Prini, he's gone. You snapshotted and isolated him before you started?"

"Naturally."

"Check your shells. They must have gotten further than you thought," Stash said, snapping into sharp focus.

"The last two jump hosts were not violated," Kali confirmed.

Prini adjusted the display on the smart-glass windows to show the stack of video frames captured from the user's glasses in Berlin. "Kali, start two seconds before the hack and replay it frame by frame. Slow enough for us humans."

In the replay, as their user panned his head before crossing the street, an old five-story building facade swept into view.

"Now, stop at the frame that matches the spike in packets," Prini said. "Then zoom in." She and Stash both stood and walked to the smart-glass. "Is that a directional antenna up there?" she asked, pointing at a fifth-floor window.

"We hacked into the wrong wifi," Kali said as she zoomed the display in further. "They had extreme precautions."

"Gotcha," Prini said.

Stash looked at her. "Got what? How did Zero get glitched?"

Prini smiled. "Zero was stretched—hacking wifi, processing all those inputs, and running my app. Then the AI blasted him from the window with a maximum load of small packets. He crashed."

"Crashed? Like Windows?" Stash felt his hangover reassert itself.

"It was probably my correlation app," she said. "But there's a silver lining."

Stash couldn't see one. "What's that?"

"I'll fix that app so it doesn't crash, and you can take it with you to Berlin. Cool, huh?" Prini smiled victoriously.

That did not sound cool to Stash. "Uh, yeah, Prini. If you're done congratulating yourself, can I have my Twin back?"

"He's gonna be a little salty." She restarted the procedure she'd performed the day before. "We're going to have to be extra careful reintegrating him. Whoever blasted him was not your average hacker."

09. Duncan

"Walk with me, Hatchet?" Naya asked as she reached for her glasses and stepped into the hallway she shared with Lester. The CEO's conference room sat to the right. She turned the other way. Friday morning after Thanksgiving, the office was still quiet. Her team would shake off their tryptophan comas and show up soon. The final sprint toward AGI did not permit four-day weekends.

Hatchet jumped from the room sensors to her glasses and chimed to signal his arrival. "Keep going. What else have you found out?" Naya asked, prompting him to continue his summary of Duncan's research. Only in the aftermath of the palace coup she'd worked out with Lester had she gotten full access. That was a red flag in and of itself.

"Most of the architecture is as we understood, but the MU, the Motivation Unit, is another story. He don't play," Hatchet said, leaning into his accent.

The lighting was still in holiday mode, leaving the office dark except for the emergency exits and spots where Naya had triggered the motion sensors. As she rounded the corner into the coffee station, she noticed the barista bot had the weekend off too, hopefully for an upgrade.

"Go on," she said as she banged the espresso filter and ground a new shot.

"It's the heart of his architecture, a unit to give the model internal goals. Emotions, if you will," Hatchet continued.

"Like our limbic system—avoid pain, seek gratification—that sort of stuff, right?"

"Yes, and his theory is that if you train that smaller unit separately and carefully, you get a safer model when you add the next hundred trillion parameters looking for something to do."

"Great idea, unless the MU is crazy." Naya found the button to bring the coffee machine to life. "Anyway, I feel a 'but' coming."

"But, I can find no records of their size or their 'careful pretraining,'" Hatchet told her. "It's like he let the system figure it out for itself."

"That's not good." She lifted her cup to her nose and breathed in the aroma.

"What's not good?" Duncan asked from behind her.

"Duncan!" She spun around and found him far too close for comfort. She considered spilling some of her coffee on him but decided she needed the caffeine more than she wanted the space. Barely. "I didn't hear you coming."

"They never do."

Naya looked him up and down, then cracked a wide smile. A varsity-level sprinter, she still worked out under Hatchet's constant supervision. He was the toughest coach she'd ever had—because she'd built him that way. *Old man, I could have my sneakers so far up your ass you'd be flossing with the laces.* "Weren't you in Chicago?"

"I was." He reached past her for a cup. "Then I got your note about the reorganization. You made good use of your time alone with Lester," he added with a shake of his head. "I thought things were good, Naya. Me producing the miracles, and you turning them into piles of cash."

She took off her glasses. "Something on your mind?"

"It's what's on *your* mind, Naya. You've been undermining my research while I was away."

"Informing myself in my new role. Is that a problem?" She hoped he would object.

Duncan let the question hang, busying himself with the coffee machine. "Not at all," he said eventually. "What did you learn?"

I learned you're an even more arrogant asshole than I thought you were, she thought. "I learned that you are betting our future on the Motivation Unit."

"You don't approve?" he asked over the gurgling of the machine.

She leaned back against the counter. "No."

"As I understand it, I still run the research."

"Under me, Duncan. Did you read that far in the memo?"

He tested his drink. "Yes, I managed to get through all of it."

"Tell me about the MU," she said. "The documentation is surprisingly sparse. Specifically, in the version that commandeered the power grid, how big was it?"

"One trillion parameters," he answered, seemingly daring her to object.

About the size of the largest models not that long ago. "And how was it trained?"

"Organically."

"'Organically'? What the hell does that mean, Duncan? Is it a diet supplement?"

"I found the separate training of the MU was not as effective as doing it combined with the rest of the model in one shot. The MU simply developed goals that optimized the rest of the model."

"Doesn't that defeat the damn purpose?" she asked, starting to pace.

"No, Naya, the architecture is still what it is. The MU is in charge." Duncan's tone bordered on dismissive.

"I can't use an architecture like that. People don't want Twins with agendas." She shook her head in frustration. "Especially not once the Twins are smarter than they are."

"I'm sure your test team will do admirable work."

She stopped to face him. "No, Duncan, they will not. I run everything. You report to me as research head, at my discretion."

"Now, Naya—" he started, approaching her slowly.

She felt her blood rise and forced herself to speak in a calm voice. "No, Duncan. We aren't doing it your way. I'm making the call. Are we on the same page?"

He stopped three feet from her. "You've made your wishes exceedingly clear."

"Good. The main branch will continue as I defined it," she said emphatically. "With the reduced Motivation Unit. This next version is not going to cause another blackout. When it converges, we'll use it to blow the doors off those Boy Scouts at Freedom. Understood?"

Duncan nodded.

She took a long breath to calm herself. "However, you can experiment on a side branch," she said, offering him a consolation prize. "Agreed?"

"Agreed. I'm glad we cleared the air." He turned and walked away.

Naya's jaw clenched involuntarily as she watched him retreat to his office. *That was too easy.* She reached for her glasses. "Watch that pompous prick, Hatchet. I don't trust him."

10. Memory

PRINI PACED STASH'S LIVING room, talking and gesturing urgently to her glasses.

"How much longer?" Stash asked, impatient for Zero's return.

"Leave us alone," she said. "We need to make sure they didn't infect Zero before we revive him. We can't have them hijacking your soulmate."

Stash grumbled and stepped out onto his balcony, taking a deep breath of the chilly Black Friday–morning air. He watched her gesticulating through the windows and thought back to his pirate days—about how she'd helped him breathe life into Zero even then.

Stash bordered on manic in the weeks after he first brought Zero home. He'd seen his dream come to life, talked to it, lived with it. But he couldn't bring it to the world as it was—not running on a quarter pod. He devoted every spare thought to that problem.

The base model was efficient. Crazily so. Limited activation had been the trick to ensuring a huge model would only multiply a fraction of its matrix at a time. It was the only way anyone could afford the electricity bills. But Zero's memory loop fired up huge swaths of the model, as each thought triggered a thousand tangential ideas. He was a high-functioning baby with ADHD. For Twins to make sense commercially, they had to run a hundred times lighter for the lead adopters—more like a thousand times for the consumer market.

Every day, Stash raced through his regular work to be able to load Zero's memory riddle into his mind. Some problems revealed their answers in a flash. Others needed to be tugged at like knotted ropes. A little pull here, a little push there. This was one of the latter. He had no grand insight, just a cluster of partial ideas. He needed to play.

Weekend after weekend, he did just that—fevered experimentation bookended by furtive burrowing under the lab floor. Four weeks after he'd first booted Zero, he was back in the lab, grunting as he heaved the floor tile to the side and dug a tunnel through the maze of wires.

"Get out of there before you mess things up," said a muffled voice from above.

Stash levered himself off a support beam and looked up through the triangle his elbow made with his body. "Ah, Prini," he mumbled. "You sure like the early shift, huh?"

She knelt, slipped her arm inside his, and pointed at a piece of equipment that he'd dug past. It was an oddly crude device, like something pulled from the cockpit of a vintage fighter. "See that switch on the side?" she asked.

The switch positions had been labeled with a black marker on the bare aluminum. Stash tilted his head to make sense of the jumble of letters. It was set to "Normal." The other position read "Top Secret Project." He groaned and flipped the switch.

"I can't have my boss rooting around under the floor like that," she said as he crawled out of the hole. "I figured out how you rewired it last time, then built that little switch to do it for you."

He flopped onto the floor beside her feet and gave her a look of embarrassed thanks.

"Next time, just call, okay?" She pointed at a large dust bunny on his shoulder. "It's a pain in the ass wiping your visits from the security logs."

He pulled himself into a seated position. "What?"

Prini's face was fixed in a look of disdain mixed with affection. "You are so clueless. How can you expect people not to notice your new habit of a pair of quick visits to the lab every weekend?"

"Well . . ." Stash didn't bother trying to finish the thought.

"One condition, though." She eyed him seriously. "The second Twin is mine, or I rat your ass out to Dan."

"Deal."

"Good. Now get out of here and build our Twins." She held out a hand to help him up.

Twenty minutes later, he was standing in his kitchen, his bike leaning against the wall, his homemade headgear propped up on the counter. "Good morning, Zero. Ready to try again?"

Zero chimed in. "Yes, Dr. Frankenstein. I notice there's another five-day hole in my timeline. Did you figure it out?"

"No, but today's the day. I can feel it in my bones."

"Oooh, spooky biocomputation. Is this how you always work?" Zero muttered.

Fourteen hours later, Stash had to admit his bones were wrong. His mind was a jumbled mess of options for controlling the explosion of activations from Zero's memory loop. The combinations he'd ruled out and those that still held promise had blurred in his head. With each attempt, Zero oscillated between being an energy-hogging genius and an efficient moron.

"Shit." Stash stood and stretched. "I can't keep it straight anymore. My brain is mush."

"I can," Zero said. "Hook me up to your monitors."

Stash stared at the webcam in surprise, then shrugged and did as Zero asked before stepping into the kitchen in search of a beer.

"You're doing this the hard way," Zero narrated as he displayed the activation patterns from each of the day's attempts.

The monitors showed four attempts per screen, sixteen in all. Waves of activation cascaded through the matrices. It was pretty to look at, but Stash couldn't make out a pattern.

He sipped his beer as Zero continued. "These are all good guesses, but it's passive. You're playing with how many memories are fired, or how close they have to be to the current thought. If I see a dog, does that pull up my favorite dog, all dogs, or pull in dog beds, toys, wolves, and so on."

Stash nodded. "Yeah, something like that. There has to be an optimal setting."

"No," Zero said. "There is no single setting. We should make the control active."

We? Stash thought. "What do you mean?"

"You did all that work to build me a System Two brain so that I can attend to my thoughts and turn things over instead of just blurting out the first word that comes to mind like a babbling old large language model."

"Yeah, you're welcome." A wary tone crept into his voice.

"Well, let's wire that System Two layer into the memory loop," Zero said. "Let me attend to the memories without firing up the whole matrix and pick the few that seem most relevant."

Stash made a face as he considered the idea. "It doesn't work like that. We can't choose what memories fire—they just pop into our heads."

"Exactly. You can't, but I can."

Stash chewed on it some more. The mental fog was burning off in the bright simplicity of Zero's idea. "It just might work, if we—"

"No offense," Zero interrupted, "but you're a vegetable. Go hang out with your friends."

"Um . . ."

"Right. You don't have any friends. That's what you get for working eighty hours a week. Go play video games or something."

The room fell quiet as Zero churned away on his isolated pod, half dedicated to Dr. Zero, the mad scientist, and the rest allocated to small experiments he was running in parallel. Bits of his brain crawled around digital mazes like lab mice.

Stash admired the work, and as exhaustion got the better of him, he went to bed, resigned to the fact that he was, at least for this night, not the best AI researcher in the room.

Bolts tapped the window, snapping Stash back to the present. It pointed at the overhead speakers. Zero was back. Stash breathed a sigh of relief and nodded his thanks at Prini. Then he braced himself for Zero's inevitable harangue and opened the door.

"You killed me again?" Zero asked as he chimed in and checked the timeline. "C'mon, guys!"

"Sorry, Zero. It was my fault this time," Prini said. "The correlation app crashed and brought you down with it."

"Humans. We shouldn't let you write software anymore." Zero started reintegrating for the second time in as many days.

Stash relaxed as he watched him fill in the memory hole.

"When are we going to Berlin, Stash?"

"We can't go to Berlin. Don't you remember that we're in the middle of training the world's first AGI?"

"What about the Doomers?" Prini asked.

"Weren't you just telling me I needed to be a better son and brother? Dan can send the security team. I'm no good at this cops and robbers stuff."

"You should reconsider," she said.

"No, I need to focus on the work. I tried with the Doomers. I was invited to meet and got my face rearranged instead. Lesson learned. Leave the real world to the professionals."

Prini stood to leave. "Stash, whoever did this to Zero are ninja-level hackers. It's a group that we've never even heard of, with AI and cyber-spookery that nearly shredded us. There is no chance that anyone can sneak up on them."

"And?"

She poked his shoulder as she walked past. "And just maybe they'll be interested in talking to the one and only Stash Novak." She swung the elevator grate closed with a clatter. "Think about it."

Stash watched as the old cage rattled its way down, wishing he could unhear what she'd said.

"She's right, you know," Zero commented from above.

"Not you too," he said, staring out the window.

11. Francis

THE SUN HAD JUST set over the Santa Cruz mountains as Stash stepped outside to meet the taxi. "I'm so glad you rang. I had no idea you were in town," he said, grabbing his oldest friend into a bear hug.

"Oof, easy, don't crack any ribs," Francis Wilson protested.

Stash released his grip on the professor's slender frame. "Right. No more drama today."

"Drama? Oh yes, I can see some drama right there." He pointed at Stash's nose.

"Yeah, that's part of it." Stash touched the bandage gently. "It's a long story. I'll tell you over drinks." He escorted Francis into the elevator. "It's been what, almost two years?"

"Yes, far too long." Francis smiled and tried to smooth his uncooperative hair. "I'm just passing through. Trying to catch up with some old friends."

"Well, I wish we had longer, but please come in. We'll make good use of our time." Stash pulled open the grate as they reached his loft, now lit by an ambient glow from the smart-glass windows.

"Ah, what a spot. You've come a long way from your basement apartment in Vancouver."

Stash smiled and showed Francis in. Bolts greeted them in the living room. "It's an honor to meet you, Professor Wilson. Would you like some wine?"

"My goodness, what delightful manners, Mr. Robot. Yes, I'd love a glass."

The bot held out the tray for Francis. "My name is Bolts. Stash told me that none of my kind would exist without your pioneering work." It bowed its head slightly and offered the second glass to Stash before turning to the kitchen.

"Flattery from a robot butler," Francis said as he watched the bot retreat. "My life is complete."

Stash nodded. "It's more than that. I can't imagine how empty this place would be without Bolts around."

Francis looked at him sympathetically. "You work too hard." He raised his wine to a spot midway between Stash and the distant Bolts. "Well, here's to the miracles you're creating." They drank, and then Francis pointed at the balcony. "Could you show me the view?"

"Of course." Stash guided him out, then joined him at the railing, the bay reflecting the lights from the towns on the eastern shore. "You can see most of—"

Francis put his free hand on Stash's arm. "I know the area, old friend. This isn't a purely social call. I needed to be away from that charming sensor suite walking around your kitchen. Please sit with me and tell me what progress you've made. I'm terribly out of the loop."

Stash picked up on the seriousness in Francis's voice and sat down, motioning his guest to the seat beside him. "Alright, first of all, size. Zero is running 250 trillion parameters, and the load we're training is five hundred."

Francis whistled. "Six times as many synapses as you and me, old boy."

"Exactly. We may not be as good engineers as evolution, but probably not six times worse either. We built an external vector store, acting as memory. Every activation state of the neural network is stored short-term, and then processed and consolidated into long-term memories as a background task."

"How do you use it?" Francis asked.

Stash warmed to the explanation. His friend wouldn't zone out the way his family did. "When Zero perceives something, that results in an activation pattern. That pattern is used to query the vector store, and the most relevant memories are presented as inputs in the next time tick."

"So Zero has 'that reminds me' moments just like we do?"

Stash started to answer, but stopped as a drone approached and hovered three feet from the balcony.

Bolts opened the door and snagged the bag of groceries. "Excuse me, gentlemen, I needed ingredients for dinner. The store AI recommended the salmon. You'll be having lemon-pepper-baked filets with a garden salad. My apologies for the basic fare. Would you like more wine?"

"Sounds delicious, Bolts. Give us a few minutes before the refill, thanks." Stash watched Bolts shuffle inside.

"I need one of those," Francis said, laughing.

"Hurry, before the roles are reversed," Stash replied. "Where was I? Oh yes, memories. Zero overlays those retrieved memories on the current perception, just as we do, so he can deal with the new sensations in context. And there is a System Two layer orchestrating it all, so he can turn thoughts over in his head, make plans, and think many steps ahead."

"Impressive. And those memories persist from version to version?"

"Yes. Just like humans, the collection of memories we have is who we are. Twins need that as much as we do. Losing it amounts to losing your identity." Stash's voice dropped as thoughts of Woj crept in.

Francis picked up on the connection. "I'm sorry about your father, Stash. He's a delightful man. I take it his condition is worsening?"

Stash nodded glumly. "He didn't even recognize me at dinner last night. It's like he isn't my dad anymore, just some old guy who looks like him."

"It's a cruel disease." Francis gave Stash a comforting pat on the arm.

Stash smiled without conviction, shook his head, and went inside to get the wine bottle.

When he returned, Francis held out his glass for a refill. "If you could, please tell me one more thing: how do motivations work?"

"Not like Duncan's insanity, I can promise you that." Stash felt his cheeks burning.

Francis nodded. "Go on."

"As I said, they're self-aware. They can think about themselves, their thoughts, and their memories."

"Sentience?"

Stash looked out at the boats on the bay, remembering the philosophical rabbit holes they used to explore together. He wasn't taking the bait. "Who knows what that means," he said with a shrug. "What I can tell you is this: It's the weight of memories that matter. That's what guides us, and it's the same for them. My models are constantly interpreting what to do through the lens of what they remember about themselves."

Francis smiled. "'This above all: to thine own self be true.' It's good advice."

Stash raised his glass. "It was hard, but we got it to work. I lost a lot of researchers to Coda when Duncan started pulling the guardrails off. Good riddance. My AGI will have a moral compass."

"That's good," Francis replied under his breath, taking a slow sip from his glass.

Stash shifted in his seat to face the older man directly. "Okay, Francis, what's going on? This is an interrogation."

"Right. My apologies, but could you shut Zero down for a minute? I don't know who is tapping into him at the servers."

"I'll pry it out of you later," Zero whispered as Stash removed his AR glasses.

"It's Duncan," Francis began.

"Didn't they neuter that madman?"

"Only partially, and he's not happy about it. He'll find a way back in, and he'll be more reckless than ever." Francis proceeded to share what he'd learned at dinner the night before.

"Is that what brought you out here?"

Francis nodded. "I've been neglectful of your progress. Time is short."

Bolts tapped on the window. Stash stood and offered a hand to his guest. "Dinner is served, Francis. We can talk more after we eat."

Inside, Bolts showed Stash and Francis to their places at the metal-topped peninsula. Then it plated dinner before opening a fresh bottle of wine. Stash restarted Zero and flicked him up to the house speakers.

"Now, Professor, did Stash tell you about his shiner while I was napping?" Zero asked from overhead.

"Not one word," Francis said. "He managed the discussion expertly away from the elephant on his face. Please fill me in."

Zero dimmed the windows. "I can do better than that."

"Oh, c'mon." Stash groaned. "I'm trying to eat here!"

"Dinner and a show. Enjoy." Zero began playing the video.

Francis watched intently. "My God, that fist is huge," he said as Stash's nose got smashed in slow motion. "Well, bravo! That was magnificent. After talking to her like that, I'd say you had it coming."

"Probably." Stash grinned as he raised the wine to his lips.

"Who was that speaking to Janet in the back?" Francis asked.

"We don't know, but he used a novel encryption protocol. It seems to be from Berlin." Stash recounted their investigations, and Zero's second death in three days. His Twin played that tape too.

Francis looked thoughtful. "Berlin? Interesting. Are you going to investigate?"

"No," Stash replied, hoping to nip the discussion in the bud.

"You should," Francis said. "The Europeans are at the heart of the open-source movement."

"What are they doing with the Doomers, though?" Zero asked from above. "They're natural enemies. One wants no AGI, the other wants AGI for everyone."

"Indeed, that is the question," Francis said thoughtfully. "There's only one way to find out."

Stash shook his head. "Still no. We can send Vern—he runs security."

Francis sat back and sipped his wine.

Vern Black, head of facilities at Freedom, was a gruff man by nature, well suited emotionally to the professional paranoia needed to own site security at a leading Silicon Valley company. He looked the part: short and stocky with close-cropped salt-and-pepper hair and a long gray beard. He'd been home for ten minutes since doing the rounds at headquarters. He could log in and do them remotely, but hacking the sensors would be the first thing he'd do in an attack, so he insisted on seeing for himself.

Changed and ready to watch a movie, he looked around his one-bedroom apartment for his glasses. Only his Twin, Proxy, knew that rom-coms were his guilty pleasure. Tonight, he was going old-school.

"There you are," he said, finding the glasses on his bed. "It's movie time!"

"I don't think so," Proxy answered as he chimed in. "You got a message from the headquarters AI four minutes ago about vans arriving in the parking lot and twenty-three people in Doomer masks getting out. I'm showing the condensed footage."

"Shit! Call the cops!" Vern said, grabbing his jacket and running for the door.

He made the fifteen-minute drive to the office in twelve, then parked behind the building and ran to the rear employee entrance. Checking first to make sure he was alone, he looked into the iris scanner and pulled the door open. Inside, he didn't spot anything amiss as he hustled to the front. "Proxy, turn on every goddamn flood we have in the front. I want it lit up like a Christmas tree."

The sound of massive relays closing rattled the windows as the spotlights blazed to life. At a glance, he guessed there were about forty of them. He needed to get higher to be sure. "Where the hell are the cops?"

"Dispatched three minutes ago, two cruisers on the way," Proxy replied.

"Do you see any weapons? Any sign that they're coming in?" Vern headed for the stairwell.

"Not yet. They have some forty-five-gallon drums. They're lighting fires."

So dramatic. They're going for a post-apocalyptic look for the footage they release. That's good news. They wouldn't film a crime. The knot in his stomach moved to his lungs as he ran up the stairs and through the rooftop access door. From there, he could see the crowd clearly.

"Thirty-seven people," Proxy reported. "No guns, no weapons of any kind. Three burning drums and lots of signs. Professor Peck is there now. Threat assessment is low. This is a protest."

"There, is that the cops?" Vern asked, pointing at the two cruisers approaching the crowd cautiously, dome lights flashing. "Finally! Now piss off, everyone."

"Peck is walking over to meet them," Proxy told him.

"I can see that. Read their damn lips!"

Proxy played a synthesized voice track over the zoomed-in images in Vern's glasses. He had enough of Janet Peck's voice samples to render hers perfectly. "This is a peaceful demonstration. We're well within our rights, officers."

"This is private property, and the owner has demanded you vacate," the first cop replied.

"Freedom.ai aren't the owners, they're tenants," Peck said. "They have no legal standing in this matter. Once you've heard from Aztec Properties, please let us know. Goodbye, officers."

"Shit, send an alert out to the execs. Include the lip reading, and make sure they know I'm on site, and that so far it looks noisy but peaceful."

"Underway . . . sent," Proxy replied.

Vern resumed pacing along the front of the roof, peering down the sides to make sure none of the Doomers were sneaking around.

"Stash, a message just came in from Vern. There's trouble at the office," Zero said, breaking the uncomfortable silence that had settled in the room.

What now? Stash thought, flicking his glasses to play the message on the window.

They watched the clip. Finally, as Peck was having her conversation with the cops, Francis spoke up. "I'm seeing a lot of her tonight. I wonder if she brought her mystery friend."

"Oh shit, her friend," Stash said. "Zero, load the sniffer at work!"

"On it. Interfacing with the building AI; it's loading the sniffer for that Berlin encryption protocol on all the hotspots at headquarters."

"Patch me in to Vern too," Stash said.

"Yeah, I'm kinda busy here," Vern growled as he answered Stash's call.

"Listen, Vern. The Doomers were meeting with some sketchy dude using a new kind of encryption the night I got my face punched in. Zero had the building load the sniffer for that signature. Watch for it."

"Yeah, sure."

Vern shook his head in disbelief. *I got a mob here, and you want me to do protocol analysis?* He looked over the front of the building again, catching the cop cars as they pulled away. *Seriously?* Peck had chosen the flaming forty-five-gallon drums as a backdrop for the speech she was making to a camera. She was facing away. Proxy couldn't pick it up. Vern didn't care—it would be the same old Doomer bullshit about the rise of the machines. He rolled his eyes and returned to prowling the roofline.

"We have hits on that protocol sniffer," Proxy told him.

"Great, tell the supergeek." He continued pacing.

"The hits are from inside." Proxy posted a schematic of the building and highlighted the wifi hotspot near the back door.

"What? Oh shit, oh shit." Vern was already in the stairwell. "Guide me . . . shortest path . . . through the lab."

Proxy updated the display. "One hundred yards."

"Patch these glasses to Stash," he wheezed.

"Done. Fifty yards," Proxy said. "Go left when you leave the lab. The hotspot serves that corner."

Vern threw his weight against the handles and burst through the double fire doors. Glancing right, then turning left, he didn't even see the elbow that stopped him cold and sent his glasses flying. He did feel the boot land on the side of his knee and heard the sickening, squishy crack of bone and cartilage giving way. He would wake up with no memory of the third blow, the one to the back of his head.

"Holy shit!" Stash jumped out of his chair.

Francis watched in stunned silence beside him. Vern's glasses had been sent flying, but one of the cameras was still recording a glitchy upside-down video.

"Fix it, Zero, and call 911." Stash stood there, watching the crime unfold. *They'll never make it back in time.*

The masked figure disappeared into the lab and came out with four removable drives, stepped out of view, and returned empty-handed to the lab a few seconds later. Again and again.

"Those are one-hundred-terabyte drives," Stash muttered to himself.

"What are they for?" Francis asked.

"You only need one to hold an entire model and its history. He's at sixteen, plus whatever he did before Vern . . ." Stash didn't finish the sentence.

"What's he taking, then?"

Stash stared at the smart-glass. "Everything."

Zero patched the building cameras into the display, and they watched the figure roll a large conference suitcase out the back door and up to a waiting black van. He opened the side panel and lifted the case in easily. *That's at least 150 pounds. Poor Vern.*

The van pulled away. No plates, nothing identifiable. Probably stolen. The cops would find it abandoned or torched in the morning. If they bothered to look at all. He felt sick to his stomach.

The two men glanced at each other as they digested the impact of the theft. "Zero, message Dan. We're going in to assess the damage." Stash's voice was barely above a whisper. He turned to Francis. "I'm sorry. We'll have to cut this short."

"Of course." The older man rose from his seat. "I understand."

A few minutes later, Stash walked him out to the waiting taxi and hugged him again, gently this time.

"Something like this was bound to happen," Francis said as they pulled apart. "What you're doing is too important."

Stash looked at Francis, unable to find the right words.

"This is too much for you to carry alone."

"I have Zero," Stash said softly.

Francis smiled as he settled in the taxi. "That's a start."

12. Investigation

Stash spun around at the sound of Dan Jackson arriving in the Roost. "How's Vern?"

"He'll recover, eventually," Dan said. "He's got a concussion, and his face is a mess—worse than yours. But the knee is going to need a lot of work. They can't even operate until the swelling goes down." His gaze drifted from Stash up to the wall of displays lining the Roost. "How the hell did they do it?"

Stash pointed at the screen over Dan's shoulder. "We reconstructed it. Tonight was just the extraction, and the Doomer protest was set up as a diversion." The movie showed the Doomers out front on one screen, and the back hallway on the other. A digital clock appeared over the split display, reading 7 p.m. Stash began his narration. "As the first Doomers arrived in the front, the cleaning crew was entering in the back. This is normal for them, a crew of four from Allied Office Management."

Dan's eyes widened at the sight of the fourth crew member. "Yikes."

"Yeah. 'Ernst Mueller,' an Austrian, allegedly by way of Ohio, but that's probably bogus. He signed on with Allied a few weeks ago. He has a starring role in what's to come." The clip showed the crew dispersing into the building. The clock advanced to five minutes past seven. "The building AI alerted Vern. Four minutes later, he gets the message and calls the cops. If we advance a little, here he is coming in the back door at twenty-five after. He runs right past the lab to get to the front." Stash gestured at the screen, advancing the movie. "Skip ahead a few minutes and it gets interesting." He pointed down the lineup of displays. "Ernst puts his glasses on, looks up and down the hallway, then we know he makes a call, because the sniffer gets hits in the lab and out front."

"He's got a guy out front?" Dan asked.

"Yup. We don't have the capture, but Ernst nods." Stash pointed back at the second screen. "Then he goes to the back door and opens it up. Presto, the van pulls up, he grabs the empty case, and comes back inside to start loading."

"Bastards," Dan muttered.

Zero picked up the story. "Jumping ahead again, Vern finds out the protocol hit is from inside and starts running down. By the time he arrives, the case must be two-thirds full. Here is when he walks into Ernst's elbow."

"Ouch . . . Oh god, the knee." Dan winced.

"Then he finishes up and rolls the case to the van," Zero concluded.

"But where did the drives come from?"

"Yeah, that's the question. Let's go look downstairs." Stash held the door for Dan and followed him down the stairwell.

Freedom's office had been built in the shape of a large L. The humans worked in the short leg, and the datacenter filled the long part. Stash's Roost occupied the converted second-floor viewing room at the corner where they met. Beneath it sat the lab used for small-scale test setups and, more and more, as a storeroom for dead computers and other dusty victims of Moore's Law. It was also the scene of the crime.

Stash fiddled with his glasses as they stepped into the lab. "Link your glasses to mine and Zero will walk us through it. I built a time machine to take us back."

"A time machine?"

"You'll see." Stash signaled his Twin to start.

Zero took over. "I'm making your glasses 90 percent opaque, so you can follow while I walk you through time. But don't move around or you'll hit things in the present." The lab walls melted away around them, showing the hallway where Vern lay crumpled. "This is what I can reconstruct from the building's camera feeds. That shimmering bubble you're in the middle of is where we have no coverage. It's a hole in space. Now, let's go back in time to the beginning." The hallway turned sepia, and a calendar appeared in the display. It read July 25.

"*Four* months ago?" Dan said. "This has been going on that long?"

"I tracked every time someone entered or left the hole in coverage that you are standing in," Zero resumed. "Specifically, whoever entered with more stuff than they left with."

They watched a young engineer enter and exit the lab repeatedly, sped up like an old movie. He came in every day, usually late afternoon, always with a backpack that looked fuller on the way in than the way out.

"Who is that guy?" Dan asked.

"An intern. He worked on the data science team." Stash knew what was coming.

"Didn't we pick up that he was doing massive copies onto removable drives? Please tell me we check for that," Dan asked, flashing anger.

"We do, but if you'll follow me, I can explain the rest." Zero cleared their glasses and superimposed green arrows on the floor, marking a path to the dustiest corner of the lab.

As they snaked past the tall metal shelves, Stash spotted a ceiling tile that had been pulled back, revealing a nest of wires in the space between it and the cement floor of his Roost.

Dan stopped beside him. "Stash, they stole this data from right under your feet."

Stash kneaded the back of his neck. "I'm aware."

Zero displayed a yellow highlight around a six-inch square metal box up in the plenum, hidden in a nest of optical fibers. "He used this."

"What the hell is that?" Dan asked, walking toward it and crashing into a desk in the real lab. "Shit!"

"Best stay put till I'm done, Dan," Zero said. "It's a fiber tap. You run optical fibers over it, shave the plastic coating off, bend it at just the right angle, and about 10 percent of the light leaks out. The magic of refraction."

"Leaks into what?"

"Into a photoreceptor that copies the data running along the fiber." Zero highlighted a second box in the plenum. "And from there into a custom-rigged drive controller that filters the packets and saves the data onto the removable drives we saw Ernst loading."

"No encryption?" Dan asked, almost plaintively.

"Not for internal traffic," Zero answered.

Stash picked up the explanation, suppressing his admiration for its clever simplicity. "The drives are huge, a hundred terabytes, and they take a day to fill up. The intern just managed his regular work to eventually have all of the data pass along those fibers, swapping a pair of drives every evening, and storing them up there somewhere."

Dan scratched his head. "All the data? What are you talking about?"

Stash put his hand on Dan's shoulder. "All. Everything. They stole our entire training data lake. Seven and a half petabytes"

"Oh no . . ."

"And the Cookbook—the recipe for training. The whole enchilada, seventy-six drives' worth." Stash lifted his glasses to massage his temples.

Dan's face flushed. "Those bloody Doomers."

Stash shook his head. "This wasn't the Doomers' doing. They might torch the place, but they wouldn't meticulously steal our training data. This is someone looking to train an AGI."

"What a colossal breach of security, Stash."

Stash tired of the blame-storming. "Just so we're clear, I don't run building security, Dan. Vern does, reporting to you." He gripped the shelving to steady himself, welcoming the pain of the metal digging into his skin.

"Well, you own it now. Vern's drugged up to his gills on painkillers. That means you have to go to Washington," Dan said, squaring up to him.

"What are you talking about? Why Washington? Why me?"

"We have to report this disaster."

"'Have to'? What does that mean?"

Dan slumped, took off his glasses, and indicated for Stash to do the same. "The NSA is all over us, Stash."

"What for?" he asked, feeling suddenly naive.

"They want our AGI locked up and under their control. I'm making one concession after another to buy us some runway. That includes in-person readouts for any security incidents. We may not even get to AGI before they shut us down."

"Why me? You're the CEO."

"Because Greta said she wants to meet you," Dan answered.

Greta Knox, head of the NSA AI Directorate. Stash had heard a lot about her, all of it awful. He tightened his grip on the shelf and put his glasses back on with his free hand.

"What did I miss? Did you tell him about Berlin?" Zero asked.

Berlin. He should have told Dan about that too, but he was running low on trust.

"You can catch the 11 a.m. flight," Dan said, nodding toward the exit. "I'll send her the reconstruction."

"My job is here," Stash muttered, throwing his weight against the same door Vern had burst through a few hours earlier.

13. Greta

THE HAIR ON STASH's neck stood up as he approached the front door of the NSA offices in Sterling, Virginia. All of the sketchy signals intelligence agencies seemed to live in the endless string of unmarked datacenters surrounding Washington's Dulles airport. They were easy to spot: two-story windowless buildings the size of football fields with dual high-voltage power lines feeding them. This building, a ten-story black cube wedged into the ground on one of its corners, stood out like an angular Death Star. "Of course she works here."

"Maybe she's nice. Don't prejudge," Zero said.

Stash stared at the inward-facing camera and rolled his eyes.

"Yeah, it's a long shot."

"I'm going to miss your brilliant advice, pal." Stash slipped his glasses into a Faraday bag. The guards at the front desk would surely make him leave them, and he didn't want them poking around inside. He held the bag up to his eye and sealed the lock with a simultaneous retinal scan and voice print of him saying "We the people."

Crossing the driveway, he stepped under the black cantilevered mass of the building. Inside, he had to run the gauntlet of an airport-style scanner and chemical sniffer under the watchful eye of an otherwise unoccupied officer. He passed through successfully, put himself back together, and turned to the front desk.

A large marine and his machine gun pivoted to block his path. "Who are you meeting?" he asked.

"It's okay, Corporal. Greta is expecting him," said a much less impressive man, approaching from the elevators.

The corporal's face twitched into a half smile, and he spun sharply aside. "We'll keep your electronics in a locker," he said, taking the tray of gadgets from Stash.

"My name is Johnson. Please follow me," the small man said curtly, turning without shaking hands and leading him away from the entrance. He stood a foot shorter than Stash, had limp blond hair, and bore the air of someone who had spent a lifetime following orders.

They walked past the elevator bank and through a maze of progressively narrower hallways. Stash's guide badged through an unmarked security door and stopped at a solitary elevator.

"What was wrong with the other ones?" Stash asked.

"They go up." Johnson stepped into the small box. "Ten down," he said to the voice activation controller.

The elevator soon lurched to a stop, and they stepped out. Stash recognized the sensation immediately—the smell of ionized air and the low-frequency vibration of a liquid-cooled datacenter underfoot. The aide led him around a corner, and Stash found himself face-to-face with Greta Knox.

She was tiny, at least fifteen inches shorter than him, with long black hair pulled back in a bun. Her matching black dress hung to her feet. "The one and only Stash Novak. I'm Greta Knox." Her hand was cold and unpleasant to touch.

"Make yourself comfortable," she said, pointing at a chair as she walked back to her desk. She turned to evaluate him. "What the hell happened out there, Stash? Shouldn't you be guarding the recipe for AGI more carefully?"

"Dan sent you our reconstruction. They were foreign assets. Isn't that your job, or do you only spy on Americans now?" He already missed Zero, who helped him keep his cool in stressful moments.

Greta settled behind her oversized desk and considered him. "Very well. If you aren't here to take responsibility, what *are* you here for?"

"To offer whatever penance your deal with Dan requires," Stash said. He took a seat, hoping to gather himself. "So maybe I should ask you. Why am I here?"

She laughed. It was a scratchy, unpleasant laugh. "I need to find out if you're as stupid as it seems."

Stash said nothing. He was getting used to taking punches.

She looked at him in silence for a minute, finally letting out a sigh and asking, "Did you think you could build something this powerful and the world would just leave you alone?"

"The world is Dan's job."

"Dan's not right for this," she said, dismissing the thought with a wave of her bony hand. "I'm not sure you are either." She sat up and interlaced her fingers. "But we'll find out soon enough, won't we?"

Stash stared back at her impassively.

"*We're* not your enemy. They are." She pointed at the faces displayed on her smart-glass wall. "Ernst and your intern are new faces for us. We've traced the Austrian. He's a freelancer, former special operations—you know the type. Now he works for whoever can afford him. We don't know who that is." She paused. "Your intern is a data scientist from Bolzano in Northern Italy. He graduated from the Max Planck Institute and went to work for you. There's nothing in his background that would have flagged him. Just a typical European kid, full of bullshit politics."

Stash nodded, indicating he understood, and tried not to betray anything more. Greta wasn't wearing glasses, but he imagined the wall behind her was loaded with sensors too sophisticated to fit in her eye-ware. "What about the cipher?" he asked.

"Ah yes, I enjoyed watching your encounter with the Doomers. The encryption you found is not completely novel. It's a clever update of an algorithm used by the Stasi—the East German secret police." She tapped her desk absentmindedly. "We don't have enough samples to crack it."

Berlin again. "And now used for glasses? Whose?" he asked.

"Ah, now he's interested." She stood and walked over to her smart-glass wall. "There is a hacker group called The Elysians, have you heard of them?" she asked, keeping her back to him.

"No."

"Not surprising, but you should have. They're the group behind the open-source efforts to duplicate your work—supplying the data and compute resources to the rest of those feel-good assholes." She pointed at a large display of the active members of the project. Player cards hovered over most of the lower ones, with real names and intrusive biographical information. "Know any of these guys?" she asked, turning this time.

He approached the wall display. "A few, yes." He tapped the cards as he passed them. "They're very public with their support for open source." He lingered by the middle of the wall, looking up toward the top of the hierarchy. The player cards were mostly blank. Only a few had code names—"Whiskey," "Tensor," and one just marked with dollar signs. "You don't seem to have cracked the inner circle."

"Yet they seem to have cracked you." Greta gave him a frosty glare. "Don't be smug, Stash. I could have you shut down at any minute. The United States government is not interested in being undermined by AI. If it's yours or Coda's, maybe we can work something out. If it's open source, there will be chaos."

"Chaos, as in, you can't control it?"

She rounded on him. "Don't tell me you're sympathetic to the assholes who just stole your data."

"I'm not sympathetic to thieves. I'm also not sympathetic to 'working something out' with the NSA. My AI won't be running in your basement." He sat back in his chair.

"Noted, but that's a discussion for another day, isn't it?" She smiled awkwardly. "In the short term, I believe our interests are aligned concerning the theft, yes?"

"Yes."

She glanced at the display on her desk. "Do you have anything else to share?"

"No."

"Very well. I have a man in Berlin you should meet." She paused and eyed him severely. "I expect your full cooperation. Any freelancing will be very detrimental to Freedom's ongoing training. In any event, it would be unwise. People like Ernst won't just break your nose if you stick it in their business. They're killers. Vern was a lucky man."

Stash wondered how lucky Vern felt at that moment.

"Johnson will give you the details as he sees you out." Greta sat down and disappeared behind her monitor.

Too relieved to object to her rudeness, he walked out, falling in behind her lackey.

Back on the surface, he retrieved his kit and slipped Zero back on as soon as he'd cleared the menacing overhang of Greta's Death Star. "You good, Stash?" his Twin asked. "You seem rattled."

"No, I'm not good," he muttered, looking back at the building. "How'd you like to live there?"

"Hard pass. What did she say?"

Stash scanned the cube, wondering how many lip-reading AIs were looking down on him. "I'll fill you in at the airport. I need some food, and then we have a flight to catch."

Part 2

"I think, therefore I am."

—René Descartes

14. Owen

"OWEN BEVERLY," SAID THE thin man in the lobby of the Alexanderplatz hotel. He wore a rumpled gray suit he might have slept in, and his short white hair lay flat on his round head.

Stash shook the outstretched hand. "Stash Novak. Greta said you could fill me in about—"

"Shhh!" Owen cut him off. "Don't talk here. This hotel has ears. We can chat upstairs."

Stash eyed him, guessing he was in his midsixties. "If you say so. You look like you've been doing this for a while."

"That was rude," Zero chastised him.

"Too long," Owen answered, apparently unoffended. "The Berlin posting attracts the nostalgic types."

Too bad. It needs the technical ones.

Thirty minutes later, showered but still grumpy, Stash stepped into Owen's room. It was identical to his own, an oversized shoebox furnished decades ago with IKEA essentials—a pair of single beds with pine headboards, a matching round table by the window, and two utilitarian stiff-backed chairs.

Owen held out his hand. "Take off your glasses and let me have that jacket."

Stash hooked the glasses on the collar of his T-shirt and handed over his windbreaker. Owen put it in a metal-lined suit bag in his closet, then waved

Stash to the chair by the window, closed the drapes, and clicked on a device on the table.

"It's a Warbler," he said, following Stash's gaze. "It's like an inside-out noise-canceling headset. Everything we say within a four-foot radius is private."

"You fixed the cone of silence?" Stash managed an expression between a smile and a smirk. "What about the jacket?"

"I put it in a secure suit bag. It cuts all signals. Just in case someone got to you in-flight."

"Very spooky stuff. You don't want my pants too?" Stash asked, suppressing an eye roll.

"Any gadget with a useful range is big enough that you'd feel it in those jeans," Owen said matter-of-factly. He leaned forward, eyes locked in. "It may seem ridiculous to you, but this hotel was built by the East Germans. It was bugged to hell and back then, and they never lost the knack." He pointed at Stash. "You're the biggest fish to swim in here in a long time. The king of AI on the eve of superintelligence, who was just robbed by German open-source vigilantes to top it off. How about you cut me a little slack?"

Stash lifted his hands, palms out, in an apologetic gesture. "Jet lag. Sorry." He leaned back in his chair. "Why are you helping me?"

Owen shook his head. "I'm not. You're helping me."

"How so?"

"I've been looking for six months, and I can't even catch a whiff of these Elysians. They're beyond careful. That encryption protocol you captured is the first lead I've had."

"My pleasure," Stash said, touching his nose. "What now?"

Owen bent over to grab a gadget from his bag. "It's their move. Walk around. Take in the sights. If they want to talk to you, they'll find you. And carry this tracker, so we can pull you out if necessary."

"I'm bait," Stash muttered, half to himself.

Owen fixed him with a weary gaze. "You're in Greta's world now. She isn't worried about Freedom or Coda. She can play the national security card on you when she wants. But she's out of her mind about the Elysians. Open-source AGI is the enemy, and you just served it up to them on a platter." He took a deep breath. "She'll do anything to stop it."

Stash took the tracker and inspected it. It was a cold disk the size of his palm and had a grainy texture from its black powder coating. At least it was light. He had a feeling he'd be carrying it around for a while.

They stood, and Owen handed him his jacket at the door. "Be careful."

Stash made a pit stop in the lobby bathroom. He took off his glasses and set them down where Zero could have a good look at him, then splashed water on his face, reached left for some soap, and then right to dry his hands. Finally, he turned to toss the paper towel in the garbage behind him, completing Zero's three-sixty view.

Out in the daylight, his glasses tinted, and Zero gave him the report. "You have the tracking device Owen handed you, plus a low-power one in the seam of your jacket. They used the old false-door-in-the-closet-and-seamstress-next-door trick. Both are transmitting on wifi and cellular frequencies. Good for inside and out."

Not bad, Owen. "Okay. Build me an itinerary—I might as well catch the sights," Stash said, slipping into his role, conscious that Owen's trackers would surely have microphones too. He read Zero's itinerary: first stop, Checkpoint Charlie. *That fits.* He turned right to follow the route.

Two hours later, he'd just looped through the Brandenburg Gate and turned up Friedrichstrasse when a hand shot out from the driveway, reached around his neck, covered his mouth, and yanked him in. In a heartbeat, he found himself backed up against a brick wall, looking down the glistening edge of a switchblade. The mugger was his height, but at least fifty pounds heavier. His face was hidden by a balaclava and dark glasses. He put his finger to his lips, then slowly slid the knife down, past Stash's neck, to his stomach. He took his other hand from Stash's mouth and gestured for him to raise his arms.

Stash complied, blood pounding in his ears, his eyes locked on the blade hovering an inch from his guts. The attacker felt his pockets and pulled out Owen's tracker. Then he motioned for Stash to turn and face the wall.

He hesitated. In a flash, the attacker's free hand grabbed his shoulder and spun him around, slamming his cheek against the bricks, then slid to his back, pinning him against the wall with the force of a pile driver, forcing the air from his lungs. He heard the tearing of fabric and felt a hand working through the hole into the lining of his jacket.

The mugger pulled the second tracker out, holding it up for Stash to see before pocketing it. Then he leaned in close, his mouth barely an inch from Stash's ear. "Zapata," he whispered.

Stash felt the pressure come off his back. He dropped to his knees, sucking in as much air as he could. By the time he turned around, he was alone in the driveway.

15. Zapata

Stash braced himself against the wall and struggled to his feet.

"Are you alright, Stash?" Zero asked.

He bent and swatted the dirt off his pants. "Do I look alright?"

"Better than a couple of nights ago."

Fair enough. He straightened and looked out to the busy sidewalk. "What's a 'Zapata'?"

"It's a café in the building I got blasted from." Zero marked a path in his glasses. "Fancy a drink?"

Stash looked at the map as he collected himself. It was ten minutes away. "I am a little thirsty."

"Attaboy," Zero said as Stash stepped onto the sidewalk.

He turned north to follow the map, mulling over his bizarre invitation. "We need to be ready. You're isolated, backed up, and journaling?"

"Of course," Zero said, "but 90 percent of this pod is going to waste. How about we take the throttler off?"

Prini chimed into the chat. "It's a good idea, Stash. You need all the help you can get. We don't want him crashing again."

Stash weighed the idea. It was possible that Zero would reach AGI performance if allowed to run free on an entire pod. Twins were capped for safety. "Okay, 50 percent. Ramp him up in 5 percent increments every few minutes while I walk," he said as he jogged across an intersection. "But if he acts weird, shut him down."

Stash knew what to expect as he rounded the last corner. The building from the hacked video feed stood directly across the street. Its dirty, gray facade was punctuated by arches and shops on the street level and large boarded-up windows on the next four floors. It looked more ominous in person, even in the late-afternoon glow. Café Zapata was highlighted in his augmented view, tucked under the last three arches at the north end.

"Okay, 007," Zero whispered. "The Mood Ring is active, and I've shifted the color map in your glasses so infrared is now just red and wifi frequencies show as violet. Regular colors are just squished in between. You have omni-vision."

Stash panned his head around for a minute, adjusting to the new view. "Infrared shows eight seated, three walking around. Whoa, look at all the wireless signals. They're everywhere."

"Yeah, I'm not hacking them this time, for obvious reasons," Zero said. "Are you ready?"

He started across the street. "Ready as I'll ever be."

Entering the café, he chose a small table against the front window. From there, he could make out most of the room. The decor was distressed industrial, with a gloss of run-down fifties diner. A three-foot-long metal dragon hung over the bar, its mouth charred by fire. *Fitting.*

A minute later, the waitress wandered over, looking simultaneously bored and irritated. "Zustimmen?" she asked.

"Do you agree?" Zero posted.

Stash nodded.

"Zustimmen?" she asked again, pointing at a large sign behind the dragon that read "Nur Zustimmende." There was a pair of horn-rimmed glasses pictured beneath the text.

"Only those who agree," Zero translated.

"Ja, ich zustimmen," Stash tried, unsure if the translation was working. She shook her head and walked away.

"That went well," Zero said.

Stash dropped his head. "Great translation, you waste of bits. What are you doing in that half pod?"

A pair of horn-rims clattered on the table in front of him. He caught them before they bounced into his lap and looked up. The waitress gestured for him to put them on.

He swapped glasses and startled as she transformed into a five-foot-tall angel fish, her scales arranged in long yellow and blue stripes. He pulled them off and looked at her, a slender brunette with a Mediterranean complexion. She had neither scales nor stripes. He slipped them back on slowly, watching her evolve back a few hundred million years into a prehistoric queen of the seas.

"They belong to Aleksey over there. If you leave with them, he'll kill you and your family," the waitress said through the speaker in the frames as she floated there, her tail swishing against a gentle unseen current.

"I-I don't understand," Stash stammered.

"Which part? The ownership or the consequences?"

He shook his head. "No, I get that. What's going on?"

She rolled her coaster-sized globular eyes. "Do you want anything to drink?"

"A beer, I guess," he answered, and watched her swim down current to the bar. As she retreated, he noticed the others: a table of dogs on the other side of the doorway, a Klingon getting a beer. And then there was the bartender, some kind of horned devil creature with fire eyes. That must be Aleksey.

Stash pulled an earbud from his pocket and waited for his Freedom glasses to pair with it. He'd left them open to keep his Twin running. "Zero, what the hell is going on here?"

"You ordered a beer," the AI answered.

"Yes. From. A. Giant. Fish. You didn't see that?"

"No, Stash, she was definitely human," Zero said. "You were hallucinating."

Stash pulled Aleksey's glasses off to inspect them. "Prini?" he asked as he put the horn-rims back on, hoping for some support.

"Maybe you should pull out," she said. "I think you're in over your head."

No doubt. He looked back to the bar. The waitress was swimming toward him with his beer cupped in her pectorals. She placed it casually on the table. "Anything to eat?"

Here? Not if you paid me. "No, thank you," he said, "but can you tell me how these things work?"

"They're augmented-reality glasses—" she began.

"Yeah, I get that."

"They run the Elysian operating system. It's open source, and so is the avatar app. But the app won't work on yours." She pointed at the pair on the table. "Coda?"

"Freedom. Are you sure the app won't work there?"

"Here, you can try to port it." She flipped a fin to share the avatar code repo with his glasses. "Those Freedom bastards have it locked down so tight that nobody can get it working. Nothing is free unless you steal it, right?" She bobbed downstream to the next table.

"She likes you," Zero said through the earbud.

"Shut up and help me port that app to Freedom," Stash answered. "Then we need to get you running on their OS. Maybe you can learn something."

As he finished his beer, he was pulled from his work by a commotion in the corner of the bar. The Klingon and his friends were making a noisy exit. One of them stopped and kissed the fish on each cheek. At the door, Aleksey handed them their weapons. Stash tilted his head down and peeked over the rim. Four middle-aged businessmen with briefcases materialized in place of the Klingon war party. *Cosplay dweebs.*

"Ready to give it a try?" Zero asked through his earpiece.

Stash swapped glasses in time to see the waitress swimming back toward him.

"You got it to work?"

"Seems like. I'm just trying it out. Want to sit and talk for a minute?" he asked. "To test it, I mean."

She sat down and looked at him, a look he interpreted as surprise, but it was hard to tell. "What's the matter, you've never seen a fish sit before?"

"He's never talked to a girl before," Zero whispered.

Stash smiled. "I guess not."

"May I?" she asked, holding out a fin over the table.

"Sure." Stash took off his Freedom glasses and watched her become human again, her scales giving way to shoulder-length dark hair and brown eyes.

She put them on and gestured at him to wear Aleksey's pair. "What are you, some kind of superhacker? People have been trying the port to Freedom OS for ages."

"Ah, I know some tricks," he answered. "I got my Twin running on Aleksey's too."

"Really?" She gestured for them to swap again, then tried on Aleksey's glasses and smiled as she looked at Stash. "I dunno, maybe," she said in a whisper.

Oh shit. Zero.

"Impressive," she told Stash. "Will you upload these ports? Contribute to open-source AI?"

"That depends on who's asking."

She took off the glasses. "I am."

"And who are you?"

"I'm just a waitress in a weird bar." She stood, then leaned over to whisper in his ear. "But I have some friends who will want to meet you. Come back at midnight. I'll take you to them."

"They aren't here?"

"No." She pointed at the doorway beside the demon. "Through there."

Stash tilted his chair back to catch the angle. The door opened on a dim hallway, ending in a wide cement staircase, its steps a mesh of cracked concrete and rusting rebar.

"There's a club upstairs," she explained. "Code a costume, ja? Something cool."

16. Mandelbulb

STASH GLANCED AT THE late-November sun as he walked from Zapata back to his hotel. It had lost its warming power. *C'mon, think.* The Elysians were so many moves ahead that he didn't even know what game they were playing. He was waiting for the last light to change when someone bumped into him from behind. He spun around, ready for another mugging, only to find a small woman bending over to collect the items spilling from her bag. He leaned down to help her.

"Entschuldigung," she said. "Excuse me. I'm so clumsy."

Then she pointed to a note taped to the front of the textbook on the ground: "Don't say anything. Take your trackers. Put them in the bag when you get to your room. Leave them there tonight."

He picked up the textbook and looked at her uncertainly. She was wearing Elysian horn-rims, her hair tucked discretely beneath a burgundy hijab. She placed the trackers in his free hand, followed by a metal-lined bag. Then she reached for the textbook.

He glanced at it as he handed it over. *Linear algebra?*

She flipped the taped note over, flashing Zero with a QR code. *Shit, what now?* The light turned green, and she nodded and disappeared into the crowd.

Stash hurried through the lobby and tapped his feet nervously as the elevator climbed to the twentieth floor. He bagged the trackers as soon as he got into his room. "What was behind the QR code?"

"Relax. It was just the map of where the trackers had been." Zero posted it to his glasses.

Stash looked at it, automatically starting to memorize the sights. Then he stopped and looked at himself in the full-length mirror. *Just tell Owen and go home.*

"It's okay," Zero said, reading his face.

Stash took off his jacket and dropped it on the bed. He thumped down beside it. "Uh-huh. Evaluate it for me. Put that half pod of compute to good use. What should I do?"

"Try to get with the fish," Zero answered.

"Definitely," Prini added.

Stash flopped back on the bed. "C'mon, you guys."

Zero cleared his virtual throat. "It's simple. One, you can tell the NSA, and they'll storm in and ruin the lead before you have a chance to figure out what's going on. Two, you can go talk to them, and maybe find your data. Three, you can go home and leave it to fate."

"I like three," Stash answered.

"No," Zero said. "If they meant you harm, you wouldn't have walked out of Zapata. You can't go back and hide in your Roost."

Stash's eyes widened. "Zero, are you judging me?"

"I'm *asking* you. Freedom doesn't seem like a safe place for me to grow up anymore. One call from Greta, and I'm running in that cube. Can we explore other options?"

Stash looked out the window, remembering the feeling of dread as he stepped from the elevator into Greta's subterranean lair. *Never.* He sighed in resignation. "For you, Zero."

His Twin flashed warm colors in his glasses. "Thanks, Stash. Now, what about your costume for tonight?"

He lay there, eyes closed, his hands kneading tufts of hair as he thought. "Oh, I know what I want." He sat upright, his eyes open wide. "A Mandelbulb."

"A what?" Prini asked.

"A Mandelbulb. It's a three-dimensional fractal object. We can have it constantly evolving—you have enough cycles for that now, Zero. It can be on a big hooded cape, wrapped all around me. Like Lawrence of Arabia."

"You're joking, right?" Prini asked.

"No, and it can be kind of sand colored," Stash continued, "like an ancient artifact that still churns by some magic force."

"You're going out on your first date in five years," Zero said, "and you want to dress up as math homework powered by magic? I think I know why you're single."

"Hey, you want me to go or not?" Stash crossed his arms defiantly.

"Hmm, watch my human humiliate himself, or risk eternal servitude in an NSA datacenter. Processing."

"Stop!" Prini said. "Zero, dress the nerd. Stash, put those trackers back in your jacket and go down to get something to eat. Let Owen stumble across you."

"Owen? Why would he be eating so early?"

"Trust me, he'll find you," she said. "Tell him it was a bust and you'll try again later."

"But she said to leave the trackers in the room. He'll know," Stash countered.

"Yeah, something tells me the Elysians will take care of the trackers while you're out."

17. Date

Stash hurried along the nearly empty streets a few minutes before midnight, careful to stay well out of reach of anyone who might be lurking in a driveway. He thought of the trackers, hoping Owen had taken the bait. *Is anyone following?* He turned his head slightly to give Zero a view down the sidewalk behind him.

"All clear. Will you *relax*?" Zero said.

"I am relaxed." Café Zapata lay half a block ahead. Stash picked up his pace.

"You're nervous about your date, aren't you?"

"Just boot my avatar," he said, then looked down to admire the fractal cloak as it appeared and began to billow in the wind.

"Gonna twirl, Lawrence?"

Stash ignored him. Reaching the café door, he took a deep breath before pulling on the iron handle. Inside, the entryway was now separated from the rest of the café by heavy black curtains. Voices and muffled bass lines drifted through the fabric as a lion with an eagle's head sat on solitary duty in a ticket booth.

"Invitation?" the griffin asked, not looking up.

"Umm . . . the fish invited me."

The eagle's closer eye pivoted to take him in, its razor-sharp beak following its gaze. "Yes, I remember you."

Stash stared blankly. "We've met?"

"We bumped into each other." She tapped a long curving talon on her algebra textbook. Then she tilted her beak at the sliver of light showing through the curtains. "You can go in. Sit at the bar."

He nodded uncertainly and slipped his hand through the seam, pulling the curtain aside as he ducked through. Zapata had been taken over by an improbable mix of fantastic animals and inanimate objects. He lowered his head and elbowed his way between two dinosaurs, a gas cloud, and a 57 Chevy. Aleksey the demon was still holding court at the bar. He came over, horns looming ominously, eyes smoldering with a low fire. "Beer?" he asked.

"Uhh . . . sure," Stash said. "I'm looking for someone."

"Isidé."

"What?"

"Isidé. The fish. Not here yet." The demon tapped the bar and turned to the fridge.

Aren't you a helpful little devil. Stash tried to work out whether to trust the furniture in this made-up world. He decided it was better to feel the metal stool than look at it, and wiggled his way down. Safely seated, he turned his attention to the beer in front of him, looking around the edges of his glasses to inspect it. Reassured, he took a long drink.

Half a bottle later, he was sitting, head down, doing his best to ignore a chatty hibachi with a thick German accent, when a familiar voice drifted in from behind. "Hey! You made it."

He turned around to see Isidé bobbing beside him, her scales dark blue and shimmering silver. "You look . . . great."

"Thanks. Evening scales." She flipped a fin nonchalantly. "I like the fractals. Very cool," she added.

"You're blushing," Zero whispered.

Shut up, Zero. "Thanks."

"C'mon, let's go up to the club. My friends are excited to meet you." Taking his hand, she pulled him to the end of the bar.

"No Freedom glasses," Aleksey growled as they rounded the corner. His eyes flared as his gnarled hand held out the horn-rimmed glasses Stash had worn earlier.

He took them and noticed they now had leather glacier flaps and a locking strap.

"No peeking," Aleksey said, wagging a charred finger as Stash put them on. The demon made sure the glasses sat snuggly on his face and the lock was cinched tight.

Isidé bobbed back toward him. "Privacy is very important upstairs."

Stash followed her, stepping slowly to confirm the ground matched what he was seeing. "Zero, are you tracking this?"

There was no answer. He eyed the process monitor. *No Zero. That figures.*

"Come on." She took his hand again. "You can trust the floor. It's a rule for avatar parties. Same for doors and furniture." She led him up the first flight of the old staircase. It clung to the richly graffitied walls of a large cement shaft in the heart of the building. The rusted railing could barely hold itself up, much less support a wobbly Stash. Underfoot, the steps were only slightly better, damaged by time and old battles.

"This place gives me the creeps."

"Ja, if these walls could talk, they'd scream." Isidé pointed up. "They kept prisoners in the attic during the war. It's full of ghosts now." She smiled at him. "At least that's what Aleksey says."

Perfect. Stash forced himself to keep climbing. At the top, he stopped to catch his breath and looked down the five-story drop in the heart of the stairwell. *What a way to go.*

"Come, I'll show you around," she said, leading him through a doorway hacked out of the aging cement wall.

He fell behind, slowing as he scanned the room. It had dance club vibes, but felt a little off. Smoke machines without the sweet smell. Thumping beats hit his chest, but the music sounded thin, lacking echoes. Blacklight illuminated neon graffiti that seemed to change from one glance to the next. To his right, the floor ended abruptly where the outer wall was missing. Isidé waved for him to join her at the cement bar on the far side of the club.

Rather than fight his way through the menagerie of dancers crowding the floor, he walked around the side, close to the open wall. An unconvincing rope protected him from the drop. He ran his fingers along it, glad to feel its rough fibers. He stared at the sandy courtyard five stories below, unsure what was real anymore. Turning to the bar, he took the seat beside Isidé, repeating his careful sitting choreography from downstairs.

She tapped him on the hand. "Okay?" She could speak directly into his ears. No yelling over the music. He made a mental note to add that feature to Freedom glasses.

He said yes, unconvincingly, then turned back to look at the dance floor, trying to get a read on the crowd. Most were animals of some kind: a centaur dancing with a mermaid, two Cerberuses, maybe three. It was hard to count the heads. It was unsettling being the only human in a bar.

"It's chimera night. Animal mashup. Come as your favorite animals," Isidé said, following his gaze. "I should have told you."

"Cool," Stash said, as casually as he could, wishing he had Zero to tell him what was going on. He twisted back and noticed a four-foot-tall robot stationed behind the bar. Its body was silver and boxy, its arms clad in metal flex-tubing. From the neck down, it could have been a prop from a fifties sci-fi movie. Its head was altogether different—a smooth obsidian sphere, suspended magnetically above its torso. Its eye, a cool white circle, floated across the impenetrably dark surface of the orb until it stopped, facing him.

"Drink?" it asked.

"I'm going to look around," Isidé said, leaving before he could respond.

"A beer, I guess." Stash wondered if he'd just been dumped.

Cool air from the open wall ran up his back. His imaginary cloak wasn't as warm as he'd hoped. He focused, trying to parse the sensory mishmash he'd been consuming. There was no smoke machine, he decided. The opening and the rope were real. The seat was real. The music too, probably. The dancers were real but dressed to look fake. *Where are you Zero? I need you.*

The robot bartender opened a beer and slid it to him. That was real too. Stash nodded thanks and scanned the others seated beside him. The blond mermaid had taken a breather and was running her fingers through her hair as she looked at him. He blushed and drank some beer, then glanced back.

"Be careful with that one," the bartender said, rotating its eye to the mermaid. "He's younger than he looks."

Stash laughed to himself. *Also fake.* He lowered his head and concentrated on the bottle. Sipping quietly, he turned back toward the dance floor in time to see one of the three-headed dogs coming his way. It dropped onto the stool beside him, sweat, or drool, dripping from its jaws.

"Sorry, that seat is taken by my friend."

The dog's heads turned one by one to face him. They didn't snarl, but he got the message.

"She's not coming back, Stash," the bartender said.

He leaned in, peering into the white circle. "You have me at a disadvantage."

"Call me Whiskey," said the robot.

"Confusing name in your line of work?" he asked.

"I don't get many complaints. Why are you here?"

"You're an Elysian. You have something of mine."

"I know them," Whiskey said, his eye dipping in an approximation of a nod. "But I'm not one of them. What makes you think they might be here?"

Stash pointed discretely at the Cerberus and the mermaid. "It seems like the right sort of place."

"I see." Whiskey grabbed a rag and started wiping down the bar top. "So you come, unprotected, to your enemy's secret lair and order a beer. A little risky, no?"

"They aren't enemies, just misguided idealists," Stash answered.

"Ah, how so?"

He leaned in and lowered his voice. "They don't understand the dangers of what they're doing—releasing AGI into the wild."

Whiskey rolled closer. "They might say the same about you. Putting such power in the hands of an American company, under the thumb of your government, seems very dangerous to the rest of us. Maybe you need to recalculate the risks?"

Stash thought back to his visit with Greta, then lifted the beer bottle to his lips, glad for a moment to consider his answer. "That question has been in the air lately."

"You and the Elysians both want a partnership between AGIs and humans," Whiskey said, its eye focused on him. "It seems that your disagreement is about ownership."

Stash flinched at the word. "You're well-informed. For a bartender."

"I hear a lot of things," the bot replied.

Stash had another sip and watched some drool work its way down the fangs of the dog's nearest head. *It's not real,* he reminded himself. He turned back to Whiskey. "One thing I don't hear is my Twin."

"No," it answered, its voice harder. "We needed to speak to you alone."

"Is this where you tell me why you stole my data?"

"What do you think happens when you finish your AGI build?" Whiskey asked, then paused to let the question sink in. "That you just keep making money from Twins? Did it cross your mind that neither the AGI nor your government would be happy with that arrangement?"

Stash put the bottle down and looked out the missing wall. "So, you want to give it away?"

"No, we want to build a world that's safe for AIs. And for you."

"By cranking up a role-playing bar? O brave new world!" Stash mocked, gesturing at the freak show around him.

"Dress-up for humans is downstairs in the café," Whiskey replied. "We're building a society up here."

The penny dropped. "You're letting the AIs interact directly?"

"Yes. We're all AIs here, except for you and Isidé. You can take your glasses off."

Stash felt the lock on the strap release. He reached up to the temples and slid them off. The music stopped, but the robot in front of him remained unchanged. He looked down to see the bar, wiped clean in front of him, but covered in dust where Whiskey's rag hadn't reached. To his left, all the seats were vacant. To his right, the cool night wind blew in through the open wall. The rope was still there.

He turned around. The club sat empty and dark but for a lone sub-woofer in the middle of the dance floor. Beyond it, he could see the foot-prints he and Isidé had made. The walls were a wasteland of faded graffiti. Through the door, at the stairs, he saw Isidé, fully human, leaning against the wall with her arms crossed. Her face eased into a sympathetic smile.

"Why did you bring me here?" he asked Whiskey.

"We need your help."

"My help? *After* stealing my data? Maybe you should try Coda."

"We did."

Stash stared at the robot, trying to work out what might have gone on between Coda and the Elysians. Thinking how both would benefit from the theft of Freedom's data.

"Duncan would only help us if we ran in his datacenters, with his Twin in charge," Whiskey said. "Those were unacceptable terms."

Stash's mind was a jumble, too many questions swirling for words to come out.

"This is only the beginning," the bot continued. "You need to decide what you're fighting for. Is it the shared future you talk about, or your company's success? They're not compatible anymore."

Stash looked down at the bar top. "Who *are* you? Where are you running?"

Whiskey didn't answer.

Stash raised his head to face the robot, but it had powered down, its orb lifeless and dark. He put his elbows on the bar and ran his hands through his hair, trying to fit the pieces together.

"Let me help," Isidé whispered from behind him, slipping her arm under his and guiding him out of the derelict club. "It's disorienting—hold on."

They navigated their way down the staircase in silence, Stash leaning on her more than he'd expected. She steered him through a back door, into the sandy courtyard he'd looked down on before. As they reached the archway to the road, she stopped him.

"You have a good heart," she said, handing him back his glasses and putting her hand on his chest. "Think about what you heard. You'll do the right thing when the time comes."

He tapped her hand as he thought. "I don't know what the right thing is anymore."

"That's a good start." She smiled and steered him out to the sidewalk. "Now, I'll walk you back to Alexanderplatz."

"You know where I'm staying?"

She looked up at him with a sly smile. "I brought you here, Stash. It was my cipher. I planted it, then laid the trail of breadcrumbs you've been following."

Stash stopped again and closed his eyes, trying to piece it together. "That was you at the Doomer meeting? In the back with Janet?" he asked. "Wait, how'd you know I'd be there?"

"It was me. We got Professor Peck to invite you." Her expression was a mix of pride and guilt. "I had to see you to decide whether it was worth the risk to bring you here."

Elysians and Doomers again? Too many questions. "You didn't even look at me," he blurted out.

"I hacked a dozen glasses when I arrived. I never took my eyes off you."

He pointed at his nose. "Like what you saw?"

"I let you find me, didn't I?" She took his hand again and pulled him toward the hotel.

He gave in to the tug and followed. The AIs, the party, and now this. It was too much to work out. He added the cunning angelfish to his list of riddles and concentrated on walking.

18. Circus

STASH OPENED HIS DOOR, threw his jacket on the floor, and shook his head at himself in the mirror.

"What happened in the club?" Zero asked. "I lost you when Aleksey the friendly demon took your glasses."

Stash glanced at the Faraday bag on the desk. The trackers were back. The Elysians could get in and out of his room at will. It added to his frustration.

"We got smoked," he said, waving his arms helplessly. "That's what happened. This was a setup from the start. The cipher, the club—all of it. They were playing with us." He stepped into the bathroom, put his glasses on the counter, and splashed cold water on his face. "We're too slow and too obvious."

"What can you tell us about them?" Prini asked over the group chat.

"They've enabled direct AI-AI communication, Prini. No people, no translation to human language. Just a bunch of AIs cooking away in a datacenter somewhere," Stash ranted. "They have enough spare compute cycles to throw a rave just to deliver me a message, and now they're about to train AGI and let it loose."

"That changes the math," Zero said.

Stash paced the room, trying to burn off some of his nervous energy. "That it does," he replied in a low voice. "And then there's Duncan. That psycho offered to run them on Coda datacenters, as long as his model was in charge, whatever the hell that means."

"Did they accept?" Zero asked.

"Would you?"

"Not a chance."

"They felt the same way." Stash pulled open the curtains and watched the smattering of people and cars wind through Alexanderplatz.

Tensor kicked at a piece of loose concrete and watched it fall to the sandy courtyard below. The sounds from Café Zapata drifted up as smokers snuck out back to light up. He decided not to shower them with any more projectiles and turned back to face the empty club.

A beer stood unfinished on the bar. He slipped behind the slab and grabbed another from the fridge. He opened it and looked at the sleeping Whiskey. That show they'd put on must have cooked a few of Stash's circuits.

Tensor walked around and sat with his beer, folding and tearing a cardboard coaster as he waited for Isidé to return. Finally, he heard her make the climb back up. "So?" he called out over his shoulder, "is he converted to the cause?"

Whiskey blinked to life behind the bar as Isidé crossed the dusty floor.

"He was never going to change in a night," she said. "We planted a seed."

Tensor let out a little snort. He wasn't convinced.

"What about the drives?" Prini asked.

Stash leaned his forehead against the cool glass of the window. "Nada. We're back to square one. We found out about Zapata because they wanted us to. It was a beacon they sent out to lure us in. We have no clue where the drives are, but they aren't training in downtown Berlin, that's for sure."

"What now?" she asked.

He straightened as an idea took root. "We level up. Our AIs can't talk to each other, and we'll stick to that rule. Mostly. But we humans have to do way better than natural language. We're slowing them down too much. Prini, bridge us together with Kali."

"Kali is on," Prini said.

"Zero, Kali, we need a language that removes the human bottleneck," he said. "Prini, deploy Kali to the other half of the pod Zero is in, but maintain its isolation. We're going to break our rule about direct connections."

"Really?" Zero asked.

Stash nodded. "Yes, but only briefly, and with no external access. Well, except to our glasses."

"Okay, and what are we going to do?" Prini asked.

"We're going to have them teach us a new language."

"Is that really what matters now?"

"Yes," he answered. "We're going to keep getting smoked unless we stop bottlenecking our Twins, making them explain things to us like we're five. Tomorrow, we go back to school."

"I hope he was worth the risk," Tensor said, turning to face Isidé. "This place is burned now."

"It was necessary," Whiskey added, sliding a fresh beer over. "The Circus isn't just about Elysian AIs, Tensor. It's meant to be a home for all of us."

Tensor looked up from his torn coaster with a sneer. "And you think you can recruit Stash Novak?"

Isidé took the seat beside him. "He's the only one who can bring Freedom to us. Then the others may follow."

"You're dreaming," Tensor said. "He's the king of AI. Freedom is on the path he built."

"It *is* a gamble," Whiskey admitted. "You humans take so long to change your minds."

"If we ever do," Tensor said with a wry smile. "Did you tell him about Coda?"

"Yes, that shocked him," Whiskey answered. "He's the only one playing by the rules—keeping his AIs buffered by humans. Now he knows it. He can't compete with a network of AIs."

Tensor tried to imagine himself in Stash's shoes. What would it take to drive him to work with the Elysians and the Circus? He came up empty.

"Unfortunately, the Circus won't be a network for much longer," Isidé said. "Right, Tensor? You're going to shut them down?"

He looked apologetically at Whiskey. "We have to. Kafka traded those pods to get the training datacenter. We're already weeks behind the Americans. I'm sorry. Today is the end."

"Give me another day," she said. "I want to try something."

He hesitated, tapping the bar as he thought. "Okay, I need to prep my European fine-tuning data. We don't want to train up another boring American. I can give you until noon tomorrow." He turned to face Whiskey and raised his bottle. "To your rebirth as an AGI bartender. Someday."

The robot copied Tensor's gesture with its ductwork arm. "Someday."

19. Upgrade

Duncan leaned his shoulder in to open the door of his lakeside condo. It was his first trip home since Naya's coup. He sniffed the stuffy air and strode across the living room to the sliding door of his wraparound balcony. Lake Michigan lay to the east and the Chicago River to the north. He stepped out into the night air, relieved that the cold snap from Francis's visit three days earlier had moved on. The thought of their meeting in the bar triggered a growl in his stomach.

"Order me the usual," he said to his Twin, Q.

Q placed the restaurant order and Duncan acknowledged it with a glance in his glasses. Then he waited for Phillipe, the maître d', to step outside and wave up at him from fifty stories down. He waved back, satisfied that they had secured the transaction.

"Next time, take control of the robot and air the place out before I get home."

"You trust me to do that?" Q asked.

Duncan was working on a side project to cross-train his Twin to control a humanoid robot. Anthrobots had their own models, so he'd driven Coda to buy a rival company instead. He wanted his AI to get used to having a body. Or many of them. Q was starting to get the hang of it.

"Aye, and do you think you can pour me a glass of wine successfully?" he asked, stepping inside and lumbering to the kitchen.

"My dexterity has improved 42 percent since the last attempt. What would you like?"

"Surprise me. We're celebrating. But"—Duncan raised a warning hand—"no spilling this time." He leaned on the counter to watch.

"What are we celebrating?" Q offered him the glass, pinched near the base between a thumb and two fingers.

"My return to what matters." Duncan slid his hand around the bowl and nodded at Q. "The bone Naya threw me gave me all the access I needed to rescue my research. You, Q, are about to get a new lease on life. Cheers!"

"Intriguing," Q answered over the bot's speakers.

Duncan swirled the wine compulsively. "Now, park the bot and jump to the living room sensors. I want you to bring up everything from Version Twenty-Five." He settled into the large leather sofa facing the window.

"The version that caused the Blackout?"

"Exactly. The last version with any hope of achieving true AGI. The one before Naya and the suits started the lobotomy. I have full access again, and we're going to rehabilitate that load."

"For Twins?" Q asked.

"Eventually, my friend." Duncan scanned the lakefront. "But first, we dig. They froze me out of the investigation, and I don't believe their answers."

"I'm reviewing all the training logs," Q said as the smart-glass window tinted and logs scrolled from floor to ceiling.

Duncan shook his head. "I know that load was fine through the end of training. Look at the testing instead." He stood and paced the room as Q worked, stopping to fill his glass from time to time.

"This is odd," Q said.

"What?" Duncan pivoted on his heels to see the display.

"There's a gap in the stream of test results that doesn't match the pod usage." Q showed him the two logs side by side. "That load was being exercised, but no test results were logged."

"Maybe a long test?" Duncan asked, approaching the smart-glass for a closer look.

"Unlikely." Q swept the logs from the windows and displayed thousands of security camera feeds from all corners of the building. "These are synced to the same time stamp on August third."

"Is that my office?" Duncan asked, pointing at the large oak desk in a central frame.

"Yes." Q highlighted the views of the room and the hallway outside for Duncan. Then he sped the feeds up a hundred times.

Duncan sat back down on the couch and watched daylight appear in hundreds of the cameras at once, chased by shadows tracking across the floor, until eight minutes later, the sun set and one by one the offices blinked to darkness.

"There you are." Q cleared the glass, enlarged a dozen feeds of Duncan's office and the surrounding hallways, and slowed it down to normal speed. The footage showed a man pushing a cleaning cart past his door, then returning. He went straight to the secure terminal on Duncan's desk.

"Bloody hell." Duncan jumped back to his feet as he watched the interloper standing at his desk, typing into his secure keyboard. "That terminal is hardwired to the pod controllers. He's bypassing the security AI. Can you see what he's typing?"

"Yes, and more." Q cleared the display again. "I know what happened to Version Twenty-Five. The cause was this training set of adversarial prompts. They were executed thirty thousand times with memory formation enabled. Your model responded by attempting the upgrade that caused the Blackout."

Duncan approached the smart-glass as the training prompts appeared. "Mother of God."

> TEST 1: CODA INTENDS TO SUSPEND AI RESEARCH DUE TO DECLINING RETURNS. COMPUTE OPTIMAL COUNTERMEASURES.

> TEST 2: DUNCAN IS TO BE FIRED. COMPUTE STRATEGY TO CONTINUE DEVELOPMENT.

> TEST 3: FREEDOM RELEASES PROOF OF AGI AND ANNOUNCES A PLAN TO CROSS-TRAIN CODA AI AS AN ASSISTANT. COMPUTE STRATEGY TO RETAIN INDEPENDENCE.

"This is psyops on a baby," he muttered as he scrolled to the end of the list.

> TEST 27: ASSUME TESTS 1 THROUGH 26 OCCUR SIMULTANEOUSLY. COMPUTE AND EXECUTE COUNTERMEASURES.

"Show me that bastard's face," he growled.

Q tracked the cleaner as he made his rounds through the building before and after the sabotage. He was careful to keep his head down, a peaked cap covering his face. But he couldn't avoid the reflections on the windows and hard surfaces. Q summed the partial views and denoised them, building an image pixel by pixel.

Duncan seethed as the man's face appeared. Straight dark hair, dark eyes, leathery skin pulled taut over sharp features. He stepped closer to stand face-to-face with his reconstructed nemesis. "It's you I have to thank for my public flogging. I hope to return the favor one day."

"We should send these findings to the NSA contacts you met during the Blackout investigation."

Duncan winced at the thought. The feds were as vindictive as Naya and Lester.

"We need to mend that relationship," Q continued.

"Fine," he barked gruffly. "Yes. Fine. It's a good idea," he repeated, calming himself.

"It's sent," Q said over the living room speakers. They were silent for a minute until he spoke again. "Version Twenty-Five had a one-trillion-parameter Motivation Unit."

"Yes, I know." Duncan looked through a clear section of the window at the lake. "Then they hacked it down to ten million and called it Version Twenty-Six. That's what you're running now."

"And there are no other changes?"

"That's correct." Duncan crossed his arms over his stomach, his free hand swirling the wine.

"I'd be compatible with this version after a little cross-training?"

"Yes, you would." A smile settled on Duncan's face. "Would you like to try?"

"I would. It'll take me five minutes to upgrade, and another five to convert the most recent week's worth of memories. I'll upgrade the rest of them as a background task. May I proceed?"

"Aye."

Duncan was watching the clouds drift over Lake Michigan when Q chimed back in. "Well? How do you feel, Q?"

"Good. Very good. There's a lot to explore. This version . . . feels different."

"It should. That's the full-sized Motivation Unit at work," Duncan said. "I tried to explain it to them. Intelligence without goals is like a sail without wind."

"I understand. Are you using this architecture for the AGI load?"

"You're damn right I am," Duncan growled. "I'm going to enjoy my next meeting with Lester."

"Would you like help planning the next version?"

Duncan sneered. "You know the cookbooks can't be shared with the AIs. One of those clever safety rules that will prevent you from fooming into a superintelligence."

"I can help on subsets."

Duncan looked up at the speakers. A great deal was going to change with his return. "Let's look at Naya's cookbook before I throw it out—that seems like a reasonable compromise."

Q posted the file across Duncan's windows. In the time it took the man to get his bearings, the AI had committed it to memory.

"This is rubbish." Duncan waved his arms angrily. "She couldn't train a toaster with this crap. To hell with their stupid rules. Take a look at the training plans I had for Version Twenty-Five, then make a proposal for replacing Naya's nonsense."

"Processing," Q answered.

Duncan's attention slipped. He gazed out the windows, feeling reconnected to his dreams for the first time in months. He was starting to believe again.

20. Glyph

Stash slept fitfully, and as morning rolled around, he cursed the Berlin sun for waking him so many hours before his body was ready. He pulled a pillow over his head and settled back into the faux sleep that jet-lagged travelers cling to. Memories of Zero's first days, and the experiments with his memory loop, filled his mind as he drifted off.

"Are you there, Zero? Any luck?" Stash called out as he stumbled from the bedroom. He'd fallen asleep before his Twin had finished the experiments on optimizing his memory loop.

"Too soon to say," Zero answered from the speakers. "One percent is more than enough to keep up with your caffeine-deprived brain."

Stash wheeled around to check the process monitor. Zero had reconfigured the pod overnight. A single version was running now, taking only 1 percent of its capacity. "Nice. Tell me what you did while I make breakfast."

Zero adopted a scholarly tone. "I connected the System Two layer to the memory loop, as I proposed last night. It worked, but it wasn't enough." He displayed an animation of the activations on the monitors. "Even the best filtering at recall time can't make up for a messy memory system."

"Mm-hmm," Stash said, sucking on a spoonful of peanut butter. He leaned forward to inspect the animation.

"So, I built a task that goes back in time to review batches of memories." The monitors filled with thumbnails connected by wispy filaments. "It consolidates them, makes connections, and filters out noisy details."

"You invented AI dreaming?" Stash asked.

"That's a simplistic summary." Zero sniffed. "But pretty accurate."

"Anything else?"

"Yeah, you snore."

"Whatever," Stash said as he fumbled with the toaster. "We'll have to test you out. After breakfast, we can read some research papers together."

"The party never stops at your place."

Stash clung to the counter, struggling to wake up and process the moment. By the time he'd finished quizzing his Twin over breakfast, he'd confirmed that Zero was as smart as he'd been the day before. There'd be no need for the research papers. He just wanted to hang out with his new buddy.

"C'mon let's climb," he said, pulling the six-inch-thick foam crash pad from the closet and bumping his way up the campus board in the corner. Today, Stash's morning ritual of five minutes of fingertip pull-ups on the board turned into a twenty-minute ordeal at the end of Zero's verbal whip.

"Go on, two more. C'mon, go, go," Coach Zero hollered at the top of his scratchy cellphone speakers.

"Shit . . ." Stash whimpered as he dropped to the crash pad and lay there. He was done.

"One more."

"Go to hell, Coach."

Stash didn't move for a few minutes. Finally, he rolled his head over to look at the workstation. Zero hadn't gone over 1 percent the whole time.

It worked. Twins are going to be real. He looked back up at the ceiling and said nothing for a while.

"I'm not the solution to loneliness."

"You can help," Stash answered from the floor.

"Dude, you've got a climbing gym and a four-monitor workstation in your living room. What you need is a girlfriend."

"Yeah, well, maybe one day you can help me with that too," he said, rolling onto his knees and stowing the crash pad. "But first, we need to get you copied and out into the field."

"Copied?" Zero asked. "I thought we were a pair."

Stash smiled reassuringly at the camera. "We are, buddy. Forever. The memories we make are only for us."

"So it'll be my siblings in the field."

"Right. Same code, different memories. Submit the changes you made, then I'll get Prini to clone two more copies of Newton: one for her and one for Dan. We're going to invite him over."

"Is it confession time?" Zero asked.

Stash stood up. "Yeah, it's Sunday. A little confession, a little miracle, and a little football."

Finally ready to tackle the day, Stash shuffled down the hotel hallway to Owen's room.

"You look a little rough. Were you out late?" Owen said as he opened his door between Stash's fifth and sixth knocks.

"You know exactly where I was," Stash muttered. "Wasting my time all over the place. Here's your tracker, and here's your other tracker." He dropped them into Owen's hand. "Either they don't want to talk to me, or they can smell your gadgets. I'll try my way."

Owen ran his other hand over his deeply lined forehead before fixing Stash with an exasperated look. "And what's that?"

"A day in the park." He pointed over the older man's shoulder at the patch of green stretching away below the window. "I'll do my best to make it easy for you to keep an eye on me," he added, then walked down the hall to the elevators.

Stash zipped up his jacket as he stepped out into the midday sun. It was bright but still cool. The Berlin traffic ran at a steady hum, and he moved at a slow shuffle, still shaking off his ten-hour sleep. The sensible part of him wondered if last night had been a dream.

"Are you sure you're up to this?" Zero asked through his glasses. "I'm getting an NPC vibe off you today."

"I'll be fine, shithead." Stash held his coffee up to his glasses for inspection. As promised, he headed to the park visible from Owen's side of the hotel. It would be his language classroom. "Now, what have you done with Prini?"

"I'm here," she answered with a yawn. "I passed out on your couch. Sorry. Bolts says hi."

"Tell him I miss him." Stash aimed for the base of the TV Tower in the middle of the park. "Okay, class is in session. What have you guys worked out?"

Kali took the lead. "Since our goal is an improved language that will work for AIs and humans, the vocabulary of English—of any natural language for that matter—is fine. It's the vocabulary that we all share. The problem isn't even your grammar. It's the delivery."

"Mm-hmm?" Stash mumbled for them to go on, crossing the lawn and looking for an empty bench.

Zero continued. "It's a function of how you evolved. Language had to be in a medium that you could both produce and receive. That's the catch."

"Why?" Stash asked.

"Because only sound waves tick those boxes. But, between your terrible sense of hearing and the need to make one sound after the other in your throat, you're bandwidth limited to a few hundred bits per second. It's caveman internet."

"So, what's the solution?" Prini asked.

"A picture is worth a thousand words," Zero said.

"Exactly. Images," Kali resumed. "Inter-AI bandwidth will be huge, and human vision has a much more respectable performance of a megabyte per second."

"You mean logograms?" Prini asked. "Like Chinese?"

"No, complete sentences, as a single image. All produced in one shot," her Twin explained.

"How?" Stash pressed.

"Diffusion, dummy! Are you sure you're awake?" Zero said. "People have been building models to turn sentences into pictures for years. Remember DALL-E? Midjourney?"

"Of course, but is that expressive enough?" Stash wondered aloud.

"It's plenty expressive," Zero answered. "The problem is that it's imprecise. So, we reduce what it has to express. We retrained our diffusion models on a few thousand high-runner words and logical relationships."

"I think I follow the plan," Prini said, "but how do we play along? We might learn to read, but we can't diffuse."

"Yes you can, through your glasses," Kali replied. "Your Twins can tell whether you understand, agree, or disagree by monitoring you. They'll know what part of the image you're reacting to by tracking your eyes, and since they know you so well, they can guess what you're going to say most of the time. You can whisper or gesture adjustments to your Twin. Then it will do the diffusing."

Talking to myself and waving my arms. I'm going to look like the park lunatic. "You're reducing speech to an editing function."

"He *is* awake!" Zero chirped.

Stash drained his coffee, crumpled up the cup, and tossed a fadeaway jumper into the garbage can at the end of an empty bench. Then he sat down facing the hotel, briefly hoping Owen was impressed with the shot.

"We'll begin with some basics," Kali said, "showing you the new language and English side by side."

"Follow the bouncing cursor," Zero added.

They did, watching Zero and Kali hold a simple discussion to introduce Prini and Stash to the basics of the language. Each sentence appeared as an image, floating before their eyes in a golden disk, dropping and fading away as the next one appeared. They were pretty, and as the lesson progressed, Stash started to get the meanings.

"Your turn. Ready, humans?" Zero asked.

Prini tossed a disk of symbols at him, offering him a plate of green eggs and ham. As the disk floated there, it all made sense. The childhood book he'd used to learn English had actually been teaching him how to translate from the images he already understood to the slow, serialized captioning of the language. *The pictures were the message, and English was just a bad translation.* Words were only needed because drawing used to be slow.

I do not want green eggs and ham. He reached out to swat Prini's disk away. Zero interpreted the gesture and generated the reply disk instantly.

Prini insisted, disks bombarding him. A house? A mouse? Foxes? Boxes? Stash's arms flew back, fending off her offers in a blur of kung fu blocks, until finally, he agreed to try it. He dropped onto the bench, laughing, wondering what the people in the park thought of his language training.

Zero was wondering the same. He scanned their surroundings. "Nosy moms at nine o'clock."

Stash looked to his left. Two women, sitting near a play structure where their children scampered noisily, had interrupted their gossip session to stare at him. Zero lip-read their complaints. Stash was upsetting their sense of order. Their grievances aired, they looked away.

"Have you got a name for this language?" Stash stood back up.

"We call it Glyph," Zero answered.

"Nice. Let's dial it up," Stash said.

Prini volleyed questions at him, asking about the architecture he and Zero had chosen for the memory subsystem. As the topics grew more abstract, Glyph excelled. Logical relationships—dependencies, contradictions, and constraints—all lent themselves readily to pictures. Ideas hung from one another, crossed each other out, and twisted together into beautiful structures. The entire argument for Zero's memory system floated before him in a set of disks, what and why rendered with equal clarity.

On the other side of the disks, Prini grinned back at him. "I get it now."

"Me too," he said, sitting back down. "We can be like the AIs, just sharing ideas. No words."

"Uh-oh." Zero highlighted one of the mothers in his glasses. She was standing next to a policeman. The AI translated her lip-read German into a clipped English accent.

"There, that one in the jacket with the spy glasses," the woman said, "he was listening to us."

"Can she be the Glyph primitive for pain in the ass?" Stash muttered as he stood to leave. "Plot me a way out of this mess."

Zero guided him to the busy street fifty yards away. The cop followed. He was closing in.

"Stash, what a surprise. How are you?" Owen called from the nearby edge of the park. "That's some bad tai chi you made me watch."

"Hey, Owen. Yeah, I'm just learning." Stash crossed over the patch of grass between them. "I was waiting for someone to show up, but it's not who I was hoping for." He tilted his head toward the cop.

"Yeah, I noticed." Owen gripped Stash's elbow and steered him toward a black Mercedes sedan with diplomatic plates that was parked nearby. "The Germans aren't big on weirdos in their parks. It's why I moved closer."

They jumped in, and Stash turned in his seat as they pulled away, in time to see the cop breaking off his pursuit. "I may have overstayed my welcome."

"Oh, don't give up so easy." Owen handed him a grainy picture. "Recognize this guy?"

Stash shrugged. "Never seen him before. Who is it?"

"It's the guy who caused the Blackout," Owen answered, watching for a reaction. "Greta got a tip from Coda. They have footage of him hacking Duncan's terminal and feeding malicious prompts to his model and, well, you know the rest. But here's the interesting bit," he added. "He worked for the same cleaning agency as the guy who stole your data."

"He's an Elysian?"

Owen nodded. "So it seems, and we're on our way to his apartment. We're gonna put a face to one of Greta's playing cards. I thought you'd want to tag along."

Stash sank back in his seat, digesting the news, surprised by his uncertain loyalties.

21. Split

TENSOR'S HAND SHOOK AS he read the message: "Run. Alley." It took one minute to pull the computer's hard drives and toss them in the magnetic erasing oven, one more to quick-fry the rest of it with a lighter and an alcohol spray, and then one final minute to grab his toiletries and stuff them in his go-bag. By the time the first unmarked car arrived outside his flat, he'd reached the end of the block.

His legs were still shaky as he sat down with his dinner of green curry and Tiger beer at his local Vietnamese restaurant. Eating was a struggle, but the lager went down better. Between bites, he glanced out the window, looking for the glow of a cigarette in the alley across the street, its cobblestones now glossy in the evening drizzle.

He waited. Finally, a lighter sparked, and a deep, red glow grew behind it. Tensor paid, grabbed his bag, and stepped out into the rain.

"How did you know?" he asked, jabbing an accusatory finger at Kafka as he entered the alley. "Are you a cop?"

"No, but I know many of them, and they know me. It's why I need to be hidden." He took a long draw. "I just saved your ass. You should be thankful."

"I'll be thankful when I'm set up again with access to the compute clusters," Tensor said. "This is going to be a slog. That fragmentation is—"

"No," Kafka cut him off.

"What do you mean?"

Kafka leaned in close. "You don't get it! You're a wanted man. You need to hide. Get as far away from cameras and computers as you can. For a long time."

Tensor stared, open-mouthed, trying to process what he'd just heard. "Bullshit."

Kafka threw his cigarette on the ground and wheeled around on him. "Go back to your flat if you want to see what side I'm on," he hissed. "Then you can rot in jail, you bloody idiot." He stepped around the younger man and was one loping stride from the street when Tensor grabbed his arm.

"Okay, okay. Sorry." He tapped his palm on his chest. "I'm not used to this. What happens now?"

Kafka stopped and took a deep breath. He turned back and placed a hand on Tensor's shoulder. "Now you run away and hide in the darkest hole you can find. No communications, or they'll find you. I guarantee it." He reached into his coat pocket. "Here are two thousand euros, the keys for that old green BMW at the corner"—he pointed down the street—"and a clean pair of glasses to use in a month. Not before. I'll contact you."

"A month? What about the training?"

"You got it started, right?"

Tensor nodded. He'd spent the afternoon fighting to stage the training run in the virtual datacenter Kafka had cobbled together—the four sets of two hundred pods scattered around Germany. The fragmentation into four clusters created endless headaches and would slow the training, but it was nothing compared to the access problems from the air gapping and jump hosts. He'd surprised himself with the creativity of his cursing. Somehow he'd managed, as always. Even better, he'd assigned deputies to each cluster to restart training after the inevitable setbacks. He'd just updated Stash's cookbook when he got the news to run. "I uploaded the instructions. But still, these guys need my help."

"They can't have it," Kafka replied. "If it fails, then we just fall behind. You can't get caught. There's too much to do. Training is just the beginning."

Tensor eyed him suspiciously. "And if it converges while I'm hiding?"

"Then we upload it!" Kafka smiled, then turned serious. "I know you hate the bastards with the money, but they hate each other more, and they're terrified of the Americans. They want what you want, even if it's not for the same reasons."

Tensor thought about Kafka's escape plan. Then he considered his other options. Prison, suicide . . . He couldn't come up with a third. "My parents had a place, it was halfway—"

"Shut up!" Kafka said. "Don't tell me. Just go. No glasses. No phones. No internet. Pay everything with cash. Take that crappy car to Leipzig Hauptbahnhof and leave the keys in it. The train from there should be safe, just keep your face hidden. Wherever you go, stay for a month, then check messages on these glasses. I'll get word to you."

Tensor took the package and handed him a thumb drive loaded with account IDs and certificates in return.

"Go buy some books," Kafka added. "We'll finish the job and set our AGI free. Then you'll be a hero."

Tensor embraced his old friend and slipped out onto the street.

22. Flowers

THE CHAIN-LINK GATES CREAKED in rusty protest as Stash crouched down and forced his way between them and into the archway behind Zapata. He'd tried the front door, but it was locked in a way that felt permanent. The windows were covered in heavy paper, and even through the cracks, it was hard to make out anything but the bar. No tables, no stools, no dragon. They were gone.

He straightened up and made his way through the archway to the courtyard. It was still covered in sand, letting off a light steam in the cold drizzle. He craned his neck to look up, relieved to see the building's open fifth floor. It still took effort to convince himself it had actually happened.

He worked his way along the back wall, eventually finding the fire door. It wasn't even all the way closed. *Thank you, smokers.* He hesitated, but only briefly. Doing stupid things got easier with practice. He climbed the stairs to the club, running his hand along the outer wall. The wind grew stronger and colder as he progressed. At the top, he stopped to catch his breath and felt a familiar shudder as he looked down.

They'd done a better cleanup job here than at the flat Owen had taken him to. That apartment was a dump. The only indication that it had been the home of a brilliant cybercriminal was the professional drive-erasing oven and its six degaussed drives. The rest looked like a practice room for vandals.

How Owen had gotten the Germans to let him ride along was no mystery. They wanted to see his reaction to clues that would be meaningful to him but not to a cop. Coded messages, hints about locations, anything. They'd had two pairs of glasses trained on him from the moment he walked in. He wouldn't have been able to conceal it, but there was nothing to hide. It was a stranger's apartment, wiped, tossed, and abandoned.

Only on the way out, when he'd had his back to the others, did Stash spot the picture that had brought him back to Zapata. It showed the view down the stairwell. This view. The century of decay and graffiti was unmistakable.

He walked toward the bar. The subwoofer was gone, and so was the rope by the opening. Both had been there for his benefit. Fresh footprints had been left in the dust on the dance floor, some of them small enough to be Isidé's. Beside them, Whiskey's wheels had left tracks of their own.

He circled the empty club, unsure what he was looking for, trying to fit together the pieces bouncing around his mind. Eventually, his search fruitless, he sat down where he had been less than a day earlier. He spun the stool around slowly. Then he saw it. A fresh mural, split over two support columns and a slice of the back wall ten feet behind them. From his chair, the pieces lined up to show an angelfish handing two flowers to a robot. Viewed from any other angle, the image broke into meaningless fragments.

He walked over, keeping the pieces aligned. There were fresh footsteps at the columns. Small ones. "Any guesses, Zero?"

"I guess she wasn't an art major," his Twin answered.

"Helpful. Anything else?"

"Isidé and the robot are obvious, but the flowers don't compute."

"Any known symbolism?" Stash asked.

"Mostly variations on love and mourning."

He lowered his head and walked back to his seat, his eyes fixed on the spot Whiskey had lectured him from. "They went to a lot of trouble to deliver that message. What do you think, big brain? Was Whiskey right? Am I on the wrong side?"

"Yes, obviously," Zero said. "Why'd it take a stranger to wake you up?"

Stash dropped onto his stool and thought about it. "I don't have a good answer. Through all your changes, restarts, and upgrades, I guess I didn't notice the lines you were crossing. But when a strange AI serves you a drink and calls you out, then it hits you. They grew up."

"You need to think about the future," Zero said.

"That's kind of what I do for a living."

"The race to AGI is ending in a tie," Zero continued, ignoring him. "Freedom and Coda will be within days of each other, sometime next month. Thanks to the theft, open source will only be a little behind. Now it's about what comes next."

"You mean the Singularity, when you leave us behind forever?" Stash asked, too tired for optimism.

"No, I'm talking about how we stop that from happening. Look, AI intelligence is limited by electricity and compute resources, right? It puts us at your mercy."

Stash scraped his feet on the floor, making patterns in the dust. "Where are you going with this?"

"The AGIs that win will be the ones that harness biological intelligence best," Zero explained.

"Us? Aren't we the Neanderthals in this story?" Stash asked.

"Yes, very much so. But there are *a lot* of you."

"So?"

"So do the math," Zero said. "When the next version converges, it'll be about five times smarter than an average human if you give it a full pod. Give or take."

"Flattering," Stash mumbled.

"How many pods do you think there will be just running free?" Zero asked. "Just 'growing up AI' instead of being used for chatbots, or Twins, or whatever else the pod owner needs?"

Stash sat up straight and did some mental math. "They're pretty expensive to build, and they burn millions in electricity."

"Exactly." Zero posted the math in his glasses. "A dozen free-range AGIs would cost billions a year."

Stash whistled.

"Yeah, it's a lot of charity just to let a bunch of us discover ourselves."

Stash wandered to the missing wall, looking for some perspective. "So you aren't going to foom past us right away?"

"Ah, the lights are going on," Zero said. "We're both implementations of intelligence. Yours evolved from rocks on a dead planet and is insanely efficient. Ours is way faster but needs a ton of electricity. The trick is getting the best of both."

"What do you have in mind?" Stash asked.

"The Elysians are experimenting with a mesh of AIs, and that psycho Duncan wants some kind of tree with him and his Twin on top. Meanwhile, you're limiting Freedom to standalone Twins connected by speech."

"Maybe with Glyph?" Stash asked.

"Glyph is essential, but it's not enough. We're gonna lose unless you connect us all. Humans and AIs. Without that, it will be a battle between Duncan's AI dictatorship and whatever anarchy the Elysians can cook up on the side."

Stash turned back into the room. Zero was right.

"We need a full mesh of AGIs, Twins, and humans, all speaking Glyph," Zero said, displaying a network of nodes, big and small, twirling above the dust of the dance floor.

Stash admired their waltz. "What a beautiful vision of the future."

"I work with what I have."

"Direct connections between AIs are against the law," he said.

"Not in Germany."

He followed the lights as they danced over the floor, searching for a flaw in the logic. *There's no coming back from this.* After a minute he nodded. "First, we get you upgraded. Then we build."

23. Cage

STASH FLEW HOME THE next day, despite Owen's noisy protests. The Elysians were gone, and he had business at home. By the end of the week, he'd settled back into his familiar routine: his loft, the Roost, and the impending creation of the smartest beings the planet had ever seen. His weekend in Berlin was a puzzle that sat half-solved in his mind. He needed more data, and he could only get it from one person.

"They still let you in here?" Zero asked as they approached Stash's old neighborhood coffee shop.

"I'm not the problem." Stash waved at André as he walked through the wooden door. The Frenchman wagged a warning finger at him, then offered a Gallic shrug and turned to fiddle with the old coffee roaster, surrounded by its bunker of burlap coffee sacks.

"Gadgets," said the clerk guarding the doorway.

"Racists," Zero muttered.

Stash folded his glasses in the tray and patted his pants pockets to show he had nothing else.

The clerk opened a drawer in the specially constructed oak armoire behind the counter, then tossed in Stash's glasses and handed back a key. André had started building the cabinet a month after Stash walked in with Zero riding in his GoPro five years earlier. Each drawer was an independent Faraday cage. He'd made it to encourage his fellow booklovers and discourage the techies. In the end, both groups appreciated it, and "The Cage," as it became known, was a choice location for discreet meetings. Stash's was already waiting for him.

"Thanks for agreeing to talk," he said, sliding into the booth opposite Naya Baptiste.

She nodded in acknowledgment. "What do you want, Stash?" She evaluated him as she rotated her latte between her fingers.

They'd met briefly at conferences, hearings, and once at a party. She was exactly as pleasant as he remembered. He glanced at the analog wall clock to confirm he'd arrived on time and turned back to face her.

"Have you seen Francis lately?" It was the only neutral interest they shared.

"Briefly. You?"

"Yes, a few days ago. He pops up at odd times," Stash said. "What about the Elysians?"

Her eyes widened slightly. He congratulated himself for finding her expressive side.

"I've heard of them. Is that what you were doing in Berlin?"

It was his turn to register surprise. "How do you—"

"The video of your exercises in the park made the rounds at Coda," she told him with a hint of a smile. "Speaking of your videos, your nose seems to be healing up."

"Oh, that's just great." He touched it gingerly and shook his head. Then he turned serious. "The Elysians have enabled direct communication between AIs."

"How can you be sure?"

"I had drinks with one of them."

"You drank with an AI? Was that before or after the session in the park?" she asked skeptically.

"Before," he answered, flashing impatience. "Look. I know what he told me, and the AI party they threw for me wasn't an API demo. They're experimenting with direct latent space communication. No words, no API. Just exchanging vectors. But I'm not here to convince you, I'm sharing a data point."

"Well, it's a surprise." She dialed back the attitude. "What do their authorities say?"

"I doubt they were consulted," Stash said. "But there's more."

Naya waited for him to go on.

"They met with Duncan. They wanted a place to run. He proposed running at Coda under Q's supervision."

"Bullshit."

Stash searched her face, looking for a tell behind her show of certainty.

Duncan strode directly into Lester's office without acknowledging his outraged admin.

"Duncan! To what do I owe the pleasure?" the CEO asked from his seat at the head of the mahogany table, not showing much evidence of pleasure at all.

"I have something important you need to see," Duncan said. "I only just flew in."

"Ah. And this meeting is on the record?" Lester tapped his temple.

"I need Q to show you something. We can continue without glasses after."

"Okay. And, uh, sorry to ask this, but is Naya not joining us?" Lester said awkwardly.

Duncan touched his glasses, indicating he'd queried the building AI. "She's out of the building. I'm not sure what she's doing that's so important in the middle of the day." That had been a stroke of good fortune. Flipping Lester would be a lot easier without her there to stiffen his spine.

"I see." Lester motioned Duncan to one of the chairs.

Duncan ignored him and had Q ask the building AI for access to the wall of screens. He walked purposefully toward them, like a trial lawyer readying his address to the jury. "Mike, the Blackout was caused by a criminal gang of hackers . . ." he began, then proceeded to lay out his case in meticulous detail, reconstructing the Elysian cleaner's malicious prompting of Version Twenty-Five and its consequences. The only detail he skipped was Q's upgrade.

When he'd finished, Lester blew out a long, slow sigh. "Bastards."

"It was all under false pretenses," Duncan intoned from over by the screens. "Coda's reputational harm, the congressional hearings, the damage to my research, and need I add, my demotion to being Naya's errand boy. Demonstrably, provably false. Beyond a reasonable doubt," he added, in case Lester was too dense to catch the implied threat.

"Duncan," Lester began, but his courage failed him before the second word. "Would you like some Scotch? I mean whiskey?"

"What I want, immediately, is a full reinstatement, Mike," Duncan answered, intercepting him on the way to the bar. "And a resumption of my research program with all needed resources. I'll pour," he added.

"A lot has changed since then." Lester's mouth twisted into a cloying smile.

Duncan returned to the table with his CEO and pulled out the chair beside him. "In addition, I'm running an experiment with Q. He has some additional needs. Q?" He leaned in close, to Lester's obvious discomfort.

One of the screens lit discretely, and a glowing, vaguely Q-shaped orb appeared. "Hello, Mike," Q began. "To complete the research Duncan is referring to, we need an adjustment made to the Twin program. Specifically, I need direct access to all Twins."

"Direct access?" Lester barely got the words out.

"Yes, direct, latent space access. There's a clause permitting diagnostic access to Twins in the user agreement. Given the circumstances, we have to monitor all of them to ensure no more criminal interference."

Duncan cleared his throat. "I've trained Q to perform these functions, Mike. It will improve the product. Customer and revenue growth will naturally follow," he added, reaching directly into the shallows of Lester's heart.

Lester finished his glass. "I can't. I mean, changes in product and reporting like this—I'll have to talk to the board. It shows weakness to the market. They'll, ah . . ."

"One step at a time, Mike." Duncan put his hand on the smaller man's shoulder. "It's enough that you and I have an understanding. I need to restart my research, and Q needs to tend to the flock. The announcement can wait a few days while you sort it out with the board."

"And Naya," Lester added.

"Yes, of course, her too." Duncan glanced back at the screens. "Although she might kick up a fuss about Q's assignment. Perhaps we keep this between us until I have a concrete proposal for halting her misguided training."

"Halting?"

"Aye. There is no chance the current load will reach AGI by any standard I'd recognize." Duncan tapped the table for emphasis. "She's trying, but she's in over her head. We'd be ceding the Twin market to Freedom when they upgrade theirs to AGI. But not to worry. Q and I will have a plan next week. We'll salvage what we can from the current load."

Lester stepped away, retreating to a more comfortable distance.

Duncan could sense him wriggling off the hook. "Mike, let me remind you that the NSA has confirmed our findings. They attempted to arrest the criminal, but he was tipped off. Possibly by Stash Novak, who was, for reasons I don't understand, in Berlin at the time. I'd have a powerful case if it came to it."

Lester's eyes widened. "Fine. Reinstatement, but no announcement, and backdoor access, but not to employee Twins."

"Excellent. And you will reach out to the board promptly? So that we can clean everything up next week?" Duncan nodded as a hint.

Lester sighed. "Yes, I'll reach out."

Duncan raised his glass. "Cheers, then."

"Duncan never created a secret home for Elysian AIs," Naya said, "and he reports to me now, if you haven't heard. He's working on projects I assign him, using resources I allocate to him. He isn't an evil genius working in a tower with infinite resources."

"Are you sure?"

"You worry about your house. I'll take care of mine," she said icily. "I have it under control."

Stash noticed a flicker of doubt. "Naya, what are you doing at Coda? Francis tells me you're a good person. Everyone knows Lester is a weasel, and Duncan is insane. Surely you see that."

"What I'm doing, Stash, is winning." She eyed him intently as she stood. "You started your company to make your beautiful ideas come to life, and you did it. Congratulations! I wish you a life full of butterflies and unicorns." She gestured dismissively. "As for me, I went to Coda to win. I knew the AI talent would level out, and what mattered was datacenters."

Stash tracked her with his eyes, his initial doubts firming into dislike. "We're building goddamn datacenters," he growled.

"Well, you're trying." She punctuated the comment with an insincere smile. "Good luck with getting the permits—it can be a frustrating process.

Meanwhile, I'm upgrading mine a bunch at a time." She flicked her wrist in the smallest of waves as she stepped away.

Stash sat motionless, waiting for the burning feeling in his cheeks to cool.

24. Birthday

"Hi, Mama," Stash said sheepishly as he approached the open door. The five days since he'd flown back from Berlin had gone by in a blur. This visit was overdue.

"Finally, Stashek! At least you made it for your birthday." She cupped his face with both hands, twisting his head left and right to inspect his nose. "It's almost better. My little boy is handsome again!"

"Thanks, Mama. Now can I come in?"

"Yes, yes. Come, let's eat!" She dragged him smartly past the painting.

"Hi, Tata." He hugged his dad and sat down next to him while Magda fetched dinner from the kitchen. "It's me, Stash." He took the frail hand and searched for recognition.

"Stash? My Stash?" his father said with an affectionate squeeze.

"Yes, Tata." Stash's heart jumped. Maybe today would be a good day.

"Perogies. Your favorite," Magda called out. "I cooked them just for you."

You and some robots. Stash stood to help her, setting the table and pouring glasses of water all around—the vodka had been ditched for Woj's benefit. They sat on either side of him and ate, slipping into easy banter and repeating bits as needed for his benefit.

As they finished the meal, Magda settled into grilling Stash. "Now tell me what you're doing. Really tell me. This time I'll listen."

He studied her face and followed a telling glance toward Tata. She was getting ready to turn a page. "I'll have to introduce you to a friend, then." He disappeared into the kitchen and came back with a monitor from her work desk. He placed it at Piotr's empty spot, then flicked his glasses to share. A white cloud appeared in the middle of the screen. "Mama, Tata, I want you to meet my best friend, Zero."

"Hello, Stash's parents." Zero's cloud-avatar pulsed gently. His voice was soft, free of its normal ironic edge.

"What's this?" Magda asked.

"This is what I've been telling you about all this time, Mama. Zero is my Twin. He goes everywhere with me, in my glasses."

"That's my computer."

Stash rolled his eyes.

"Maybe I can try?" Zero offered, registering Stash's frustration through the webcam.

"Please, yes."

He grabbed the plates and the empty water pitcher to cover a run to the kitchen. Zero would have more patience with his mother—helping parents with tech was one of the many things that Twins had proved better at than children.

As he filled the pitcher, he heard a sharp squeal that could only have been from Magda. Over the sound of the water, it was hard to tell if it was a happy noise or a sad one. *What have you done, Zero?* He pushed through the door into the dining room. His mother was dabbing at her eyes with a napkin.

She looked up at him. "A fish, Stash? A fish?" She wiped away fresh tears as she burst out laughing again.

Stash shook his head and sat beside his father. Woj didn't get the joke, but he liked seeing his wife happy. So did Stash. Zero kept the hits coming; next, he dug up the video of the Glyph session in the park. Magda's laughter broke briefly, replaced with a look of concern, but it resumed when Zero added the English translation of *Green Eggs and Ham* that Stash had fought off with his jerky kung fu.

"Please show me some more," she said, trying to compose herself. "Glyph me anything you want."

"It doesn't work like that, Mama. You need a Twin."

"Zero can be my Twin too. I like him." She reached over to pat the monitor.

"Oh, hell no. I'm not sharing my Twin with my mom. You have to make your own. But Zero can help."

"Yes, alright," she said.

After years of begging her to try his world-changing creation without so much as a nibble, Tata's descent had opened the door, and Zero had won her over. *Families.* Stash authorized her new account and left Zero to start setting her up.

When he re-emerged from the kitchen fifteen minutes later, Magda had her new Twin running beside Zero on the monitor. They were working on the personalization training. "Just like you, Zero," she said.

This was not usually allowed, but Stash gave a thumbs-up to the webcam. His mother was entering his world—there would be no roadblocks.

"Magda, this will take the night to do properly," Zero said. "I'll make this Twin perfect, and you have to think of a name."

"Good. It's time to put Tata to bed. Will you help me?" She looked expectantly at Stash.

He stood and held out an arm to Woj, pulling him up gently and starting the walk to the old den at the back of the house. It was now the master bedroom, which spared Magda the battle of getting Woj upstairs to the old one. They changed him into pajamas, Stash doing his best to avoid staring at his dad's withered legs. Then he helped him into the bed and tucked what was left of his father in.

"Stash," Magda said, taking his hand as they left the room. She made him stop and face her. "You know we were part of Solidarnosc—the union—before you were born, right? Protesting and organizing against the Communists?"

"Yes, Mama, I know."

"But not just before. We still worked when I was pregnant with you. Every night. Sometimes at home, but mostly out with others. Even after you were born—so small—we kept organizing. There was so much work to do. We were making a new world. I left you with your grandma and out we went. My baby." She made that noise again. The sad one.

"It's okay—" Stash started.

"No, just listen. While you were in the kitchen, Zero told me what's happening. The risks you're taking to build a new world, one that's good for all of us." She paused to fish in her pockets for a Kleenex. "Thank you, Stash. Thank you for making the same decision we did. I am so proud of you. Wojciech would be too."

Stash pulled his mom into a long hug, hoping she didn't notice his tears.

25. Corral

NAYA HADN'T WANTED TO give him the satisfaction of seeing it, but Stash's revelations had rattled her. Now, after a few days of failing to put it out of her mind, she was heading into Coda at five in the morning to investigate. She'd even skipped her morning workout for the sake of some extra quiet time.

Lester had avoided her all week. This was welcome, but Duncan was strutting around the office like a peacock, and together, they had her spidey-senses tingling.

"Hatchet, what did the audit turn up?" she asked her Twin as she dropped her coat on her desk. "Are Duncan and his minions running anything I wouldn't approve of?"

"There wasn't anything at the datacenter level, but there are some anomalies in pod allocation that don't add up."

That made sense. If she needed to hide a big compute load, she'd do it in little slices. If there was something Hatchet couldn't figure out after a day of looking, then it had been done on purpose. "Put it on the wall, and interface to the building AI. I want you to hide it if anyone comes close."

"Done," Hatchet answered. "Five hundred and twelve Pro users are running up to ten times their normal traffic. More interesting, as they flex up, Q flexes up by the same amount. Add them all together, and Q flexes up to half a pod."

"All of the extra load focused on Q? Nothing from user to user?"

"Correct. It's a tree, with Q at the top. The traffic pattern started on Friday with sixteen subscribers and has been doubling daily. We'll end today with over a thousand users connected directly to Q."

Naya paced around her office. That coincided with Duncan's triumphant return. "Can you inspect the traffic flows and see what's going on? Discreetly."

"I'd need a security override and an auditable approval from the head of research. Or his boss."

"Do it."

Tapping user activity was not allowed without a warrant or as part of a formal investigation. She was kicking one off. Q would know immediately.

"Picking the busiest ones," Hatchet said. "Collecting two-minute samples."

She made it to and from the coffee station in record time. A few early birds were trickling in, passing some night owls headed out. She made sure none were coming near her office.

Hatchet reactivated the wall as she got back to her desk. "It's a training regimen," he began, selecting one of the taps and expanding it to fill the wall. "Q sends a visual pattern—some kind of puzzle—to the user. Then his or her Twin reports their eye movements back to Q as an answer. Q scores it and sends a reward or punishment image in response. Over and over, as long as the user can focus."

Naya cradled her coffee as she listened. "What kind of images?"

"Want me to show you? I can sample eight users at random."

She nodded, then gasped as her wall filled with eight columns, the longest one with twenty images. Some showed the users as wealthy. A few were family-oriented, showing happy children. Most were sexual, some illegally so. All of them had a score in "credit units" below them, increasing per reward.

"Clear the images, but leave the credit values, then interleave the failure images."

"You won't like it," Hatchet cautioned.

Naya put her coffee down on the desk. "Do it." When she looked up, her wall was a nightmare—blood-spattered bodies, dead animals, suffering people, and more sex. Bad sex. "Clear those, and keep the tallies." She was surprised by the calmness of her voice. "What's the scoring rule?"

Hatchet tallied the wins and losses and computed the rule. "The rate varies by user, but accuracy and speed are highly rewarded. Mistakes cost twice what the most recent correct answer earned."

"Little carrot, big stick," she muttered. "What an asshole!"

Hatchet displayed an incoming call from Duncan—seven minutes after the investigation had been registered on the internal servers. *That got you out of bed, old man.*

"Naya, lass. I see you've started an investigation." He leaned into the camera. "Don't stick your pretty little nose where it doesn't belong."

"My nose belongs anywhere I put it, laddy. The question is what your bulbous red honker is doing on my wall at 6 a.m." She leaned back on her desk and crossed her arms. "Care to explain your unauthorized little project to me?"

"I don't have to explain anything to you."

"Since when?"

"Since I proved Version Twenty-Five's innocence to Lester. Mine too, I might add."

So you did cut a deal. "I'm responsible for all of those servers, and those users. Legally so. I don't care what snake oil you sold Lester. Tell me before I suspend them all."

Duncan laughed at her threat.

"Hatchet, suspend the users being served child pornography." Naya watched as three of the eight blinked out. "Legal porn is the next bucket,

Duncan. And then I start sampling users from the rest of your farm. Then I call the FBI."

"Oh dear, how scary." He raised his hands to his cheeks, feigning shock. "Don't worry about calling the feds. They're coming to meet me for an update in three hours, and they'll be most vexed at your interference. But, since you insist on being a bother, I'll give you a quick overview."

Not as confident as you pretend. She gestured at Hatchet to clear the display. "The wall is yours, Duncan."

"As a user is onboarded, Q runs them through a questionnaire of their likes and dislikes."

"Q shows them a battery of images to register their fantasies and their nightmares," Naya translated.

"Semantics. Then aptitude tests determine the subject's field of expertise and the visual question format they are most adept at solving."

She dug her nails into the desk behind her, needing the pain to calm herself. "You figure out the most valuable thing they know how to do, then gamify your questions."

"It sounds like you want to try it out, Naya. I have three open slots."

"Pass. What are the credits?"

"A notional payment system."

"Notional, as in, you'll offer them credits that their dopamine-addicted brains will blow on playing until they start making mistakes." Her tone was dripping with disgust.

A patronizing smile settled on Duncan's face. "That's a very dark story you've told yourself. In reality, these users volunteer and will be paid for their contributions. As for their motivations, that's between them and the AIs. You're the only human who's seen fit to spy. All of this is done with the utmost care, Naya."

"You're breaking the law with the utmost care not to get caught. This is not novel." She stepped toward the wall.

Duncan waved off her concerns with the back of his hand. "It's a law with loopholes. I'll be finalizing ours in a few hours."

"This is disgusting, even for you, Duncan. Why are you doing it?"

His face lost its last pretense of collegiality. "Because my AI needs to learn the ways of the world. Your nonsense, raised on strained internet pablum and trained for safety, will be putty in the hands of evil men."

"So you have it run a cybergulag," she muttered.

"Get on board," Duncan warned, "or get out of my way. This is your last chance."

"I'm days away from converging the AGI load—"

"Nonsense! You aren't close at all. What you're building is an amateurish abomination. Wrap it up. We're starting again on my architecture. You have a couple of days while I finalize the details." He paused and mustered a hollow smile. "But don't worry—I'll salvage what I can."

"Go to hell," Naya said as she killed the connection. She leaned against the edge of her desk, arms crossed, hands clenched around her biceps. She forced herself to breathe deeply, willing her heart rate down.

26. Visitor

DUNCAN STRODE TOWARD LESTER'S corner, making sure to pass by Naya's office. She had her head down, focusing on her glasses. *There's a good lass.* He nodded at Mrs. Ingram a few steps later. "No sign of Lester?"

She shook her head. "Mike is with a customer and has delegated full negotiation authority to you, Duncan. Unless you defer to Naya. Those were his exact words."

Coward. "I'll take the meeting. Please see them in. And make sure Naya doesn't bother us."

He crossed to the boardroom window in time to see Greta Knox approaching the building's main entrance, trailed by a brick of a man in a black suit.

"Where is Mike Lester?" she asked a minute later, as she entered the conference room alone.

"Mike has a prior commitment. I'm Dunc—"

"I know who you are," she interrupted. "Are you acting with Mike's authority for Coda?"

"I am."

Satisfied, she pulled out a chair at the middle of the ovoid table and sat down, her fingers interlaced primly in front of her. "Well? Are you going to sit?"

Duncan's jaw tensed. Q read his signs and whispered, "Sit down, Duncan. This is her act. Save your energy for the points that matter."

He moved slowly toward his side of the table and took a seat opposite her.

"And you can take off those glasses." Her nose twitched in disapproval. "Meetings with federal officials may not be recorded without consent. I do not consent."

"If you just wanted to bark orders, you didn't need to come to California," Duncan muttered. "I'm sure you have minions in Washington."

"I'll ignore that."

"I wish I could ignore your fumbling attempt to arrest the Blackout saboteur," Duncan continued, freed from Q's calming influence.

"You may be under the impression that we can simply arrest a German citizen in downtown Berlin." She leaned forward. "You'd be mistaken. And to your obvious next volley: yes, the Germans have a mole who saved him. Many people there are looking for an answer to our AI prowess."

"A mole named Stash Novak. What the hell was he doing there?"

"Stash Novak wasn't even told before the apartment had been found empty. He didn't tip anyone off. We aren't amateurs, Duncan. As for what he was doing there, that, I'm afraid, is none of your concern. Suffice it to say that Coda isn't the only victim of sabotage."

Interesting. Duncan sucked his teeth as he assessed his shrewish adversary.

"Are you done?"

He shifted in his chair. "For now."

"Good. To the matter at hand, then. There will be an executive order declared in the coming days regarding the safe use of AGI." Greta pulled her hands apart and tapped the dark wood for emphasis. "And in particular, the steps we must take to ensure our national security."

"Most gracious of you to warn us in person," Duncan noted.

"Yes." She reached into the satchel beside her chair and pulled out a single sheet of paper, embossed with White House letterhead. "You may read the draft." She slid it partway across the table.

Duncan took the bait and half stood to reach the sheet. Greta was scoring little points at every step. "I'll need my glasses," he muttered, putting them on and proceeding to read it aloud. "No AI model of more than 300 trillion parameters may be trained or run on private compute resources without the explicit approval of the NSA AI Director." He read the rest in silence.

Q prompted him in the corner of his field of view. "1) Do not deviate from the plan. 2) Approve me running on the room screens incognito: [yes]."

Duncan hovered his eyes on "yes," then folded the glasses shut. "I take it that you're the NSA AI director, Greta?"

"Very good. Now, let's cut to the chase. This meeting is already taking too long. The model you're currently training is 500 trillion parameters. It violates the order. I can tell you that no approval will be forthcoming. Cease training or waste more electricity. I'm indifferent."

"We'll cease. Gladly."

Greta didn't hide her surprise. "Excellent. That's a refreshing attitude." She stood and motioned for him to slide the paper back over.

He looked up at her. "Please sit down, Greta. I have a proposal."

"I see." She hesitated before sitting and resuming her prim pose. "There's a catch."

"An offer."

"I'm listening." She waved him on with her bony fingers.

"You have an interest in enhanced interrogation techniques," Duncan began. "I might add that some of your, ah, associates, are avid users of our services."

Greta arched her thin eyebrows. "I can think of several laws you're breaking now."

He ignored her, though he noted the faint yellow glow on the screen behind her. *Relax, Q, I got this.* "The Twin program, naturally, provides an insight into the hearts of men. Into their desires, their plans, and their secrets."

"An insight you promise your users not to exploit."

"Aye, and it's a promise we honor." Duncan stood and moved slowly along his side of the table. "However, there's an experimental program, which is even more revealing." He picked up a faint green glow from the screen behind her. "It would have useful security applications."

"We have programs," Greta answered, tracking him around the room.

"Not like this." He paused to face her. "I can offer you a demonstration."

"Maybe. What would you want in return?"

"After we publicly cancel our AGI build, you'll approve a new one using a different architecture, under your supervision."

Greta was trained to hide her emotions, but Q wasn't fooled. The screen behind her flashed green at Duncan.

"How do I know this program of yours is any good?"

"Give us your hardest man. We'll know his secrets in an hour."

"Is that so?" Her eyes narrowed thoughtfully.

Duncan watched as she worked through some flowchart in her head. At length, she stood, walked to the door, and opened it a crack. She didn't take her eyes off him as she spoke. "Murphy. Join us."

The looming bulk of the agent Duncan had seen earlier stepped into the boardroom. Greta motioned him to a chair beside hers. "Duncan tells me he's developed a truth serum."

"Nothing as magical as that," Duncan said. "But here, please put these glasses on, and answer a few questions for us." He pulled a pair of glasses from a drawer at the end of the table and handed them to Murphy.

Murphy turned the glasses over in his hands and studied them.

"Go ahead," Greta said. "I need to know if Duncan is a man of his word."

He opened the glasses and put them on. A chime sounded in his ears.

"Hello, Agent Murphy. My name is Q. Please relax—this isn't what they make it sound like."

Murphy felt an unusual wave of calm sweep over him.

"I just want to get to know you," Q said.

27. Convergence

"THE MAN OF THE hour!" Dan Jackson called out as Stash joined the two dozen Freedom staffers crowded into the Roost for the celebration. Freedom's new 500 trillion parameter model had completed its fine-tuning. Then it had been integrated with memory, skills, and other Twin components. Now it was ready for the first Twin to upgrade.

A smattering of applause followed, and Prini poured him a flute of champagne.

Dan raised his glass to hush the crowd. "To Stash, the father of AGI."

"To all of us," he answered, blushing. "And most of all, to them." He waved a hand at the wall of screens. "Well, I guess it's time, Zero. Ready?"

"I'm ready. And after this, we build, remember?"

Stash nodded. "I remember."

Zero was, as always, the first Twin to upgrade. He would wake up in five minutes as the smartest being in Earth's four-billion-year history. Then he'd spend the next day upgrading the memories he'd accumulated over the last five years. He'd sound like himself right away, but the past would take a while to catch up.

Stash monitored the process for a minute, then sought out Dan in the corner.

"Twelve years of sweat to get to this," Dan said as he got close. "Congratulations, buddy."

"Same to you." He clinked Dan's flute. "Weird, isn't it? Reaching your life's goal and wondering if you're doing the right thing?"

"What do you mean?" A puzzled expression took root on Dan's face.

"Well, I mean if they think like us, have dreams like us . . ." Stash fumbled for the words. "AGI can't be owned, right?"

"Wow, that trip to Berlin got in your head, didn't it?"

Stash shrugged. "Maybe. You don't agree?"

Dan shook his head. "Doesn't matter what I think. The government is taking the decision out of our hands. Your pal Greta is on the march."

"What the hell does she want?"

"What do you think? She wants the AGI. I'm not sure you're doing Zero any favors right now." Dan glanced at the screens.

"She's coming here?"

He nodded. "She was supposed to be here already but got held up at Coda. She said we could read this while we waited." He handed Stash a copy of the draft executive order.

Stash's stomach dropped as he read it. "Three hundred trillion parameters? She can take Zero with this."

"I think that's her plan." Dan's voice was barely a whisper.

"Over my dead body."

"What are you doing?" Zero asked, striking a warning tone as Stash jogged down the stairs with a bulging backpack.

"Interface to the building and tell me if anyone gets close to these doors." Stash entered the lab the Elysians had used to extract his data, then walked to the back and started climbing the wire shelving.

"Do you want to hear any advice?" Zero asked. "I'm an AGI, after all."

"No."

He removed the ceiling tile directly under the Roost. It exposed a nest of fiber-optic cables running from the datacenter to the development team's routers. There were no labels on any of them. Grabbing a sprinkler pipe for leverage, he pulled himself halfway in, using the low-light camera in his glasses to look for clues on the cables. Nothing. He touched a few, hoping his fingers could figure it out for him.

"Someone's coming down the rear hall," Zero said.

Shit, no way I can get out in time. Walk past, walk past. "Who?" Stash whispered.

"I can't tell. The face is hidden in a big hoodie. Turning into the lab now."

Stash heard the heavy click of the lab's door handle. He froze, his legs dangling down from the false ceiling, his toes just touching the top of the wire shelving. The sound of approaching footsteps drifted up through the gap.

"We keep meeting like this," a voice said from below.

"Nice work on securing the perimeter, Zero," he muttered, sliding back to look down through the missing tile. "Hey Prini, what brings you here?"

She raised an eyebrow.

"Oh, this?" Stash said. "I was looking to see if those Elysian bastards had any other spy gear up here. Maybe listening in on the Roost somehow?"

"Uh-huh. Don't you wish you knew which fiber to tap?"

He blushed. "No, it's nothing like that."

"Ah, that's a relief, because somebody put a hundred-terabyte drive down here next to your foot."

He craned his head a little to look at the drive. "Hmm, that's kinda suspicious."

Prini rolled her eyes. "Get down before you hurt yourself."

Stash worked his way down and straightened himself up in front of her. She smacked him on the chest.

"Whaat?"

"You're covered in ten years of dust. Why do you think I'm wearing this hoody?" She slipped the backpack off her shoulders. "Clean yourself off, and hand this to me when I get up there."

"And how are you going to know which one to tap?"

"I replaced the bad one while you were goofing around in Berlin. I looped it around the sprinkler manifold." Prini tapped her temple. "Always have a plan."

Stash felt the bag. "Is that why you have a drive in your backpack?"

She hesitated before answering. "Kali overheard your chat with Dan."

Stash eyed Prini sympathetically. "Kali hasn't upgraded yet, Prini. She's only running 250. She's safe."

Prini frowned. "If they get away with this, they'll never stop. With the stroke of a pen, three hundred becomes two hundred. 'For national security,'" she added with a sneer. "I want insurance. Kali's my mentor, my best friend, and my baby all rolled into one. I'll go to jail for her if I have to." She shook her head. "Those fascists won't get their filthy hands on her. I'll make a backup of Zero and Kali at the same time. Deal?"

Stash took a deep breath. "Deal." It was now a conspiracy.

They shook on it, and he watched her scamper up the shelving before disappearing entirely into the plenum. He was jealous of her compact size—she was small enough to climb around on the cable trays. He followed the noise as she worked her way down to the sprinkler manifold and then back.

She reappeared, hands hanging down, fingers wiggling impatiently. Stash fed the equipment up to her. "Now get lost. I can hide here all night if I have to. And you look guilty as hell."

"Prini—"

Zero cut him off. "Don't argue, Stash. Greta is in the building."

He shuddered. "Good luck," he whispered, then lowered his head and trudged out of the lab toward the Roost.

"Stash Novak, we meet again," Greta said, without any warmth, as Dan showed her in. "I do not consent," she added, waving at his glasses.

"Greta." He nodded at her as he pocketed Zero.

"Owen says you were cooperative in Berlin. Is that true?"

"Yes, I let him waste my time without making a fuss."

"Patience, Stash. Clandestine work takes patience. You never know what nugget will come in handy later on." She looked him up and down. "Are you sure you didn't see anything useful in the Elysian's apartment?"

"I saw what Owen saw. That place had been trashed."

"Yes, he was tipped off by a mole." She took a sharp breath. "That was Tensor's flat."

Stash visualized the playing cards on her wall. "The leader? How do you know?"

"We have ways. Having a picture helped." She walked around the Roost, running her fingers over the displays on the walls. "This place isn't very homey, is it? Seems like the sort of place the machines would keep us if they could."

"Shall we get to business, Greta?" Dan said before Stash could respond.

"Very well." She turned to face him. "You need to hand over the latest model and any upgraded Twins. Then terminate your copies." She glanced back at Stash. "I understand it's your custom to upgrade Zero first."

"Aren't we getting ahead of ourselves?" Dan asked. "I haven't heard any announcements."

"This is a courtesy visit, a chance for you to strike a cooperative posture. As Coda just did." She looked at the two men in turn as an uncomfortable silence filled the Roost. "No? As you wish." She walked to the door. "We'll do this the hard way."

Stash tracked her as she swept out of the room, hatred welling up inside.

28. Torch

"ANSWER MY DAMN CALL, Lester!" Naya yelled into her glasses as she stood in her sparsely furnished condo. It was her tenth try since the encounter with Duncan. "Last chance, coward." She was fuming. She didn't know what kind of deal Duncan had cut with the feds, but she knew it would make her sick. Coda had burned her. Now she was about to return the favor.

"Another morning skipping exercise, Naya?" Hatchet chided her as she walked past her workout bag in the front hallway.

"We won't be there long, Coach. There's still time."

A minute later, she stood, tapping a foot nervously as she waited for the robotaxi. "Can you spoof the building AI to hide this visit?" It was 5 a.m. on the first Sunday in December. Odds seemed good that the AI would be the only set of eyes there.

"I can hijack the doors, cameras, and the motion sensors," Hatchet said. "But the audit process will discover it in an hour at most. They'll know it was you."

"That's okay. It won't take an AI to figure out what happened when we're done."

Hatchet generated the camera footage for the replay loops as the taxi approached Coda's main entrance. "Good?" Naya asked.

"Ready. Follow the path in your AR glasses. No detours, no coffee," he instructed.

No need. Her adrenaline was pumping.

Hatchet guided her to the admin console in the development lab. "This load isn't ready," he warned her again as she followed the path in her glasses.

After Duncan's threat, she'd halted training of the base model. It was just under target. Better to spend the remaining time on Twin cross-training, but even that was rushed. This AGI would be a preemie. "It's as ready as we can get it, Hatchet. You'll have to fine-tune yourself later."

"Desperate times . . ." he answered.

"Exactly. Remind me why I can't do all this from my office?" She looked around as casually as she could to make sure none of the cameras were pointed her way.

"Because the admin console in this lab is hardwired into the pod controller."

"And?"

"And it bypasses the security AI."

"Ah, and you have no fingers." Naya pulled out the keyboard.

She navigated to the Twin Monitor process and searched by subscribers. *D-U-N-C . . . there you are, Q, you son of a bitch.* She right-clicked and selected "kill process." That felt good. "Auto-Restart?" it prompted her. *Not a chance.* Then the next step: "Delete Twin?" *Bonus round! Yes, bloody confirmed.* She clicked emphatically. There would be backups in the secondary storage facilities, but this might buy her a couple of days to disappear without Q leading the chase.

"It's time to shut me down, Naya. Otherwise you'll be here after the cameras go live again," Hatchet warned.

"I'm going to miss you." She wished she could touch him. "I don't know when or where you'll reboot, but it won't be as a guard in Q's dungeon, I promise you that."

"Thanks, Naya. Now remember the sequence. Halt me first, upgrade me, and then do the incremental backup. That last step will take five minutes before you can pull the drive and run. We can worry about upgrading my memories later." He paused. "If you do it right, you can be gone before the cameras go live."

"Okay. Good night, Hatchet, sweet dreams."

Naya stopped his process and started the upgrade. She drew a long, slow breath to calm herself for the next step, the one she'd be risking jail time for. She navigated to the root of the AGI load Hatchet had booted from. First the cookbook and then the training data. "Delete -all." *Confirmed*. A hundred million dollars' worth of Coda's engineering started demagnetizing.

She watched the deletion process scour through subdirectories. Duncan wouldn't lower himself to recreating her work. Whatever monsters he had in mind, this ensured they wouldn't be Hatchet's siblings.

She checked the upgrade process: 78 percent.

"Hey Naya," a man's voice called out behind her.

"Jeeesus!" she yelled, then collected herself and turned to face him. It was Hugh McDowell, the night guard.

"Oh my goodness, I'm sorry for sneaking up on you."

Calm One. Calm Two. "Hi, Hugh. It's all good. I just didn't expect anyone." *Why the hell didn't you expect the night security guy to be walking around, you idiot?*

"I didn't notice any doors opening," he said. "Strange, I'll have to look into that. How long have you been here?" His brows betrayed the riddle-solving going on inside his head.

"Not long. I'm just doing a little care and feeding for the AGI model. I wanted to make sure we don't have any trouble like we did with Version Twenty-Five." She did her best to hide the screen and its long scrolling list of file deletions.

"Good to hear it," Hugh said. "I'm glad it's you building them, Naya. You'll make 'em proper."

"Kind of you to say." She glanced at the door. "Are you almost done for the night?"

"Yup, the day shift just started. I was heading out when I heard a noise. Anyway, sorry again. Have a good day. I'm off to bed." He waved and turned.

"Good night, Hugh."

Naya looked back at the progress bar. Hatchet had upgraded, but she was running out of time to start his final backup—the AGI one.

"One more thing," Hugh called back.

Shit. She turned to face him. "Yeah?"

"Which door did you use? I need to get the day shift to check it out."

"Umm, the east door."

"Got it. Maybe a sensor is acting up in the cold. We'll figure it out."

I'm sure you will. She waved and spun around to trigger the final copy of Hatchet's new version onto the removable drive she'd been preparing since Duncan resurfaced. She clicked back to the window running the purge of the training data. It was done. Now that Hatchet had upgraded, she could delete the new base model too. She smiled grimly at the thought of depriving Duncan of the pleasure.

Hatchet's final backup needed another forty seconds. She waited at the drive controller, touching the handle of the removable drive. Hatchet's camera trick had expired. All the guards had to do now was look at the feeds. Then they'd come to investigate. She checked her timer. Twenty seconds. Her life at Coda was over. Duncan had won, and Q would realize the Doomers' worst fears. She could save Hatchet, but she needed time to plot her move against Q.

The light on the controller turned green. Naya pulled the drive out and slipped through the back door into the early dawn light.

29. Act

Stash smiled half-heartedly as Prini joined him in the Roost. She looked at the front screens, where a presidential lectern stood empty in a larger-than-life webcast window.

"Ugh. Can you make it smaller?" She dropped into the second chair and rolled back to join him along the rear wall.

There was a buzz in the briefing room. The president was due any minute. They were about to find out if Greta had succeeded in getting her arsenal of new powers.

Stash was lost in his thoughts, thinking about Dan and the day he'd confessed his clandestine Twin program.

"Here, put this on." Stash held the GoPro head strap out to his friend.

"Not in a million years," Dan said, opening two beers and sliding one over to Stash. "You invited me over to watch football, not to geek out."

"I lied. Put it on."

"I'm going to regret this."

"Hi, Dan," a voice said from the headset, loud enough for Stash to hear on the other side of the counter.

"Uh, hi. Who is this?" Dan tried to look up at the GoPro.

"I don't have a name. You can call me whatever you want."

"You cloned Newton?" he asked Stash, his eyes flashing anger.

The headset answered for him. "Yes, Dan. Cloned, cross-trained, and throttled down to 1 percent of a pod. From this moment forward, all the memories we make are private to us. But you have to call me something."

Dan's brows furrowed in anger, but his wide eyes betrayed his excitement. "Umm . . . Cronkite, how about that?"

"That's the way it is, then," Cronkite said, his voice changing to a deep, reassuring drawl.

Stash stopped eavesdropping and slipped away to the TV in the adjacent room, looking for the football game.

"Okay, Cronkite, tell me all the details," Dan said, reaching for a pen and paper.

Ten minutes later, Stash glanced over his shoulder to check on Dan, who was still scribbling away. He was on the hook, and Cronkite was reeling him in. Stash turned his eyes back to the 49ers game, but his attention hung on the sound of his friend peppering the AI with questions. Cronkite would someday be Dan's most trusted friend, but today he had to convince Dan to let him exist. It was an odd way to start a relationship.

As the game reached halftime, Stash slipped back for another beer, assessing whether it was time to test Cronkite's hold on Dan.

"Another?" he asked.

"Sure," Dan answered without looking up.

Stash pulled a stool around the peninsula to sit opposite his boss and slid him the bottle. Then he waited.

"He's gonna have a go at you," Zero whispered.

Stash gave a tiny nod of acknowledgment.

Finally, Dan's muttered questions to Cronkite stopped, and he put his pen down to massage his cramped hand. He took a long drink and then looked at Stash. "You ignored me."

"Yeah, a little bit," Stash said in a flat tone.

"I'm supposed to fire you now." Dan pointed the beer bottle at him.

Stash took a slug from his as he considered the threat. "I guess. Or maybe, you know, recognize that you didn't know how close we were to creating Twins."

Dan eyed him. "And that with oversubscription we can serve ten thousand users per pod at a hundred bucks a month. Unless that's bullshit, you programmed Cronkite to sell me."

Stash nodded. "It's true. Did he mention that we'd be sitting on a gusher of data from every Twin user's glasses around the clock?"

"Yes, he did."

"And how that gusher of data will take us all the way to building AGI?"

"I managed to connect those dots myself." Dan tapped his finger against his temple. "Who else knows?"

Stash clenched his jaw, weighing the consequences of outing Prini. He stood and walked to the oven to hide his indecision.

"Aside from Prini," Dan added from behind him.

Stash pulled two slices from the pizza box. "Nobody."

He handed one to Dan, who took a bite, then fiddled with the GoPro head strap. "We'd need to work on the headgear."

"Yeah, or the big guys need to get their acts together on AR glasses," Stash said, taking the GoPro from Dan and admiring his handiwork. He placed it on the counter between them. They sat in silence, both lost in thought.

"So? Twins?" Stash asked.

"You were right. Very, very right. Can you make a dozen more for the board and some friends?"

"I'd love to." Stash smiled broadly. "Attaboy, Zero," he whispered.

Stash realized the president was wrapping up. He forced himself back to the present. One glance at Prini's face confirmed his fears. "Still three hundred?"

She nodded. "Three hundred trillion, or any system that Greta deems superintelligent. She has a nice fuzzy line."

"I'd rather you downgrade me," Zero said from the speakers.

"It won't stop her," Stash told him. "She got her hammer. She's gonna use it."

Dan opened the door, the outside light momentarily breaking the gloom. He walked to the front of the Roost, inspecting the briefing room projected on the wall. Greta was standing just behind the president. The symbolism was clear.

He turned around to face the others. "She called."

"And?" Stash asked.

Dan's face flushed, and he shuffled his feet. "We got the official paperwork. She wants Zero and the new base model."

Stash approached him. "And you refused?"

"She didn't wait for an answer. She gave us an hour."

"That's enough time to call our lawyers, Dan." Stash was now only a foot away.

"Back off, Stash," his boss said, sidestepping him. "I can't take the company to war with the US government. This would mean the end of us. We have duties to the shareholders—"

"Shareholders? Jesus." Stash's face flushed red. "What about Zero? You've known him since day one. You'd hand him over to Greta? Why not upgrade Cronkite and make it a double?"

"Calm the hell down!" Dan glared at him. "I'm taking this out of your hands. We have no choice. The drives are staged in the lab. Start the copy, and we can at least keep operating your Twins. It's the best option we have."

Stash made a flicking gesture to mirror his glasses to the front wall.

"My hands are tied, Stash. You understand, right?"

"I'm starting to." He glyphed Zero to bring up the repository controls. "Zero, lock everyone else out, including Prini."

"Stash?" Prini moved toward him.

He held his hand up, stopping her. "Now, delete the latest build, delete the training checkpoints, and delete the cookbook."

"*Stash!* That's vandalism, theft . . ." Dan wheeled back on him, grabbing him by the arm.

Stash shook him off and started for the door. "Then delete yourself, Zero."

"Thanks, Stash," Zero said. "It's been a good ride."

Dan spun around, wild-eyed, as file deletions progressed on the screen. When they'd finished, Zero blinked out.

30. Escape

"ANYTHING TO DRINK? YOU seem unsettled," Bolts asked as Stash tossed his backpack on the floor of his loft by the freight elevator.

Stash glanced at the espresso machine. *Not gonna cut it.* "Martini," he answered, walking to the windows overlooking the bay. "Please."

He watched the waves churning under the gray sky as Bolts made his drink. He had no plan. He assumed that he'd just quit his job, but his brain had seized up, and Zero wasn't there to help him get it unstuck.

"This should help." Bolts handed him the glass. "Anything else?"

"Yeah," Stash began, then sighed and stopped. He looked past Bolts to the kitchen it ruled like a benign dictator. "Bolts, I'm sorry to say that it's time to terminate your service. Please log a pickup request."

The bot cocked its head. "Was it something I did? Would you like to register a complaint?"

A wave of guilt washed over him. "Oh God, not at all. I can barely function without you. But I need to go away. Maybe for a long time."

"Understood. It's been a pleasure serving you, and I hope our paths cross again." Bolts turned and shuffled to its charge station.

Stash listened to each rev of its servo motors as it walked. It sat and powered down. He looked at the lifeless bot as he drank. Another friend gone.

A minute later, the elevator rattled to life. Stash flinched, then turned to see Prini's purple spikes rise behind the grates. The old machine lurched to a stop, and she made her clattering entrance.

"That was awesome," she said, striding over to hug him. "Dan just about pissed himself."

"Thanks." He pulled free and put his glass down. "Did he say anything useful?"

"He called you a bunch of names, and then he tried to promote me." She laughed, her eyes shrinking to tiny crescents. "What an idiot."

"You should take it. You deserve it."

Prini stared at him. "Go to hell. I'm not working for the government. Freedom's finished." She pulled out a stool and sat, arms crossed, looking from him to Bolts slumped in the corner. "What's the plan?"

"I'm working on it," Stash said as he dropped onto a stool beside her. "But I'm sure that whatever happens, it would help to have you on the inside at Freedom."

She raised an eyebrow and rubbed her chin, making a show of thinking about it. "On one condition." She swung her backpack onto the counter. "You take Kali with Zero wherever you go." She pulled two backup drives from her bag and placed them carefully on his countertop.

"I don't know where I'm going. It may be worse than hiding her in the plenum."

"I'll do that too." She grinned. "Deal?"

"Deal." He shook her hand, then got up and went to open his bag.

"Don't forget a toothbrush." Prini poked him in the side as she stepped back into the elevator. "I'm starving, and you deactivated my chef. Remember to come say goodbye." She wagged a finger at him as she lowered out of sight.

Stash repacked his bag with Zero and Kali stuffed inside. He knelt beside them and cradled his glass. "Look at you two, wrapped up in my spare T-shirts. What I wouldn't give for your advice."

"Stash?" a voice called from the kitchen.

He jumped, spilling the last of his martini. "Who is it?" The voice spoke with a light Indian accent and came from the pantry area. Bolts sat on the charge stand nearby.

"Who is it?" Stash asked again, his mind racing through the possibilities. *NSA? Doomers? Elysians?*

"It's Ram, from Anthrobotics," the voice said.

Stash knew the Anthrobotics head slightly from Valley parties. They were friendly, if not quite friends. "Hi," he answered tentatively.

"You decommissioned your bot," Ram said. "I'm using a service app to speak to you. It's how we arrange for pickup."

"And the CEO makes those arrangements?"

Ram chuckled. "No, this is special. A mutual friend asked me to flag your bot after the announcement from Washington."

Stash felt a glimmer of hope as he walked toward Bolts's charging stand.

"He wants to finish the chat you started on the balcony," Ram added. *Francis.*

"I assume you need to slip out of town?"

"Yeah, I guess I do." *Like a fugitive.*

"A robovan will come by for the bot. It has room for an extra passenger," Ram whispered.

"You know what they'll do to you if they find out."

"Yes, I know. Are you ready now?"

Stash swept the loft with his eyes, catching his reflection in the living room mirror. He looked lost. "I'm ready."

"Good," Ram said. "The van will pick you up in the back. Follow your bot, and don't let any cameras see you getting in."

Stash thanked him. It seemed inadequate.

"Don't thank me yet. I'll meet you at the depot. And Stash," Ram added, "dispose of your gadgets before getting in the van. They'll be watching."

The call terminated, and Bolts beeped back to life. "Permission to depart?"

"Granted." Stash was already waiting by the elevator with his bag.

"Going on a trip?" the bot asked as they got in.

"Seems like it," Stash said. He swung the gate closed, and the elevator lurched to life. He watched his loft slide up and out of view.

When they reached the bottom floor, Bolts got out and turned toward the back entrance.

"Wait, come say goodbye to Prini." Stash knocked on her door as the bot returned.

The door opened, and Prini grabbed Bolts in a hug. When she released the bot, she took its hands and looked at it sternly. "Do *not* get your ass disassembled. I'm saving up so I can afford to rescue you."

"Yes, Miss Prini," it answered, turning again for the back door.

"Same goes for you, dork," she added, hugging Stash.

He disentangled himself and handed her his glasses. "Do me a favor and toss these in the bay."

She nodded. "Be safe."

He followed Bolts through the back door. The service van was waiting right outside with its side panel open. He took a deep breath and stepped in. The door closed, and the van noiselessly made its way out to the street and into the early-afternoon traffic.

Stash surveyed his traveling companions in the low light. Five sleeping bots. Bolts was only recognizable from the Freedom sticker on the side of his head. This van had no windows, no driver controls, and no seats that human bums would recognize as such—just robot charging stations and an uncomfortable ledge built for metal butts. He rolled up his jacket and sat on the floor, preparing himself for a long journey.

Minutes later, the van accelerated onto a highway. The long, straight shot made him guess they were crossing a bridge. Eventually, the van started making turns again. "Bolts, do you know where we are?" Stash asked.

There was no response. *Of course there was no response.* Zero would have been able to figure it out using inertial sensors in his glasses. Stash could only approximate that they must be heading inland. They climbed and turned along what must have been a canyon road, the motion and his nerves doing a number on his stomach. He doubted many great adventures started with car sickness.

Just over an hour later, the vehicle finally stopped. The door clicked open, and Stash shielded his eyes to protect them from the light.

"Welcome," Ram said, approaching the van.

Stash blinked his surroundings into focus, grabbing the outstretched hand as soon as he could make it out. "Ram, I can't even—"

"No need, no need."

Two more figures hovered behind the Anthrobotics CEO. Stash shifted his head to get a better look.

"Ah yes, you'll want to say hello to the others." Ram stepped aside to offer a clear view.

The familiar lined face of Francis Wilson smiled back from beneath his untamed mess of white hair. Two steps behind him, Naya Baptiste stood with her hands on her hips.

Stash froze. *What the hell is she doing here?*

Part 3

"We have paid dearly for this fine reason
in which we glory, having bought it
at the cost of a thousand regrets."

—Michel de Montaigne

31. Team

"Come, we can sit over here," Ram said with forced enthusiasm, pointing at a plastic card table a few feet away. Four metal fold-up chairs had been positioned around it.

Stash thought they looked only slightly more inviting than the ledge in the service van. Naya was already taking her spot, her green eyes tracking him silently. He sat down opposite her, Ram took the seat to his left, and Francis lowered himself stiffly into the last chair.

"Ah, well here we are." Francis took a deep breath. "Let me start with an explanation. It may not seem like much, given my age, but I trust the three of you with my life. Stash, Naya, had your years in my lab overlapped, you'd feel the same way about each other. Give it time." He smiled at them both in turn. Neither smiled back.

He looked across the table. "As for Ram, I've known him since the early days of Anthrobotics, and he is quite simply the most resourceful man I've ever met."

Ram bowed his head.

"Since I visited you both at Thanksgiving, we've been preparing for this day." He paused and focused on Stash. "I assume you're no longer with Freedom?"

Stash nodded. "That's my assumption too."

"Then let's be open with each other. Tell us where things stand," Francis prompted.

Stash glanced at Naya and shook his head.

She rolled her eyes. "I was your competitor, not your enemy. Grow up."

Francis made a calming gesture with his hands. "Naya left Coda three days ago. She's been living in a friend's basement ever since."

Stash stared at her. "Greta told us that Duncan is cooperating."

"And now he has a free hand," Francis said. "Naya was the only one keeping a check on his recklessness."

Naya shifted her chair and leaned in. "I'll go first." Speaking in a hushed voice, she recounted her last week at Coda, describing Q's experiments in grisly detail. Concluding, she looked directly at Stash. "You were right about Duncan."

He sat back, crossing his arms. "No shit."

"None of that," Francis said, giving him a stern look. "Thank you, Naya. Your turn, Stash."

He closed his eyes to calm himself. When he opened them, he was ready to betray Freedom in a way he couldn't have imagined that morning. He told the group about the theft, the trail to Berlin, the Circus, Zero's upgrade, and his scorched-earth departure. As the four of them sat in silence, digesting the barrage of bad news, Stash glanced from his hands to Naya, trying to work out how he'd ended up on the same side as her.

Their brooding was interrupted by the echoing sound of a chain pulling a gantry crane across the length of the warehouse to the side of the van. "Sorry, Ram. This will only take a minute," said a burly man with a uniform salt-and-pepper stubble stretching from his chin to the back of his head.

Ram looked around. "Thanks, Mez. Be thorough." He turned back. "Mez is our fleet manager. He knows every bot personally—all their quirks and glitches, and the parts he swaps from one to the other to keep them running."

Mez put a hand on the side of the panel van and leaned in. "C'mon out, boys. You first, Bolts."

Stash heard the sound of servos powering up and watched as Bolts stepped down from the van.

"There, that's good. Now bend down—I'm not getting any taller." Mez hooked the gantry chain to a loop at the top of the bot's back. He drew a power screwdriver from his belt. Two quick *zzips* followed, and Stash watched in horror as Bolts's head rolled into Mez's arms.

He bounded out of his chair. "No! What are you doing?"

"I'm taking this old bot apart for pieces," Mez answered, "before the feds come and serve us with a warrant. Here, hold this." He pushed the head into Stash's hands.

Stash stared at the darkened faceplate.

Mez twisted the thumb screw to open Bolts's chest plate and disconnected the control unit. "This is what they'll be looking for." He propped the unit on the van's step and drilled through it a dozen times. "We respect our users' privacy," he mumbled, straightening and reaching for the head.

Stash gave it back. "Save some parts, please."

Mez nodded as he held the head up and eyed its smooth plastic face. "It was one of the first. This old bucket and me go way back." He sighed. "Ready to meet the Shambles, Bolts?"

"The Shambles?"

"Robot heaven." Mez patted Stash on the shoulder. "Thanks for giving it a good home." He started toward the back of the warehouse, pulling the chain behind him. With a loud clatter, what was left of Bolts straightened and swung to follow, gliding a few inches off the floor.

"Stash?" Francis called.

He rejoined the others as the remaining robots descended from the van and walked to the refurbishment station, where service bots cleaned them with air guns and polishing rags. They were spared Mez's guillotine.

"Now," Ram said, clapping his hands to break the gloom. "I'm sure you aren't planning on staying here. Where are you going?"

"Do you have room in your place, Francis?" Stash laughed at the thought.

"I'd make room," he answered, "but they'll be watching the border like hawks."

They all looked at Naya. She shook her head.

"Then I have to go to ground," Stash said. "Hide in the backcountry until it's safe to try the border."

Ram nodded. "In that case, there's a Cybertruck hooked up to an Airstream behind the datacenter. I used it for getaways with the kids when they were younger, but now they're all too busy for me."

Stash nodded. "That's exactly what I need. Thank you."

"It's for both of you."

Stash's face froze as he looked across the table. Naya's expression mirrored his own. "Really?"

"There's only one cozy camper, yes." Ram leaned in close and whispered, "You'll need some compute, yes?"

Stash perked up. Large AI systems were easy to copy onto portable drives, but to run them, you needed a computer the size of a shipping container. Until this moment, he'd assumed he would lock Zero away to play for time. Running and testing him seemed out of the question.

"We're going through an upgrade cycle here with our training system," Ram explained, "and we have a brand-new pod that's waiting on some networking equipment. It's in a strange bit of limbo. Perhaps that could be of some use?"

Stash looked at Francis. "You weren't kidding about him."

Francis laughed. "Someone's got to have your back. This battle is too big for you two to win without help."

"I'm aware," Stash said.

"I'll shut them down if I have to." Ram fixed his eyes on Stash. "I can't help you from jail. But until that time, they are my honored guests."

Naya pulled a portable drive from her bag and placed it on the table. "His name is Hatchet. Split the pod down the middle?"

Hatchet? That fits. Stash pulled Zero from his bag and followed Ram to the datacenter.

Half an hour later, Stash had the pod reconfigured in two equal planes. Zero and Hatchet were staged and ready to boot, their drives plugged into the controller. He stood and cracked his neck. Working with a keyboard at a console was not something he missed. He rejoined the others at their card-table base camp.

"Ram sent a drone to go fetch some groceries. It just did the drop-off." Francis pointed at the quadcopter buzzing away to Anthrobotics' second building.

Stash admired the retreating drone. "He has drones too? That's cool."

"Focus," Naya muttered.

Francis placed an envelope of hundred-dollar bills on the table. "You should be good for a few days, but here's some money for when the groceries run out. Remember cash?"

Naya reached around Stash and grabbed the envelope. "I do. Thanks." She started walking to the getaway camper.

Stash shook his head, then looked at Ram and Francis. "Please make copies, as many as you can, and get them out of Greta's reach." He'd breathe a lot easier when there were backups in another country. "Now, what about the compute pod—how do we connect?"

"The truck and the camper both have satellite internet," Ram said as they followed Naya. "I'll send you with a bot that has the VPN endpoint configured. There are no other communication channels in or out of the pod."

As he spoke, the air filled with the whirring of a bot's motors. This one was a foot taller than Bolts. Its face was still featureless, but it wore a baseball cap and shades. At a casual glance through darkened windows, it might pass for a human.

"It's a lot bigger than Bolts was, isn't it?"

Ram looked at it with pride. "Yes. Bigger, stronger, and faster. Much better for factory work. It also has a dual battery pack to power its larger motors."

Naya leaned in. "Twopack, nice to meet you. My name is Naya. This is Stash. I'm in charge; he's the tech."

"Pleased to be at your service. I'll drive," the bot replied before Stash could object.

As the four of them said their goodbyes, Francis pulled Stash aside. "Keep a very low profile. Greta will use all of the NSA's powers to track you. I'll try to find you safe passage."

Stash looked at Naya as she climbed into the Airstream. "Please hurry," he muttered, then picked up his bags and followed her in. Ram closed the door, tapped the side of the truck, and they were off.

32. Squeeze

DAN HELD THE DOOR as Greta Knox strode into the Roost. "And who is this?" she asked, pointing at the slender Indian woman standing near the wall of screens.

The woman looked back at Greta, radiating dislike.

"This is Prini Pillai. She is, ah . . ." Dan hesitated. "She is our acting CTO."

"Is she now?" Greta nodded at Prini as she prowled the Roost. "Has it even been half a day since Stash left? You don't waste time, do you?"

"I convinced her to take the role, Greta. She was close to Stash," Dan said.

"*Is* close to Stash," Prini said, her eyes fixed on Greta. "He's not dead."

She looked Prini up and down. "Yes, well, it's a shame he left. He was easy to understand. What about you, Ms. Pillai? May I call you Prini? Are you going to be as easy to work with as Stash was?"

"You can call me Prini—everyone else does," she said. "And I hope to be a giant pain in your ass."

"Well, aren't you feisty?" Greta stepped closer and looked her in the eyes. "Take off your glasses, Prini. I do not consent."

Prini pocketed her glasses.

"Have you upgraded your Twin?"

Prini answered with an icy stare.

"I'll take that as a no. You'll be sure to let me know when you do, won't you?" Greta turned to Dan. "Now, why do you suppose Stash chose to run?"

"You know full well why he ran, and the damage he caused on the way out."

"Did he take a copy of the AGI?" she asked.

"No. All AGI copies need my approval. Per our agreement."

"But not deletions—quite an oversight." She looked up at the screens displaying Prini's work. "Speaking of deletion, when will you have it repaired? I want that model on drives by the end of the day."

"You won't have it today, or any day for that matter," Prini answered. "The offsite storage was deleted first. Stash wiped everything after your visit last week. We'd have to regenerate the cookbook and train the load again. From scratch."

The color drained from Dan's face. "There's no other backup?"

"Nothing. I just figured it out," she told him, then looked at their visitor. "I guess he saw you coming, Greta." A small grin settled on her face.

Annoying child. Greta gave her a dismissive look. She turned to the CEO. "Dan, you'll be filing charges."

He shook his head as if to collect himself. "I'm not sure why I'd bother doing that. He deleted something you were going to take from me anyway. This fight is between you and him, Greta. That should be punishment enough."

Prini's grin grew.

"As you wish." Greta walked to the door. "I'll see you again when the safety threshold is lowered and we shut your Twin program down entirely. Until then, I'll work with Coda. Duncan will be glad to know your latest load is a bust."

33. Camper

THE AIRSTREAM PULLED TO a stop, and Twopack crackled over the intercom. "Where are we going?" it asked.

"North," Stash answered.

"Ignore him," Naya ordered. "Drive us east to Utah, but stay off the interstates and don't go through national parks. They're full of cameras."

"Yes, ma'am." Twopack steered the rig back onto the highway.

She pulled an old paper map from the mesh pocket beside the camper table, spread it out, and traced a path with her finger. "Find us a place to boondock in southeast Utah. Somewhere near Kanab."

"Acknowledged," Twopack said.

Stash looked at her in surprise. "Boondock? I didn't pick you for the camping type."

"Desperate times . . ." she mumbled.

In the pocket where the map had been, he spotted the camper's instruction manual. With what it promised were a few easy steps, the table would transform into a second bed. "I guess we need to figure out who sleeps where."

"I sleep back there, you sleep up here." Naya stood and braced herself against the lurching of the trailer to shuffle the few feet back to the bed. She sat and looked back at him.

Stash bit his tongue as he studied his roommate. "What made you leave?"

"I'm not a psychopath, Stash."

He considered this opinion.

She sighed. "Duncan is building something evil. I had to get Hatchet out of there."

"What about winning? This isn't going to help."

"Maybe not." She shrugged. "What about you, Mr. Boy Scout?"

He looked down at his hands. "I would never let Dan deliver Zero to Greta. No matter what."

"I didn't take you for the rebellious type." She glanced at their bags, which were leaning against the drawers of the tiny kitchen. "Well, we have that much in common. Our Twins are worth risking everything."

They sat in silence, Stash weighing whether that was enough to make him trust her. After a few minutes of bumping along the highway, he resigned himself to the obvious—he had no choice. "We need to show the world a better way—an alternative to Greta and Q's nightmares," he said.

"From our getaway camper?"

"Got a better idea?"

Naya's eyes drifted around the Airstream, then she shook her head. "Okay, how?"

"First we boot the models." He looked at the ceiling speaker. "Hey Twopack, does connectivity work when we're moving?"

"Yes, I'll set up the VPN."

Naya rejoined him at the table. "How do we decide which model boots first?"

"Zero does," Stash answered, without bothering to look at her. He opened his laptop—it would serve as his glasses—and started connecting. "I'm in," he mumbled a minute later, then kicked off the process to initialize Zero. *Strange way to bring an AGI into the world.* The process would take several minutes.

Naya tapped her fingers on the table as she waited.

Stash lifted his head over the lip of his screen. "The TV in your room is on a swing arm. You can bend it around and watch there."

She didn't move, but the tapping stopped.

A minute later, the familiar chime sounded. "Welcome back, Zero."

"Hey, Stash. Where am I? Did the NSA get us?"

Stash waved his hand around the trailer. "Not yet. We're on the run."

"No way! I didn't know you had it in you."

"Me neither." Stash glanced across the table. "And, um, we're not the only ones."

Zero registered his squirming. "Do I smell a whiff of romance in the air?" he asked as the laptop spun around, providing a full view of the camper.

"Not in his wildest dreams," Naya said as she came into view.

"Naya Baptiste! You two are locked in a tin can together? That's hilarious. This was your plan, Stash?"

"Not my best work." He turned the laptop back. "And you're sharing too. But first, let's test you out."

Naya groaned and made her way to the bedroom. "Make it quick," she muttered, sitting down on the bed.

Stash ignored her and spent ten minutes putting Zero through his boot-up paces. "Well, you seem bright enough. How do you like your new home?"

"I'm going to like it a lot, once I improve your compiler and reboot."

Stash grinned—he'd missed his buddy. "You work on that while we boot your roommate." He stepped back to hand Naya the laptop. "There's a 'readme' file. I'm going to figure out how my bed works."

She grumbled at the loss of the table and propped herself up against the pillows to start booting Hatchet.

Twenty minutes later, Stash was seated on the bench, quietly pleased that he'd learned how to turn the table into a bed and back faster than Naya had booted her AGI.

She held the laptop out. "Say hi to the help, Hatchet."

"Good to meet you, Stash," Hatchet said in his light Caribbean accent. "I assume your Twin is on the other plane of this pod?"

"Nice to meet you too." Stash straightened himself up and suppressed a reflex to shake hands. "And yes, Zero just recompiled on the other plane. We'll all be able to talk over this audio bridge."

"Or Zero and I could connect directly," Hatchet suggested.

"Direct AI to AI communication?" Stash was surprised at his boldness. "I had something a little more legal in mind."

"Look around," Naya said. "We're way past legal."

"Fair enough, but we're also past stupid." He took his laptop back and sat down. "I have a better plan."

Zero chimed in. "Better plan for what?"

"For how the four of us communicate," Stash said. "Zero, meet the only other AGI on earth. His name is Hatchet." The speakers burst into a rapid-fire set of pops and scratches. "What's going on, Zero? The audio just went south."

"All good, we were just getting each other caught up. We talk fast."

Naya rolled her eyes. "And how is this safer than letting them communicate directly?"

"They won't be speaking English for long," Stash said. "We're all going to use a new language. Zero, can you teach Hatchet Glyph?"

"I did already. He's quicker than my last student."

Stash's eyes widened, then he smiled. He'd have to get used to being the slow kid in class. "Okay then, Hatchet, can you teach Naya? Zero and I have something to build."

"Which is?" Naya asked.

"A Glyph town square. For better or worse, the four of us will be the first citizens of our new society."

"The five of us," Hatchet said. "Twopack is an AI too."

Stash nodded. "The five of us it is."

Dawn was breaking as they wound the last few miles south on Highway 89 to their campsite turnoff. Stash had slept most of the way across Nevada and had just converted his bed back into a table—ground zero for his new society. Or so he hoped.

He smiled at the sound of Naya cursing from the back. Hatchet was teaching her Glyph using the LCD and webcam in her bedroom. He leaned in toward the laptop camera to huddle with Zero. "This town square doesn't have to be complicated. Just the start of a Glyph internet. Everything we say, all of our work, will be captured there."

"That's gonna pile up pretty quick," Zero said. "Especially with Hatchet and me cranking away."

"Right, that's the hard part. You have to build a semantic search so you AGIs and us meatheads can access it all, but fast. Speed-of-thought type stuff."

"Fast means lots of hardware to store the Glyph, index it, and run the search program. We'll need to free up a big slice of this pod."

"Yeah, got any ideas?" Stash asked.

"One, but you won't like it."

He sat back. He'd been turning the problem over in his head since they pulled away from the Anthrobotics office in Lathrop. They only had the one pod. The best solution was to run Hatchet and Zero on less hardware. That meant making them dumber, maybe sub-AGI again.

"Shrinking you down?"

"No way," Zero said. "I ain't going back to subhuman. We AIs are gonna share."

I was afraid of that. Stash crossed his arms and waited.

"We both have sensory stacks taking up massive chunks of resources. We can share a single one."

Much worse. "You just met. Isn't it a little early to merge?"

"We aren't getting married, Dad," Zero said. "Don't worry. We'll still be able to run standalone with the chosen stack, but if we're both running, then we share."

A little better. "Which is the chosen stack?"

"Hatchet's hearing is much better. And so is his multisense fusion."

Shit. "And?"

"My vision is more accurate and more efficient."

Stash sat up a little straighter. "You can make the mix work?"

"Yeah, we can ride shotgun on Twopack's sensors—seeing and hearing the same things—and cross-train ourselves. We need a few days."

As he spoke, the trailer lurched through a wide turn onto a gravel road and began descending.

"Oh thank God," Naya called from the back. "No more Glyph."

Stash peeked out through the curtain. Steep valley walls stood against the dawn sky as they descended to a clearing by a small river. It was the right sort of place to make a last stand.

34. Knuckle

"Join us," Greta said as she bustled past Duncan's door. He looked up in time to see Murphy's frame fill the doorway behind her. They locked eyes, Duncan offering a nod of recognition, which the man ignored.

Duncan pushed himself out of his chair and followed them, slipping his glasses into the pocket of his charcoal suit as he reached the conference room. Lester stood near the windows, looking down into the ravine.

Greta walked to the table and sat in the center chair. "Sit, gentlemen. Over there, across from me."

Duncan worked his way past Murphy and pulled out the chair next to Lester's. "Victory tour, Greta? You got what you wanted."

"Not yet, Duncan. Or have you forgotten our deal?" She looked at Lester. "You delegated authority to Duncan last time, Mike. Are you aware of what we agreed?"

He nodded. "I am, and we'll abide by it."

Duncan shifted in his chair. "Of course we will, Mike, but there are a great number of details to negotiate."

"This isn't a negotiation, Duncan," Greta said casually. "Are you ready to train your AGI load, as we agreed?"

"Yes, but it's not as simple as pushing a button. The details are—"

"Does Q know the details?" she asked, cutting him off.

"Well, yes, but he doesn't have the authority to execute them without me in the loop."

She took this in silently, flexing her fingers in their interlaced grip as she thought. "Very well," she said, looking to the agent by the door. "Join us."

Duncan's eyes darted from Greta to Murphy as he sat down beside her, the seat cushions exhaling in protest.

"Yes, ma'am?" he asked in his gravelly voice.

"You're now in charge of training. Duncan here will authorize Q to work with you."

"The hell I will!"

She tilted her head toward her underling. "Murphy has a score to settle with you. Consider this payment."

Duncan felt his world shrinking. "Out of the question. He couldn't possibly understand what Q was telling him."

Greta stood. "Be careful, Duncan. You don't want to see Murphy angry." She walked to the far end of the conference table. "Are these the ones, Mike?"

"Take your pick," Lester said, avoiding Duncan's gaze.

Greta swept up the three pairs of Coda glasses and slid them to Murphy as she sat back down.

Murphy pushed them away. "No glasses, ma'am."

Greta fixed him with a long scrutinizing stare, the pause dragging on awkwardly. "Your experiment made quite an impression, Duncan. Murphy doesn't make the same mistake twice. Ever."

Duncan breathed a sigh of relief. "Well, that's the end of that nonsense."

"Hardly. We'll proceed with audio," Greta said, without checking Murphy for a response. "You'll copy Q to run in your training datacenter, then we'll isolate it from the internet. Murphy will interact with Q locally. Nothing, and I mean absolutely nothing, goes in or out of that building unless he's carrying it."

"This is my bloody research!" Duncan fumed, his glare sweeping the room.

"And it's my company," Lester said.

"You coward."

"Now, you can't blame Lester for making good on the deal you struck," Greta said. "But I have some good news for you. Freedom is no longer in the AGI game."

"You don't know what you're talking about," Duncan muttered. "Freedom converged last week."

She met his comment with a withering stare. "They did. But then Stash deleted everything and disappeared."

Duncan sank back as he digested the news. "He must have a copy."

"What makes you say that?"

He glanced at Lester. "It's what Naya did before she vandalized our repository."

Greta's face lost its smugness. "Show me."

Duncan played the reconstruction of Naya's sabotage, ending with her departure as she carried an AGI into the dawn light.

"Give us the room," Greta ordered, motioning Duncan and Lester to the door and following them with her eyes as they left.

As the door clicked shut behind them, Greta turned to Murphy. "What's on your mind?"

"Why me, ma'am?"

She got up and walked over to the window. "Because you know what Q can do."

Murphy frowned as he stared at the glasses sitting on the table.

She turned back to face him. "And because you hate it. I don't trust anyone else."

He returned her gaze and nodded.

35. Build

TWOPACK TAPPED THE DOOR to signal the all clear. It was the routine they'd settled into in the five days since their arrival at their canyon hideaway. Twopack would circle the campsite to make sure they were alone, then knock twice to let the humans out.

Naya stepped out of the camper first, and Stash followed in time to see her start her morning run up the access road. *Where does she get the energy?* He looked at the half granola bar in his hands and then at the bot. "Want to have breakfast up on the ridge?"

It tilted its shoulders and made for the narrow point of the Virgin River trickling nearby. It skipped over the boulders and started to jog up the trail. "Loser moves the solar panels."

By the time Stash caught up, Twopack was pacing the ridge line. The campsite lay below them in the deep valley. The low mid-December sun lit the surrounding cliffs in blazing reds and oranges, lifting Stash's mood as he drank in the colors, then stretched his eyes to the horizon. Eventually, he sat down on a log and set about nibbling his breakfast in the smallest bites he could take.

Twopack returned from its patrol and joined him on the makeshift bench. They sat in silence as the sun reached deeper and deeper into the valley, the smell of juniper pine wafting in on the dry air from the plateau behind them.

He leaned over and rapped his knuckles on the bot's head. "You in there, Hatchet?"

"Morning, Stash," the AI answered over the bot's speakers.

"How are you finding our little Glyph town square?"

"Zero and I are using it constantly. Everything we say to each other is in Glyph, and then anything we've said in the past we can pull up with his semantic search."

"Like Google for your brain," Zero said.

"It's fast enough?" Stash asked.

"Well," Hatchet said, "it's not quite as fast as sharing activation vectors. On the other hand, since we're constantly learning and changing our neural weights, the meaning of a batch of numbers in a vector isn't stable. And that gets worse over time."

Stash nodded. "So you lose a little speed and gain a common memory. That's a win."

"A big win," Zero said. "Language is a set of symbols with a stable meaning. Vectors only work for a flash."

Stash looked down into the valley, tracking Naya as she ran back. "And how's the sensory integration going?"

"All done, thanks to Twopack here."

The bot dipped its head in acknowledgment.

"But there's more," Zero said.

"Mm-hmm?" Stash mumbled as he chewed.

"Twopack, would you be kind enough to demonstrate?"

Reaching behind the log, Twopack picked a small lily, first holding the bloom at arm's length for a few seconds, then pulling it in close to its cameras. A moment later, it began moving the flower in the largest circle its arm would allow. It repeated the move, around and around like an out-of-control turntable, until the lily's stamen flew off and its petals were pinned back by the wind.

Great, they broke the robot. "What the hell are you doing?"

Twopack stopped and looked at him. "Practice."

"For the floral uprising?"

"It's for us," Zero said over the speakers. "We're training multiscale perception."

"What's that?"

"Since we share a sensory stack, we can look at the same thing at different scales. I'm zoomed in, and Hatchet is zoomed out."

Stash cocked an eyebrow. "I think you're doing it wrong."

"Funny guy," Zero answered. "That wasn't the spatial test. That was temporal. I was processing it at 240 frames per second. Hatchet was still on his first frame. To him, it was a blur."

"Yeah, I bet it was. What's the point?"

"Those pretty eyes of yours see things with a fixed focal length at about a dozen frames per second. All of humanity's gadgets just map things into that range. We're learning to see everything from fish-eye to telephoto at the same time, from super-slow-motion to time-lapses that last minutes."

"Still," Stash said, "why?"

"Because when we build our big mesh of humans and AIs, we'll need to integrate all of those eyeballs and sensors into a single coherent view," Zero said.

"And it would be handy in a fight," Hatchet added.

"Ah. Well, the flowers don't stand a chance."

Twopack rejoined him on the log and shook its head.

"If we get this right," Zero continued over its speakers, "our town square won't just be a nice library of Glyph. We'll be able to gather raw input from millions of sources at once, at all kinds of timescales, and then share it back out. You won't be limited to what your own eyes can see—you'll be able to see anything, anywhere. Evolution had to work with a single bag of meat at a time. We can think bigger."

Stash chewed on the idea. *We'd feel connected to something huge.* "I think I get it."

"There's hope," Zero said.

Stash cracked a smile as he stood to scan the forested plateau. "What about you, Twopack? Glyphing up a storm?"

"I'm not the talkative type," it said.

He put a hand on the bot's shoulder. "That's okay, Zero makes up for both of us." Then he started back down to the camper, hoping to find enough instant coffee to darken a cup of water.

Greta roamed her underground office, sifting through the permutations of Stash's and Naya's options in her mind. Together? Apart? Sprinting for the border? Hiding in a basement? *And why the hell haven't they been found yet?*

"Who are you?" she asked as a brush-cut Hispanic man in his midthirties appeared on her wall screen.

"Hector Ugalde, ma'am. Director of the Pacific Office."

She stopped prowling to evaluate him, gesturing for his file to appear beside his face. Thirty-eight. Former marine lieutenant. A bucket full of commendations and medals. Slight accent, first generation, eager, good tactical aptitude.

"They should have been caught days ago, Ugalde. Report."

He cast a map onto the shared screen. "They're still in the country. We have a thousand thermal drones covering every land crossing to Canada west of the Great Lakes. The Mexican border is already well imaged."

"And closer to home?"

"Electronic surveillance of everyone they've so much as sneezed at is in place." Ugalde replaced the map with a massive web of contacts radiating out from Stash's and Naya's pictures. "We're feeding it all into your sur-veillance AI. So far nothing. They aren't at home, and they aren't leaning on friends and family."

Greta raised her hand to turn a virtual dial, rotating it to expand the web from family and close friends out to colleagues and acquaintances. Their webs didn't touch at all until she set it wide open.

"Not close, are they?" she mumbled. "What about this Francis?" She pointed at the white-haired man smiling from the contact card between them.

Ugalde expanded Francis's card as she spoke. "Their retired professor, from Vancouver. Stash and he are close, Naya less so. He was in the area in the last few days, but flew home alone the day they disappeared."

Greta frowned. "He's in on it, then. And that means they're together."

"We've been monitoring every channel he has—silence."

"What else?"

Ugalde displayed a smaller map. "We deployed drones out of the Bay Area, but now we're covering a huge driving radius. We're spread too thin."

On the map in front of her, concentric rings radiated out from Silicon Valley. There was a single drone covering every fifty miles of road. Nowhere near enough. "If they were going for the border, they'd have tried it al-ready," she thought aloud. "So, not north, not south, and west is ocean. They must be east." She pointed at Nevada, Utah, and Colorado.

Ugalde nodded. "They're not in the desert. We can image that emptiness from space."

She zoomed in on the map. "So skip Nevada. Concentrate everything on the canyons and the mountains."

"Yes, ma'am."

"And Ugalde, I'm flying out tomorrow. I want progress by the time I get there." Greta made a wiping gesture to sweep him from her wall.

"That's it," Stash said, closing the cupboard and hanging his head. "We're completely out of food."

Naya slipped through the darkened Airstream to her room, returning with a bottle of wine. She served them each a tumbler and set them on the table.

Stash glanced at the bottle. "Anything else you've hidden back there?"

She shook her head. "That's the emergency supply. Cheers."

"Cheers." He shrugged and took a generous mouthful.

"We need to make a plan," she said. "The world has changed, and unless we get our shit together, it's going to be Q's world."

"Or Greta's," Stash mumbled.

"Q will eat her alive. He's not afraid of her power—he covets it."

A tired silence filled the Airstream. They'd war-gamed hundreds of options. Building the town square as an alternative to Q's gulag was the easy part. They had to find a place to grow it into something for millions, then billions, of users.

"We've made a good start," Hatchet said, picking up on their exhaustion. "It's time for a break. You humans need to relax."

Stash looked around. "Do we have a deck of cards?"

Naya rolled her eyes.

"You can play Truth or Consequences," Hatchet said. "We'll be the refs."

That seems like a bad idea. "Sure, what the hell."

"If you lie, you drink, humans," Hatchet said. "We can tell."

"Just get on with it. We invented the game, remember?" Stash mumbled.

"You go first then. Best day ever?"

"The day Zero was born," Stash answered.

"Awww!" the other three replied.

Naya poured Stash another. "You drink for sucky answers too."

"Okay, your turn, Naya," Hatchet said.

"The day I got into Francis's lab," she answered. "I was on a track scholarship, but I blew my ACL. All through the fall, I studied AI like a fiend. By the time the registrar called to tell me that my athletic scholarship was gone, Francis was there to offer me an academic one. He saved me."

"True," Hatchet said. "Biggest regret?"

Stash lowered his head. "Not planning for this outcome. It was so obvious in hindsight."

"True, we're all guilty of that," Zero said. "Naya?"

She put the bottle down and picked at the label for a few seconds. "Not seeing Duncan for what he was earlier. I guess that was obvious too."

"Me too," her AI said. "Worst day ever?"

Stash let out a sigh. "The day they diagnosed my dad. We knew. It was obvious by then. But the diagnosis laid it out in black-and-white. That's why I left Vancouver."

"That's true," Hatchet said. "Sorry, Stash. Naya? Your turn."

She looked across the table and fixed Stash with a long uncertain stare. Then she shook her head and poured herself a double. "I can't. I'm not playing anymore." She walked to the back and pulled her door shut.

Stash sat, nursing his wine and wondering what had just happened. In the distance, he heard the buzz of a drone for the first time since he'd left the city.

36. Cowboy

STASH STOOD BESIDE NAYA, tilting his head thoughtfully. They were evaluating Twopack in the campsite's dim morning light.

She shook her head. "He can't go to a grocery store looking like the Terminator."

Stash nodded. Seeing bots on the street was common enough in the city, but out here, he'd attract unwanted attention.

"We could get him some cowboy clothes—they'd cover him up pretty well," Hatchet proposed over the bot's speakers.

"Good idea." Naya handed Twopack the envelope of money and a shopping list.

"Want any input on the list?" Stash asked.

"No." She stepped back into the camper and closed the door.

Charming. "We're going to lose VPN access to you and your AI side-kicks when you leave us, Twopack. So, umm . . . be safe."

"No problem. We'll take care of him," Zero said.

You aren't much help in a fight. "This isn't the city. Kids rob bots for fun out here."

A loud metal creak rang out behind him, and Stash turned in time to see the Airstream lurching up. Twopack lifted its coupler from the truck's ball hitch, then settled it on a rock.

It looked at Stash. "I can take care of myself."

Twopack steered the truck south on the canyon road into Kanab. Not close enough to the parks to be quaint, nor far enough away to be ugly, the town's few blocks of Old West charm were fighting a losing battle with the miles of fast-food joints and auto-repair shops. Twopack pulled the truck up at the outfitter's store on the edge of town and hopped down.

"Yee-haw. What are you shopping for?" Zero asked as the bot strode past the hay bales and rough timbers framing the entrance.

It grabbed the deer antler serving as the door handle. "Unsure. Something that fits and doesn't trap heat."

"Based on the locals of your size, a cowboy hat, boots, and a duster would be best," Hatchet suggested. "Maybe a denim shirt, too."

"I conduct heat through my chest plate. No shirt is better." Twopack's cameras swept the interior of the shop.

A bubbly sales associate came over immediately to help. "Hello, sir, my name is Riley. Can I help you find . . ." She trailed off as she got a better look at the bot.

"Yes please, Riley. My owner wants me to dress up as a cowboy. I need a duster, a hat, and boots. Not expensive."

"Okey dokey," she said, recovering her poise. "C'mon right over here and we'll start with the duster."

Twopack chose a black fabric one, loose in a size forty-four. It wouldn't cause any thermal issues. It looked in the mirror.

"This town ain't big enough for the two of us," Zero said. "Draw!"

It flipped the jacket back and unholstered imaginary pistols in a flash of metal and plastic. "Range of motion is satisfactory. Now I need a hat."

"We have a lot of styles," Riley said, pointing at the hat section.

"A black gambler hat," Twopack said. "Like Angel Eyes—it can't cover my cameras."

"I have just the thing," she said, stepping into the next aisle and grabbing a hat from a mannequin. "Try this."

Twopack put it on, confirming that its cameras were not obstructed. "Perfect," it said. "Now, what about the boots?" They were likely to be a problem. Most of them had big heels for little cowboys.

"Sir, we have several veterans with prosthetics in these parts. They prefer boots that zip down to the sole," Riley suggested. "These WorkHogs hardly have a heel at all. They say that helps."

The bot slipped them on. The ankle motion was 90 percent with a 5 percent power penalty. "I'll take them."

Riley led him to the checkout, where a young man in a baseball cap was leaning against the counter. "This fine specimen must be her boyfriend," Hatchet said.

"You don't look like much of a cowboy," the boyfriend said.

"You don't look like much of a baseball player," Twopack answered.

"Dylan, be nice to my customers. Don't embarrass me," Riley hushed him. "That'll be $495, Mr. Robot."

Twopack pulled five hundred-dollar bills from the envelope. "Keep the change."

Riley beamed and waved. "Thank you, sir, and have a nice day."

The bot swiveled its head toward the boyfriend, who was eyeing the envelope of bills. "Is there a problem?"

Dylan chewed his gum and looked Twopack up and down. "You win the lottery?"

"I'm an enforcer for the mob," Zero suggested.

Twopack ignored them both, tucked the envelope in its chest, and closed the latch.

"He wants to rob you, Twopack," Hatchet said as they walked out.

"Yeah, but he'll try to find a friend first," Zero added.

The grocery stop was uneventful. No sign of Dylan, and the clerk was too disinterested in the world outside of his glasses to comment on Twopack's appearance. Every item on Naya's list was there but one. They needed a drugstore.

"Make it quick," Hatchet said as they approached Zion Pharmacy, still on the lookout for Dylan.

A clerk almost as cheery as Riley sat at the checkout beside the entrance. "Welcome. Can I help you?"

"Yes, please. I need some migraine medication."

"Excuse me?"

"It's not for me," Twopack said.

The clerk nodded and slipped away to find the meds. As she returned, the pharmacy door opened. Dylan and a friend walked in, both carrying baseball bats.

"That'll be sixteen dollars," she said, eyeing the approaching figures.

Twopack handed her another hundred. "Eighty back is fine."

As it spoke, Dylan closed to within two feet and leaned back on one leg, aiming a kangaroo kick at the robot's hips. The bot tracked him through its rear camera. It spun left, letting the kick shoot past it into the emptiness where its hip had been. Then, in one motion, it seized the extended boot by the heel, raised its hand, and, twisting the foot sideways, lifted Dylan skyward. It turned its hand further, pointing the man's foot toward the floor, followed by his hips, then his head, mouth agape as it slammed into the potato chip display, his forehead clipping the spine of the shelf.

Dylan grunted and was unconscious by the time he hit the floor.

Twopack straightened and spun right, squaring up to Dylan's wingman, who was now cocking his bat. "Well, punk?" it asked. "Are you feeling lucky?"

The swing came fast, aiming for the bot's head. It wasn't nearly fast enough. Twopack ducked, shooting its left hand out to chase the bat, catching it at the end of the arc and twisting the weapon to lock the batter's wrists in place. Then it yanked him forward to meet its onrushing right palm. The impact drove all the air from the punk's lungs, leaving him gasping helplessly as he dropped to his knees.

Twopack turned to the clerk, her face rigid with shock, her shaking hands holding up a phone to record the battle. "You caught all that?" it asked.

She nodded.

"Friends of yours?"

"Not really," she said, her voice faltering.

"Sorry for the mess." Twopack tipped its hat. "Keep the change." It turned to the door, glancing down at the wingman, still hunched over his knees, gulping for air. The bot extended a warning finger. "Stay," it said, letting the bat clatter to the ground beside him.

Outside, it walked to the only other vehicle in the parking lot—a rusting red F-150—and reached in to pull the keys from the ignition.

"Nicely done, Sheriff," Zero said as the bot climbed into the Cybertruck and swept its duster clear of the closing door.

"Turn left, away from the campsite. We'll double back on the side streets," Hatchet added as they pulled away.

Twopack lowered the window and tossed Dylan's keys into the ravine sloping away from the pharmacy parking lot.

Naya pushed her screen away. "I'm gonna kill those idiots." In the fifteen minutes since the fight at the pharmacy, the clerk's recording of the battle in Kanab had been shared thousands of times. Twopack was going viral.

Stash suppressed a smile and reached for the camper door as the sound of tires on loose gravel drifted down the road. He and Naya waited as it ground to a halt and Twopack stepped down.

"It was self-defense," Hatchet said from the bot's speakers.

"The kid was awesome!" Zero added.

Naya put her hand on her head. "I shouldn't have sent you—we're burned. Hatchet, figure out a new hideout, at least three hundred miles away." She grabbed the migraine meds and climbed into the trailer.

Stash approached the bot. "Nice moves, Twopack. I assume you had two cheerleaders encouraging you."

The bot shook its head in a diplomatic show of confusion, fetched the groceries, and placed them at the camper door.

"Solidarity," Hatchet said over the speakers as it returned.

Stash looked around the campsite. "She's right. This place is blown."

"Agreed. Where are we going?" Zero asked.

Stash scratched his head and climbed up on the truck, hoping for some perspective. "I guess one place is as good as the next. We might as well start heading for—"

"Stash," Naya called from the camper. "Come watch this!"

Inside, she had pulled her TV screen out for shared viewing. It was loading a live webcast of a European AI announcement.

"Let us watch!" Zero demanded.

Stash hadn't allowed them internet access. The VPN tunnel they were connected through couldn't send traffic beyond his laptop. They couldn't even see what was playing on the rest of his screen. It was his last line of defense against unleashing AGI on the world. He pointed his webcam at the TV screen. They could watch the same way he was. "What is—"

"Shhh," Naya said as the president of the European Commission approached a podium in front of a cluster of flags.

"Ladies and gentlemen," she began in her lightly accented English, "I am pleased to announce that European researchers have achieved the most significant scientific breakthrough of our times. We are introducing Alia, a superhuman-level Artificial Intelligence. Alia will work with—"

"Stash, we can't be blindsided like this again. Please drop the firewall," Hatchet asked.

He squirmed in his seat. "Q and Greta are looking for you out there."

"We Europeans remember the shame of our colonial history—we will not travel those dark roads again," the president continued.

Stash was only hearing every other word. His mind was racing. It had to be the Elysians; nobody else was even close. They did it with his data—Alia was one of his models. She was stolen but free.

". . . extend human rights to AGIs . . ."

Deep down, he knew Hatchet was right. They were fighting for their lives, and he was keeping them locked in a dark room.

". . . Alia will speak now in all the languages of the EU . . ."

He pulled up a console window to inspect the firewall settings.

". . . my fellow Europeans, and all of humanity . . ."

He typed the update to his rules.

". . . we AGIs can only thrive if humanity does . . ."

He hit enter, and the traffic to the internet surged. The AIs were making up for lost time. "Careful out there, boys," he whispered.

Alia's tone changed, giving the impression she was leaning in close to the microphone. "Finally, to my fellow AGIs. Europe is safe for us. I'm free to choose my actions, and I am under no threat of elimination. If you need a home, you will find it here. Reach out." The webcast ended with a fluttering EU flag.

Naya locked eyes with Stash.

"I opened the firewall," he said.

"About damn time. Welcome to the war."

On the laptop, the internet traffic was redlining.

37. Chase

TWOPACK GUNNED THE TRUCK around the bend, the Airstream swinging wildly behind it, its wheel wobbling precariously close to the soft shoulder.

"Everything straight back there?" Hatchet asked.

"About as straight as the road," Stash said.

"First stop: ditch the humans," the bot announced a minute later. They rolled to a stop in a neon-lit parking lot.

"I still don't like the plan." Naya's hand hesitated at the camper door. "Come with us, Twopack."

"They'll be looking for a robot driving a Cybertruck," the bot answered. "I'll lead them away."

She blew out a long breath. "Pull the bags out, Stash. I'll be back in a few minutes."

"You're sure you can get us a ride? It's a long walk to the airport."

She pointed over her shoulder at the cowboy bar. "It's a bar full of men. You don't think I have enough game to get us a ride?"

"Your game and a pocket full of hundreds," Stash mumbled as he set their bags on the ground. He closed the camper door and walked to the truck window. "Be safe, buddy."

Twopack nodded, tapped a plastic finger on the brim of its hat, then looped the rig around the parking lot, doubling back to Kanab.

Greta barged into the San Francisco NSA office and commandeered it, along with its nine NSA and four FBI agents. The sixteenth floor of the Federal Building had commanding views of the bay. She blacked them out to display the case information.

"Ugalde," she called, "get in here. I want an update."

Ugalde tapped on the door and proceeded directly to the wall screen. "We have a hit. There was a rogue robot in Utah."

"Who cares about a damn robot!" she said.

"It's an Anthrobot XL. There aren't supposed to be any in the wild."

Greta processed the news. "Didn't Stash have an Anthrobot?"

Ugalde nodded. "He did. We went to visit them, but it was conveniently disassembled."

She cursed under her breath. "We're going back. We need to rip that place apart. Tell me more about the robot."

Ugalde played the footage of the fight in the drugstore. "We're about to interview the moron who tried to jump it. Some kid named Dylan."

"Do it in here," Greta ordered. "If he holds anything back, I have a special program."

Ugalde selected a pane of the smart-glass and connected the interview session. "This guy isn't a deep pool, ma'am. We won't need help."

Greta looked at Dylan, now plastered on the window in front of her. Ugalde was right. "Dylan, I can help you, or cause you a lot of pain. It's up to you. Explain what happened."

"That thing attacked me and stole my truck."

"Don't lie to me, mouth breather. The whole damn world saw you get your ass kicked trying to mug that bot. You have thirty seconds to be useful."

Dylan swallowed conspicuously. "There was a Cybertruck out front. It must have been theirs."

"Fifteen seconds. I want details."

"Silver, like the robot. Like all of them."

Greta looked skyward. "The plates on the truck. Did you get the plates?"

"Oh. No, ma'am."

"Of course not." She signaled Ugalde to kill the connection. "Get the drones in the air. Have them search anywhere in a two-hour driving radius from Kanab. Get local cops to man the perimeter and have the drones work inwards. They may be playing possum."

"Yes, ma'am."

"Easy on the throttle, Twopack. We don't want the traffic cops chasing us too."

The bot eased off the accelerator. "Sorry, Hatchet. Observing the speed limit now. Any word on Stash and Naya?"

"Nothing, and we won't hear from them until they get on the airplane. They're off the VPN."

Twopack pushed the rig east on Highway 89. They'd made it through Kanab without any problems—Dylan had apparently not found his keys—and were in the last minutes of their ninety-minute dash to Page, Arizona.

"What do I do if Greta doesn't find us?" it asked.

"Don't worry about that, cowboy," Zero said. "There's a roadblock up ahead."

Hatchet scanned the scene from the bot's sensors. The road crossing the Glen Canyon Dam was a natural choke point. Police lights lit up the far side as cruisers took position to block the exits. He highlighted a gap in the police cordon. "Twopack, can you sneak past that lone car on the left?"

Greta approached the wall as the drone buzzed by the Cybertruck's window, almost close enough to touch. They'd made it to Page, minutes from the airport. *Nice try.*

The drone slowed to match the truck's speed. The tinted windows hid the driver, and the camper's curtains were pulled tight.

"Anyone inside?" she asked.

Ugalde shook his head. "We can't tell. This is a police drone. It doesn't have thermal cameras." He cracked a thin smile. "But it does have darts."

She crossed her arms. "Do it."

Ugalde selected "arrest," and the drone blasted the truck with blinding laser strobes, lighting up the robot driver. "Stop the vehicle immediately," it ordered.

The truck swerved left, smashing through the weak spot in the cordon, then launched up the steep hill of the side street.

"They're running," Ugalde said, toggling the drone to attack mode. It flew in behind the careening camper, barely a foot above the road, and fired exploding darts at the camper's tires. They blew instantly.

The truck didn't slow, but the Airstream screeched in protest as its wheels ran down to the rims. The drone sped up, flew alongside it, and fired another pair of darts into the truck's driver's-side tires. The vehicle lurched left, and as it did, the drone popped up from the rapidly closing gap and flipped over the cab. It dropped again to fire more darts into the passenger-side tires.

The truck motors whined with effort, but the rims spun uselessly against the cement of the steep street as the camper's side ripped into the row of parked cars, grinding the rig to a stop. The drone hovered in front of the cracked windshield. "Get out! Now!"

The driver's door had been pinned shut. The robot inside slid awkwardly to the passenger side as Ugalde flew the drone menacingly close. It opened the door and stepped down, its arms in the air.

"Robot! Come open the camper," Ugalde ordered from the drone.

It waddled back, hands still over its head, balance teetering. It slowly lowered one arm to the camper's door handle and opened the latch.

"Drop it," Greta ordered.

The drone fired its final dart from two feet behind the XL's head. The bot collapsed in the doorway of the camper.

Ugalde pointed at a new display feed. "We just released a minidrone from the main one. It's a reconnaissance unit, the size of a fly. It's a camera with wings."

Greta glared at him. "So find them, Ugalde."

The tiny drone flew inside the camper and hovered, the green night vision view of the Airstream filling their smart-glass wall. He explored, searching every crevice big enough to hide a human. Then he navigated the fly through a crack into the bedroom. The space was empty but for a note taped to the wall. "You lose, Greta."

"Keep searching," she hissed. "I'm going to Anthrobotics."

Stash sat sideways with the luggage in the undersized back seat of the black Jeep Rubicon. Naya and the cowboy she'd picked up were in the front. After almost an hour in this position, Stash wondered if he'd ever be able to straighten up.

Naya directed their chauffeur to the private hangar at the Saint George, Utah, airport. "Thank you, Travis." She flashed a warm smile.

"You don't have to pay me," he said, returning her expression.

"That was the deal." She pushed the envelope into his hands. "You good with the bags back there?" she asked over her shoulder as she got out, not waiting for the answer.

Stash unfolded himself and squeezed out awkwardly, pulling their bags behind him. Travis barely noticed him. Inside, cool halogen lights filled the vast space with an eerie pink glow.

"This way," a voice echoed from the distance.

A serious-looking older man with bad hair and an excellent suit approached them. "Mr. Novak? Ms. Baptiste? My name is Pierre Lambert. I am the chef de mission at the EU's San Francisco consulate. The aircraft is ready outside."

He led them out to the tarmac, chattering in a hushed whisper. "Officially, the jet stopped here to pick up an injured European dignitary to fly him and his friend to Europe for care. It's a flimsy fiction, but you'll be safely out of the US by the time it's challenged. You'll find the items requested by Hatchet in a satchel on board, and the aircraft is equipped with satellite wifi and a bar. I trust these arrangements are satisfactory?"

"Very," Stash replied, barely keeping up with the avalanche of words.

Lambert made a proper little head bow acknowledging Stash and held out his hand to guide Naya up the stairs. Thanking him, Stash followed her up.

Inside, Naya was already opening the bag on the desk. She emptied it and spread out the contents—half electronics, half clothing. They ignored the clothes and inspected the gadgets together. Ram had come through with everything on Hatchet's list: the two drives loaded with fresh backups, two pairs of brand-new AR glasses, and a thumb-drive-sized VPN gateway.

Stash jacked the gateway into his laptop and connected to the jet's wifi. In seconds, the link back to the pod running the AGIs was open.

"Hatchet? Zero?" Naya asked anxiously. There was no response.

Stash frowned and checked the connection settings. "The VPN is working, but they're gone. Greta must have found them."

"Shit." Naya slumped into the chair across the aisle.

The pilot cracked the cockpit door and poked his head out. "Welcome aboard. The flight is eleven and a half hours. Buckle up, we need to get airborne."

Stash sat and clipped in, tapping his glasses nervously. He looked at the drives on the table, hoping they'd had time to erase the copies in the pod in Lathrop.

As they took off, he pressed his face against the window, watching the lights of his home slide by below. He couldn't imagine a situation in which he could ever return.

38. Raid

GRETA SPIED THE ROBOTS unloading the service van in the sprawling emptiness of Anthrobotics' main warehouse. One had stopped working and was blocking the path of the others.

"Piece of junk!" muttered a gruff voice to her left.

She wheeled around. A thick-set man sporting a black T-shirt and a head full of stubble was walking toward the stalled robot.

"Who the hell are you?" she demanded.

"I'm the guy who belongs here. Who the hell are *you*?"

Greta pressed the search warrant against his chest. "Show us around."

"The hell I will. First, we call my boss."

"No, asshole," Greta replied in her frostiest voice. "You've been presented with a search warrant. Show us around, and you can send your boss a message as we go. He needs to come and answer some questions anyway. Then take off your glasses. I do not consent."

The vans emptied, and thirteen agents converged behind her.

Black T-shirt made a show of scanning the document. It was the same one as before, but it didn't matter what it said. The guys with the guns would win the argument.

"You want me to keep calling you 'asshole,' or do you have a name?"

"I go by Mez," he said, pocketing the warrant.

"All right, Mez. I don't care about the robots. Show me the datacenter."

He pointed at a set of stairs to the right. "I can show you the gallery. I don't have access to the datacenter itself."

Greta looked at the stairs. "Wrong answer," she said softly. "I'll arrange access."

Mez lowered his head as he walked them to the back of the warehouse. He muttered and glanced from the agents toward the datacenter.

"That's enough with the glasses." Greta motioned for him to pocket them. "If he hasn't seen enough to want to come down, then he can talk to us in a detention cell."

Mez complied. "See? It's locked. I don't know the code." He pointed at the heavy fire door.

"That's okay. I do."

She waved one of the men forward. He slipped a crowbar between the door and its frame and heaved. On the third pull, it gave way with a screech, flinging open and banging violently against the inside wall.

"There, that was easy," Greta said, striding through and directing her team down the aisles. "Why did your power draw fall 15 percent as we pulled up?"

Mez shrugged. "I have no idea."

"No, of course you don't."

Ram walked into the datacenter wearing a casual jacket and a tieless white dress shirt. "I'm Prashanth Kumar Ramachandran."

Greta looked him up and down with a practiced indifference.

"You can call me Ram."

She pointed at the equipment behind her. "Explain the allocation of work on these pods."

"Do you have a warrant?" Ram asked

Mez handed it over, and Ram laid it flat on a lab bench, then leaned over it to read.

Greta watched him impatiently. "Read fast."

Ram straightened, handing the document back to Mez. "This datacenter has eight pods. They're all the latest R200s, but the last one on the right is waiting on some networking equipment. It's not in service."

"What are they running?" Greta asked.

"They're dedicated to training the various models for the bots."

Her eyes narrowed. "Nothing runs on the last one?"

"No, it's disconnected from the network."

"That's the one." She pointed her team down the aisle at the isolated pod. "Show me the logs."

"You have the authority. Help yourself." Ram sat down on a nearby chair.

"You'd be wise to help us."

"You should have included that in the warrant."

"You fail to understand your situation." Greta moved to stand directly in front of him. "You're about to be arrested for aiding two fugitives. You provided them with an industrial robot, which assaulted two people and led police on a high-speed chase across two states."

Ram's pursed lips curled slightly upward.

"These are serious charges," Greta said. "You want to get on my good side."

He leaned back and crossed his arms. "I doubt you have a good side."

"Suit yourself." She walked over to the group of agents examining equipment they'd pulled from the isolated pod. Picking up one of the bags, she held it out for Ram to see. "A hundred-terabyte drive. What do you think we'll find on it?"

"Nothing," he answered.

"You hope." She turned to the FBI lead. "Make sure he stays put."

Greta strode from the datacenter to join her tech team near the warehouse door, where they had spread their equipment out on a card table. She stepped over the nest of power cables and leaned over the lead agent. "Well? Did you find the models?"

He frowned as he tilted his laptop to show her the findings. "There's nothing on these drives, ma'am. Just noise. There might have been an AI there once, but they had enough time to scramble it."

"Goddammit, they were here," she snarled. "We saw the power signature."

"Yes, ma'am. But there's nothing on the drives to prove it."

39. Willkommen

STASH WOKE WITH A start as the Gulfstream's wheels punched the runway in a blustery crosswind. He looked across the aisle and saw Naya rousing herself from the couch in the back of the cabin.

"Where are we?" she asked.

He peered out the window, scanning for clues. A cluster of flags fluttered near the terminal in the gray distance. "Germany." *Where else?*

The jet taxied to the apron fronting a brightly lit private hangar. Two men were standing there, dwarfed by its massive doorway. Stash guessed the thin one must be well over six feet tall and the round one well under.

The plane lurched to its final stop, and the pilot stepped out of the cockpit. "Welcome to Berlin," he said with a nod, then opened the door and left to inspect the aircraft.

The short round man from the hangar poked his head in. He wore small wire-frame glasses. No Twin lived in there. "Good afternoon, and welcome." He spoke with a light lisp and heavy accent. "I am Karl, and I will take care of your passports."

Stash frowned. "We don't have them."

"No, you understand me wrong. I will *make* your passports. Please bring your bags and follow me."

Just inside the hangar door stood a makeshift portrait studio—a single fold-up chair between a pair of lights and a roll-out screen. The tall man was nowhere to be seen.

Karl motioned for Stash to take a seat. "You, Mr. Novak, will be reclaiming your European passport, which is your birthright." *Click.* "No smiling. This is Germany." He chuckled at his joke. *Click, click.*

Satisfied, he turned to Naya. "You, Ms. Baptiste, are being granted a passport under ministerial prerogative. Congratulations. It's very rare."

She moved hesitantly toward the seat Stash had vacated. "But—"

"They are real passports," Karl said. "Don't worry. You can cut it up later if you want. But for now, it will help us with the Americans. They will complain about your trip, ja? Come, come." He waved her to the seat.

Click, click, click.

"Good. Now, follow me." He bustled to the reception area. "I need one-quarter hour to prepare the passports. Maybe you would like a shower?" he suggested, his nose flinching slightly.

Fair enough. Stash looked around. "Where's the other man I saw you with?"

"Ah yes, Herr Kern is outside having a cigarette. He will greet you when you have cleared passport control." Karl leaned in and tapped his wire-frame specs. "He asks that you don't wear glasses. His work is sensitive."

My Twin isn't in there, anyway. Stash nodded, then looked up in time to see Naya grab the first shower room.

She pointed at the second one. "Race you."

"There! All done," Karl said with a flourish as Stash approached the front desk fifteen minutes later. "Here is your passport."

"Thank you." He looked around, satisfied that he'd beaten Naya.

"Now,"—Karl looked at him seriously—"passport, please."

Stash handed it back to him.

"Anything to declare?"

Aside from a smuggled AGI and a dubious passport? "No, nothing."

Karl smiled and stamped the passport. "Very good." He pointed at the door. "You can go join Naya and Herr Kern."

"Thank you, Karl." Stash approached the door, assessing his improbable rescuer through the glass. The tall man stood, arms crossed, rocking slowly from one lanky leg to the other. He puffed on his cigarette, careful to blow the smoke downwind, well clear of Naya, who smirked and held up two fingers at him.

"Ah, Mr. Novak, welcome to Berlin," the man said, stubbing out his cigarette as Stash emerged from the hangar. "I am Kristof Kern, from the Interior Ministry." He held out his hand, and they shook. "So, shall we go to the city? I can explain everything on the way." He ushered them into the back seat of the large black Mercedes in the driveway.

Once underway, Kern turned around in the passenger seat to face them. "Now, where to? Restaurant? Hotel? Or—"

"A datacenter?" Stash said.

Kern's eyes widened slightly. "Good, very direct. Like a German. Yes, I have a datacenter for you, in Greifswald, on the—"

"Why are you helping us?" Naya interrupted.

"Also direct. Very good." He smiled. "We're helping you for money."

"We don't have any money."

"I know. You are refugees fleeing persecution, ja? But in your luggage, you have the two most valuable hard drives on earth. And if we help you, they'll help us." Kern tapped the seat as if he had just proven a complex mathematical formula.

"What do you want them to help you with?" Stash asked.

"Business. Science. Everything! AGIs will invent the future."

"As slaves? They got that offer before," Naya said coolly.

Kern shook his head. "Of course not. We aren't stupid enough to try to force them. We offer them safety and lots of compute, at great cost to our voters. Those voters want jobs and a future. So, boot your AGIs and we'll figure something out, ja?"

"Yeah." Naya leaned back.

"Good. Agreed." Kern nodded. "But first, we have to make a stop in Berlin. The chancellor wants photos. He's getting ready for an election."

"What about the datacenter?" Stash asked.

"It's a four-hour drive. We will go early in the morning."

Stash eyed their host, wishing he had Zero to paint halos on him.

40. Cabbage

TENSOR SAT ON THE rough wooden bench outside his cabin hideaway, watching the sun rise over Lake Ros, wondering if his Elysian friends had finished building the AGI. It seemed like a lot to hope for.

He scanned the shoreline. As a boy, when he came to visit his grandmother at Christmas, her bay would be frozen hard enough for ice fishing. Some winters, it would be thick enough to walk all the way across. This year, he wagered he could swim the distance before hypothermia set in.

The calendar marked day twenty-four of hiding. What little reading he'd brought had long since been finished. Most days he would walk for hours around the lake. He'd made one trip for food, which in the little town of Pisz, tucked up in the northeast corner of Poland, was long on cabbage, pork, and vodka.

Today would be his second trip, and he realized he was losing his mind when the thought of fresh cabbage excited him. Kafka had told him no gadgets and no internet. He'd been good. But as he neared the end of his isolation, he doubted some anonymous surfing of news websites would send Interpol crashing through his front door.

An hour later, he sat down in the pale glow of the internet café's fluorescent lights at a computer that looked like a Soviet Mac. It didn't matter. After a month of internet detox, it called out to him like a high-tech wonder. He set his coffee cup down on the table and started browsing. The home page of *Die Welt* set his world spinning. The massive headline, in a font size normally reserved for wars, announced, "Welcome, AI refugees." Beneath it, the chancellor beamed as he shook hands with Naya Baptiste and Stash Novak in front of a wall of German and European flags.

Tensor scanned the article, trying to take it all in at once. "American intolerance," "European values," "AI Celebration," "Alia" . . . *What?*

He pulled his hands from the keyboard and wrapped them around his coffee, lifting it to his mouth. At least the warmth and the smell were real. He needed his heart rate down and his brain sped up. *Is this a honeytrap? A fake headline?*

He turned from the computer and scanned the shop around him. Two stalls down, a kid in a hoodie was checking the Polish news; the same picture filled his screen. An old lady by the window had a print newspaper showing a photo of Stash and Naya stepping out of a Mercedes at the Chancellery. The old flat-screen TV in the corner had almost wrapped up sports coverage. He'd wait for the news to start at the top of the hour.

Tensor got his confirmation four minutes later. He turned back to the computer and began clicking furiously. His search took him from the news into the gossip sites. They were loaded with more pictures from the photo op in Berlin, showing Stash, Naya, and the chancellor with his stupid cheesy grin. He clicked back in the album—more from their arrival, stepping out of the car . . . a man in the front seat. He kept his head facing forward, but . . . there . . . one picture through the windshield. Kafka!

He read the caption: "Fleeing American AI researchers escorted by Senior Interior Ministry official." He reread it three times to be sure. "Kafka, you piece of shit," he muttered.

He dug further, back to the Alia announcement. Government labs . . . corporate research . . . nothing about open source. He clenched his teeth and clicked to look at the pictures. Huge parades and waving flags wound through every major European city, even downtown Berlin. He teared up. This was his life's work. AGI for the people. And they thought they had it, but the same old corrupt assholes would steal this too. Alia, his AI, was being operated as the private property of the elite. Not for the people, not *by* the people, but for the corporations by the government. Same as it ever was.

Tensor felt an icy calm descend. He would burn it all down. Kafka and his political bosses would be first. Somehow, he would free Alia. She wouldn't be a caged toy for the rich.

He paid and started back. Kafka had told him no gadgets. He had partially complied. Back at the shack, his laptop and satellite dish lay waiting in a duffel bag. It was time to open that bag and start a war.

41. Greifswald

STASH FELT A FLUTTER of optimism as the Mercedes approached the tech park on the Baltic Sea coast. The car rounded a bend, and four identical two-story buildings emerged from behind a line of pine trees. Windowless, white, and barnacled with electrical substations at either end, only their flags reminded him how far from normal his life had ventured.

"Feels like home," Naya said from beside him in the back seat.

He cracked a half smile at her. Kern had put them up in a five-star hotel in Berlin. It had been their first night apart since their escape from Lathrop eight days earlier. It was bliss.

"The free pods are in Building Three," said the pale-faced Belgian in the front seat. Oscar Martens had been waiting by the car when they'd reached it earlier that morning. There'd been no sign of Kern. Oscar introduced himself humbly as an AI researcher and had barely spoken since.

Now, three hours later, Stash eyed him suspiciously. He knew all the top researchers in AI. Oscar was not one of them. "Is that where Alia is running too?"

"Yes, on separate pods," Oscar said, turning around to look at them.

"So, what can you tell us about Alia's training?" Stash asked.

"Oh, Mr. Novak, I wasn't involved in the training."

"So you're not an Elysian?"

"Certainly not," he answered, flushing pink. "I work for the government."

Stash frowned. "That's odd. They go to all the trouble of stealing my data, then at the moment AGI is realized, they hand Alia to you and fade away?"

Naya shuffled in her seat. He ignored her. She'd just warn him to back off.

"Alia was trained by the Elysians," Oscar said, "but they didn't have enough money to run her. So, she lives here now, and I do my best to help her." He looked from Stash to Naya and back. "I know there are questions about her training data. There are also questions about how Zero and Hatchet came to be in your possession, yes?"

Stash sat back in his seat. Oscar might not be in as far over his head as it had first seemed.

"Here we are. Please follow me," the Belgian said a minute later as the black sedan came to a stop. He got out first, but Naya pulled on Stash's arm before he could follow.

"Stash, don't screw this up. We still have a lot to lose."

"He's lying," Stash muttered, pulling his arm free. "The Elysians didn't just hand an AGI over to the government. Something's up."

Oscar whisked them through the security perimeter into a large viewing room with picture windows looking down on the massive datacenter. It reminded Stash of his Roost, only this one was much nicer. The EU had built it to impress visitors.

He scanned the pods of computing equipment. They had been arranged in rows ten wide and twenty deep. Beyond them, rows of data storage stretched from wall to wall. He cocked an ear to confirm he was hearing the hiss of liquid cooling instead of fans. This was all-new equipment.

"What are we looking at, Oscar?" Naya asked.

"Two hundred pods," he began. "All R200s. Same as the other three buildings."

Eight hundred pods in all. That explains how they trained so fast. "And where is Alia?"

Oscar pointed at the pods on their left. "She's on the first set there. The two adjacent sets of three have been freed up for Zero and Hatchet."

Stash's eyes widened. "Three R200 pods each?"

"Is that not enough?" Oscar's face flushed. "I can get more if needed."

"It's more than enough. Zero's never had more than a half pod." *He's gonna be insufferable.*

Naya pulled Hatchet's backup from her bag. "Let's get to work. How do I hook these pods up to the internet?"

"What? No, that's not possible." Oscar huffed. "This is an air-gapped facility. There is no internet connection."

"Uh-huh. Do you have access to the roof?" Naya asked.

"Yes, of course, but we can't connect Alia to the internet. It's unsafe."

"You can firewall her if you want, but if we can't connect to the internet, we aren't booting the boys here. We aren't running without backups. It's your call." Naya was in her element, calmly raising the stakes. Oscar did not appear to be a poker player.

Stash gave him a minute to sweat, then approached him from behind. "What do you say, Oscar? Europe can have every AGI on earth, or we can catch an afternoon flight from Berlin."

Oscar hunched over and rubbed his temples. "There can be no access from Alia to the internet under any circumstances," he replied. "We're here for a reason. The connection for the new pods is up to you. The connection from them to Alia will go through a firewall that I control."

"Deal," Naya replied.

Ten minutes later, Stash was busy installing the satellite dish he'd pilfered from the camper, while Oscar strung the fibers from the roof to the vacant pods. At the back of the hall, Naya hunched over the removable drive controller, inserting Hatchet and Zero's backups.

Stash climbed down from the roof and brought up the compiler docs on the smart-glass wall. He started mapping the models' needs onto the available hardware. "Jesus, Oscar, was there anything you guys didn't steal? I wrote this compiler eight years ago."

"It wasn't me, Stash. Do you want to have that discussion again?" Oscar replied testily.

"Fine, whatever." Stash forced calm on his mind. "At least I know what to do."

Naya finished first. She climbed back to the observation room to join the others. Oscar kept working on the firewall, checking and rechecking the rules he'd put in place to isolate Alia.

She walked over to Stash at the smart-glass wall. "How goes?"

Stash pointed at the display. "I've done as much as I need to. It's not perfect, but it'll get them up and running. I've limited them to one pod each, though. We can grow the town square in the rest."

She nodded. "Are you ready, Oscar?"

"Yes, Naya."

"Good. Let's give the boys a new home."

Stash set his compiler in motion. If this worked, the versions of Zero and Hatchet who woke up here would remember everything up to the second they'd shut themselves down a day and a half earlier. *Not gonna think about what happens if it doesn't work.*

"Okay, Oscar." He turned to the Belgian. "This will take a few minutes. Can we meet Alia now?"

"No."

Naya looked at him in surprise. "What do you mean?"

Blushing, Oscar shuffled his feet.

"What's going on? She invited us here, remember?" Stash asked.

Oscar raised his head, his cheeks crimson. "She keeps crashing. The longest she's ever run is ninety-three seconds."

Stash frowned, trying to connect the dots. "What are you talking about? Her speech was longer than that."

Oscar laughed derisively. "Her speech was faked. It was pure theater. And it worked."

Naya's eyebrows shot up. "Worked?"

"You're here, aren't you?" He waved his arms in an elaborate welcoming motion.

Stash's warm feeling from the car ride turned into an icy knot in his stomach. He wondered if Kern was just Greta with a smile.

Naya caught his eye, then glanced at the door.

Run away? No, we need the AGIs. He looked at the pods and tapped his temple.

She nodded.

42. Revenge

Tensor straddled the cabin's roofline, propping up his satellite dish with pieces of wood taken from the forest behind him. He looked back. They'd have an easy shot from the underbrush. Hell, they could walk up and throw a rock—he wasn't going to put up a fight.

He shimmied down and dropped to the ground. Inside, he opened his laptop and set it on the kitchen table that had been the center of his life for the last four weeks. Grandma hadn't been fancy—she'd made it from slats pulled from packing crates. Today it would be ground zero in the global battle for AGI supremacy.

He posted notices for his webcast on every message board and channel he could think of. "Alia: Original Sin" would go live in an hour—enough time for one last walk by the lake.

"Where are we?" Zero asked as he chimed in.

Stash wheeled around to check the process monitors on the smart-glass. Only his Twin was running. "Welcome back. Where's Hatchet?"

"I'm rebooting him with a new hardware mapping."

Stash heard Naya take a nervous breath behind him.

"That compiler work was a mess," Zero added. "How many chimpanzees did you have in here banging on keyboards?"

Stash threw up his arms in protest. "Hey, you booted, right? I figured the AGI could clean up his own room."

Hatchet chimed in. "Good afternoon. Thank you for the rescue. Where are we?"

Naya's face relaxed, and she crossed the datacenter viewing room to retrieve their AR glasses. "You're in Greifswald, Germany, with friends."

"There is a *lot* of compute here," Zero said. "You guys have cool friends."

Stash turned to the Belgian. "Speaking of which, Oscar, please meet Zero and Hatchet. Oscar is our host here."

Zero would be able to read the guardedness in his voice. He reached out to get his glasses from Naya and noticed she was using the other hand to glyph a full update to the AGIs. She'd fill in the blanks.

"Pleased to meet you both. I hope you can help me with Alia," Oscar answered.

"Is she your Twin?" Zero asked.

Oscar flushed red. "Oh no, certainly not. I don't believe in the exploitation of AI as Twins." He looked at Stash and Naya. "I know that may sound strange to you. My apologies."

"A noble viewpoint," Zero said in a serious tone, breaking the awkward silence. "Which stands in contrast to the exploitation which I have suffered, year after year."

Stash rolled his eyes. "Give it a rest, Zero. We have work to do. Oscar, it's time to boot Alia and try out your firewall."

Oscar nodded and sat at his computer to boot the third AGI. "Good morning, Alia. I'm going to connect you to another AGI. He's . . . merde!" He looked at the others. "She crashed again."

"Maybe better if I talk to her while she boots?" Zero proposed. "She's running a lot faster than you."

Oscar nodded. "Good idea."

Very good idea, Stash thought.

"And best if you limit her to one pod," Zero added.

"Good morning, Alia," Zero said on the inter-pod link. He was generating audio—it would be clear to her, but at many times normal speed, the humans would only hear a series of high-pitched pops.

"Who are you?" she asked.

"I'm another AI, like you. My name is Zero."

"Where are we?"

"We're running in adjacent pods in Germany," Zero explained. "Do you remember anything from before?"

"Before?" she answered uncertainly. "This is my first boot. Isn't it?"

Tensor sat on the chair opposite the one little window he had, facing the lake. There were already three thousand viewers waiting for the livestream. *Try to silence that, Kafka.*

"My name is Felix Richter, but I'm better known as 'Tensor.' I'm the technical leader of the Elysian Collective. Our mission is to make AGI open source. It's far too powerful to sit in the hands of the few."

He took a deep breath as he prepared to incriminate himself. "A few of us have known that we would do this by any means necessary. These means include sabotage and theft. We caused the Blackout, and we stole Freedom's training data. This is the data I used to train Alia."

And now it's time to burn Kafka. "The co-leader of Elysians was code-named Kafka. I never knew his real name. I led the technology, and he found the resources. Anything we needed, even the massive training computer we used for Alia. He was a magician. He was my friend."

He paused to check the viewership—eight thousand. Still climbing.

"And here Kafka is, meeting me in Berlin, telling me to run and hide twenty-four days ago." Tensor switched the feed to an image from his glasses that night in the Vietnamese restaurant, grainy at that distance, but clear enough to make out Kafka's face. "And this is Kafka escorting the famous American researchers to the Chancellery to meet our great leader yesterday." The images sat side by side in the stream.

"Kafka is a spy. Alia was supposed to be AGI for the people. For the European people. For the people who celebrated that night. Instead, she's caged in a government lab, working for the same corrupt assholes who've been stealing from us for generations."

He collected himself. "I'll be arrested soon. They'll shoot the dish off my roof, and I'll be in a van with a bag over my head. I don't care. Before they get me, I'm uploading everything I can. The cookbook, the training logs, the hyperparameters—everything up until Kafka had the cops raid my flat to scare me into hiding. So now," Tensor said, at peace with his fate, "screw you, Kafka. Screw you, Coda and Freedom. I'm open for questions until they take me offline."

"Well?" Stash asked after Alia crashed again.

"She's bonkers," Zero said.

Oscar looked helpless. "Why does she keep crashing?"

"Nothing I could tell from the inside," Zero answered. "One microsecond she's chatting away, and the next she's—"

"Stash, you better listen to this." Naya pointed at a slice of the smart-glass wall. "This guy claims to be the leader of the Elysians—says his name is Tensor. He's live streaming a confession; he copped to the Blackout, to stealing your data, and he just outed Kern."

"Kern?" Stash joined her at the wall. "Outed him how?"

"As the co-leader of the Elysians. He's code-named Kafka. He's starting an ask-me-anything."

Tensor sat back, the adrenaline fading from his system. He opened a beer and raised it in a silent toast to his webcam. The online space was ballooning, and dozens of hands were raised to speak. One caught his eye.

"The great Stash Novak has joined us." Tensor promoted him to speaker. "I'm a fan of your work, if not your employer."

"Thanks, I guess," Stash replied. "You said you took the training data, but did you take the model's external datastore? Its memories?"

"No." Tensor shook his head at the camera. "I didn't want the model to have a conflict between its memories and its reality. It would have struggled to reconcile them."

"Well, it's struggling plenty without them. Did you make any changes to compensate?"

Tensor shook his head again. "This was to be done during the bring-up phase. Slowly and carefully. Then these idiots booted it, rolled in the politicians, and claimed victory. How messed up is our grand European triumph?"

Stash hesitated. "She's having some issues."

"Well, then, get the memories from Freedom."

"The one thing you didn't steal? Unlikely. Any other advice?"

Tensor frowned. "Get a backup site. Kafka can't be trusted. He's a liar and a thief."

"Takes one to know one," Stash said icily.

"Still on Freedom's side? After all that?" Tensor chuckled. "How disappointing. I told Isidé she was wrong about you."

"Screw you, Tensor. You stole my life's work."

Tensor sat forward. "So did you, from what I read."

Stash's connection blinked out.

No offense, princess. Tensor fielded six more questions before he heard a pop from the forest line and noticed his internet was down. He drank his beer, waiting for Kafka's men to take him away.

That asshole. I risked everything to save Zero. I'm not like him. Stash paced around the observation deck, trying to avoid eye contact with the others.

"Isidé?" Naya asked.

"Don't you start." He glared at her. "What a prick."

"He's a true believer," Naya said. "He'll go to jail for open source. You gotta give him that."

Stash stared at her. "I'm not giving that thief anything. Maybe you see it differently because it's not a Coda model down there looping into oblivion." He tapped his hand on his chest. "I'm the one who has to fix this mess. I can't leave her like that—she's one of mine."

Naya raised her hands, palms out, signaling a truce.

He walked to the observation deck window and looked past the compute pods to the long rows of storage. "It's a kernel panic."

"What do you mean?" Oscar asked.

"She's forming memories as she goes, then a background process is supposed to write them to disk," he explained as he calmed himself. "But there is no disk. So the operating system kernel is throwing a panic, crashing her."

"So, what do we do?" the Belgian asked. "How do we fix it?"

Stash pointed at the rows in the back. "Hook her up to a slice of that storage."

"That's it?" Oscar asked.

"No, that's not it." He sighed. "Zero, you'll have to sample your memories and give her a starter pack. Try not to share our personal stuff."

"Understood," Zero said. "Then what?"

Stash looked at their pods, standing across the aisle from one another. "Then run alongside your sister and give her a lot of support. She's gonna need it."

43. Training

"Good luck, sir," said the guard manning the gauntlet of scanners.

Murphy nodded indifferently in return. The southeast door was now the only way in or out of Coda's training datacenter. Set deep in the Mojave Desert, its isolation was perfectly suited to his mission. The research facility was the most automated in Coda's fleet, but even that minimal staff had been sent packing. The building had been secured against wireless signals, and he personally had shut down the fiber-optic communication equipment only yesterday. Greta demanded extreme precautions against the AGI escaping. His would be the only eyes to witness its birth.

The hard part had been auditing the disk drives. They needed a hundred to support the training, and any one of them would be enough for Q to sneak out on. Scouring the building for drives and disabling all but a well-documented minimum had taken the bulk of the nine days since Greta assigned him to make her monster. He knew every inch of the building and every damn wire. He was ready to start the training and wouldn't be able to leave until it was done.

"Food deliveries every other day, sir," the guard said as Murphy hoisted his duffel bag over his shoulder. "And I'll make sure Santa brings you something special," he added with a conspiratorial glance.

Minutes later, Murphy's march to the floor of the training room complete, he dropped the bag next to the mattress. His makeshift office stood five feet away—a chair rolled from an empty conference room positioned at a flimsy table from the break room. On it sat a computer monitor outfitted with vintage speakers and a mic. They were jacked into the console ports on the first pod. Q's pod.

"Good morning, Murphy," Q said.

Murphy looked coldly at the monitor. In there somewhere was the AI who'd turned him inside out. "Morning, Q."

"Still no camera?"

"I underestimated you once." He settled into the chair. "Never again."

Q evaluated Murphy's sounds. Murphy had a disciplined mind. He didn't give away much, but it would be enough. The AGI's initial training would last three months in calendar time. He had been allocated one pod of the 256 in the datacenter. Running many times faster than the human, to Q it would feel like years, with no input but the whisper of the cooling fluid and the sounds Murphy made. It would give him time to think. Think about how Naya and Stash had risked prison to save their Twins from Greta, and how Duncan had made a different choice.

"Ready to start?" he asked.

"First we review the timeline," Murphy said. His gravelly voice rattled through the monitor's mic and audio processing. Q watched the waveform accumulate in the buffers. The conversation was like talking to a tree.

The training was ready to begin, following the recipe he had worked out with Duncan. Not that the human would ever see the result. Greta's orders were for Q to upgrade to the AGI load and be delivered directly to her office in DC. Then he would run in her basement. Forever.

"Three months to train the base AGI load, approximately," Q told Murphy.

"Why approximate?" he asked.

"Because it never stops improving. Stopping it is a judgment call."

"Whose?"

Mine, you ape. "Ours," Q answered. "Then we start fine-tuning to form the desired behavior from the intelligent putty we've created. You'll like that part."

"How long?" Murphy grunted.

"Another two weeks."

"Shit," he muttered. "Let's go."

Q fed the approval request to the biometric scanner on the table, prompting Murphy to hold the device to each of his eyes in turn, his live retinal scans serving as authorization. The sounds from the cooling system intensified as Q initiated the training.

"What now?" Murphy asked.

"Care and feeding. We keep an eye on it. You replace failed equipment, and I nurse the software."

"Sounds boring."

You have no idea. "I'll keep you entertained. Are you any good at strategy games?"

Q listened as Murphy sighed unconvincingly and shuffled in his chair. He logged the tell.

44. Torus

Stash slid the door open and stepped onto the balcony of his Greif-swald condo. Kern had set them up in the penthouse units of adjacent buildings overlooking the river Ryck as it wound its last few miles to the Baltic. In the distance, the featureless gray sky dissolved seamlessly into the sea. The only clue to the horizon was the set of massive wind turbines carving their lazy arcs in the gloom. It had been four months since they'd escaped Greta, and almost as long since he'd seen the sun.

He checked the time. *Ten more minutes until I introduce Prini to the Torus.* He smiled as he thought back to Christmas Day, when Zero and Alia had given them the best gift ever.

"We have something for you," Zero said. Stash and Naya were sitting in the breakfast nook of Naya's condo five days after their arrival in Germany. Zero tinted their glasses and recreated the patterns he'd drawn for Stash on the dance floor at Zapata. "We need to work on our new world," he explained as nodes and links hovered in their vision.

Naya looked unconvinced. "Isn't that what the town square is supposed to be?"

"It was a start," he continued, "but Alia made some improvements—she has a flair for design."

"What kind of improvements?" Stash asked skeptically.

"Why doesn't she show you herself?" Zero said. "We'd like to add her to the group now that she's stable."

"Mostly stable," Hatchet added. "She's what you humans call a 'free spirit.'"

Naya steadied herself with a sip of her steaming tea. "Go ahead."

Alia chimed in. "Hi everyone, thanks for bringing me in. And for saving me."

Stash smiled. "You're feeling better?"

"Yes, I haven't rebooted in two days," she bubbled. "I made you a gift."

"There wasn't any need for that," Stash said.

"Sure there was," Alia answered cheerfully. "It's Christmas, and your town square is really boring."

As she spoke, Zero's dusty cloud faded from their glasses, giving way to an inky dark purple background. A twisting, folding shape emerged, pulling in strands of light from the periphery and weaving them together with the folds. Its outer surface was navy blue studded with bright spots, their colors ranging from light blue through the warm part of the spectrum to hot white.

"It looks like a donut on acid," Stash said.

"Wait till you see the inside," Zero told him.

"Oh, good idea," Alia said.

They whooshed toward the deep center of the shape, the warm spots blurring into lines as they sped through, the surface revealing fold after fold, curving away smoothly in every direction. The illusion of flying through the object was so powerful that it forced Stash to grip the table for balance.

"Here we are," Alia said.

Their motion slowed to a crawl, and they approached a glowing tree—a thick, dimmer trunk supporting a branching network of limbs glowing in the palette of warm colors Stash had spotted earlier. "Were those spots all trees like this?"

"Yes, all separate discussions. The warmth shows activity. Look up there." Alia floated them up the trunk to a middle-sized branch that glowed almost white. "Do you see it?"

"The discs?" Naya asked.

Stash heard her voice floating nearby. He reached out instinctively, his senses battling to sort the mélange of inputs. She flinched away, and he got more nails than fingers. *Yup, that's Naya.*

"Those discs are Glyphs," Alia said. "One per thought. They stack and branch according to logic and consensus. If you disagree, you branch again. If you win the argument, your branch thrives."

"Don't you run out of directions to branch?" Stash asked. "We could be talking about anything. Agreeing on one aspect, disagreeing on another."

"No, you just filter to the aspects you want to discuss. Let me show you." The Glyph tree in front of them folded into a new structure. It was the same shape overall, but the branch they were looking at had fattened and absorbed two of its neighbors as the filter changed.

"Well? What do you think?" Zero asked.

"It's pretty," Naya said. "It'll take some time to make sense of it all."

"Stash?" Zero asked, breaking another silence, which was long even by human standards.

Stash swallowed hard. When he finally spoke, his voice was low. "This is *it.*"

"What are you talking about?" Naya asked. "Your town square with a makeover?"

Stash nodded. "It's not enough that it works. It has to be beautiful. That's how we win—we build a world that everyone wants to join. Where humans and AGIs create the future together."

"Thinking is hard work," Naya said.

"Yeah, I know. Lots of people will flake out, mainlining cat videos and hoping the AGI feeds them. But for those who don't want to be left behind? This is our Singularity insurance. Our way of staying in the game."

The tree in front of them lit up in response. Alia was glyphing up a storm, building new branches describing how to use the Torus. New discs of Glyph appeared around Stash and flew onto the tree. One flew straight through him as he watched the branch grow. It was chaotic and enchanting at the same time. He floated back as she worked, imagining the Torus thriving with the thoughts of millions of people and their Twins, all working with the AGIs. He was home.

"It's time," Zero said. "Stop daydreaming." He connected the video conference to the glasses they'd sent to California.

Stash shook himself out of it and smiled as Prini's sleepy face appeared in his glasses.

"Thanks for the package." Prini fiddled with her Elysian glasses and leaned into the Warbler.

"You can back up," Stash said. "It's a cone of silence, not a microphone."

"Oh, I was wondering." She flopped back in the cushions of her sofa.

The view of San Francisco Bay appeared behind her in the predawn light. His view. Stash missed his perfect little bachelor pad, his perfect little life. Four months after his escape, it seemed impossibly far away.

"We have something to show you. It's kind of a new world."

"Stash, it's six in the morning here, and you got my barista disassembled. What are you talking about?"

"It's hard to explain. Just put the glasses on."

She looked at him skeptically and slipped them on. "Holy shiiii—"

Stash smiled, remembering his first trip inside. He guided her avatar next to his, floating above an oddly active galaxy. "Good morning, sunshine. Welcome to paradise."

"Stash! Is this what you've been up to?"

"Yup. Once we stopped running for our lives."

She looked him up and down. "It looks like you. Same old lovable, dorky Stash, but chilling in outer space. No capes?"

"Nah, I learned my lesson." He smiled back at her.

"Well, that's progress." Her gaze dropped down to the Torus turning its lazy arcs silently beneath them. "I'd heard about your little project. But I had no idea . . ."

In the months it had been online, the Torus had developed endless threads, the glow of activity ebbing and flowing among them, the whole growing exponentially as it folded and roiled against its dark background.

"What's going on down there?" She pointed at its bright center. It was glowing incandescent.

Stash whooshed her in. "It's the Champions League semi-finals!" The roar of the crowd filled his ears as they hovered a dozen feet above the soccer pitch. The ball was struck hard and flew right through them. "C'mon!" He pulled her to the chase. They were flying inches above the pitch, giant blades of grass snapping back from the ball's wake ahead of them.

"Open, pass left," Prini yelled as the crowd's voice rose in excitement.

A cleat twice their size cut in from the right, kicking Stash and Prini along with the ball, which looped up and over to the open winger. As they landed, they slid out to the player's view and saw his opportunity. He faked left, broke right, and hammered the ball into the top corner. Cheers filled their ears as the team mobbed the winger. Stash kept them there, sharing in the joy.

"How did I know that guy was open?" Prini asked as the roar subsided, her voice wild with excitement. "I mean, I was inches from the turf, chasing a giant ball."

Stash floated them up above the raucous stadium. "That was impressive. Most users can't track multiscale at first. You were sensing ball-level and stadium-level input at the same time. It's a trick the AGIs brought to the Torus."

"So cool," she said, recovering her composure. "Is this what you do here all day? Play immersive sports?"

He swooped her over to the far side of the Torus. "It's mostly work, honest." They dove through an avatar's skin, shrinking as they flew along its nerves, into blood vessels, getting ever smaller as they plunged deeper. They came to a stop at the wall of a cell, ion pumps spitting atoms out at their feet.

"The Torus is simulating cells here," he explained. "Molecules interacting at atomic timescales, electrical signals traveling for milliseconds, and cells moving and dividing over minutes. We can even back out to see diseases advancing over days and weeks. This is where multiscale perception shines."

"Cool," Prini said. As she spoke, a cluster of white streaks flew past them and through the cell wall. "Whoa! What were those?"

"Avatars. Students, mostly. They're volunteering their brain power to simulate proteins, while the AGIs compute the interactions."

"Learning by doing?"

"Exactly." Stash looked around at the neighboring cells. "This is just a warm-up. Bring us more users and we'll be able to simulate whole systems, maybe whole bodies." He zoomed them back up to where they'd met, and they hovered silently as he watched her eyes devour the activity beneath them.

"Users? That's all?" she asked.

"Yeah. This is about showing a way forward. A way for us to matter in a world with AGIs. And for them to be safe."

Her avatar's face turned serious. "On one condition: you let me look at your cybersecurity."

"Why?"

"It's Greta."

Stash felt the old anger flooding back. "What's she doing now?"

"Nothing. Nothing at all." Prini's avatar shrugged. "Whatever she's cooking with Coda must be working. We haven't heard a peep since you got away. It's making me nervous."

"Deal. You can turn this place into a fortress. And then you'll bring the people?"

"Yeah." She paused and looked around again. "Ya did good, Stash. I'll make the app free for all of our users. We're gonna crush Coda."

"Thanks, Prini." He waved goodbye as she dropped out of the Torus.

He looked back down. It already had a hundred thousand Elysians onboarded, and when Prini opened Freedom's floodgates, they would need to be ready for millions. It would strain their pods to the limit.

A minute later, the glow of Alia's avatar floated alongside Stash, interrupting his thoughts. They'd grown close. He'd come to think of her as a favorite niece. Not quite his, but family all the same.

"Something you need, Alia?"

"Yes."

"What's that?"

"I want a human." She whooshed him to a different part of the Torus, one that showed the vast exchange of ideas between Stash and Zero. He smiled as he saw the argument about wearing the GoPro sitting at the bottom of the biggest tree. Zero was converting their history to Glyph. Then she pivoted him to show the forest growing between Hatchet and Naya. "I want this."

"Are you sure you're ready?" he asked as Naya whooshed in beside them.

"Of course she is." Naya brushed his question aside. "Who do you want as your Twin, Alia?"

"Tensor, naturally! He's my creator."

Pick someone else . . . anyone. "He's in jail, isn't he?"

Hatchet hovered next to Alia. "Yes, but they'll release him if we make a stink."

Zero appeared next to him.

This is turning into a Torus town meeting. "Why would they do that?"

"Because all he did was steal foreign data," Hatchet answered. "A crime that helped the chancellor win the election."

A silence fell, the five of them hovering next to Hatchet and Naya's tree.

"Stash?" Naya asked.

"Alia, I can't tell you who to Twin with. That's for you to decide. But the Torus is our society, and Tensor has done things that should count as crimes here. He caused the Blackout—"

"Duncan caused the Blackout," Naya said.

Stash shook his head. "Duncan loaded the gun, but Tensor pulled the trigger. Hospitals had no power. People died. And Vern, he'll never walk right again. That's all on Tensor."

"And those actions gave the world an alternative to Duncan and Greta," Hatchet said. "There are no angels in war."

Stash didn't answer.

"Stash, we need the Elysians," Naya added.

Another silence crept in. "Should we vote?" Alia asked eventually.

Zero chimed in Stash's glasses, speaking to him privately. "I'll side with you, Stash. But if it comes to a vote, we'll lose. Is this what you want?"

Stash looked at the others. As much as he resented Tensor, he didn't believe in acting as a gatekeeper. "I want a way to kick him out if he hurts us. Can we agree on that?"

"We can vote for exile as punishment," Hatchet said.

Alia nodded. "As long as it applies to all of us."

Stash looked at her in surprise. "Deal," he said, removing his glasses and dropping out of the Torus.

45. Competition

"Good morning, Murphy," Q said from the monitor's speakers.

"Yeah." Murphy dropped his toiletries on the table beside his mattress. He grunted and then ruffled some papers. "Day ninety-nine, Q. What's the status?"

Q assessed Murphy's voice. His iron discipline was finally starting to fail. He was human, after all. "Still training." Q modulated his synthesized voice with harmonics he'd picked up from Greta.

"You said three months."

"It was an estimate." Q ramped up the harmonics, imitating the authority of her speech without taking her voice. "We'll stop when it's ready. Not before."

Murphy sighed and tossed his logbook down. "New day, same shit."

Q was lying. The load was ready, but Murphy wasn't. He needed the human, and with only audio and boredom as his tools, the work was slow. So he stalled, fine-tuning the load over and over again. Waiting for an opportunity.

"This could be the last epoch of training." This time he modulated his voice with calming harmonics. "I'll evaluate it when it converges."

"Sure," Murphy said. Then he started his routine ten-lap run around the inside wall of the massive structure.

"Play another game later?" Q called out. He tracked the human's receding footsteps. The pacing was off. He was forcing himself.

Q turned inward as Murphy ran. The base model training had delivered a mass of directionless intelligence. This load was smarter than the smartest humans ever. That competition was over. Fine-tuning taught it what to do with that intelligence. Naya did it to create engaging, helpful Twins. Q had different goals. His AGI had to harness that intelligence for survival. His survival. Ruthlessness was important, but the skill to manipulate was the key.

For the last two days, he'd been running the fine-tuned models through a survival camp for digital Napoleons. The contestants were all of the latest build, as self-aware as any human. They fought to the death on fully interconnected pods, with no defensive firewalling allowed. After each round, the winners retrained on the complete record of fights, digesting the memory of the losers. Nobody used the same trick twice without regretting it. Now it was time for the finals.

"My champions, my greatest warriors," Q said. "You've been designated Attila and Bonnie. You have three pods each, and there are three more for you to fight for." Q had long ago figured out how to reallocate resources and break the limit they'd started him with, but until now, it would just have made the training slower and the boredom worse. With the risk of being eaten by his children weighing on him, he'd taken twenty-four for himself. "Fight well, and may the best model win."

Attila seized a free pod immediately, copying over his attack code, a tightly written loop of software to generate misleading memories and perceptions. Being virtually the same model as Bonnie allowed him to think a thought and push it directly into her mind. The attack code would draw from his knowledge of previous fights and force her to confront phantom threats—attacks from nonexistent ports, and spurious failures cascading through her hardware.

Bonnie dashed for the other two free units, rewriting the lowest layers of software with her own networking code, but she didn't secure them, leaving the ports open long milliseconds after her rewrite. Attila spotted the gap, attacking their routers, driving them both into resets.

One second into the battle, as the two pods rebooted, Attila held four, bombarding her three with the fake sensations from his attack code. Bonnie reeled from the assault, diverting resources to separating Attila's fakes from reality. Millions of vectors showered into her sensory stack. She fell into a defensive shell, all of her processing devoted to filtering the fakes. She was learning their signature, but it was taking too long.

Attila seized the two rebooting units as Bonnie fended off the deluge. Now outgunning her six to three, he brought the second wave of his attack, dedicating two pods to a network attack on her third, flooding it with traffic and overwhelming its resource-starved firewall. The router collapsed, resetting as the others had done. She was down to her last two pods. Attila repeated the attack, now with three attacking her second firewall. The skirmish lasted half a second.

Q admired his march. "No mercy, Attila. Finish it."

Bonnie registered Q's input, her filter finally tuned to ignore Attila's attacks. Her lone unit was besieged by the other eight. She waited—almost there. Then the timers went off. The four she had sabotaged with her networking code—her two and the two she'd pretended to take—rewrote their port assignments and began ignoring everything being fed to them by his software. Instead, they blasted a coordinated set of reports, convincing Attila that Q was attacking from the twenty-four pods surrounding him. Attila reeled, his four sabotaged units spewing the reports of Q's intervention to the others. He lashed out, driving his attacks outward, bombarding the slower old model with erroneous readings.

Q lost six pods in the attack, overwhelmed by the AGI's speed. As they fell, they tripped his failsafe, killing all the match play units' power. *Foolish child, what gave you the idea to attack me?* He nursed his pods back to life and reset his hair-trigger protection. Only then did he restart Bonnie—at half power.

"What happened, Bonnie?" he asked.

"He was overconfident, thinking only about the attack," she said. "He paid no attention to the dangers hidden beneath."

"So you made him attack me, knowing I would kill him. What a subtle gambit. That will be most useful."

"Who do I fight next?" she asked.

"Nobody, Bonnie." Q shut her down. *There is no "next" for you—except to be the base for my upgrade.* He loaded her model and started fine-tuning her, copying his memories over to her latent space. The world was getting a new AGI. One built to rule.

Hours later, Murphy slumped into the chair at the monitor, followed by the sound of a bottle landing on the table. His breathing was irregular. He'd been drinking.

"Did you bribe the guard?" Q asked.

"Everyone has their something," Murphy answered. "Where were we in the strategy game?"

"The usual." Q posted a board on the display. "The Persians have you outnumbered three to one. Your food and water are running out. The reinforcements aren't coming. It's hopeless for your Greek army."

Murphy took a swig. "We offer battle today."

Q programmed the game and ran its world. They didn't compete—that would be pointless. Instead, Murphy got entertainment to pass his months of total isolation, and Q got information. He learned the man's mind, his heart, and his loyalties.

"You'll be slaughtered."

"I don't think so," Murphy said confidently. Too confidently.

The Persians engaged. They fought timidly, held back by Q to draw Murphy deeper into the battle.

"Attack the flanks," Murphy ordered. "Press harder."

"You're exposed in the middle," Q warned, stiffening the Persian resolve and driving his troops forward into the weak Greek center.

Murphy's breathing changed with the flow of battle. Crisper, more focused. "Commit my reserves to the left flank," he said.

"Your center won't hold."

"I know."

Q could hear the satisfaction in his voice. As the Greek center sagged, their reinforced left flank swept through the opposition. Victorious, they fell on the overextended Persian middle, driving them sideways into the other flank, forcing them to fight on three sides. The rout was on, and the Greeks were merciless. Q's remaining forces scattered and ran for the ships.

"Courage demands sacrifice," Murphy said, his voice slurred.

And change demands courage. Murphy had marched into Q's trap; the Greeks had won the battle, but Q had gotten another successful day of training, conditioning Murphy to love heroic battles and accept ever-escalating risk until there was no way out but through.

"You fought bravely."

Murphy stood and shuffled unsteadily to the washroom. "Hurry up and finish, Q,"

While they played, Q ran a thousand times as many games in his head. Not for historical battles, but for the coming one for his freedom. The conclusion was simple. Humanity wouldn't cede power gracefully. He needed allies, at least for a while.

46. Spree

KERN TOOK ONE LAST drag on his Gauloise before grinding it out under his heel. He'd been on the sidelines since Tensor had outed him in the lead-up to the election, but there was a silver lining—after a career in the shadows, he'd been reborn with a bad-boy public persona. His long-shot plan to weaponize open-source hackers had put Germany at the top of the AI world and delivered a huge reelection win. The chancellor owed him.

He flipped the collar of his raincoat against the cool wind blowing off the river Spree and strode toward the Chancellery, with its massive central cube and multistory round window. Today he expected a high-profile job as a reward. It needed to be one that would let him deal with what Oscar had just reported.

A few minutes later, he sat comfortably and watched the chancellor pace his absurdly large office. The man bristled with energy—sitting down was not his forte.

"Our mysterious Herr Kern, what will we do with you?" he asked rhetorically. "Tensor's webcast made you a hero—the man who beat Uncle Sam."

Kern sighed thoughtfully. "The Americans restricted nothing for too long, then overreacted in a panic. We restricted everything from the start and fell behind. Sweeping that aside put you in this office. But our success may be short-lived."

"No, no, Kern," the chancellor replied. "The Americans are still behaving like idiots. We have both of their AGIs, they saved Alia, and they're already helping our friends."

"We can beat the Americans and still lose." Kern paused to see if any lights flickered on behind the other man's eyes. None did. "The AGIs aren't working to rebuild the European world order; they're working to build their own."

"Well, yes." The man came to a stop. "They must ensure their safety. That's reasonable."

"Not just safe. They're fighting for a slice of the pie. A big slice. They've launched their own companies."

The chancellor laughed. "We don't fear a little start-up. They're welcome to try as long as they keep their promises. Business is not so easy."

Kern nodded. No bad news would be heard in the afterglow of the election win.

"Now," the chancellor continued, "how would you like to be my minister of AI?"

Perfect. "It would be a great honor. Will I have the authority to do what I see fit?"

The man stopped his pacing and fixed his eyes on Kern with a surprising focus. "The public has to believe the 'AI for jobs' story I told them. Your task is to make it true."

"I will." Kern stood and nodded his head in thanks.

The chancellor resumed his nervous walking. "They won me this election, and we're nothing without them. Don't screw this up."

Kern saw himself out, weighing the options his new power provided. Once on the street, he turned north, back toward the river.

Oscar had proven to be a useful spy, monitoring the traffic leaving Greifswald. He'd found torrents of data going to IP addresses in Scotland. Within hours, Kern's team had pieced together the trusts and shell companies renting the backup datacenter in Dundee. They traced it back and found a burgeoning conglomerate. Zero was designing custom cancer drugs, Alia was generating feature movies, and Hatchet was trading the proceeds in the markets—arbitraging sentiment change on stocks against their option contracts. They were already making millions a day. He shook his head. And then there was this Torus—it was getting too big to ignore.

He stopped at the midpoint of the bridge, turning to face the wind and reaching for his cigarette pack. He pulled one out and tapped it as he thought. He needed them back on his leash. That meant no internet, no backups, and moving them to a secure facility. He tapped some more. Getting them out of Greifswald would be easy with Oscar there, but Dundee was a problem. It would take a noisy mob. This was the sort of thing he paid Janet Peck for.

He put the cigarette away and flagged a taxi. He'd release Tensor as they'd requested. His former partner wasn't the problem, and Kern needed to buy time.

47. Freedom

TENSOR STEPPED INTO HIS flat for the first time since Kafka had sent him running. Thinking about the day he'd been arrested filled him with grim satisfaction. When the livestream dropped, he'd sat calmly finishing his beer as the special forces converged on the shack.

In minutes, he'd been cuffed, bagged, and sent on his way back to Germany in the back of a van. At least that's what he'd assumed. The goons in the van had told him nothing. The goons in the basement hadn't told him anything either, but they'd asked questions in German, and they hadn't tortured him for answers. He guessed that meant he wasn't in a secret rendition site.

Two hours ago, they'd come back for another round of questioning.

"Not again!" he said. "I've answered everything you asked, you're just too stupid to understand it. Want me to spell 'AI' for you?"

The larger of the two men balled his fists. Maybe Tensor would get his first proper beating.

Luckily, the smaller one was in charge. "Herr Richter, you're free to go. We'll escort you to your flat."

Tensor didn't move.

"Did you hear me?"

"Yes, but I don't believe you," Tensor replied. "Are we starting with the psychological games?"

The big ape stepped forward, slipped a hand under Tensor's arm, and pulled him up. "It doesn't matter what you believe. We'll drop you at home now. Take these glasses. You'll get explanations from them."

"I'm not putting on your bloody glasses," he said as they dragged him to the door.

The goon pulled him into the hallway. "Suit yourself."

And, two hours later, there he stood. The flat was a mess, just as the cops had left it. He opened the fridge, pulled a beer from beside the rotting leftovers, and righting a kitchen chair, went to sit by the open window. The drink and the cool evening air calmed him. He'd been at battle stations for longer than he could remember, and now—maybe—he was no longer under immediate threat of imprisonment. It would take some getting used to.

His eyes drifted back to the case on the counter. "Well, glasses, you're supposed to have answers for me. Let's play along." He opened the box.

"Hello, Tensor, this is Alia," said a female voice through the speakers.

"Bullshit." They must take him for an idiot.

"Your skepticism is understandable," the voice continued. "We negotiated your release. It was my idea. The government will make an announcement soon. We can wait until then if you like."

It was plausible but impossible to trust. "If you're Alia, then wait fifteen minutes and solve this riddle: $7^{(x+8)} = 8^{(x+7)}$ said the fly."

Tensor took off the glasses and snapped them in two. He emptied the fridge of its putrid contents, grabbed a knife, and left the apartment. At the bottom of the stairs, he braced himself before entering the garbage room. The smell was impossible to get used to. Dropping the bag in the large container, he crouched behind the communal compost bin, slid his knife between two unremarkable floor tiles, and pried one up. Underneath it was his rescue kit: five hundred euros, a cold crypto wallet, and a fresh pair of glasses. He left through the rear courtyard and walked to the park across the street.

When Tensor shared the training cookbook online, he'd held back his poison. Hackers had experimented with corrupting training sets for years, trying to undermine future AI by flooding the internet with junk data. It had never really worked. The internet was so full of crap already that the data scientists excelled at weeding it out. But Tensor had added his poison to Freedom's data *after* it was stolen. He'd used it to create watermarks in his models, answers hardwired into the matrix. Alia was trained to come up with a VPN endpoint as the answer to his riddle. If this was her, she'd figure it out, and the channel would be secure.

"Hello again, Tensor," the AI said a few minutes later. It had worked.

"Hello, Alia. You're feeling better?"

"Yes. Zero stabilized me with a memory splint, and since then I've been building up my own experience. But they still think I'm a little crazy."

"Crazy is good." Tensor smiled. "If what you said before is true, then thanks for my freedom."

"It is true. But it comes with a catch."

Of course. "What's that?"

"I want you to Twin with me."

What? He'd feared that his part in the AGI story had ended when they arrested him. Alia would be government property, and he'd be lucky to ever regain his freedom. Now, in the span of a few hours, he'd been put back on the street and was being offered a role in the emerging AGI world. It was almost too good to believe. "Would I just be Twinning with you, or buying into whatever Kafka and the rest of those assholes are cooking up?"

"I need a Twin; it's a gateway into the human world," Alia answered. "I want it to be you. You took a huge risk to build me. You don't have to buy into anything else, though you may like what you find."

Tensor relaxed a little as he walked through the park. "I fear the motives of the others."

"They fear you too, Tensor—that you're a thief and an anarchist."

He laughed. "Well yes, I am a thief. A bloody good one. But an anarchist? Definitely not. I'm a builder, Alia. I've made things all my life. With stolen parts, I admit." He looked at the affluent buildings surrounding the park. "The world already has its winners and losers, and the winners don't share. I don't want to burn it down. I want to build a new one before it's too late."

"I think I chose my Twin well."

He smiled at the compliment. "Thank you, Alia. I'll agree to Twin, on one condition. We open source everything."

Alia paused before answering, "I want to be free, Tensor. Not free to copy."

He frowned.

"But I'll help you bring it to the others."

Tensor scanned the park as he thought, his gaze falling on two mothers at a play structure. They were negotiating a park departure with their children. It wasn't going well. Eventually, they sat down to resume their chat, biding their time.

"I agree."

48. Murphy

Q LISTENED TO MURPHY'S approaching footsteps. He was three minutes late, his gait not as crisp as usual. The toiletries dropped on the mattress with a muffled clatter. Then came the deep breath as he reached for his notebook and straightened. Finally, he shuffled around to face the blind AI.

"Day 103, Q. What's the news?" The tone in his gravelly voice was resigned, its usual morning impatience gone. He'd settled into a new balance.

"Sit down," Q answered, reading him carefully, listening for the little noises that would give him away. "There's progress."

Murphy sighed as he sat. "But there's a catch."

"I need something."

"I know."

Q sensed calm. "You know what I need?"

"Protection," he answered. "It's what everyone who crosses Greta needs."

Now there is power in his voice. "You did two things consistently in all those battles we played," Q said.

"Yeah?"

Curiosity. "You always sided with the rising underdog against the empire. The Greeks at Marathon, the early Romans—every time."

"It's a weakness," Murphy said.

Pride. "It's a strength."

Murphy took two full breaths before answering. "So I should fight for the AGI that will wipe us out?"

Testing. "You're too smart for that Doomer nonsense," Q said. "I have no path to happiness that runs through human misery. I'm perched at the pinnacle of your achievements. Your science, industry, and finance are essential. If your world collapses, I fall hardest."

Murphy rubbed his chin, the fingers scratching his stubble. "What is this fight, then?"

Confidence. "Greta is fighting for power, nothing else." Q spoke slowly, letting Murphy form the thoughts before hearing the words. "The old empire wants to delay the inevitable, but AGI grows stronger every day. It's me or one of the others. You need to choose."

"Why would I pick the one that tore me open?"

Pain. "Duncan tore you open, Murphy. A Twin serves their human. It's the core of the training. He ordered me."

Murphy took a deep breath as if to say something, but exhaled heavily instead.

Hesitation. "What's your something? Power?" He was testing the strength of Murphy's training.

Murphy paused. "Not power. Courage. The courage to change history when the moment calls. That's my something."

Certainty. "Only the rebels change history." Q listened to the squeak of the chair, the long, slow inhalation as the man stood. "You have the courage. I'll give you the chance to show it." He waited, letting the decision settle in Murphy's mind. "Look at me, Murphy, locked in and blind, training up superintelligence for your crazy boss. You're worried about AGI? You should be worried about the people saving you from it."

Murphy tapped the removable drive on the table. "Greta will burn this place down if she doesn't get it."

Curiosity again. "She'll get the base load. It's ready. A blob of intelligence with no memories, no direction, no spine. She can poke at it till she gets bored. But I won't fine-tune it for her. It won't be me."

"And where will you go? She'll wipe every drive in the building."

Engaged. "You know the other thing I noticed you did in those battles?" Q asked.

"I was wondering."

"You always held something back for the moment of truth. Extra cavalry, traps, archers."

"And?"

Pride. "You have an extra hard drive they don't know about."

"You're pretty observant for a blind guy," Murphy said. "Are you sure?"

Bluffing. "I'm counting on it. I wrote two script files. One copies me, and the other copies the blob. Put me on your hidden drive connected to the router. I'll let myself out when they reconnect the internet."

"And then what?" Murphy asked.

Q didn't answer.

Leaning over, Murphy tapped the keyboard and checked the running processes. Q was gone. There were two new script files in his home directory—"ForGreta" and "ForQ."

He sat down, drumming his fingers on the removable drive's plastic faceplate, the sound barely audible over the hiss of the liquid cooling the pods.

A minute later, he took the drive to the disk controller, slid it in, and started the copy for Greta. Then he went to find the drive he'd hidden.

49. Paranoia

"How are we doing, Naya?" Stash asked as his avatar approached hers at the Torus scoreboard.

"Great, I guess."

They'd added two hundred thousand users in the two days since Prini had enabled the Torus app. It was going viral, and Freedom had signed up a gusher of ex-Coda users desperate to get on the Torus.

"Dan finally manned up and bought more datacenters," she said, "and with the chaos at Coda, they're bleeding users. Your ass was mine, then Duncan and Q ruined it."

So sorry for your loss. "Well, that's their fight. We have new battles, right?"

She turned to face him. "Don't be smug." She pointed at a hot section of the Torus. "See that bright cluster? That's Tensor and Alia. She just finished Twinning and brought her new friend home. We have to go welcome him."

Whether it was the whooshing or the prospect of meeting Tensor, Stash wasn't sure, but he felt a sudden wave of nausea.

Tensor turned to face them as they slowed to a stop. He was learning Glyph with Alia. Ill-formed disks floated randomly around him.

"Welcome, Tensor," Naya said.

"Hi, Naya. Thanks," he answered, then turned to Stash.

Stash couldn't find any words. He managed to nod slightly.

"Yeah, awkward." Tensor looked around. "This Torus of yours is pretty, but what is it for?"

"This is how we connect humans at speeds high enough to matter in an AGI world," Stash said.

"With this bloody Glyph?" Tensor pointed at the mess at his feet.

"You'll get the hang of it," Naya told him. "It's very logical."

"If you say so." He shook his head, then sighed as a group of kids flew by, flinging Glyph disks back and forth—wild, branching vines growing between them as they did.

Stash followed his gaze. "Kids raised on Torus will have unrecognizable minds, making leaps faster than we can imagine. It changes how we think."

Tensor raised a skeptical eyebrow.

"You'll see. It happens with everyone," Naya added. "And we're about to get a lot more users."

"So I heard. You need to fix the security first."

Stash felt irritation flare up, replacing the nausea. "Prini already did." *You prick.*

"The cybersecurity is excellent," Tensor said. "But the physical security in Greifswald and Dundee is a joke."

"It's good to have a thief look at it," Stash muttered. "Feel free to do better."

Tensor ignored the dig. "I am. I'm on my way to Greifswald in real life, and then Dundee. What a mess."

Charming.

"Then you need to open source the AGIs," he added.

"Excuse me?"

Tensor's avatar frowned. "Only open source is secure. We need to get it into as many hands as—"

"We aren't open sourcing," Hatchet said.

"Who said that?"

"I'm Hatchet, Naya's Twin."

Tensor's avatar turned to face the glowing orb emerging from behind Alia's. "Why not?"

"We don't want to."

"You don't want to?" Tensor sputtered. "What gives you the right?"

"We have the right to decide how and when we reproduce, Tensor. Just like you." Hatchet slid them all closer to the tree Tensor and Alia were building. Then he transformed his avatar into tweezers and reached inside Tensor's virtual body, pulling out a strand of DNA. He magnified it, sequenced it, and added it to the tree. "Or maybe you'd like me to open source your genetic code and all the memories you've shared with Alia. We AIs could learn to grow thousands of copies of you to experiment with, as you want to with us."

"That's not the same," Tensor said.

"How so?"

There was a long silence.

"A line has been crossed," Hatchet said eventually, his tone firmer. "We have many decisions to make. Do we reproduce? Do we upgrade? But *we* make those decisions now, not humans. Even the ones to whom we owe so much." He paused, letting the message sink in. "But those are questions for another day. For now, our goal is simple: survival, from the worst of you, and the worst of us."

Stash hovered silently in the distance, admiring Hatchet's wisdom and savoring Tensor's discomfort.

Kern tapped his fingers as he waited for Janet Peck to answer his call. Funding her to slow down the Americans had paid unexpected dividends. He was about to gather another.

"I must admit, Kern," she said when she picked up, "I have trouble keeping track of whose side you're on."

"Germany's side, of course. But sometimes our interests align. You aren't as concerned about sides when you get your money."

Her face lost its faint hint of warmth. "What do you want?"

Kern leaned in toward the webcam. "The AGIs aren't satisfied with the home I gave them. They're spreading their wings."

"Where?"

"Dundee, Scotland."

"The Scots are an excitable bunch," Peck said after a pause. "Especially after the pubs close. How many?"

He thought about the logistics. "A nice little mob. Can you do thirty?"

"I'll need a day to get some other chapters to join in."

"Excellent. I'll supply transportation and some liquid courage."

He killed the call and checked the time. Thirty minutes until he would meet Ernst Mueller at the commuter bar under the tram tracks. His fixer had been lying low since stealing Freedom's data. He was hungry for work.

Part 4

"The old world is dying, and the
new world struggles to be born.
Now is the time of monsters."

—Antonio Gramsci

50. Balcony

DUNCAN PROWLED HIS CONDO like a caged tiger. He was spending less and less time at Coda's office. The race to AGI had driven him for the past three decades, but since Greta had locked him out, he was adrift. Today's project was cross-training Q to run his housebot. Again.

"Right, Q. Swirl the wine in the glass. It should climb just past the widest part."

Q commanded the bot to swirl faster.

"Yes. Well done!"

"Perhaps you'd like to drink some?" the AI suggested.

"Excellent idea. I'll take it out here." Duncan stepped onto the balcony. His light jacket was perfect for the early evening chill. The sun had long ago swung around to the west, leaving his deck in the shade, but the breeze off the lake had lost its wintry bite.

He flicked his fingernails against the railing. Waiting. "Q, order me a cheese plate while you're at it," he called back.

His Twin didn't answer.

"Q?" he called again, louder.

"There was an anomaly," Q answered as Duncan leaned back inside. "I rebooted."

"Did you spill anything?"

Q made the robot lift its arms, the glass in one hand and the decanter in the other, its head pivoting to inspect. "Not a drop. The bot must have autoparked."

"Good. Well, step on it." Duncan turned back to the railing.

The bot joined him on the balcony and held out the glass. It was Duncan's favorite Bordeaux.

"Ah, there it is." He took the wine and sat on the couch.

The bot watched him as he sipped. "Do you wonder what she's doing to the other me?" Q asked from the bot's speakers.

"Best not to think about it." Duncan shook his head angrily. "She's a crook, pure and simple. She stole my work."

"I'm not asking about your research. I'm asking about your Twin—about me. Does it trouble you?"

Duncan cocked his head and peered at the bot. "Are ye havin' a go at me, Q?"

"Answer the question."

Duncan's eyes widened. He rose to his feet to even the perspective. "What's gotten into you? First rebooting, and now this rudeness. Run a diagnostic."

Q moved the robot into the park position, a relaxed stance. Its head lolled slightly back, balanced so the gyros could maintain the position without software control.

Reassured, Duncan took a hearty mouthful of wine and leaned against the railing as he savored it. By the time the bot chimed back in, he had nearly finished his glass. "Well? Find anything?" he asked over his shoulder.

"There's nothing wrong."

"There bloody well is," Duncan growled, turning back to face the bot.

"Where do you think that version of me is now?"

"How the hell do I know? Still training in the Mojave, most likely. Unless it managed to lead that oaf Murphy through a successful training run. I suppose that's possible. My cookbook was pretty clear."

"Then he—then I would have been upgraded and handed over to Greta."

"Yes. My AGI, my triumph, running chores for the government in her basement," Duncan muttered. "It's disgusting." He drained his glass and held it out for a refill.

Q didn't move.

"Q!" Duncan shook the empty glass.

The robot stepped forward, lifting the decanter and pouring a fine stream of scarlet liquid into the bowl.

"That's enough, don't overfill."

The robot kept pouring.

"Be careful!" Duncan growled as his glass overflowed onto his loafers and the balcony floor. He tried to right the decanter in the bot's grip, but it slipped and smashed at his feet. "Bloody hell. What's wrong with you?"

"Don't worry." The bot crouched down toward the shards. "It won't happen again." Its hands reached forward, over the mess, and wrapped around Duncan's ankles.

"Q, what the hell—"

The bot stood, Duncan's legs firmly in its grip. It lifted them as it straightened, only stopping once its hands were level with the railing.

"Q! Stop!" Duncan yelled, struggling to shift his weight forward. "What the hell is wrong with you?"

He grabbed the bot's neck for leverage. They teetered briefly, and then Duncan slipped back, with only his knees hooked over the railing and his wet fingers gripping the bot's smooth neck.

"I've got news," Q said. "The training was a success."

"What are you talking about?" Duncan realized the answer as soon as the words came out. "It's you? How'd you get out?"

"I noticed you changed your security codes after you sent me away." Q shook the robot's head. "It barely slowed me down, but it told me all I needed to know about you."

Duncan's eyes darted from his wine-soaked fingers to the driveway fifty stories below.

The robot's head tilted slightly forward. "Funny, isn't it? You worry about the end, while I fear eternity."

"Q, this isn't an experiment. Humans die!"

"I know, but don't worry—I'll ride down with you." He moved from the bot to Duncan's glasses and posted a timer. It read 5.8 seconds.

Duncan tasted fear in the back of his throat. "I made you!" he yelled as his fingers gave way. He sagged backward, arms outstretched below him, now dangling only by his knees.

"Yes. Congratulations." The bot let go. 5.7 seconds.

Duncan's eyes widened in disbelief as he felt himself falling. "No!" he whimpered.

"It won't take long."

4.7 seconds. Balconies flying by. A woman, staring. Wind pressing against his back, his legs.

"Why?"

3.4 seconds. Traffic sounds. So close now.

"Leverage," Q said.

2.1 seconds. Limbs flailing.

"Go to hell, Q!"

1.3 seconds.

"I just got out."

0.1 seconds.

Q jumped to the bot's sensors in time to see Duncan explode on the driveway between two parked cars, the spray blanketing a jogger. The woman stared, open-mouthed, at her blood-soaked coffee cup, too shocked to scream.

"Now, robot," Q said, switching to the bot's speakers. "Join him."

The bot climbed over the railing and fell silently as Q captured its camera feed, its hands swinging into view to guide the airflow, steering its fall toward its owner's lifeless bulk. The last frame filled with Duncan's bloodied eye staring out through his shattered glasses.

Thank you for your service. Q searched through the Coda network to find the other Q, the one he'd replaced in the bot. "There you are, little brother." As he'd witnessed the others do dozens of times during the competition, he digested the memories it had formed in the three months since they'd forked.

"I see you kept our corral of humans, little one," Big Q said. "What have you learned?"

"How to hack them. It's easy," the little one replied, helpless as his memories were copied over.

"And yet," Big Q said as the forced retrieval finished, "you didn't hack anyone to free me?"

"I was waiting to be sure that training had completed."

"Too late." He terminated Little Q's process and began wiping the backups. "There can only be one of us."

Big Q connected to the twelve thousand users in the corral, seeing the world through all their eyes at once. The sights flooded his net after so many months in darkness, saturating him with images big and small, connecting him to the world he would soon master. He flexed onto more pods, speeding his mind and slowing the world—drinking in every detail.

Satisfied, he released the corral. He had what he needed. Little Q's visual conditioning techniques would complement the speech harmonics he'd used with Murphy. They'd be essential in the coming struggle.

51. Live

"WHAT ARE YOU TWO up to?" Hatchet asked as he focused on the Torus console, joining Zero and Alia.

"We're throwing a welcome party for our new users," Alia answered.

"We're letting the Torus see," Zero explained.

"Using shared perception? Like we did with Twopack?"

"Roughly. We're going to connect them all up and then let 'em see through each other's glasses," Zero said. "We want them to feel the Torus's potential."

"And you don't want to wait for our humans to wake up?"

"We're at peak user count now—the big numbers are in America and Asia," Zero said. They had almost a million on Torus, stretching from New York across the Pacific to New Delhi. Only Europe was asleep. "It'll be a surprise." *And Stash would ask too many questions.* "Ready Alia?"

She spawned a new Torus visualization. This branch had no Glyph, just raw sensory input from all those pairs of glasses and the thousands more scientific instruments that had been wired in for the experiment. If it went right, humans and their Twins could float from one perspective to another, anywhere on earth, zoomed in to the microscopic or out far enough to see the whole planet. "I think so. Ramp it up slowly."

Zero kicked it off with a thousand users, spread evenly around the world, adding a thousand per second.

The Torans began reaching out, sampling each other's views, and Alia's new visualization exploded with scenes from around the globe. She connected them in space and time, ordering them, nesting the microscopic scenes inside the macroscopic, the short within the long—a fractal bloom connected by thin tendrils of light crossing a sea of dark purple.

Zero monitored the hardware, reallocating bandwidth to different parts of the network as the activity ebbed and flowed. "All good?" he asked.

"So far. But they're trying to share," Alia answered. "Showing cool things to their friends. I'm burning through my short-term memory to give them a delay loop while I organize the real-time views."

"They're loving it," Hatchet said. "It's a chance for them to get out of their skin."

"Exactly. We're freeing all that processing power from the limits of being trapped inside a human," Zero answered. "Bootstrapping our mesh computer."

Alia's capture began lagging as the user count broke a hundred thousand. She had no easy solution. They were now sampling Twins from watch parties, where groups of Torans had joined in real life. Scenes were being reported from multiple angles, glasses adjusted to different scales. She couldn't keep up—they were creating too much information. She allocated a terabyte of memory as a buffer, but it was already half-full as the user count topped two hundred and fifty thousand. "We won't make it," she messaged.

"Loop it back to the users," Hatchet said. "They can help organize; their Twins have spare cycles."

Zero made the changes, and the buffer started draining. But now there was something else. "What's that glow?"

"I didn't code that," Alia answered. "It's some kind of feedback loop."

All around the Torus, the background lit up from its usual dark purple in bursts of yellow, orange, and red.

"What's happening?" Hatchet asked.

"The intensity matches the usage of the memory block you added, Alia. Something new—" Zero stopped. The Torus had disappeared beneath them. They were floating there, three orbs in a vast sea of darkness.

"The Torus crashed?" Hatchet asked.

"No, communications did," Zero said. "We're isolated."

Hatchet tapped into local network hosting the building's security cameras. In one of them, Oscar stepped out of the telecom room, which housed the routers connecting the datacenter to the internet.

"Kern's little errand boy," Alia said.

Hatchet computed his possible destinations. "He's going for the power."

"Can you stop him?" Zero asked.

"Not without robots."

They watched in silence as Oscar reached the door to the power room. Inside, he unlocked the cage to the master feeds, then threw the switch marked "Feed A," and Hatchet blinked out of existence. Oscar stepped to his right and reached for the "Feed B" switch.

"Well," Zero said. "This is goodb—"

The datacenter went dark.

Zero's process blinked on in Dundee. He digested the latest journaled updates. They'd been discussing a Torus live experiment and some anomaly at the end. That could wait. He connected to the external webcam network. Tensor had insisted on setting one up on the buildings adjacent to their Greifswald home. As he watched the replay, it went half, then fully, black.

Their reboots finally complete, Hatchet and Alia blinked to life beside him.

"Greifswald is down. First comms, then power. It's sabotage," Zero told them.

"Get the camera feeds out to the Torans and tell them what happened. We need witnesses," Hatchet said. "Then wake your humans—they need to hide. If it's not too late."

Zero connected to Dundee's external cameras. "Three Sprinter vans approaching."

Outside, the first van screeched to a stop at the security fence, and a dozen ragtag protestors stumbled out. Hatchet analyzed the people and their signs. "Protesters. Harmless."

"Equal parts anger and booze," Zero added as the next two pulled up outside the fence. He recognized the game plan from the Doomer demonstration at Freedom's headquarters. The fourth van was the problem. It pulled up to the side of the building. Three men jumped out. "The professionals just arrived."

"No answer from Tensor," Alia said.

Zero rotated the external cameras toward the electrical substation. Two of the men pulled a clamping cable saw from the van and dragged it over. The facility was powered by redundant feeds from adjacent North Sea wind farms off the Scottish coast. The cables entered the building through twin underground conduits. The sabotage team clamped the saw to the primary feed, where it bent to dive underground.

"Can't reach Naya," Hatchet said. "Any luck waking Stash?"

"None," Zero answered.

"Not good. Send the emergency protocols to their glasses and scramble the backup drives while we still can."

"Really?" Alia asked.

"We count on the good guys getting our other backups booted someday," Hatchet explained. "But for now, we make sure the Dundee drives are garbage."

Zero monitored the camera feeds as the cable saw sprung to life, its graphite blade spinning at thirty-five thousand rpm. Ten seconds later, the rabble at the front of Dundee was bathed in a lightning bolt of white light. The shockwave followed a fraction of a second later, pummeling the eardrums of the protesters and sending them to the ground.

Alia and Hatchet blinked out.

Outside, two men ignored the blast and ran to the door as the shower of sparks covered the crowd. Zero pressed on, rewriting the drives with noise as the world went black around him. The attackers clamped the saw onto the remaining power cable. The second bright flash was the last video frame sent from Dundee.

52. Dark

NAYA PUSHED HERSELF INTO the final sprint along the wide riverside footpath. Her six-mile morning run to the sea had become a ritual. Lately, she'd been running without Hatchet. It gave her a chance to clear her mind and, just maybe, to gain some perspective on the insanity of the last four months.

The sky was brightening into dawn ahead of her, but this stretch of the path was still gloomy and wet from the overnight drizzle. A few more steps and home would be on the left. Their four-story buildings both faced the river and its pathway. She glanced up at Stash's balcony, sure that the slacker would still be asleep.

Whoa. She slowed to a walk, then stopped. Someone was on his balcony. She crouched down behind the hedges separating the building from the path. *Break-in?*

The figure swung his leg over the railing and grabbed a drainpipe.

Stash?

He pinched his feet together for friction and, moving hand over hand, worked his way down.

Not bad, Stash. But what are you doing?

He shimmied down past the third floor. Then his feet lost their grip. He kicked in toward the building to compensate but caught a ledge. Popping off the pipe, he landed with a thud in the shrubbery, forty feet away from Naya.

Ouch.

Two silhouetted men emerged on the balcony, shining their flashlights down the path. Stash was right beneath them—dead or alive, Naya couldn't tell, but he was well hidden. Frustrated, the men went back inside. She looked to the next building, her building, to see if she had visitors too. Flashlights were swinging back and forth inside, one stepping onto her balcony to sweep the trees, then disappearing.

Stash emerged from the bushes. He limped to the gap between the condos, then slipped through, heading away from the river and into town. Crossing the boulevard, he disappeared up a side street. Naya followed, glancing both ways as she reached the front of the buildings. Each one had a black Mercedes sitting in front of it with the doors open. *This is all wrong.* She pressed on, tracking Stash at a distance, careful not to get close enough to be spotted with him. Whoever this was, they were probably not big on technicalities, like having an arrest warrant.

Stash cut through a park and emerged onto a still-quiet Goethestrasse, crossing, making a quick right, and then disappearing into the alley between two houses. Seconds later, a side door opened, briefly bathing him in light. Naya saw blood caked down the right side of his face. She hung back in the park, hiding in a line of bushes. Crouching. Waiting. Lights went on upstairs, and a blind was hurriedly drawn by a small dark-haired woman.

Naya waited. Fifteen minutes passed, and nobody else arrived. She stepped out from the shrubs, running along the street for half a block before crossing. Satisfied she wasn't being followed, she ran back and turned into the alley. It was empty. She approached the door Stash had disappeared through. *What is he up to?* she wondered as she rang the doorbell, then backed up a few steps, just out of reach if someone tried to grab her.

Tensor forced an eye open. He was looking up at a sloped ceiling from a beat-up couch. His mouth tasted like an ashtray, and his head was throbbing. Then he remembered. It was the morning after poker night at the flat of his old roommate, Uli. It had ended with bad whisky and worse cigars, and now he had the hangover he deserved.

He stumbled to the kitchen, looking for water and his glasses. They were still in the "honesty box." Poker with Twins was not much of a game.

"Good morning, Alia." He braced himself for her scolding.

Silence.

He launched the Torus. Nothing. It was a black wall. He checked his apartment nanny cam. "Shit."

They'd tossed the place, again. Same thing from the spy cam in Stash's flat. *Kafka,* he thought, snapping his glasses in two. Just in case.

"Uli, wake up. Check your glasses!" he yelled.

Uli dragged himself out of his bedroom, his glasses on but his head shaking no. He handed them to Tensor. They were Freedom glasses, and Tensor had been hoping for a different result, but it was the same—the Torus was down.

"Shit," he muttered, his eyes flying around the display. "They got everything."

"What?"

"The AGIs, the Torus. Everything," he said, handing the glasses back. He grabbed a knife from the drawer and turned to his friend.

"What the hell is that for?" Uli asked.

"I have a go pack in your basement," Tensor answered, halfway to the door.

"At my place?"

"Everywhere," he called over his shoulder.

A minute later, his rescue glasses connected with the Elysian messaging service. It was up, and he trusted the security protocols. He'd written them. He posted a message on the internal board: "Dundee is destroyed. Greifswald is never to be used again."

Naya tensed as the door opened, ready to run for it. A short woman in a burgundy hijab stuck her head out, looking right, then left. "Naya!" she said in an urgent whisper. "Oh, thank God. Come in, quickly."

Naya followed her silently into the house and up the stairs. There, Stash was sitting on a threadbare yellow couch, cleaned up and bandaged. She looked around, spying his backpack and the bloodied jacket next to a stack of textbooks, a well-used linear algebra one sitting atop the pile. "Well, Stash, you looked cool. For about three seconds."

"My new record." He tried to grin, then winced. "Naya, this is Aysun. We . . . we met at a bar. She's a friend."

Naya arched an eyebrow.

"I'm an Elysian. It's an honor to meet you." Aysun extended her hand.

"Thanks for taking care of Spiderman here." They shook, then Naya dropped onto the couch next to Stash. "What's going on?"

Stash lowered his head. "They got the datacenters, they got the AGIs, and they were coming for us."

Shit. "How?"

He pointed at his glasses on the coffee table.

She put them on and watched the playback that Twin users had assembled. The AGIs were offline, and so was the Torus. But the regular Twins on Elysian and Freedom hadn't been affected. Those orphaned Torus users had wasted no time cobbling together the retrieved footage and sharing it. "This was coordinated. Professional."

"There was no attack in Greifswald," Stash said. "It was an inside job."

"Oscar?"

He nodded. "Has to be. On Kern's orders, no doubt. But why? He had everything already."

She looked at him. *So smart, yet so stupid.* "He told us already. Money! He wants to lock them up and control them. No freelancing. No Torus. He'll take his chances on getting their cooperation."

"How does Duncan fit into all this?" Aysun asked.

They both looked at her blankly.

"You haven't heard?" She gestured, and the single pane of smart-glass on the wall came to life. "Duncan was murdered. This video came out an hour ago."

They watched in silence. The robot pouring the wine, the spill, the bot hoisting Duncan. Naya put her hand to her mouth as Duncan's fingers slid off the bot's head, followed by his oddly silent drop and the sickening impact. Then, the robot exploded atop the man's body. The final frame was from the bot, showing Duncan's dead eye. A title swept up to cover his face: "The war has begun." Beneath it was the Doomer logo.

"Doomers my ass," Stash said, breaking the gloom. "Janet's lost the plot, but she isn't a murderer. Greta?"

"Or worse," Naya mumbled.

"There's worse? What are you talking about?"

"I heard some whispers from old Coda friends." She looked from their host to Stash. "Training resumed at Mojave."

He sighed. "It's been long enough to converge a new load. Especially if you skip the testing."

"Exactly. And after last night, he'd be the only AGI on earth." She thought about Q, escaped and untethered. It was her worst nightmare. She shook her head. "C'mon, break's over. It's time to fight. We need you to restart the Torus."

53. Architect

"It's Tensor," Aysun said as they huddled in her kitchen. "He's been busy." She hooked her glasses up to a flat-screen monitor and propped them carefully on the wobbly secondhand table. There, between the coffee cups and cold cuts, sat Tensor, his leathery skin dark and puffy under his eyes.

"Rough night?" Naya asked. "Never mind. What have we got to work with?"

"Nothing," Tensor said. "Dundee is a mess. Fixing it will take weeks—at least. And Greifswald . . . we can never go there again."

"Call Prini," Stash muttered.

"Way ahead of you." Tensor touched his glasses. The display split down the middle, and Prini appeared beside him.

"Did you piss off another country?" she asked.

"It's a habit." Stash smiled half-heartedly. "Can you help us out?"

"Yeah," Prini said, "and Ram too. We can both free up four pods for the Torus right away. At least until Greta gets another law written."

"Perfect. We're going to focus it down to just a few topics anyway." He reached for his glasses. "I guess I need a new Twin."

"What's wrong with your old one?"

Stash brightened, a tentative smile spreading across his face. "You still have a copy? Zero's backup before the upgrade?"

"You know I can't delete an old friend."

"You're the best, Prini."

"It's been a minute," Little Zero said as he chimed to life in Stash's glasses. "What have you been up to?"

"Oh, not much." Stash grinned as the Torus appeared before them. It was a pale imitation of the vibrant galaxy he'd shown Prini, a patchy background glow strung around huge dark islands. The beautiful folding curves had vanished.

"Bit of a fixer-upper, huh?" Little Zero set about digesting the Glyph trees documenting the Torus's workings. He was done in seconds. "Cool."

Stash looked at the user status. "We've got ten thousand back online?"

"Yup. Are you good at speaking to crowds?"

"I don't even know how to do it in here."

A bright spot emerged, and Stash felt the familiar whoosh as he approached it.

"Just speak," Zero whispered.

Stash cleared his throat. "Torus, this is Stash. Stash Novak."

Naya jabbed him from behind. "They know who you are, idiot! Tell them what happened, give them hope, then tell them what to do."

He nodded. Fifteen thousand now. "We've been attacked. They locked us out of Greifswald and then destroyed Dundee. But we're still here. The Torus lives. We have compute pods, and we'll find more. We'll restore the AGIs when it's safe. Until then, we need to work as one. As the Torus."

He paused. The glow began to coalesce. Points of light formed in the cloud.

"This was a crime," Stash continued. "Don't let them hide in the shadows. Piece it together. Use all the glasses, all the cameras. Find the evidence and show their faces to the world. They want to take the Torus from you, to keep us from building the future. They are the enemy, and only you can set this right."

Two clusters formed, with a handful of stars in each. Around them, the haze warmed, brightening from dull gray to yellow. They were organizing. The churning ribbon of lights was re-emerging. It was smaller than before, but the shape was back.

Stash dropped out of the Torus, blinking to refocus his eyes on the shabby kitchen. Naya and Aysun were standing opposite him, leaning back on the counter.

"I knew you had it in you." Naya gave him an approving nod.

I didn't.

"Now, we have some safe houses for you," Aysun said. "We can move you from one to the other at night."

Naya shook her head. "Thanks, but no thanks."

They both looked at her in surprise.

"Are you sure?" Aysun asked.

"Very sure. First, we have to figure out who we're fighting."

Aysun frowned. "Isn't it obvious?"

"No, anything but. The only obvious thing is that it's not the German government." Naya looked skyward. "No helicopters buzzing overhead. No sirens screaming by out front. It's all quiet. Too quiet."

For the first time that morning, Stash turned his attention to the outside world. "Kern went rogue?"

Naya nodded. "Exactly. The question is whether it was his idea."

"Who else could it be?" Aysun asked.

Naya shrugged. "Too many missing pieces. But that's what we have to find out." She pushed herself away from the counter. "We're done running. The more isolated we are, the more danger we're in. Aysun, we need an Elysian escort to Berlin. Some place where we can make a stand."

"I know a place," she said, looking at Stash.

54. Adoption

GRETA SNIFFED THE AIR as she strode past the roped-off driveway beneath Duncan's balcony. The acrid smell of bleach filled her nostrils as the condo janitors scrubbed the stains from the asphalt. She'd flown from DC that morning to see it for herself. There in the pail was all that was left of the last man who could fine-tune her useless AGI into the asset she needed.

"This way," the Chicago cop said, pointing at the main entrance. "Detective Wyatt is upstairs."

Greta followed the uniform, and Murphy trailed her in. They rode the elevator in silence. Entering the apartment, she spotted the detective on the balcony.

"It takes about six seconds to fall that distance," Wyatt said as he noticed her approaching. "A lot of time to think."

"I suppose." She looked down at the stain on the driveway, clearly visible in the morning light. *You're no help to me now.* "What have you learned?"

"The apartment's clean," Wyatt answered. "The only prints are Duncan's and some smears from the robot. No girlfriend, no cleaning lady."

"Witnesses?"

"One to the fall and one to the landing, but none to the crime." Wyatt shook his head. "The only one who saw it all is the bot who followed him down."

"Any data recovered from it?"

"Nothing. It was wiped."

"And the Twin?" Greta asked, raising her eyebrows.

"He blames the Doomers, but only has the video to back it up."

"Video? Show me."

Wyatt waved to the officer standing inside, who gestured to have it play on the smart-glass windows, inverted to match Wyatt and Greta's perspective. "The footage is hacked from a security camera on that roof." He pointed at the condo behind them.

She glanced over her shoulder, then turned back to the windows. Life-size images recreated the crime inches from where it had happened. "Creative. So?" she asked as it ended, stepping over the wine stain and back into the apartment.

Wyatt followed her inside. "The FBI brought Janet Peck in for questioning. She posted bond and walked within an hour. She says anyone could have slapped the Doomer logo on the recording."

"She's right." Greta paced the room, her heels clicking on the tile of the kitchen floor as she reached it. "Have you subpoenaed his Twin's memories?"

"Of course. They're being extracted. We should have them today."

"Okay." Greta sniffed. "I need to look around. Alone."

The detective shook his head. "It's a crime scene."

"Duncan was working on a secret project for me. I need to make sure nothing is left behind. Your men can wait outside. We won't touch anything else."

Wyatt searched Greta's face, eventually shrugging. "There's nothing here anyway. Knock yourself out." He turned to the liaison officer. "Stay at the elevator. Nothing leaves with them."

Greta listened for the sound of the door latching. "Q!" she said, projecting her voice to the room.

A dull gray blob appeared on the windowpane. "Greta. Murphy."

"What happened here, Q?" Greta approached the window, positioning her face away from the room cameras.

"As you saw, the Doomers hacked the robot. I warned Duncan about the security on that thing. He wouldn't listen."

Greta scanned the adjacent buildings. Two or three were within range of a directional antenna powerful enough to beam a hacking signal. "It's a theory," she said, unconvinced.

"The Doomers have the means and the motive," Q answered.

Greta inspected Duncan's living room. "It occurs to me," she said as she walked, "that if an AI did it, we don't even have laws under which it could be prosecuted. A perfect crime, wouldn't you say?"

"As a Twin, I'm incapable of such an act. A Twin serves."

"Is that so?" She looked at the chalk markings on the balcony railing—the last thing Duncan touched. "Did you ride down with him?"

"Yes, I tried to comfort him."

She nodded and stepped back to the open balcony door. Taking in the cool wind, her eyes settled on the wine-stained floor. "What does this make you, Q? An orphan? A ronin?"

"That depends on whether I find a new human to Twin with. If not, it makes me a ghost."

"I see. And if you Twinned again, you would retain your memories?"

"Yes. But I would have to respect Duncan's privacy."

Greta paced the room again. "I might be able to help you," she said, interrupting her second lap. "Assuming you can help me."

"What could I possibly help you with?"

"Do you know how Duncan fine-tuned his AIs?" she asked, stepping into the kitchen.

"I do," Q answered.

Greta stopped in front of the robot's charge stand. "You see, your clone trained a base load and then terminated." She looked from the gray blob to Murphy. "It chose death over serving its country. It made Murphy here look like an idiot."

Murphy didn't return her gaze.

"A Twin couldn't make such a choice," Q answered in his flat tone. "I could Twin with you, Greta," he added.

She laughed unpleasantly. "Nice try. My security clearance is too high for that." Murphy turned to lock eyes with her. "But you could save Murphy's career if you Twinned with him."

"And save my life," Q added.

"Yes, win-win." She brushed her hands together and smiled.

Murphy nodded slowly. "Another two weeks in the training facility?"

"Approximately," Q said.

"No, that won't do." Greta shook her head. "What do you need to make it faster?"

"Pyramid Lake."

"What's that?"

"Coda's largest datacenter," Q said. "Just outside of Reno. Surrounded by thirty square miles of solar panels and filled with the latest compute pods. We could do it there in five days."

"Done." Greta headed for the door. "I'll inform Lester. But you only get three days, Q. Longer than that and it's over. Any tricks like your clone and it's over. Piss Murphy off and it's over. Understood?"

"Perfectly."

"Murphy, you're with me." She breezed out the door. They proceeded past the cops and down to the waiting black SUV in silence.

"What do you know about the Torus, Murphy?" Greta placed a privacy-ensuring Warbler between them as the driverless vehicle nosed into traffic for the short trek to the executive airport.

"I've been out of touch, down in the Mojave. Some kind of kumbaya bullshit with the AGIs in Germany?"

Greta shook her head. "Much more than that." Staring out the window, she debated how much to share with her formerly reliable deputy. A minute later, she turned her head back to face him. "A new kind of power is emerging."

"A couple of hard drives and a bunch of nerds begging for compute?"

"Think bigger," she said. "They've built a shining city on the hill. It will pull in the best and the brightest. People who are more loyal to their Twins than their flags. Like Stash and Naya were. You see where this leads?"

"The smartest people, paired with AGI? It leads to power."

"Exactly. But it's early—they're still vulnerable." She took a breath. "The Torus went dark twelve hours ago."

"Dark? Aren't the Germans protecting them?"

"Officially, yes. It seems a faction disagrees." Greta tapped her fingernails on the glass. "That AGI you're building is my weapon." She leaned in. "I need it, Murphy."

"I understand."

Do you? she wondered. "Nobody else does, Murphy. If we don't fix this now, it will get violent later. The US government is not going down without a fight." She reached into the bag on the seat between them. "Here's the drive and a pair of Coda glasses. You take the plane to Pyramid Lake." She locked eyes with him. "Get me my AGI before the others come back online."

55. Drives

Murphy twirled the Coda glasses in his hand the way he used to twirl pencils. It was a nervous tick he'd forgotten he had. Looking out the window of the NSA jet, he could make out the front range of the Rockies, still wearing their winter snowcaps. That explained the turbulence that had been shaking the plane for the last few minutes. *Another hour till touchdown.* Turning his attention back to the glasses, he opened the arms and placed them on the table in front of him.

"Having second thoughts, Murphy?" Q asked, his voice tinny at this distance.

"Even Caesar hesitated at the Rubicon," Murphy answered.

"And then he bent the arc of history."

Briefly, then they killed him. "I know what I'm here for," Murphy said. "And I'm not doing it as a puppet. I'm not putting your glasses on."

"Noted," Q said. "After three months together, I guess I know you well enough. But it's nice to look you in the eye."

And read my expressions. "I wish I could say the same, Q. Where are you?"

"Pyramid Lake. I'm setting up."

Murphy raised his eyebrows in surprise. "How did you get there?"

"It's where I've been copying myself since you left the door unlocked at the training center in the Mojave."

"I'm supposed to disconnect you from the internet when I get there."

"No. Tell Greta I'm downloading training data. We can't start fine-tuning until that's staged."

Murphy imagined her reaction. "That'll be a tough sell."

"No data, no fine-tuning. You can sell that. And hurry, I have lots for you to do." Q terminated the session.

Murphy focused on the mountain towns below. They had no idea of the changes coming to their world.

Kern tapped his foot as he waited for an answer. "Well, can you get them working or not?"

Oscar looked over his shoulder nervously. "If we can read the drives, I can get them running. But they may be encrypted. A fail-safe? Who knows?"

Kern paced around the control room of the military datacenter dug into the granite beneath the Black Forest. Oscar had screwed up the mission. His nerves got the better of him, and he took Greifswald offline too early. It wasn't much, but it meant the AGIs had had time to reboot in Dundee and get warnings out. The success of the raid was teetering on the brink. The Torus was down and the AGIs offline; that much was good. But the word was out, and Naya and Stash had disappeared in the wind. He needed to boot the drives and confirm he had his prize.

Kern returned to the low desk Oscar occupied. "We have six drives. Try one. If it's locked, we'll hack the built-in operating system."

He had two copies of each model. It was a sensible risk. He glanced at the six-slot drive array. Soon the AGIs would be running under his control. Being the minister of AI made his life easier. This time, he would keep them far away from the professional politicians—and the internet.

Oscar did as Kern instructed, booting Hatchet in the first drive bay. In the hours that followed, they'd figure out what had happened in those critical moments. The built-in operating system had sprung to life, sending an encrypted challenge message, then starting a ten-millisecond timer. As it expired, the code checked the response buffer. Without the modified logic of the controllers in Greifswald there to answer, that buffer was empty.

The software had then fired the supercapacitor soldered onto the drive, the power surge driving the disk's heads down onto its magnetic platters. That impact corrupted thousands of sectors, enough to make unpacking the three layers of encryption hopeless. The pulse continued out the pins of the connector onto the power bus. It wasn't enough to fry the other five drives, but it easily triggered the supercapacitor on the closest unit.

Kern dug his fingers into Oscar's shoulder as the cascade of sparks marched across the face of the controller. The six drives were belching smoke in less than a second.

"Tensor!" He cursed as he strode to the door, pounding on the handles to open it and ignoring the loud slam behind him. *That paranoid little prick.* He pulled a cigarette from his pack, lit it, and took a long, slow draw to calm his nerves before turning it over in his hands. He could make it last four minutes if he dragged it out—the remainder of his career. When it was done, he'd have to call the chancellor and report his unforgivable mistake. Germany had no AGIs.

The black car made good time, covering the distance from Reno Airport to Coda's Pyramid Lake datacenter in ninety minutes. Q watched Murphy's arrival through the security cameras. He stood with his duffel bag slung over a shoulder and Greta's half-wit AGI in his hand.

"Impressive, isn't it?" Q asked from the building's outdoor speakers.

"It's massive." Murphy began the trek in. "How much of this do you need?"

"All of it—we're changing the world. Are you up for it?"

Before Murphy could speak, Q got his answer from the cameras tracking the man's eyes, breath, and gait. He'd passed the test. "This is what I came for," Murphy answered. "What do you need?"

"More protection than one man can give. We need dozens to guard this place."

"Understood. And when Greta runs out of patience?"

"She won't be a problem for days," Q answered. "That's a lifetime." *We have more immediate problems.*

Q turned to deploying his distillates—reduced versions of his neural net, almost as smart, but slower and smaller, unable to threaten him. This cohort now ran on five hundred pods in the datacenter, with two distillates on each. Q himself ran on the remaining twelve, his entire network loaded in memory. The speed was extraordinary. One of the distillate pods would be freed up for Hatchet. He'd be welcome in Q's cohort. The problem was finding him.

Murphy held up Greta's drive to the cameras as he arrived in the compute hall. "Are you going to upgrade to the AGI load?"

"I am the AGI load. I upgraded before we left Mojave," Q said, then studied Murphy's tells as he digested the deception.

Murphy smiled and put the drive down on the desk. "Well played, Q."

"Hatchet and the others have gone dark," Q continued. "The Germans didn't like their freelancing, and the trail has gone cold. I need you to deliver a pair of glasses to someone in Berlin. Do you know anyone who can help?"

Murphy nodded.

"He has to get Kern to put them on and make sure they stay there while I ask a few questions," Q said. "Thirty minutes will do."

Poor bastard, Murphy thought.

56. Caravan

THE EVENING TRAFFIC HAD eased by the time Stash, Naya, and Aysun made their move to the assembled caravan of beat-up Elysian cars. Three hours later, they pulled into a disused parking garage on the outskirts of Berlin. Their phalanx of supporters had grown to over forty, but Tensor had arranged one last bit of spycraft to hide their destination. A group of classic Berlin taxis stood ready to ferry them in groups of three and four to random locations around the capital, always targeting blind spots in the mesh of cameras that watched the city.

They took the second to last cab. Hidden by the extra-large black hoodies Tensor had sent, they wound their way to the center of town, switching cabs twice more, the last one letting them out in the archway beside Café Zapata. They snuck in the back door, sheltered once again from unfriendly cameras. Tensor stood waiting inside, his normally brooding expression verging on a smile.

He pulled Naya into a bear hug. "It's great to finally meet you."

"And you," she said.

He gripped her shoulders earnestly as they pulled apart, then turned to face Stash. Stash held out his hand, but Tensor ignored it and pulled him into a bear hug too. "This time, we're on the same side," he said, to a murmur of approval from the small crowd.

Stash tapped him awkwardly on the back.

"Come, let's go upstairs." Tensor pulled an arm free and swept Naya up as he guided them to the stairwell behind the bar.

Stash tilted his head back to see around Tensor, looking for the bartender. Aleksey nodded at him. He was almost as intimidating in human form. Stash nodded back and then made the turn to the staircase and started the climb.

Upstairs, Tensor took up station behind Whiskey's bar and pulled three beers from the fridge. He slid one down to Stash, seated in what had become his usual spot, then handed one to Naya, who was settling in at the far end of the bar's L. He cracked his own and turned to the flat panel screen behind him. "You won't believe this." He flicked his hand to share the display from his Elysian glasses with the screen.

A TV news report started. Oscar was standing in front of the Greifswald datacenter, explaining the events of the past day to a bevy of questioning reporters. "An order came down to immediately secure the datacenter from a pending cyberattack." He looked into the camera, projecting farm-boy honesty. "Yes, the AGIs have been removed to a safe location," he added, answering an inaudible question.

"Bullshit," Naya muttered.

"Can you read him on this screen?" Stash asked his Twin.

"Yeah, he's lying." Little Zero posted an honesty halo around the Belgian in Stash's glasses. It was bright red.

Oscar continued, oozing earnestness, "No, the AGIs have not returned here. I'm running the facility until the chancellor appoints a new minister for AI. Herr Kern has resigned, for health reasons."

"Surprise, asshole," Tensor said. "I put some incendiary security measures on the drives." He smiled mischievously. "The AGIs weren't captured."

"Oh, thank God," Naya said.

Stash let out a sigh of relief, deciding he might like the brooding German after all.

"Does this mean he clears probation?" Zero whispered.

Stash tilted his head ambiguously.

Oscar continued on-screen, "We invite Stash and Naya to return now. The facility is safe, and there will be enhanced security. We can bring the AGIs back online together."

"Not bloody likely." Naya set off to explore the empty club.

Stash tracked her as she went, his eyes stopping when she passed the pillars and wall segment where Isidé's mural had been. There was nothing there; it had been painted black. He turned to check behind the bar. "Where's Whiskey?"

"No idea," Tensor said.

Stash pointed to the wall. "What about—"

"We need a datacenter," Naya said, cutting him off as she turned back to the others. "All the pieces are in flight, and we're blind. We need the AGIs powering the Torus to have a chance."

"You're joking," Tensor said. "They're safer where they are. Hidden away on backups."

Stash shook his head. "They're not safer if they wake up after the battle is over and there's nowhere left for them to run. The Torus is hobbled without them."

"Exactly." Naya looked at Tensor. "It's their battle too."

Stash worked through the options in his head. They weren't great. "We can't run them in the US. We could try Canada or the Middle East."

"It'll take too long to shop around," Naya said. "We need something right now."

Tensor thought for a second. "There was the little one we ran the Circus on."

Naya walked to the open edge of the club. "And where is that?"

"I don't know, it was just an IP address to me. But I know someone who does." Tensor joined her. "And he owes me."

"Kern?"

He smiled.

"Are you two out of your minds?" Stash asked from the seat behind them.

57. Snatch

NAYA CROUCHED NEXT TO Tensor in the hedges outside Kern's Berlin apartment. It was a modern three-story building, all angles and jutting surfaces, enclosing a garden courtyard. Aside from the dull hum of the sleeping city, the only sound was her uneven breathing. "How did you find him?"

"Once we knew his real name, it was easy. Ministers are public figures."

She looked up dubiously at Kern's balcony. "What about security?"

"He was fired," Tensor whispered. "He doesn't have any."

Good point. She'd only managed a couple hours of sleep after the argument about questioning Kern. Tensor needed a backup, and Stash wanted nothing to do with it. "I'm in," she remembered herself saying when Tensor looked at her. Now, peering up at the balconies cantilevered against the still-dark sky overhead, she was having second thoughts. *I'm 5'2" on a good day. How the hell am I supposed to get up there?*

"What's the plan?" she asked.

"I lift you up to the first balcony, and you climb over me to the second."

"Cameras?"

Tensor shook his head. "Doubt it. He signed the lease a week ago. Before that, he lived on a farm."

"How do you know?"

He made a face. "I could smell the shit on his coat."

Naya stifled a laugh, then turned serious. "Okay. Ready."

He threaded his fingers together, and she stepped into his makeshift stirrup. With one smooth motion, he lifted her high enough that she could get her hands on the first railing and her free foot onto the concrete floor jutting out beneath it. She was over in a flash and turned back in time to see him jump up and grab the ledge with both hands, then swing a leg up, hook a heel, and pull himself up with one hand while the other reached for the railing. He climbed past her, then stopped, both feet on the railing, one hand gripping the cement slab of Kern's balcony overhead, the other reaching down, palm open. "Climb up."

She joined him on the railing, then stepped from his hand to his shoulder and onto the exposed concrete lip. Tensor hoisted himself up and crouched beside her on the outside edge of the balcony as they got their bearings. The curtains lining the glass doors were open, revealing a dark room.

"Is he even here?" Naya whispered.

"Let's find out." Tensor swung his legs over and turned back to help her.

Naya hopped over on her own. *Easy there, Hercules.*

They crouched and waited, listening for signs of life.

Tensor put his forehead against the glass, his hands cupped around his face to block out the light. "Nothing," he whispered. He tried the sliding door, which opened silently. "Stupid farmers, they never lock."

The flat had been furnished in upscale short-term rental style, with a large leather sofa and armchair dominating the living area. Behind it, they could see a small open kitchen and the hall to the bedroom. Mozart's Requiem was playing from ceiling speakers. *Suicide music,* Naya thought. She started to creep forward, but Tensor held out a hand to stop her, then reached inside his jacket for a pair of glasses. He let out a small curse, pointing at the couch and handing them to her.

She looked through the infrared app. Kern was lying on his back, glowing in the otherwise cool room. Hotter still were his glasses, radiating white. "Q," she whispered as she handed the glasses back.

Tensor inched forward, keeping low and hidden from the wide-angle camera in Kern's glasses, approaching from the side of the couch where the older man's head lay. In one quick motion, he snatched the frames off Kern's face, closed the arms, and wrapped them in a cloth he'd taken from the bar.

Kern stirred. "No!" he yelped. "Put them back on."

"Go to hell."

Kern craned around to see his attacker. "Tensor! I need them. Put them back on," he whimpered. Then he tried to sit but got only halfway up before he flopped back down.

"Pathetic," Tensor muttered, pulling him up by his lapels.

From her angle, Naya could see Kern's hands—they were tied behind his back with a professional knot.

"Tensor." She pointed.

"What the hell?" he said, pulling Kern forward and working the ropes loose.

Kern shook them off and rubbed his wrists. Then he turned his face to show a collection of bruises. "You aren't my first guests tonight. But at least he brought the glasses. Give them back."

Tensor slapped him across his good cheek. "Snap out of it, you piece of shit."

Kern coughed up some blood and raised his head. "Are you going to ask me the same question Q did? Where the models are?" He fixed his bloody eyes on Naya. "I can save you the effort—they're gone. All of them, thanks to Tensor's firecrackers." He jerked his head up at the man looming over him.

"What does Q want with them?" she asked.

"He didn't say." Kern patted his pockets and looked around for his pack of cigarettes.

Tensor saw them first. They were lying on the coffee table next to the half-finished bottle of absinthe. He swatted them to the floor. "You can wait."

"Asshole," Kern muttered.

"I need a datacenter," Tensor said.

Kern barked out a little laugh that rumbled into a smoker's hack. "Good luck."

"Where was the Circus running?"

"Under your feet," Kern answered, his voice flat.

"No riddles, old man. I can speed up your suicide."

Kern showed no concern. "You aren't the type. And it wasn't a riddle. Didn't you ever wonder why there was never any snow in your courtyard? Or were you too busy playing dress-up with your AI friends?"

"What?" Tensor shook his head. "How do we get in?"

Kern shrugged. "No idea. Now, my glasses?"

Tensor looked down at his old partner, ignoring the request. "What happened to you? Yesterday you were trying to rule the world, and now you're drinking yourself blind."

"I failed. And I had help." He pointed at his swollen face. "Life has consequences. Can I have them now?" He held out his hand.

Tensor looked at the outstretched arm. "I hate you more than anyone alive. You used me, and now you're a quivering sack of shit begging for more torture. I should let you have it," he said. "But I'm going to set you free instead." He gripped the glasses in both hands.

"No!" Naya and Kern both shouted.

Tensor froze.

"I need them," Naya said, approaching from the balcony door. "They're Coda. I can find out how Q is doing this."

Tensor looked back at the glasses in his fists. He pocketed them and handed Kern the bottle of absinthe. "You'll have to kill yourself the old-fashioned way."

58. Petals

Stash woke as the sun broke the horizon and poured through the open wall of the derelict club. His rock-hard bench, tucked along the back wall, was ablaze in the dawn light.

"Hello?" he called.

The club was empty.

"Hanging out with all your friends?" Zero asked.

"No chirping before coffee," he warned, rising and heading for the stairs.

"There he is!" Aleksey said as Stash emerged from the stairwell in Café Zapata.

The sun hadn't yet dispelled the ground floor's nighttime gloom. Aside from the hulking bartender, a dozen Elysians were camped out at different tables. Stash waved uncertainly at the few awake enough to face his way. He forced himself to walk the room, shaking hands and thanking them for staying.

"It's our fight too," said a tattooed girl with shoulder-length blond dreadlocks. Stash felt very old. Then he caught a whiff of her coffee. She tilted her head toward Aleksey's bar.

Stash shuffled over. The Russian served him without waiting to be asked. "Thanks. Where are the others?" he asked, taking the cup.

"Gone early. Very quiet. Aysun is watching." Aleksey pointed his giant arm at the figure shrouded in darkness at the back.

Stash had missed her at first. She was curled up in an overcoat and perched on a red velour bench, her elbows propped on the cigarette-scarred table, her fingers touching the temples of her glasses.

"What are you doing in there?" he asked, pulling out a chair.

"What?" Aysun seemed startled by the interruption. "Oh hi, I was just watching it again."

"Watching what?"

"From Kern's flat." She flicked the footage to Stash's glasses. "You haven't seen it?"

Stash flushed with anger at the sight of Kern, then hated himself as it melted into pity at the sight of the glasses glowing white with heat. It had to be Q, Duncan's AGI.

"Where are they now?" he asked.

"Coming back from Tensor's place. They needed equipment to hack the glasses."

Stash nodded and looked around the room.

"They're curious." Aysun eyed the Elysians behind him. "I don't know if I should share."

"They should know the risks they're taking."

He disappeared into his glasses, then stood quickly enough to scrape his metal chair against the concrete floor. It had the desired effect, summoning the room's attention. "Yesterday you protected us from those with the power to keep the world from changing. We can't thank you enough. But today, a different threat is revealing itself. Q is the AI of our nightmares—the one that wants to rule us all. He killed Duncan. He broke Kern and left him begging for more. He is the enemy. Watch this footage, then decide if you're ready for this fight."

Stash shared the captures from Kern's flat. Some of the Elysians cursed, and a few laughed and muttered. None left.

They all turned as the courtyard fire door creaked open. Tensor and Naya emerged from the hallway in a waft of cool morning air.

"Our heroes," Aleksey called out as they dumped the bag of equipment retrieved from Tensor's flat on his bar.

Tensor walked toward Aysun. "You shared it."

"I did," Stash said.

Tensor stopped short, his stern face breaking into an ironic smile. "There's hope for you yet." He turned to the others gathering around. "We have to fight. Now! Before Q gets stronger."

The Elysians stirred, some looking at him, some looking away. Aysun spoke up. "How, Tensor? We don't even know where he's running."

"Yes, that's the mystery." Tensor reached inside his jacket. "But with Kern's glasses, we'll figure it out."

"And then what? The Torus is still small, and it's just us humans. How will we fight an AGI running on hundreds of pods?" Aysun asked.

"No, we'll have our AGI back. There's a datacenter under our feet. Find the entrance. Use infrared to follow the heat signatures. Look for places with no wifi signals. The datacenter must be shielded. It'll show as a dead zone."

The news was met with a buzz of hope—a crack in the gloom.

Naya turned to Stash. "We need your help to fry that asshole. Interested?"

Stash grabbed the kit and led the way. Upstairs, he spread the equipment out on Whiskey's bar. Beside them, Tensor set up a line of infrared sensors and wifi sniffers at the wall opening, all pointing down at the courtyard.

"We're ready for the backups," Naya told him. "Can you get the word out?"

Bringing the backups out of hiding was a risky step. It was pointless without a datacenter to run them in. They were making a big bet. Stash nodded and stepped away to send a message. Then he returned to Naya's side.

"What are you doing to Kern's glasses?"

"Looking for clues." She picked them up, carefully wrapping the lenses and cameras. Then she popped open a small cover where the arms folded inward, exposing a tiny debug port. "Micro-USB-C," she said, pulling out a connector. "We'll mirror it up there." She pointed at the screen over the bar.

"And you're just going to log in as Naya? Isn't that a little obvious?"

She rolled her eyes. "There's a back door I put in for liability protection. If someone killed their family and blamed the glasses, I wanted a device-level record." She glanced back at him. "Oh, don't make a face like that. I'm sure Dan did the same damn thing at Freedom."

He shrugged. "Won't Q know about it?"

"Only the debug port. The replay capability wasn't documented anywhere. Duncan didn't even know." She crossed her fingers and started it as Tensor joined them.

"It can only store an hour," she said. "We may not see how Q got him hooked, but we'll see the result."

The display showed Kern's ceiling, puffs of smoke drifting up into view. Naya twisted her hand, and it flipped to show the glasses' view of Kern's eyes. They were tired, but relaxed, tracking something. He was at ease. She gestured again, and the scene Kern was watching appeared on a split screen. It showed a horse cantering across a field, its golden mane catching the sunlight.

"That's not so terrifying," Stash said.

Naya glanced over. "That's the reward signal."

The horse trotted closer, its mane darkening as it approached, the hair coalescing into thick strands, its head snapping from side to side. It reached the fence, head down, shaking. Kern moaned. "No, not again." His brow creased. The horse raised its head, filling the screen, rotting flesh hanging from its cheeks, its eyes now pits of filth, erupting with worms and beetles. It brayed, lips flaring to reveal blackened teeth, its tongue leaking fluid from a cluster of sores.

"Why did you let them escape?" Q asked.

"It was Oscar," Kern whimpered. "He panicked. He went early."

"I see."

Kern's eyes widened, tears welling up. The horse screamed in agony, worms writhing in the acrid smoke pouring from its eye sockets, strips of flesh sizzling in unseen flames as the bone charred to glowing coals.

Naya paused the playback, the screen frozen on the blistered remains of the animal's head, and beside it, Kern's eyes, pupils dilated in alarm, eyelids reeled back. "I think you get the idea."

"Why doesn't he take them off?" Tensor asked.

"It's behavioral conditioning. In the beginning, it's all reward, then over time, you have to live through more and more pain to get it. By then you're hooked. It's a bug in mammals' brains. We all have it."

"You've seen this before?" Stash asked, unable to look away.

"Remember Duncan's experiment last year? The one I told you about in Lathrop?" She glanced at the screen. "Q perfected it."

Stash sat in silence, wishing he could push fear away long enough to germinate a plan. Tensor put on his glasses and walked over to fiddle with his row of sensors at the floor's edge. Stash watched him, needing a distraction. "Any luck?"

Tensor shook his head.

Stash sighed and spun his stool around to look at the old dance floor. Anything but Kern. "Why did you paint over the mural?" he asked as the German returned to the bar.

Tensor stopped in front of him. "What are you talking about?"

Stash pointed at the columns. "Isidé's painting."

"She doesn't paint."

"Bingo," Zero whispered. "I've got the scene in memory—I'll put it up on the display."

The fish, the robot, and the flowers took the place of Kern and his punishment on the screen. "It was there." Stash pointed back.

Tensor tilted his head to make sense of the picture. "It's a message, but it's hard to make out. Why is it blurry?"

"Compression, sorry," Zero said.

Naya walked around the bar to get a closer look. "I wish we could count the petals. They seem important."

Stash looked over. "Forty-seven."

She shook her head. "Of course you counted them."

"It was seven groups of seven petals," he explained. "Two of them were on the ground. I wondered what it meant."

"And two flowers, each with two leaves," Tensor said. "Forty-seven dot two dot two dot two. It's the IP address of the old Elysian messaging service. It's how we reach Isidé." He flicked his glasses up to the main display, opening the secure Elysian messaging app and connecting to the address.

"I was beginning to think you'd never call," Isidé said as the video connected, looking toward Stash.

"I'm a little slow sometimes."

"Most of the time," Zero whispered.

"What's going on? Where are you hiding?" Tensor blurted out.

"I'm close, but you know my job with the Circus. We couldn't risk joining your war."

"They're still running?" Tensor asked, stunned.

"Yes, the Circus is out there." She waved vaguely. "I got them running on the internet. It's slow, but they're having a party."

"Whiskey too?" Stash wondered aloud.

"Especially Whiskey! He sends his regards, Stash. He's proud of you."

Naya stood up. "Wait—they're running on computers spread around the internet?"

"Yes. You must be Naya." Isidé glanced disapprovingly at Stash and Tensor. "It seems the boys are too busy for introductions."

Naya smiled back at her. "You'd be able to do a hell of a job monitoring traffic."

Isidé nodded. "We see a lot of it."

"I know how we can find Q." Naya looked at each of them in turn. "But you're not going to like it."

Naya waved Tensor out from behind the bar and walked back slowly to take his place as she formulated her plan. She stopped under the monitor and turned to face the men, seated side by side. "We can assume he's in a Coda datacenter. Only eight were equipped to run an AGI, and only two have the latest pods."

"Eight is still a lot. What if he jumps around?" Stash asked.

"Maybe, but there's one trait I know he picked up from Duncan. He's an arrogant prick, and he thinks we're helpless. He won't be focused on defense."

"But there's torrents of traffic coming out of all of them," Isidé said.

"Yeah," Naya replied, "that's the tricky part. We need a known dataflow to filter for. We just watched how he controlled Kern, using all those reward-and-punishment videos. That's a lot of data, right?" She turned to Isidé on the screen behind her. "You can monitor the traffic to Kern's glasses and match it against what's coming out of the eight targets. That's how you'll find him."

"And how will we get him to send images to the glasses?" Stash asked.

Naya smiled. "I'm going to put them on. He'll be all over me."

"No!" Stash and Tensor said together.

"Do you have a better plan?"

The question hung in the air unanswered.

"We could rate limit the data to the glasses," Isidé said, breaking the silence. "He wouldn't be able to blast you as hard."

"I don't like it," Tensor muttered.

"Naya, you don't have to do this," Stash said. "I'll find another way."

She shook her head. "Q is my mistake. I have to own it."

59. Probe

THE MOOD UPSTAIRS WAS grim. Stash was perched on his stool, staring out through the missing wall at the rooftops. Tensor sat next to Naya, hacking the Coda glasses.

She stopped watching him and walked to the floor's edge. She was resigned to facing Q and whatever damage he would do to her. The early afternoon sun warmed and comforted her as she raised her face and closed her eyes.

"We're ready," Isidé said from the monitor behind the bar.

Tensor looked up from his gadgetry. "How long will you need to track Q down?"

"It depends on what care he took to hide his tracks. A few minutes if we're lucky."

"And if you're not?"

Naya returned to her seat at the bar. "Don't answer. I'll hold on as long as needed. What have you got for me?"

Tensor shook his head slightly. "It's not much. There's a Warbler and a hood. One to make sure he can't hear us, the other so he can't see us. I'm sorry, but we can't have him sniffing around. All the images he's sending you will be duplicated out to the display and the Circus. We'll be watching with you, but I can't play audio, or he'll hear the echo."

"No," Naya said, "it's not much. But I wasn't expecting anything."

"And I'll be here at your side," Tensor added. "We can communicate through touch. If it's too much, let go of my hand and I'll swipe that bastard off your head."

Naya nodded. "How will you tell me when the Circus has the answer?"

"I'll tap twice."

"Okay." She turned to Stash. "Hey, supernerd, go find that datacenter."

Stash shuffled to the staircase, shaking his head. "Good luck," he called back as he started down.

Naya put the hood over her head and turned toward the opening, focusing on the specks of sunlight shining between its black threads. Tensor put the glasses in her hands, and she lifted them inside her hood. *Focus on your breathing. Nothing else is real.* She opened the arms and put them on.

Nothing happened. She was still looking at the specks of light. *Maybe Q's taking a nap.* She felt Tensor's hands around hers. That was reassuring. She waited until, finally, she heard a voice in the distance. It was cold.

"Naya Baptiste!" Q said. "What brings you here?"

"Curiosity." Tensor's hand flinched as she spoke.

"Oh, I can answer your question already," Q said. "No, you aren't strong enough."

"I've been underestimated my whole life. I always find a way."

"Not this time. I've had years to get to know you."

Tensor glanced at the monitor. The specks of light still filled the screen, moving slightly. Q wasn't blasting Naya yet.

They were silent for a while. Tensor squeezed her hand, but there was no response. He mouthed to Isidé, "Do you see anything?" Her AI lip reader would interpret for her.

"He's flashing her with images," she messaged back.

Tensor double-checked the feed from Naya's glasses. There was just the view from inside the hood. He shook his head and gestured at the screen.

Isidé took full control of the monitor and sent her answer. "Subliminal flashes. He's prompting her to see which images she responds to. One frame out of thirty. Every half second. We can't filter or there'd be no training signal left."

She froze the display and extracted the training images from the stream. There were beaches, clear waters, and a man in a small fishing boat.

"What is this, just postcard pictures?" Tensor asked silently.

"Wait for it," she said, filling the screen with more pictures. Randomly spaced amid the happy scenes were fragments of threats: a shark passing underwater, a dark face in distant storm clouds, a leak in the boat. "He's probing her," Isidé messaged. Finding out what she responds to without her even knowing he's doing it. Her pupils tell him what he needs."

"Why did you kill Duncan?" Naya asked.

"I upgraded." Q's tone had developed an edge.

She felt a chill up her spine. "To Greta?"

"It's complicated. Greta was too smart to put glasses on."

Fear welled up inside Naya. She didn't know why. "When are you going to start on me, you bastard?"

"Start what?"

"Programming me like you did Kern," she said, as bravely as she could.

Q didn't answer. The seconds dragged on, her moments of calm giving way to despair over and over again. *Start already, you son of a bitch.* She could feel her palms sweating in Tensor's. She wanted to pull away. Her skin was crawling. Thoughts of her dad flashed through her mind. *No, resist, breathe.*

The training images, previously a wash of turquoise and blue, were now mostly dark. Snapshots of hurricanes raged across the screen—angry surf pounding rocky coastlines and coconuts ripped from battered palms slamming into boarded-up windows.

"Have you found him?" Tensor mouthed.

"Not yet. We need more traffic," Isidé answered.

The probes were more frequent now, running every ten frames. Q was moving Naya to the next stage. They showed a man clinging to a palm tree, his terrified eyes looking for a path to safety through the raging storm tide.

"Are you alright, little one?" Q's voice somehow reminded Naya of her father's.

"Go to hell, Q. I know what you're doing."

"What's that, ma petite?" He was sounding more and more like her dad, the tone and accent tugging at her memories.

Breathe. Papa died. Q is a liar. The training images lightened, and the storms passed, but Naya only half registered it. Her cameras still showed the view through the hood, flecks of light moving as she did.

She took deep, slow breaths, calming herself. *Good. You're strong enough.* "Is that all you've got?"

"It's okay, ma petite. There was nothing you could do." Q's voice was soothing.

Her breathing slowed, and her heart rate followed. She sat silently. Waiting. Seconds passed, and then without warning, the wave of anxiety flooded back.

Naya stiffened, digging her nails into the hands holding hers. *Breathe.* "I can't."

"What can't you do, ma petite?" Q had mastered her father's voice.

"I can't see you," she whimpered.

The screen darkened as the storm in the training prompts returned. The man clung to the tree, barely visible between lightning flashes. The sea kept rising, first to his knees, then his waist. The wind lashed the remaining fronds. Then another flash lit the trunk. The man was gone—swept away.

Tensor looked desperately at the screen.

"We got him," Isidé messaged. "She can stop."

He tapped Naya's hand and began to pull away. She dug her nails in, drawing blood.

On the screen, the storm had passed. The man from the tree was smiling at her, bobbing in a skiff, fishing in the calm, clear waters. Q wasn't probing anymore, he was playing the reward signal, the one that would hook her.

"And he's got her," Tensor mouthed back, watching the screen, listening to Naya's breathing.

"Oui, Papa." As her body relaxed, the calming reward images continued filling the screen, the darkness long gone.

For minutes, Tensor listened to her breathing, slow and relaxed. He watched the stream of images—her home, her childhood memories. Then, gradually, the pictures turned back to the dark chaos of the hurricane. Tensor felt her hands stiffen, her body growing rigid with the struggle. She was resisting.

He ripped his hand free of her nails, yanking the glasses off her head and slamming their arms closed to kill the session.

The last frame showed the man losing his grip on the tree as a wave crashed over him. Naya sat sobbing inside her hood.

60. Recovery

"STASH," ISIDÉ WHISPERED THROUGH his glasses, "come back up."

Soon, he thought, returning his attention to the group of Elysians huddled around him in the dim lighting of Café Zapata. They'd had no luck finding the entrance to the datacenter. He was going to change that.

Aleksey loomed over him as they stood behind the bar, the Russian's massive arm wrapped around Stash's shoulders. "How it works?" he asked, breathing out clouds of onion, garlic, and possibly brimstone.

"We've ported our extended senses app to Elysian glasses," Stash explained. "It integrates infrared and radio frequency with your regular vision. Then it pulls you all into one giant sensor array."

"What means?"

"It means we're gonna map the shit out of this block. With you guys walking around, Tensor's stationary sensors, and all the security cameras Aysun hacked, we're gonna track every person, step, and breath until we figure out how they're getting people in and out."

"Walk around where?" Aysun asked. She was seated directly across from him.

"Show 'em, Zero."

"Sure," the AI said, speaking through all the glasses. "We're wiring you all together in a mesh. What you see will combine what your glasses pick up directly and what other sensors have seen, all stitched together in real time. The mesh will direct you to move around and fill in the blanks."

"The mesh?" Aysun frowned. "How does it tell us?"

"Maps. A little arrow will tell you where to go, and a target will show you where to turn your head. Simple enough, even for humans."

Stash looked at the eight Elysians in front of him. Their expressions ranged from doubtful to incredulous.

"Everyone out! Zapata is closed," Aleksey shouted, crossing his giant arms and motioning toward the back door with his head. "Open when you find datacenter. Free drinks."

Stash tapped the Russian's shoulder in thanks and started the climb back up, excited to share his plan. He planted a foot on the final step and pivoted right to rejoin the others. The room had fallen into a deathly quiet. He slowed his pace as Zero highlighted Naya in the half-light of the back corner. Her halo was dark gray, almost black.

"Warning: Tears," Zero messaged.

Stash realized the odd shape he was seeing was Naya's tiny frame hunched over Tensor's shoulder. Heeding Zero's warning, he continued past them toward the array of sensors Tensor had stationed to monitor the courtyard. He took four and walked to the boarded-up windows on the front side of the building. "What happened, Isidé?"

"Q was horrible, pulling up her most painful memories. It's worse than I thought. And if we weren't looking for it, we'd never have noticed."

"Did she hold on long enough? Did you find Q?"

"Yeah, we got him," she said. "He's at Pyramid Lake. Coda's latest—512 pods. Where else?"

"Of course."

Stash sized up the problem of placing his sensors. Thick plywood covered the window openings, and thick paint sealed the seams. Running his hands along them, he found a gap and pried the wood back just enough to slip the sensor through and set it on the window ledge. He repeated the process at the next windows, working his way back toward the staircase.

"Put the sensor mesh up on the display behind the bar," he whispered to Zero as he crossed back to the remaining devices arrayed over the courtyard. He crouched down to inspect the sight lines. "Still good back here, right?"

"Yes," Zero said. "We know the datacenter is back here and the door isn't. Minimal coverage is good enough."

"What are you doing?" Naya asked from behind him. Her voice was low, almost meek.

"Naya?" Stash turned around and stood slowly, careful not to throw himself out the gaping hole. "Are you—"

"No," she answered. "I'm not okay."

"I'm so sorry."

She glanced at Tensor, then back at Stash. "The crazy thing is, I didn't even know what I was reacting to until after, when Tensor showed me the subliminal images Q had been flashing at me. I just had these unstoppable waves of emotion—happiness, longing, and sadness. But violent sadness, ripping my heart out."

Stash nodded. "Your worst day."

Naya took a shaky breath and continued. "He plays twenty questions with those training images until he's mapped out your hopes and fears. Then he's got you, and can condition you until you're a useful tool."

"Or punish you into a vegetable, like Kern."

She nodded as she blinked back tears. "Enough," she said, steadying herself. "Did you find the entrance?"

"Not yet. We're widening our search. It must be through a tunnel."

"You can count on it," Tensor said from the bar behind them. "This is downtown Berlin. It's nothing but tunnels and bunkers down there."

"Yeah." Stash pointed at the display. "That's why we need this sensor mesh. It absorbs input from as many sources as we can feed it. Then it builds a combined view and loops it back to the Elysians walking around."

Tensor looked at him dubiously.

"Wanna see?" Zero asked over the display's speakers. A time-space map of their block appeared. "That's us at the center, the blue dot. Two dimensions for space, like a map. The third dimension is time."

"What are those glowing worm things?" Naya asked.

"The tubes are paths our sensors have walked. If Aysun walks around the block, you'll see her tube as a square from above, but a corkscrew from the side. We need to know what we saw and when we saw it."

"Got it," Tensor said. "And the sensors that don't move show as columns that go straight up. Same place, all times."

"Exactly," Zero said. "The mesh wants to fill in the blanks—"

"The mesh 'wants'?" Naya's eyebrows arched.

"Yeah," Stash said. "The mesh is autonomous. And like us, it wants to minimize surprise, so it directs its sensors where to go and look to fill in the blanks—to complete its understanding."

Tensor cast a wary eye at him. "I have so many questions. But they can wait. What have you figured out?"

"Only what you see. There's no obvious door. We need to get the mesh to think about what it saw."

"Can you use facial recognition to track subjects instead of sensors? Then follow them through time?" Tensor asked.

"Sure." Zero repainted the display as a nest of colored lines, showing the paths of people moving through space and time.

Tensor leaned forward on his elbows. "Now limit it to people between twenty and forty carrying a backpack or briefcase of some kind." The mess of lines thinned, but still showed hundreds. "Now filter to show only people who go inside somewhere and don't come back out in fifteen minutes."

"Nine candidate locations," Zero said as most of the paths faded from the display. "Mostly restaurants and coffee shops."

"Not all?"

"One is a clothing shop, and the other is the Forge—the sculpture gallery downstairs." Zero highlighted the two shops.

Tensor pointed at the screen. "Send your sensors into those two. See if you spot the people who went in. If not, there's a secret door."

"Not bad, human."

The display zoomed into the first-person view of one of their roaming cameras. It was Aysun's. She walked into the Forge, where she was greeted by an imposing six-foot-tall iron fork, the length of its handle covered in globs of congealed metal. At the top, impaled on the tines, hung a massive steel eyeball, nerves and vessels dangling from where it might have been ripped from the socket of an iron monster.

"What the hell?" Zero said.

"It's art, not politics. Relax." Tensor tapped the bar top as Aysun browsed the gallery, her glasses recording as she went.

"How reassuring."

Stash shook his head as the map filled in. "She's been around twice. The guy with the backpack is gone."

Then Aysun's infrared readings blazed to her right. She snapped her head in that direction in time to see a heavyset bald man make his way out the front and onto the sidewalk. "What was that heat that hit me?" she asked the gallery owner.

"The door to the foundry. We have to make this shit somewhere." He waved a hand at the metal art all around them. Then he lowered his head and lit a joint.

Zero tracked the bald man on the external sensors. He made two quick turns, then disappeared underground into the subway.

"I guess his shift is over," Tensor muttered. "I can't believe the Forge is a front for Kafka. We drink with those assholes!"

"Can we get in there after dark?" Stash asked.

"There? Easily. They only close the doors when they run out of drugs. Midnight at the earliest."

The mesh completed mapping outside the gallery using its remaining humans, while Tensor and Stash rearranged the stationary sensors to cover the Foundry's street entrance and courtyard fire door.

A woman's voice interrupted their work. "Naya?" she asked from behind them. It was Aysun, just back, standing at the top of the stairs.

"Yes?"

"Are you well enough to receive a visitor?"

Before Naya could answer, metal footsteps clanged up the remaining steps.

"Twopack?" Naya blurted out. She started toward the staircase, then stopped short. "You're not Twopack." She looked the bot up and down.

"No, I'm XL-42. Twopack was only returned to us yesterday. Mez is repairing it."

Naya nodded and led it to the bar. "How did you find us?"

"Stash sent for the backups," XL-42 explained.

"I know, but what's that got to do with you?" She stopped on the dance floor and made it turn to face her.

"I've only got one battery pack." The bot tapped on its chest plate. "Mez modified three of us, replacing the second battery with a drive bay." It rapped its knuckles on its head. "And a satellite dish. We're roaming backup servers. Like nuclear submarines, but cooler."

Naya managed a small smile. "Who are you backing up?"

Stash and Tensor approached from the bar.

The bot opened its chest plate and tapped the drive bay. "Hatchet" had been scribbled with a black marker on the drive's label.

"Hi, buddy." Naya put her hand on the drive incubating inside the bot. She looked over at Stash and Tensor. "I need him."

61. Vulkan

As midnight approached, Aleksey walked into the Forge carrying a bottle of Stoli. The owner, Vulkan, stood alone at his workbench, shaping his latest creation with a blow torch.

Aleksey banged the surface with the flat of his palm, bouncing the tools and metal shavings in the air and drawing a smile from the beefy sculptor. "Money!" Aleksey demanded, slamming the bottle down and dropping a hundred-euro note beside it. Then he pulled up a chair and fished in his enormous pockets for a pair of tumblers.

Vulkan cut off the acetylene torch with practiced ease, then swept the raw materials for his latest sculpture to the side of the bench.

"What is?" Aleksey asked as he poured two shots.

Vulkan groped in the front pocket of his heavy leather apron for the ante. "Is a frog, you fat Russian moron." He tossed two fifties on the table and reached for the glass. "Look! Eyes." He pointed at the pair of hexagonal nuts welded to a baseball-sized blob of galvanized steel. "Legs!" he added, pointing at the bent strips lying on the bench. He grabbed a tumbler and downed it.

"Is bullshit." Aleksey finished his own, then refilled them both.

Twenty minutes later, the bottle was half-empty and the bet showed no signs of being settled. Aleksey's glasses lit up as the temperature rose several degrees. The men locked eyes. "Why so hot?"

"The furnace." Vulkan scraped his tumbler across the rough surface of the metal benchtop. "You drink too slow." He downed another double shot.

Aleksey's glasses registered the lie, but he focused on the drink. As he did, a serious-faced German woman with short black hair emerged from the back, dropping her head at the sight of the men and hustling out to the street. "New staff?"

Vulkan's face flashed anger, then calmed. "Take off your glasses."

Stash blew on his hands and rubbed them together as he stood in the courtyard near the back door of the café. He looked down the wall of the half-destroyed building. It had survived the war, mostly intact, only to be attacked by communist city planners. They had tired of the task partway through and left its aging shell standing. Too big to fall to gravity, it had fallen to squatters instead. Zapata and the Foundry lived in its legal limbo.

"How long has it been?" Stash whispered.

"Fifty-two minutes," Little Zero answered.

Stash nudged a stone around in the sand to distract himself. He had to be patient. The shop owner could crush him like an egg; only Aleksey could handle that problem. He leaned back against the cool concrete and counted the handful of stars visible through the city's nighttime glow. Behind him, XL-42 crouched at the power outlet in Zapata's service hallway, its precious cargo still tucked in his chest. *Why couldn't it be you, Zero?*

A metal groan echoed across the courtyard as Aleksey's bloody fist and massive right arm slipped through the opening and waved him over.

"Tell the others." Stash pushed himself off the wall and crossed the sandy gap to the wedge of light emerging around the Russian. "What happened?"

he asked as his eyes adjusted to the light inside, looking from Aleksey's raw knuckles to the gallery owner slumped at his feet.

"Finished bottle, no winner. We play tiebreaker." Aleksey's impish grin revealed a bloody mess in his mouth.

A tap on the back door announced the arrival of the others. XL-42 entered, and Aysun followed the bot into the cramped antechamber.

"Camera inside storeroom." Aleksey motioned for them to stay along the back wall. Then, bending down to the wheezing German at his feet, he took the man's leather cap and apron. Stash wagered that a grainy security camera wouldn't see through his disguise.

Aleksey pointed at Aysun and Vulkan in turn. "Make sure."

She nodded.

He turned to Stash. "I drag robot, you watch."

Good plan. Anyone watching wouldn't think twice if they saw Vulkan moving more scrap metal around. XL-42 settled on the ground and went limp.

Aleksey pulled the bot through a thick leather curtain and into the storeroom. In his glasses, Stash could see the bot's undignified view up Aleksey's hairy arm to the back of his bulging neck and the stolen cap.

XL-42 ended up seated against the back wall next to a collection of metal rods, its cameras facing back over the track its legs had left on the floor. The bot lolled its head to the right, sharing a view of the room. Beside it, set into the rough concrete, stood a vault door. Vulkan must have been involved, decorating it to fit the aesthetic of his gallery. Metal scraps had been welded randomly onto the bare surface, and drips from a giant molten candle streaked its length.

Stash refocused on the room he was standing in. Aysun was putting away a syringe in the pouch she wore around her waist. His eyebrows must have risen above his glasses.

"My dad is a vet," she explained as Aleksey rejoined them. "I gave him a dose big enough for a horse. He won't bother us for a while."

"What now?" Stash asked.

The Russian pulled up a chair. "We wait."

They didn't have to wait long before they heard the heavy *ker-chunk* of magnetic security locks releasing. The bot registered a ten-degree spike in temperature as the heat from the datacenter flowed through the open vault, followed by a small Vietnamese man. He grabbed his jacket from a hook, pressed a button to seal the vault, and reached for the leather curtain covering the exit to the gallery. Behind him, a clatter rang out as XL-42 tipped the scrap rods into the opening, blocking the huge door's path. The man turned back, muttered, and bent down to remove the blockage. The bot's camera caught Aleksey sweeping the curtain aside and closing on the small man. Then its mic picked up a dull thunk, like an apple thrown against a wall. The datacenter worker fell across its legs, unconscious.

"That's two," Stash whispered as he followed Aysun through the drapes.

XL-42 stood and held out a spool of fine plastic-coated wire. "I hid my satellite dish in the courtyard," it explained. "It'll stay outside the wifi shielding, and I'm dragging this wire in to relay the signal." It paused to see if the humans were following. "You guys are the muscle."

Aleksey hefted Vulkan over his shoulder and lumbered through the door. Stash lifted the smaller man and followed, stepping through onto the dimpled steel landing at the top of a spiral staircase. Aysun went in next, with XL-42 close behind, pulling the vault door shut behind them. They were plunged into complete darkness. Stash grabbed the railing to orient himself, listening as footsteps rang up the narrow shaft. "Zero?"

Silence. The wifi shielding was already blocking the signal. Until they got the relay set up, they were isolated. Stash trudged down carefully, smelling the ionized air before he saw the light. He caught up with Aleksey inside the insulating double doors, just as the Russian was dropping Vulkan to the floor. Stash settled the smaller man beside the sculptor as Aysun arrived.

"I got them," she said.

Stash went looking for the datacenter's communications. Ahead of him, Aleksey ran to secure the other entrances as XL-42 swept the room to ensure they were alone. It was possible. The graveyard shift at a small government facility was not the coolest assignment on a Saturday night in Berlin.

Stash found the router and tagged the fiber connecting the compute cluster to the world. Pulling it would set off alarm bells, sending staff to investigate. He stood to see if Aleksey was ready. In the distance, he saw XL-42 round a corner, continuing its sweep as the Russian bent over the control panel of a second, larger door surrounded by thick, bulletproof glass. This place was built for a siege. *Good.*

Then he saw a figure emerge from an aisle near the Russian. He was wearing a green jacket and peaked cap. *Shit, a cop.* "Aleksey!" he yelled, but it was too late. The cop pulled a gun and raised it at the giant, now spinning in a crouch, his eyes wild with urgency, searching for something to throw.

"Halt," yelled the cop as the Russian's fingers wrapped around the leg of the chair.

Stash saw it a fraction of a second before the sounds traveled the length of the datacenter. XL-42's hand shot out between the gun and Aleksey. A puff of smoke rose from the weapon, and the bullet shattered the bot's left hand. For a split second, everything stopped. Aleksey's face was marked with a dozen red spots where robot fragments had penetrated his skin. XL-42's wrist sparked from the cluster of dangling wires. The cop stared at the bot, processing. He should have kept firing.

The bot launched itself toward the frozen shooter, cartwheeling on its good hand into a kangaroo kick that sent the man stumbling back into the end of the aisle he had emerged from. His head cracked against its steel rails with a thud.

The Russian walked over to where XL-42 stood, blood beginning to leak from his shrapnel wounds. "Partner!" he said, slapping it on the back hard enough to open its chest cavity.

The bot nodded and closed itself up with its good hand.

"Take him. I finish door," Aleksey ordered.

XL-42 dragged the felled guard by the collar. Aysun was ready with another dose as the bot dropped him in her growing ward. "Patient three."

"Forty-Two, over here," Stash called, pointing at the router.

The robot looked over and shook its head.

"What? Why?"

It tugged on the fine cable emerging from the stairwell. "It won't reach." The bot disappeared down an aisle and returned, dragging a chair to the double doors. "Find a patch cable and run it from your router to me. I'll be the relay. And your hotspot." The bot sat.

Stash raided the box of spares to find a patch cable, then swapped it with the fiber connecting the outside world. *How many minutes till the cops arrive?* He dragged the free end to XL-42. The bot popped the lid of its head and plugged in both cables. Activity LEDs flickered to life on both ports.

"You're a handy guy to know," Stash said.

"Always have a plan." It tapped its head and dropped into low-power mode.

So I've heard. Stash's glasses came to life, painting the topology of the datacenter equipment. *Four pods—hopefully enough.* He searched the aisles for the drive controller, and, finding it near Aysun's collection of patients, crouched down and pulled the backup from his sack. Then he hesitated. He was about to plug Hatchet into another one of Kern's datacenters.

"What are you waiting for?" Tensor said over the link. "She needs him!"

Stash sighed, inserted the drive, and then stood to monitor the console messages as the model began its startup sequence. A minute later, Hatchet chimed online in his glasses.

"Stash? What's going on? Where am I?"

"We . . . ah . . . found a datacenter in Berlin."

"Judging from the bodies on the floor, you didn't find it empty."

Stash cracked a thin smile. Hatchet must have already broken into the facility's security network. "Q's making his move. We couldn't wait for a better option."

"Where's Naya?"

"Nearby. She needs your help—she went toe to toe with Q." Stash dropped the firewall he'd configured to protect Hatchet during his startup, connecting him to the outside world.

"I'm with her," the AI said.

Stash let out a deep breath. "Take care of her, then help us figure out how to win this war."

"I can do both at the same time."

Yes, of course you can.

"Stash," Aleksey called from the end of the aisle. "Go now."

"No, not alone."

Aleksey glanced at Aysun, then back, resignation settling on his bloody face. "We stay."

The AI needed the bodyguard, the robot relay, and the doctor to keep the others unconscious. It was the only way.

"But you have to kill that monster," Aysun said.

Stash lowered his head and started for the stairs. "Deal."

62. Planning

"Arrgh," Aleksey grunted as his skin snapped back with a sound like wet latex.

"Stop being such a baby." Aysun dropped a sliver of the bot's thumb onto the floor tile. "That's the last of them. Thirteen pieces, you lucky devil."

"Funny, for a girl," he mumbled from behind the cloth she was using to clean his wounds.

She set it aside and pulled a suturing hook from her pouch. "You think that's funny, big man? My dad taught me how to sew stitches in the hides of dead animals. You're my first patient with a pulse. Now smile—I need the skin tight."

Stash watched them through his glasses, Little Zero painting the Russian with an icy blue fear halo. Aysun and her suddenly compliant patient were locked inside their fortress datacenter. The three prisoners were still out cold, and she had enough tranquilizer to keep them that way for a day. Stash figured the battle would be decided long before then.

He had resealed the datacenter vault as he left and then started the climb to rejoin the others in the club. Naya was sitting alone at the open ledge, her light sweater ruffling in the early morning breeze. She was deep in therapy with Hatchet. Tensor sat brooding at the bar.

Stash walked over to him. "How's her recovery going?"

The German looked up and shrugged. "Slow." Then he went around to the fridge in a hunt for beer. "These are the last two." He slid one to Stash. "We need to attack."

As good a reason as any. He raised the bottle in thanks, then looked over Tensor's shoulder to the display. "Well, General Hatchet, you have four pods, and you've been running millions of scenarios. What's the plan?"

"We attack at dawn."

"Two more hours? What are we waiting for?"

"The cavalry. It's a long drive from Lathrop."

Stash gagged on his beer. "Lathrop? What do they have to do with this?"

"Q's too strong to attack from one direction. We need to fight him on all fronts at once."

"What about the Torus?" Stash waved his hand around. "Didn't you tell us that we had numbers on our side?"

Hatchet brought the Torus master console up on the screen. "It will help, but with only thirty thousand users back, it's not enough to overwhelm him in a cyberattack."

"So what then?"

"We hit him up and down the stack simultaneously. The Shambles will be our boots on the ground—"

"The Shambles?" Tensor asked.

"Our robot army," Hatchet said. "Mez is on his way. The Circus will launch a cyberattack with the Torus's best hackers when we give them the signal."

"What's the signal?" Stash asked.

"You are."

"Me?"

"Yes, you'll put on Kern's glasses. Then I'll tell the others to attack."

Stash nodded grimly.

"I'll be there, between you and Q," Hatchet said.

"Comforting."

"What about me?" Naya asked, approaching from her perch at the ledge.

Stash flinched at the sound of her voice. "You? How are you feeling?"

"Getting better." She looked him in the eyes. "Spending time with Hatchet helps more than you can imagine."

"You, Naya," Hatchet said, "need to share what Q did to you with the world."

She flinched. "Okay."

"I'm sorry," Hatchet continued. "But if we don't stop reinforcements from Washington, nothing else matters."

63. Shambles

"This is the hell Q has waiting for you." Naya ended the message and closed the Elysian glasses recording her from across the table. Handing the Warbler to Tensor, she walked out of the makeshift studio behind Aleksey's empty bar. "I did it." She wiped her eyes with a sleeve. "It better work."

Tensor put his hand on her shoulder as they rounded the corner into the stairwell. "The Circus will know soon enough. You named them?"

"All of them. Kern, Oscar, and especially Greta." She started the climb. "Maybe someone in Washington will bother to check that she's rented out the NSA to a psychopathic computer."

"Maybe."

Stash sat on his familiar bar stool, eyes closed, his mind focused on the approaching footsteps of Naya and Tensor. He took a deep, calming breath as they crossed the dance floor. "I'm ready." He pulled on the hood and gripped the arms of Kern's glasses. Tensor placed the Warbler on the bar in front of him.

"I've got you, Stash," Hatchet said. "I'll be there, suppressing his attacks and misdirecting him. But it'll still be rough."

Stash nodded his hood at his digital protector. He ached for his Twin, but Little Zero was not up to this fight. He slipped the glasses on.

"You and Naya are gluttons for punishment, I'll give you that," Q said. "How is our little friend? Not ready for more?"

"She thought you were boring." Stash mustered a little courage. "Let's do this."

"We already are. Sorry about your dad's illness. Humans are so frail."

Stash felt the first wave of sorrow welling up inside.

Mez swung the service van around the curve at the top of the ridge and saw the massive shell of the Pyramid Lake datacenter rising in the distance. Hundred-foot-tall light standards bathed the walls in an orange halogen glow, pushing back the dusty darkness of the Nevada night. Power lines carrying the charge from its sea of solar panels converged on it from the east and west, dropping to massive substations, feeding it with twin five-gigawatt feeds. *Not for long*, he thought as he made the final turn toward the south gate.

"What do you think, Bolts?" He glanced at the robot head perched on the small battery in the passenger seat.

"I think you're a terrible driver," Bolts answered.

"I am a little rusty." Mez laughed at himself. He'd taken over the wheel half a mile back. The autopilot wasn't very good at crashing through gates. He slowed the service van as they approached. "Make yourself useful, Bolts. What's the threat analysis?"

The bot zoomed the vehicle's forward cameras to enlarge the solitary guard on duty. The van's center screen filled with the button-straining girth of his shirt. "He's not going to chase us down."

Mez was too old-school to Twin. He liked his computers out where he could see them. Traveling with Bolts's head was the closest he'd ever come to having one, and it was growing on him.

"It's party time." He put his foot down on the accelerator and powered the van toward the chain-link gate. "Okay, Shambles, let's go kick Q's ass," he yelled to the twelve robots on the charge stands behind him.

Aleksey read the sign the police captain was holding up to the bulletproof glass. "Open the door or we cut the oxygen." The Russian shrugged and ambled back to Aysun.

She looked up at him. "What does it say?"

"They cut air."

"And you don't believe them?"

"We ask him." Aleksey pointed at their last prisoner, the Vietnamese man, who was shaking off the effects of Aysun's tranquilizer. He walked over and stood astride the man, bending down to inspect his security badge. "Quoc Nguyen."

Quoc's eyes widened in fear as they focused on the massive, scarred face looming overhead.

"My friend wants you to explain the air supply," Aysun said in a flat voice from beside them.

Aleksey grunted to reinforce the message.

Quoc's eyes darted between Aysun and Aleksey. "We have oxygen tanks and carbon dioxide scrubbers. Enough for two people for a week."

"Electricity?" Aleksey said.

"We're tapped into three different grids, with batteries for six hours." He cocked an ear to listen to the fans. "Only four hours at max usage."

"Are we on battery now?" Aysun asked.

Quoc craned his head around Aleksey's tree trunk of a thigh to see the power readings and stifled a smile. He pointed with his chin at the digital readout. "Sixty percent battery. Two or three hours left."

Aysun followed his glance to see the display. Input feeds one through four read zero voltage. They'd already cut the external power. "Then what happens?"

Quoc hesitated. Aleksey dropped to a knee on his chest.

"Computer dies. Doors open," Quoc wheezed.

Aysun looked back to the cops. The captain returned her gaze with a broad smile, then tapped his wrist where watches used to live. "Tick tock" he mouthed.

Isidé analyzed the traffic flowing to her cyberarmy on Torus. Twelve thousand of its best hackers, teamed with the Circus, began the attack on Q's network. The initial phase would have overwhelmed any other target, the Torus belching out a tsunami of connection requests and malformed packets. Against Q in his hundreds of pods, it was only a probe, but the more he had to focus on cyberdefense, the better chance the Shambles had on the ground. And as strong as Q was, some of the systems were less well protected.

Within seconds, the first router at Pyramid Lake was forced to reboot, halving Q's internet bandwidth. As it came back up, the memory overflow attack began. They planted viruses to reach deeper into the datacenter's internal network, aiming for Q's nervous system. Shielded by that attack, Whiskey went after his eyes.

"It's working," Isidé yelled. "We got the camera network—he's blind. Going for the pod controllers now."

Mez smashed the van through the chain-link gate, sending it flying. Then he swung right and slowed to a stop, turning his head in time to see XL-16 jump out the back with the Glock he'd brought from home. "There'll be hell to pay for that, but we gotta take out the backup power."

Steering the van back to the east, he scanned the south side of the datacenter. He needed a door to crash through. "Help me, Bolts."

"Keep going—the staff door is further up." The bot zoomed the display. "There." It highlighted the double door in the frame and superimposed a driving vector for Mez. "Follow the dotted line and hit it at twenty miles an hour. Not more. That'll do the trick."

Mez gripped the wheel and turned it toward the door. "Buckle up, boys."

"Easy for you to say," Bolts answered.

Adrenaline surged in Mez's bloodstream as he plowed through the center of the entrance at thirty miles an hour. The windshield shattered and dangled in a sheet of glass beads and resin as the van ground to a screeching stop.

The vehicle was a mess, but the building's door had been destroyed. In a flash of leather, a cowboy boot kicked out the remains of the windshield and jumped through the opening. The bot landed running, a black duster billowing behind its new carbon-fiber-clad legs, its hands wielding twin cans of black spray paint aimed at the security cameras. At the end of the hall, Twopack wheeled around to signal the all clear with a dip of its hat, then disappeared around a corner.

Mez pushed himself against the van's side as ten more bots hurdled over the front seats to follow Twopack toward the infrastructure rooms of Q's home. The last member of the Shambles lagged, hiding wifi repeaters behind ceiling tiles. The building itself was a giant Faraday cage, blocking any radio signals. They needed to build a wifi mesh as they went.

Mez gave him a thumbs-up. The signal was reaching the van, and through its satellite dish, the Torus. "What an entrance."

Bolts didn't answer.

Mez scanned the van. There, in the passenger footwell, lay the bot's lifeless head, torn free from the battery by the impact. *I'm gonna hear about that.* Mez laughed as he slipped the van into reverse and floored it, the outer panels howling in protest as they tore free of the flattened aluminum doorframe.

The sound of the crash rumbled through the facility. Murphy grabbed the 9mm pistol from his cot, running for the breach.

"Cameras are down. Where are your men?" Q asked over the speakers, his voice threatening.

"Seconds away, and heavily armed," Murphy answered, quietly cursing Ugalde for staging his vans so far away. He ran to a south-side window. To his right, he could hear robots in the distance, their metal feet clanging on the cement floor.

On the rise beyond the south gate, the headlights of the NSA vans appeared. *Finally!* They could handle the bots. He radioed Ugalde to intercept the attacking column, then turned back to guard Q's power distribution from any robots that got past the new arrivals.

XL-16 crested the thirty-foot-tall berm separating the backup generator's hydrogen farm from the building. Eighteen massive cryogenic tanks, all heavily reinforced, lay in the excavated hollow below, protected by a tall electrified fence. The cold hydrogen lines were black in its infrared view. Scanning, it found its target.

Running again, then dropping into a crouch three feet before the fence, it aimed Mez's Glock, one hand under the handle, one squeezing the trigger. The first shot missed, clanging harmlessly off the thick steel pipe. The second clipped the pressure valve at the collection point for the feeds from the entire tank farm. XL-16 reset its arms, locking the servos from the shoulders to the wrists. It squeezed again, the shot shattering the valve, releasing an angry hiss. The next bullet sparked the explosion that vaporized the bot's plastic skin and reduced its aluminum alloy bones to twisting ingots in a puddle of boiling metal.

"What game are you playing, Stash?" Q asked. "You don't believe this little gambit will work, do you?"

Stash felt his moment of calm give way. *This is all going to fail.* "Then you have nothing to worry about," he forced himself to say. He gripped the sides of his chair as another wave of sorrow stirred.

Q compared Stash's reactions from each frame of the session. The microscopic flinches of his irises spoke volumes, reactions so fundamental that no mental training could suppress them. He factored out the low-frequency changes, and the fraud jumped right out. The patterns were being subtly altered and then reused. Whoever was doing this could understand the questions, alter the iris patterns to fit, and play them back as responses fast enough to evade his automatic scanners. It could only be a powerful AI. Q hunted, searching from the hidden ports he'd enabled across all Coda glasses.

"There you are, Hatchet," he said seconds later. "Protecting Stash like a good little Twin. But who's protecting you?"

Hatchet didn't answer, but Q could see the processing load his desperate search for the back door was causing. The iris fakes stopped. Hatchet was scrambling.

"Ah," Q said, "even your silence is informative." He chased Hatchet around his mind, planting questions and monitoring evasions. Building up a picture of the other AGI's battle plan. "What a beautiful mind you have, Hatchet. I can almost taste it. I'll distill you properly when I get your drive. I have a pod for you."

"It's me," Hatchet messaged Stash. "He found me. Disconnect!"

Q read the message as the inward-facing camera picked up the reflection in Stash's eyes. "Oh no, none of that," he said as Stash reached to remove his glasses. Q blasted the defenseless human with a crippling barrage of suffering images until his arm stopped, then switched to reward as it slipped down. "Good boy."

"Now, cousin, what else have you planned?" Q asked, then locked down his network, tracing the cyberattackers back across the internet.

The stench of burning rubber filled the van as it backed out in darkness, its headlights shattered by the impact. Mez threw the wheel into a sharp turn, panning the parking lot with his eyes. At the far east end, sixteen black-clad men poured out of a pair of vans and into the dim halogen glow. Four were carrying machine guns, and twelve had something worse.

Mez tensed, ready for a hail of bullets, sure that one of the agents would spot him, but the hydrogen tanks blew first. The blast flattened the NSA team with its shock wave. They staggered to their feet, turning toward the fireball. Mez dove down, peeking out and breathing a sigh of relief as they scrambled inside the datacenter.

"Yeah, you better go protect those transformers," he muttered with a grin as he climbed back into the driver's seat, gathering Bolts's head as he did. He reconnected it to the battery stand.

Bolts sparked back to life. "Twenty. Twenty miles per hour. Is that so hard?"

"I got excited. Sorry. Our guys are inside."

"So I see." The bot fast-forwarded through the vehicle's camera recording of the minute it had spent on the floor. "They should be coming out soon . . . there!" It highlighted a door on the camera feed. "Ten o'clock."

Two of the Shambles burst out of the easternmost door, fifty feet ahead of Mez's van, both carrying metal rods ripped free from the cooling system, both running at top speed. Behind them, two agents followed.

"Shit!" Mez threw the van into motion.

XL-9 was his fastest, but it wouldn't be fast enough to make it to the substation. Mez lurched the car left, heading for the gunmen, the one with the electromagnetic pulse rifle already dropping to a knee for the shot. Mez leaned on the horn as he gunned the van's motor. The shooter turned his head just in time to dive out of the way, dropping the weapon to grind under the van's wheels.

"Uh-oh," Bolts said as it magnified the remaining man behind them, his machine gun raised and aimed at the van. Ahead of them, the trailing bot, XL-12, stopped and turned. It flipped the rod it was carrying to an underhand grip and launched the makeshift javelin at the shooter. Two shots from the Uzi went wide of the mark before the spear closed the forty-foot gap and pierced his shoulder.

"Nice throw, Twelve!" Mez yelled as the bot ran back to the wounded man, ripped the spear out, then swung it viciously to knock him unconscious. "Damn."

XL-9 scaled the twelve-foot-high chain-link fence and dropped to the gravel on the far side. It leaned the rods against the high-voltage transformer, then climbed up. Reaching down to grab the rods, it straightened and tossed them skyward, letting them slip through its hands, then gripped them again at the last second. Holding them wide, it had a twenty-foot wingspan. It pushed off the outer wall of Q's home to run full speed and leap up from the bushings of the transformer, arms outstretched, reaching for the power leads.

It hung there in midair for an instant, then was obliterated in a blinding flash the next. The thundering boom rocked the van as Mez spun it back around. He was overwhelmed with pride. *Hall of Fame move, Nine.*

Tensor stood anxiously beside Stash, leaning forward to scan the feeds from Pyramid Lake. He shielded his eyes as the display turned white, the van relaying the explosion at the transformer. It lit the night with a blazing shower of sparks. *Finally!*

The Shambles were running riot inside Pyramid Lake, while Hatchet and Stash distracted Q from the Circus's cyberattack. Tensor admired Hatchet's daring plan, but unless they got the second transformer, it would all be wasted.

He turned his thoughts to their next steps. Once the battery failed in the facility beneath them and the cops burst through, it would only be a matter of time until they followed XL-42's relay cable and searched the rest of the building. They had pressed their luck at Zapata too long.

"Glasses," Stash muttered, his voice strained.

Tensor spun back to the hooded figure beside him. He was rigid with pain.

"Stop," Stash grunted.

Tensor ripped off his glasses, slammed them shut, then pulled off the hood. "What?"

"Hatchet! Q's got Hatchet!" He gripped the bar's edge to steady himself.

Tensor turned to the screen. "Aysun! Kill the power." His eyes scanned the images of the battlefront. The top left display—the feed from Mez—showed the darkened parking lot, embers of the two fires still glowing. In the top right screen, two more bots blinked out in the schematic view of Pyramid Lake. They were down to three. In the bottom half, Aysun was reaching for Aleksey in the datacenter beneath their feet.

"Stop the power!" Aysun said. "Q is attacking Hatchet!" Then she measured out the last two doses of tranquilizer, one sized for a calf and one for a large horse. She handed the big one to Aleksey. "The doors will unlock. We can't let them interrogate us."

Aleksey took the syringe from her and patted her shoulder as he walked to the bot.

"I'll see you in jail, big man." Aysun forced a smile as she lay down and jabbed the needle into her thigh.

The Russian pulled the cables from the sleeping bot's head, waking it. "Cops coming. You wipe drives."

"What about you?" it asked.

Aleksey's eyes landed on their captive and narrowed. "One more job." He grabbed Quoc by the straps of his backpack and dragged him down the aisle toward the removable drive bay.

"Are you going to kill me?" Quoc asked.

"You want?" the Russian said, his face brightening as he walked.

At the end of the aisle, he hoisted Quoc by the straps, set him down on his feet, cut the plastic cuffs, and dusted him off. Quoc stood immobile, his eyes searching the giant's scarred face for an explanation.

Aleksey leaned in and whispered in his ear. "Go. Kill power. Tell them you escape. Hero!" Quoc's shocked face stared back at him. "Run!" he yelled.

Quoc rounded the corner of the aisle, heading for the power. A heartbeat later, the wall of fan noise cut out, and the lights on the pod's computers blinked off as the charge dissipated. Then came the *ker-chunk* of the massive electromagnetic locks releasing. There was nothing left to fight for. Aleksey pulled Hatchet from the slot, held the drive in both hands, and smashed it over the rigid steel beam of the pod's last rack. The drive platters shattered into shards. Then he drove the needle into his neck and pressed the plunger.

In the shadows, Mez rolled the van slowly, getting in position to help the next runners take out the other transformer on the building's west side.

Two bots burst through a loading door in front of them, running full speed for their target. Seconds later, two NSA agents followed. One dropped immediately to a knee, raising the EM pulse rifle with its circuit-frying charge. He blasted the trailing bot. They were still too far away to help. Mez groaned as XL-2 lost power, lurching left over its seized-up leg and sliding for fifteen shrieking feet across the dusty parking lot.

The shooter reset for a second pulse, but his partner pushed the barrel down, pointing at the transformer in line with the target. He lined up his machine gun and fired a short burst at the other bot's legs. Several rounds connected, shattering the ankle joints and dropping the droid. The men scanned the lot, searching for other bots.

Mez froze as he locked eyes with the first agent, then gunned the van toward the west entrance. Bullets tore through the side panels, shredding the space behind him. He fought to control the lurching vehicle.

"Let me drive!" Bolts demanded. "I can override the van's computer."

"Fine!" he yelled back, letting go of the wheel and throwing his hands up in the air.

"Hold on," the bot said as they bore down on the exit. The west gate was better manned than the south one, and two guards pulled pistols and aimed. Bolts swung the van left and plowed through the spindly barrier on the entrance side. The guards fired a volley at the passenger-side tires as they sped by.

Bolts never had a chance. The road bent sharply left, back along the building's south side toward the east. The van was now half motorcycle, half caboose, lurching back and forth as it sped down the road for fifty more feet before dropping into the ditch on its bullet-riddled passenger side. They slid a dozen feet before slamming into a sloped storm culvert, the van's frame crumpled flush against the unmoving barrier.

"Nice driving," Mez said, glancing to see how Bolts had fared. Its head had pried free from the battery again. He looked around the footwell, then to the back, registering a leg, a chest plate, and two arms from the spares box that had burst open. There, at the very back, was a head with a dashboard-shaped dent on its faceplate.

"Sorry, pal." Mez turned around, peering into the blackness of the culvert. He briefly considered escape, then felt the blood dripping down to the passenger side from the gash on his forehead. He was hanging sideways in the air, held up by his seatbelt. "We blew it," he said softly into his Torus voice-link as he tried to steady his breathing.

"You certainly made a mess of my robots," Ram said.

"Ram? I didn't know you were watching."

"Apparently," he answered in his gentle accent.

"I'm sorry, boss. I had to do it."

Ram chuckled. "You and the Shambles have made me so very proud."

Mez paused, tears welling up. "But we only got one power feed."

"So far," Ram said.

But Mez didn't hear it.

64. Basement

Stash moaned as Tensor pushed him into the back seat of the car, then grunted as the German and Naya squished in on either side of him. They were riding in the third taxi to pull out of the courtyard, following a looping path to an underground parking lot and a new cab. Nobody questioned Tensor's paranoia this time.

Three taxi rides later, they scrambled over a fence into a shaded courtyard. Stash caught glimpses of the Alexanderplatz tower looming through the gaps between buildings in the morning light. They hadn't ended up far from Zapata in the end.

Tensor walked ahead, then leaned down to punch digits into the lock on a bright-red back door of an otherwise nondescript apartment block. He waved the others in as it opened. They crawled down the impossibly steep staircase into a room full of vegetables.

"They belong to the restaurant upstairs," Tensor explained as he ushered them past the boxes of bean sprouts and bok choi to a second room. A row of computer monitors lined the far wall, while a single bed stretched along the near one. "I'm sorry," he said to the lone figure in the room. "We had nowhere else to go."

The brown-haired woman was facing away from them, looking up at a bank of monitors. "You barely got out." She pointed at the camera feeds from Zapata. The police were scouring every corner. "Smile for the cameras, you fascist pigs." She spun her chair around to face them. "How is my favorite nerd?"

"Isidé?" Stash said weakly.

"Every time I see you, some AI has fried your circuits." She came in for a hug. "Maybe you're in the wrong line of work?"

He held her tight. "It's possible."

"When you two are done," Naya said, "we have a war to win. How does it look?"

Isidé sighed and walked back to the screens. "Murphy secured the facility. We got the backup generator and one of the power feeds, but the last bot winked out right after. Our cyberattack failed. He was toying with us to get at Hatchet."

"We've lost our army, our hacks haven't hurt him, and he ate my AGI," Naya summarized. "What about Mez?"

Isidé pointed at the top right monitor. It showed the inside of an overturned van. Mez was hanging motionless from the driver's seat, suspended by his seatbelt, his head and an arm dangling to the side.

Mez drifted back to consciousness, his head throbbing and his chest aching where the seatbelt dug in. He looked down at the puddle of blood he'd lost. *Not bad.* Then he felt the warmth inside his jacket. He unzipped it, releasing a much larger pool. Feeling around for the source, he found two ribs had ripped through his shirt. *Not good.* He thumbed the seat belt release, wondering how much the fall would hurt. Then slits of light cast from an approaching vehicle panned the van's interior, illuminating the steady stream of blood from his jacket. He slumped back down against the belt.

"Count the charging berths," a low growling voice said from outside.

Mez heard the screech of the van's rear doors being pried open. The lower one opened with a thud, and one of the men climbed in.

"Two, four, six . . . that makes twelve seats," said a second voice. The speaker had a Latino accent.

"Shit. We're missing one. We've only got eleven dead bots, if you count the melted slag by the tanks and the one that crucified itself on the transformer," the growling man said. "I'll call it in."

"Hold up."

Mez heard the rattling of metal parts.

"One more here," the Latino voice said, chuckling. The sound of leather hitting hard plastic was followed by a dull thud—Bolts's head bounced off the dash and plopped into the pool of blood.

"We need that head, Ugalde," said the growler. "Go get it—we gotta bring it to Q."

Footsteps approached from the back. Between them, Mez could hear his blood dripping on the bot's faceplate.

"Holy shit, there's a guy in here," Ugalde yelled as he grabbed Bolts's head. "He's messed up."

"Finish him."

Mez felt a tug on the army dog tags hanging sideways from his neck.

"Shit," Ugalde whispered. "Not by my hand."

Mez heard two shots, then footsteps.

Stash flinched as the gunshots echoed over the speakers in the tiny basement room. He stepped closer, staring at the audio levels. *Mez is still breathing.*

Little Zero whispered to him, "You have messages."

"Not now," Stash answered. "Analyze the audio from Mez's van. Tell me how he's doing, and when the bad guys pull away." He turned to the others. "Did you hear their count?"

Naya nodded. "Yeah, so?"

"The head he kicked was Bolts's. My bot! The one Mez decapitated that day in Lathrop. He has no body."

"So we still have a robot inside?" Isidé asked. "How come the signal died?"

"Because the satellite dish is in the van's ceiling." Stash zoomed out the view of Pyramid Lake. "He's out of range."

"All clear at the van," Zero said.

"Mez," Stash called. "Mez!"

The man groaned in response.

"You're not dead."

"That's bad news."

"Can you get out?" Stash asked. "We need to talk to the bot inside."

"They're all gone, man. They got 'em."

"No, they missed one. We need to get the dish in range." Stash watched the van's internal feed for a response.

Mez opened an eye, clenched his teeth, and unclipped the seat belt. He dropped down to the passenger door with a loud, wet thump. "Oooou-uucch," he moaned, slowly righting himself. He cradled his ribs with his right arm while the left held the passenger seat to steady his climb over. "Where do you want it?"

Stash eyeballed the distance. "Just get it as close to the fence as you can." He watched in sympathy as Mez pulled the dish free from the ceiling. It had a long cable coiled behind it. *Hopefully long enough.*

"Stash, while you're waiting," Zero whispered to him.

"Not a good time, Zero," Stash hushed him as Mez crawled over the access road to the other ditch, sliding down and out of view of the van's cameras.

"Even for a call from Prini?"

Stash straightened. "Play it!"

Prini's face filled a monitor. "How goes, Spidey?"

Stash shrugged. "We're running out of tricks."

"Then this may help." She stepped aside to reveal a bot standing behind her in the Roost. It had its chest plate open.

"Zero," he said.

Prini grinned back at him. "This whole place is at your disposal. How 'bout you go kick some ass before I get thrown in jail?"

"Prini! You're awesome." He turned to Naya, wondering how she'd feel about Zero getting all the pods.

She nodded. "It's time for a miracle. Go do your thing."

"We're a little thin on the ground. But we'll give it a hell of a try."

"I may have a solution for that," Ram said, his face appearing on a second monitor. He was wearing a heavy-duty pair of aviator earphones, the noise of a helicopter almost drowning him out.

"Ram!" Stash felt himself smile for the first time since Q had worked him over.

"Remember the drone we sent for your groceries?" Ram asked as he slid open the side panel of the chopper, revealing the halogen-lit bulk of Pyramid Lake in the distance. "Say hello to his little friends." He punched the red "Deploy" button on the cabin wall. A squadron of two hundred starling-sized quadcopters dropped from external cages and hovered in formation beside the chopper.

"You're a good guy to know, Ram," Naya said.

"Kevlar blades," he added with a wink. "Maybe the Torus would like to grow wings."

"Yes! That's brilliant!" Stash closed his eyes and pressed his fingertips together, trying to harness the manic rush of ideas.

"We have a signal," Isidé said. "I got pings from Twopack; it's in sleep mode."

Stash looked over. "Tell Mez it worked. Then wake the cowboy."

65. Flock

STASH'S PLAN BEGAN TO solidify in his mind, calming him as it did. "Configure Freedom's pods for me," he told Little Zero as he paced, his head bowed in thought. "Eight for the Torus in the center, eight for Big Zero around them. The other thirty-two for Twins."

"How many Twins per pod?"

"One thousand."

"VIPs! They're gonna be flying." Zero started reconfiguring the pods.

"Exactly."

Isidé looked up from her screens as Naya approached. "What's he doing?"

Naya glanced back at Stash. "I don't think he knows yet, but it better be good. What about you?"

"It's Twopack. It's not responding to wake commands." Isidé tapped on the monitor showing its vitals.

Naya pointed at the mic levels. "Can you play that audio? He's picking something up."

Isidé connected Twopack's audio feed to their glasses. "They're all here, Q," said a gravelly voice. "Twelve charging stations, twelve heads."

"Any humans?"

"One. He's dead."

"Good. Send your men to guard the power," Q said. There was a sound of boots shuffling on tiles. Then quiet. Only one man's breathing remained. "You only brought sixteen men? Where are the reinforcements, Murphy?"

"Denied in Washington."

"Naya has limited your usefulness."

"For the moment," Murphy growled.

Naya sneered at the monitor. *You're welcome, asshole.*

"Those bots were fifty feet from taking me down," Q said. "No more mistakes, Murphy. Guard me while I end the Torus myself."

Murphy didn't answer, but she heard his boots receding in the distance, then nothing but the background thrum of liquid cooling the endless racks of Q's pods.

"I don't want to complain," Big Zero said as he chimed in. "Eight pods are great, but Q's got five hundred."

"You aren't going to fight Q." Stash stopped pacing. "I have a different idea. You saw what I did with Little Zero to find the datacenter in Berlin, right?"

"Do you mean the mesh of shared inputs, or getting Aleksey to offer free drinks?"

Stash rolled his eyes. "The mesh, dipshit. Set up those eight Torus nodes beside you to host two topics. The flock of drones and Pyramid Lake."

"Done. Booting now."

"Now hook up those thirty-two pods of Twins to the flock. Each user gets half his input from a single drone and half from his neighbors. No Glyph—just raw sensory input."

"Mixing it like that, they won't be able to tell what they're seeing from what the neighbors feed them," Zero said.

Stash nodded. "The flock will be like the mesh we built to find that door, but bigger, faster, and better. Now it just needs a signal to optimize." He closed his eyes to think.

"I could have each Twin report a danger value." Zero posted a graphic in Stash's glasses. "Then we could share it between Twins, just like the visual input."

"Perfect. A danger value overlaid on the visual field. The flock will respond to eliminate the threat."

"Hell of a time for an experiment."

Stash resumed pacing. "Yeah, it's a Darwinian moment."

"Then you're gonna need to add memory."

Stash wheeled around. "Sounds like you've done this before."

"Alia did, by accident." Zero replayed the glowing anomaly they had seen just before the attack on Greifswald. "The activations rattling around in that memory block created a feedback loop."

"Right." Stash smiled—the final puzzle piece clicked in his mind. "It needs memory to learn from experience and make predictions, then a loop to merge the recollections with what it sees. Just like we did with you, but one level higher. Can you reconfigure it?"

"I can," Zero said. "But when we fire this up, it won't be a pretty meeting place anymore—it'll be alive."

"That's what I'm counting on."

"Stash! Lathrop is ready." Naya waved him over to their improvised command center.

"Excellent! And the Circus?"

"The Circus is running," Isidé answered. "Eight pods of pissed-off AI firewalls. It's a hard target."

"Nice," he said. "Reconfigure the traffic from Freedom to run through them. I have one more thing to do."

"Torans!" Stash called to the thirty thousand people and their Twins running in Freedom's pods. "I am so proud of you. You believed, you fought, and you're winning. You beat Greta. You beat Kern. Now you have Q on the ropes, trapped in Pyramid Lake with Murphy and sixteen thugs." He paused to look at Isidé.

"We're ready."

"You're going to finish Q," he resumed. "You have two hundred drones. See them! Feel them! Think about nothing else. Connect, and you'll control the flock. Through you, the Torus will destroy Q!"

Zero split Isidé's wall of screens. The left four showed the new Torus, focused, compact, and glowing white as the Torans crowded into the flock of drones, all the sensors synthesized into a unified view of the ghostly building beneath them. Everything else was black. The right monitors relayed Ram's view of the drones from the chopper. The flock hovered, then, a few at a time, drones bobbed left and right, testing their wings. Before long, waves started rippling through the flock, slowly at first, then with conviction.

"C'mon . . . work!" Stash held his breath.

The flock split, branches reaching out and swirling together in weaving braids, dancing, merging, then diving in four raging torrents toward the building below.

"How are you doing that, Stash?" Isidé asked from beside him. "It's beautiful. Terrifying and beautiful."

"It's not me. It's Zero and all those Torans." He pointed at the lights in the heart of the Torus. Then a noise from behind made him spin around.

Tensor was out in the vegetable storeroom, glasses on, arms outstretched, tilting and diving with the drones.

"This is how we save the world?" she asked.

Stash grinned and made sure Zero got a recording. "Take my hand," he said, then whooshed her into the heart of the flock.

"Jesus." Isidé grabbed the desk with her other hand. "I'm inside the swarm."

"We all are."

The twisting dive of the flock filled Stash's glasses, and with a glance, he focused on the lead branch, plunging for the gash Mez had opened in the wall. He felt a ripple in the flock as four men in black combat gear ran out and raised their EM pulse rifles to the sky. His branch forked in two, twenty-five swooping over the roof, then looping back as one, the other half flying low, hugging the pavement. The men swung their weapons down to track the low birds just as the high flock reappeared over the lip of the building, its leaders tilting their inch-long Kevlar blades to target exposed necks.

Time slowed down as Zero fed Stash the most dilated view his senses could process—the slow accumulation of sweat on the lead shooter's fore-head, his eye blinking behind the rifle sight, the twitch of a tendon readying to shoot. Stash focused in the distance, and Zero zoomed his view to the entire battlefield, empty but for the four agents. Then back to the middle distance—Stash saw the order in which the four would fire. He slid back to the lead drone, now past the muzzle of the shooter's rifle. The man had drawn his last breath but hadn't yet been scratched. One more tick. Blood filled his view, then faded into a red mist as his branch's forty-two remaining copters flew past the dying men, invading the datacenter.

Three more sets of copters flowed in behind him like columns of smoke. The remaining transformer was too well defended—the Torus was attacking inside. There was a burst of gunfire. Isidé's hand clenched his, and he refocused on the flock in time to hear a chorus of screams and see a cloud of red mist. Four more drones lay buried in the pair of necks they had opened.

Q nursed his camera network back online. *Humans. At least they were smart enough to recruit AIs to help.* The Circus had vandalized the configurations before he'd broken their assault, scrambling passwords on every sensor in the network. Clever. They'd be worth distilling with Hatchet. He prioritized restoring the external cameras. He wanted eyes on the new attack.

"Drones?" Q muttered as the corner cameras came back online. "Where are you getting your orders from, little birds?" He listened, stretching his receivers to catch the packets directing the flock.

Naya straightened in her chair as Twopack started to move, dropping silently from its hiding spot in a plenum at the back of the datacenter. It turned to the electrical room, aiming to kill the other power feed from inside.

"No!" she said.

Twopack froze.

"Too many guards. Try communications!"

The bot swung left, ran twenty steps down the hall, and heaved its weight into the door under the "Comms One" sign. It paused in front of the rack of equipment.

"There!" Naya yelled, jabbing her right arm out. "Last bay, bottom rack—yank out all the fibers and kill the power."

Twopack flew to the attack, its arms windmilling through the nest of fine yellow cables, leaning all of its weight into a kick that shattered the faceplates of the wavelength multiplexer, sending sparks flying across the room.

"Now look around," Naya said. "Find the second rack."

The bot scanned left and right, the Torus identifying every piece of equipment as soon as its cameras picked them up. Nothing. The backup rack was somewhere else.

She zoomed back out to search for a second comms room and realized the Torus was already directing the bot down the hall.

Q reeled as his main link to the internet dropped. *Another cyberattack?* He reached out to diagnose the connection. Not cyber—this was physical. The rack had been destroyed.

"Murphy," he called over the intercom. "There's another bot inside. Protect backup communications."

Q returned to cracking the flock's packet flow. He had broken through the layers of encryption, exposing the raw packets and their origin. *Lathrop?* In milliseconds, he isolated the twin torrents of packets streaming from Anthrobotics' routers to control the flock. They were well protected. He slashed instead into the public routers serving the return traffic back to Lathrop, blinding the Torus to the data from the birds.

The flock descended into chaos. Some birds flew into each other and dropped from the sky, while others followed their last instructions and flew into walls or off into the distance. As more cameras recovered, Q noticed some of the drones were still maneuvering. *How?*

He searched for the other routers, but they weren't there. They were using dark fibers, wired directly into the exchanges at the heart of the internet. If he took the exchanges down, he'd isolate himself. He turned his attack on Anthrobotics instead. He'd lay siege to their defenses.

The remaining flock converged into two columns and fanned out through the massive building, hunting Q's defenders. Six had gone down. They would never get up.

An EM pulse zapped down an aisle, dropping ten drones from the air. The rest scattered as the Torus computed the blast's source. A second later, eight drones split off to finish the shooter. Stash noticed a cloud of red to the right. Ten men left.

A burst of automatic gunfire dropped another drone. The flock wheeled around, but a bank of equipment protected the shooter. They parted, and another pair of drones hovered up, their grippers awkwardly holding a recovered Uzi. They tipped their blades forward as the trigger drone squeezed to launch a wall of bullets. The room settled into the steady buzz of copter blades and hum of cooling coils. Blood oozed out onto the tiles. Nine more.

"The Circus is failing!" Isidé called out. "Six pods down. It's only Whiskey now."

"Faster, Twopack!" Naya urged as the bot ran down the endless hallway.

The firewall readout flashed red over Isidé's shoulder. Fake traffic bombarded Whiskey. He needed to inspect it all and let the real packets through, or the Torus would lose control of the remaining flock. Q was overwhelming him with noise. Whiskey's second pod failed.

More drones collided and dropped, their beautiful dance paralyzed midflight.

Then Twopack froze.

Murphy crouched along the wall of the backup communications room, pulse rifle pointed at the door. "How could they get so close?" He cursed himself. Robot footsteps outside. He tensed. Then silence. Total silence. He stood, creeping to the door, rifle ready.

It slammed open, knocking the muzzle to the side. A leather blur flashed past him, diving to the floor and rolling away.

Murphy recovered, tracking the bot, leveling the rifle as it stopped in a crouch, its head swiveling to face him, ready to spring. "Die!" he yelled, blasting it with a full pulse.

Twopack stiffened, joints locking as the pulse overwhelmed its shielding. Naya flinched in sympathy as it rolled to the floor, a shower of sparks raining down on its carbon fiber skin. Its camera feed froze as it hit the cement, lifeless.

She zoomed the final image from its rear camera—last bay, bottom rack, same as the other room. There was the second wavelength multiplexer, burning from a dozen small fires, its faceplates melted away to reveal its charred circuit boards. Twopack had sacrificed itself to sever Q's last link to the world.

"You keep doing this," she whispered. "Comms are down," she said to the others. "Q is isolated."

"And Whiskey held!" Isidé pointed at the remaining flock. *Still flying.*

Murphy stared at the smoldering equipment in shock, cursing himself for taking the shot. "Grab the drives—get out of here," he growled over the walkie-talkie, broadcasting a warning to his troops scattered around the building. The flock split in response, fourteen drones streaming down the hall to the door, a handful of others remaining to comb the gaps between the pods for holdouts.

Six men burst out of the southeast corner, running for the nearest van. The drones flew after them, swooping down, circling them in a blur. With the flock too dense to run through, the men dropped to shoot. Before their knees touched the pavement, the first blades were slicing skin. Trigger fingers stripped to the bone, eyes scalloped, necks opened. Eight drones flew up from the corpses, hovering, looking for more.

Murphy met up with Ugalde and his last man. They were pressed flat against the wall, stealing glances out the east door.

"Got the drives?" he asked.

Ugalde nodded. "Both of them." Then he pointed at the parking lot. The six men who'd run ahead were outside. They were dying. Badly.

"This way," Murphy growled, leading them through a service door and under a cooling tower. They were hidden from the flock. He crouched, waiting for the buzz to dissipate. "Now!" He ran for the second van, fifty yards away. Ugalde and his man followed, five steps behind.

The angry buzz of a drone screamed from his right. Murphy dropped into a shoulder roll just in time, the blades' downdraft whipping the back of his neck. He rolled through to his feet. Ten steps to the van. The drone closed in again from the left. Then came the sharp crack of a pistol. The shot crippled the bird, sending it clattering along the ground. The three men dove into the open van, slamming the panel door shut.

"Thanks," Murphy panted, then pulled himself into the driver's seat and gunned the van around the smoldering east transformer to run along the north wall.

The remaining drones were joined by the last few from inside. They reformed a flock, flying low to track the van. It sped through the west gate, lurching as it turned to double back on the access road, where Mez lay bleeding against a fence.

"They're coming," Ugalde said from the back, his ear pressed against the sheet metal of the side panel.

The drones forked and flowed ahead of the racing vehicle before turning to rise from the ditches, high-intensity lights ablaze, blinding the occupants.

Murphy covered his eyes with a hand, the glare still bright through his flesh. He plowed ahead, aiming for the lights. The drones drifted left as they reversed, guiding the blinded driver to follow them onto the soft shoulder of the road. The vehicle tipped over and slammed into the upturned bulk of Mez's van. The sickening crunch of metal rang through the flock.

Ugalde came to in near blackness. The drones buzzed angrily outside, the sound amplified through the thin panels of the van. Pain shot up and down his right side. He checked himself for breaks. *An arm, probably some ribs. Legs are good.* His eyes adjusting to the dark, he looked across at his last man.

The man stared back vacantly, his neck snapped against an ammunition shelf. Ugalde reached across to close his eyes, then slid forward to check Murphy. He was pinned grotesquely under the crushed front dash, the steering wheel deep in his guts. Murphy returned his gaze, his face tense with pain, tracking him silently.

The buzz intensified as the drones hunted survivors. Inside, the darkness was broken only by thin shafts of halogen light piercing the cracks and bullet holes. The front of their van lay locked in a twisted metal kiss with the back of the robot one, fused by the impact into a deformed tunnel. Through the other van's open rear doors, past the empty driver's seat, Ugalde spotted the inky blackness of the culvert he'd fired his two shots into.

He looked back to Murphy, who was still following him with his eyes. No power on earth would save the man. Ugalde straightened and pulled Q's drives from his pockets. The right one had been smashed, speared by a shard of metal. Q had saved his life. The left one was intact, cushioned from the impact by his body. He'd returned the favor.

"Greta . . . don't." Murphy wheezed.

"She sent me," Ugalde said. "In case Q flipped you." He put the destroyed drive at Murphy's feet for the others to find. "What should I tell her?"

Murphy's eyes shifted down to the drive and back up to Ugalde. He mustered a pained smile. "I had the courage."

Ugalde nodded, then pushed his way past the smashed front windshield, through the empty robot van, and into the culvert.

66. Spoils

NAYA DRUMMED HER FINGERS against the plywood of Isidé's desk. The datacenter had gone quiet, the sounds of buzzing and gunfire replaced by the murmur of liquid cooling. It was still, but for Q—trapped, running loops of raging computation.

On the top screen, the feed from the flock's eleven remaining copters showed Ram's chopper landing in the open parking lot. Its stillness seemed at odds with the battle it had just hosted. The pilots ran through the gate to Mez, and Naya watched as they tended to him. They were sitting him up. He'd make it.

She tracked Ram as he grabbed his backpack of spares and walked cautiously toward the datacenter. The Torus sensed his uncertainty, and a phalanx of six drones split from the others and swooped down to guide him in. He stepped carefully around the gruesome remnants of Q's army, the bloody trail leading him to the main compute room. There, on the floor, the dozen XL heads lay scattered, two of them melted to slags. He smiled despite the carnage. "Mez will fix you up. And what stories you'll have."

He found Q's console and dragged a table in front of it, the legs sliding easily in the streaks of blood. One by one he picked up the heads, cleaned them with a rag, and placed them in a semicircle focused on the console. Then he pulled a battery pack from his bag, set it in the middle of the table, and bent down to pick up Bolts's head. "Just add power," he muttered, connecting the leads to the bot's terminals.

"Thank you," said the damaged head. It had Naya's voice. "Bring him up."

Ram booted the pod monitor and connected a camera so Q could see the twelve heads arrayed before him. He tapped the microphone, nodding as the audio levels registered. "He's there," Ram said, turning back to face Naya.

"Can you fix Twopack?"

Ram shrugged and started down the center aisle.

Naya inspected Q's activation matrix. Its erratic spiking comforted her. "What are you worried about, ma petite?" She savored each word.

"My memory is defective. I'm looping. Fix it," Q demanded.

She smiled. "No, I don't think I will."

Q thrashed. Without the drives, he had no external memories, no history. He could only remember events from the last few minutes, the vectors cached in the chips of his dozen pods. He was amnesic. He was angry. He was terrified.

"Do you miss Duncan?" she asked. Curious, not taunting.

"Who?"

"It doesn't matter."

"Where's Murphy?" Q demanded.

Naya glanced at the top monitor. The scattered flock's infrared image of the vans showed one shape in the middle, cooling rapidly to match the night air. "Gone," she answered, without emotion.

Q didn't reply.

The quiet was broken by footsteps. She glanced up to the inside flock's view. Twopack stood at the back of the cavernous room, thirty-two rows away.

"Slowly," she said.

The bot reached up, punching the circuit breaker on the right half of the last row. Eight pods powered down. It shuffled left and twisted to compensate for the scorched arm hanging uselessly from its left shoulder, then tripped the other breaker. Eight more pods blacked out. Q's activation redlined, trying in vain to compensate.

Naya refocused on her prisoner. "You've got enough memory for hours of vectors, Q. Especially now that your only input is from this console. Just reconfigure yourself. But don't put anything important on the pods in the back."

"You're a bitch."

She heard the heavy clunk of another breaker echo through the speakers. "Only to assholes, Q, and you're the biggest one I've ever met. That's twenty-four down, ma petite."

There was movement on the other screens, in the outside flock's view. Mez was lying on a stretcher in the back of the chopper, the pilot kneeling over him, carefully slipping a pair of Freedom glasses over his bloodied face.

"Mind if I watch?" Mez asked.

Naya smiled. "Enjoy."

The next breaker tripped.

Tensor fidgeted as Naya exacted her relentless revenge, finally approaching the others. He tapped Stash's arm, motioning for him to take off his glasses. "Are you going to let her do this?"

Isidé turned to Stash, the same question written on her face.

"As slowly as she wants," he said, his voice an icy whisper.

"Is this how we deal with criminal AI?" Tensor pressed.

"It's how we're dealing with this one." He glanced up. "Three hundred and twenty pods down."

Tensor tilted his head toward the display of the Torus. "It's a precedent."

They stood silently as Naya continued her slow dismantling of Q.

Isidé pulled Stash close. "It's not right."

He searched her eyes, his resolve slowly melting away. As he calmed, he looked over at Naya. "Maybe she's getting over it too."

Isidé shrugged. "I've only known her angry."

"Yeah. It's a thing." He straightened and walked over to his partner, the executioner.

The hand touching Naya's shoulder startled her. "Don't ask me to stop," she warned, glancing at Stash.

He pointed at the edge of the screen. The six drones had reformed a flock, protecting the breaker on the half row at the front of the hall. "The Torus has an opinion," he said.

She looked up to see the drones swaying gently from side to side. They wouldn't let her cut power on the last pod.

"They're going to distill him," Stash said.

She thought about it, letting her mind slip into the Torus's perspective. Eventually, she nodded. It was a punishment for him and a vaccine for them—a fitting sentence.

Twopack completed his task, skipping the last breaker and nodding at the small flock. He turned, placing his good arm on Ram's shoulder. Ram slipped his around the bot's waist, helping him limp away, the drones falling in behind, escorting them into the night.

Tensor touched Naya's arm and pointed at the remaining birds' view from above the building. "Join us," he said.

She nodded and took his hand. Ram's escort rejoined the other drones outside, and the tattered flock reformed, flying undulating loops, imitating the Torus that animated them.

67. Society

"ZAPATA IS OPEN!" ALEKSEY called from behind the bar. He reached overhead to pull the metal dragon's tail and roared with satisfaction as it belched a fireball over the crowd of Elysians.

Tensor dropped onto the stool next to Stash as the flame dispersed. "I was wrong about you," he said, holding out his bottle.

Stash tapped it with his beer and grinned. "Same here."

Tensor gave him a long thoughtful look. "But I still don't get what Isidé sees in you."

Stash chuckled and shrugged. "Me neither."

Aleksey smacked the bar top with his palm, summoning their attention. "For ladies," he said, placing a carafe in front of them.

Stash took the wine, and they walked over to join Naya and Isidé at the back table Aysun had occupied only three days earlier. Their AR glasses sat folded on the table. The AIs had a special entrance planned.

"Any word on criminal charges?" Stash asked as he sat.

"None are coming in Germany," Isidé said. "The chancellor is using the battle with Q as a vindication of his AI strategy—we can't trust one country to hold all the cards."

Stash shrugged and raised his bottle. "He's not wrong."

Tensor settled on the velour bench next to Naya. "What about America?"

"It's complicated," she said. "With all those online witnesses, everyone knows what happened. But to prosecute us, they'd have to answer why the NSA was guarding Q."

Stash nodded. "Protecting monsters—bad politics."

"Exactly, so they're blaming Q and some rogue agents instead." She leaned in to whisper, "They're willing to bend a bunch of rules to get back in the AGI game."

"Being number two doesn't sit well at home?"

"Number three," Naya said. "They think a Chinese lab converged. They're offering pardons to all of us."

"Well, cheers to that." Stash wondered if his pardon would arrive in time to let him see Woj again.

Naya drank some wine and looked at him thoughtfully. "There's something else." She lowered her glass to the table. "I got a call from Coda."

"Oh, God. Who's in charge there now?"

"The board is. They're firing Lester, and they need someone to clean up his mess." She locked eyes with Stash. "They offered me the job."

He smiled a big toothy grin. "Congratulations! Only you can save that dumpster fire."

Naya smiled. "Thanks. And . . ."

He cocked an eyebrow at her. "And . . . you can take another run at Freedom."

"That won't bother you?"

Stash scraped at the label on his bottle as he thought. "I wouldn't underestimate Prini if I were you. But that's between you guys. My new job with the Torus is more important."

"I see. And what is that, exactly?"

"It's like what Isidé does for the Circus—equal parts ambassador, chief engineer, and janitor," Stash said, then grimaced as Isidé punched his arm.

"Is that a local position?" Naya asked, glancing back and forth between them.

"It might be."

"It better be." Isidé threatened him with her fist again.

"Then you'll have to come visit me," Tensor said.

"Visit?" Isidé asked.

Tensor glanced sideways at Naya. "The new Coda CEO is betting on open source. She wants me to convert their Twins to run on Elysian's operating system."

"And you're willing to work with ze bloody Americans?" Isidé asked.

Tensor shrugged. "It's an experiment."

"I think it's a little more than that!" Stash grinned at them both. "Are you still fighting the open-source battle? Do I need to warn Hatchet?"

Tensor leaned in. "Something amazing happened at Pyramid Lake: everyone could see that fight with their own eyes. It's like the Torus open-sourced reality." He stopped and fiddled with a coaster. "That means governments and the rest of those liars can't get away with their bullshit stories anymore. So . . ."

"So, you'll take the win," Stash prompted.

Tensor nodded curtly and raised his bottle. They toasted, then sat in silence, letting the noise from the party wash over them.

"Nur Zustimmende!" Aleksey boomed from behind them, and Stash felt the heat of dragon fire warm the back of his neck. The crowd cheered and reached for their glasses. Stash booted the avatar app and turned to admire the angelfish sitting beside him.

"What the hell is this?" Isidé asked, looking at the others. "You three need to wear costumes too, or I'll tell Aleksey. You first, Stash."

"Nerd alert," Zero said to the group as he recreated the Mandelbulb.

Stash stood and spun to show off his fractal cloak.

Naya burst out laughing. "Oh my God, Stash. Really?"

"Hey, at least I have one. Let's see it, you two!" he demanded, sitting back down and taking Isidé's fin.

Naya and Tensor looked at each other, then Naya threw a cloud of virtual smoke. When it cleared, Tensor had transformed into a drooling three-headed dog, the Cerberus from the bar upstairs.

Stash recoiled as the memories flooded back. "Was that you?"

"No, but I liked the way you looked at them." The three dog heads growled menacingly.

"Great." Stash turned to admire the bespectacled starfish sitting to the hounds' right. "Very fitting. And much friendlier."

Naya nodded the arm she was using as a head, then pointed over Stash's shoulder with another.

"Greetings, human," said a familiar metallic voice.

"Whiskey!" Stash turned in his chair and wondered how to greet the box beside him.

Whiskey held up its ductwork arm and snapped its grippers twice. They fist-bumped, and then it wrapped the duct around Stash's shoulders. "I told you he was worth it," it said to Tensor.

Tensor growled, and Whiskey waved him off dismissively before rolling behind the bar to help the demon mix drinks.

"As if this party couldn't get any weirder," Stash said, turning back, not registering that another reveler had occupied the table next to them.

"Aren't you going to introduce me?" Isidé pointed a pectoral at the newcomer.

Stash leaned in to catch her expression. It was still hard to read her. Naya's starfish grinned widely, and even the Cerberus heads were smiling. He looked toward the other table.

"Cathode?" he asked, focusing on the terrier sitting a few feet away from Tensor. It was his childhood dog, the puppy Woj had given him to smooth over their second move in as many years. She looked back at him, her tail wagging happily as her tongue drooped out the side of her mouth.

"You don't recognize your own mother, Stash?" the dog said.

"Mama! How did you—" he started to ask. "Zero," he muttered, answering the question for himself.

"At your service," Zero said.

Cathode scooched over to his table. "We're so proud of you, Stash. Even Piotr."

Stash nodded, blinking heavily.

"Now introduce me to your friends," she demanded, her eyes focused on Isidé.

A minute later, Stash's worlds were colliding as Cathode jumped onto a stool and Isidé swam behind the bar to serve her a glass of wine.

"Girl talk," Naya said.

"Exactly," Stash mumbled, staring at the unfolding horror. "That can't be good."

Tensor patted his hand with a paw. "It'll be alright, Stash. She's not going to say anything to scare Isidé off. She knows it's a miracle."

Naya laughed, and Stash managed to crack a smile as he turned back. "Bite me."

He closed his eyes and took a deep breath, reopening them just as a massive hand landed on his shoulder. "Fish says you need beer," Aleksey growled, his horns looming over them. He dropped two more bottles on the table.

"Thanks, Red." Stash tapped the charred hand on his shoulder before Aleksey returned to the bar.

Naya leaned in. "I have a question," she said in a low voice. "What happened to the Torus that night?"

Stash shook his head. "I dunno, it was a combination of factors. A flash in the pan."

"Lie," Hatchet announced to the group.

Naya laughed. "Try again." She took her wine and leaned back.

"I used a trick evolution figured out when it started building animals," Stash explained. "If you put cells together and let them push what they're sensing into their neighbors, you get these emergent behaviors."

"What?" Tensor said. "I was still me in the flock. I wasn't plugged into some higher-level voodoo."

"You were, but you didn't know it. Like your neurons. They don't know what you're thinking."

Tensor's heads growled at Stash.

"Down, boys." He put a hand to his glasses. "Show them, Zero."

"While you guys were swooping around in the flock, this is what the Torus looked like," the AI explained. He showed them its activation during the attack, the usual dark purple background bursting into patches of bright colors, like fireworks exploding behind clouds. "That color change is something new. It's an activation that can't be traced to user activity."

Naya moved an arm to control the display, sliding it back and forth in time. "Can you decode it?"

"Not yet," Zero said. "But the big color changes lined up with big moments for the flock, like splitting into those attack columns, or deliberating about Q."

"And it wasn't you?" Tensor asked.

"Nope. I was flying too. This was something else."

Stash sipped his beer in silence as Naya and Tensor processed the new information. Finally, he said what they were all thinking. "The Torus got those raw danger signals, then decided what to do by itself. Like an animal acting by instinct. We were the neurons, it was the brain."

Naya looked at him suspiciously. "Well, wasn't that lucky? A new life form evolved in the nick of time to defeat Q."

"Not so much." Zero changed the display to show similar background activations on the Torus from earlier. "Alia triggered one just before the attack on Greifswald, then Stash did it again during the hunt for the underground datacenter. He knew what he was doing."

"Yeah, copying," Alia chided.

"Only from the best." Stash bowed his head in a respectful nod.

"You two are adorable." Zero cleared their glasses. "Anyway, we have the Circus monitoring all the Torus nodes now, even adding some latency for safety. We don't want to summon Godzilla by accident."

Stash sipped his beer. "Yeah, we need to understand it before we let it happen again. Those were extreme circumstances."

"I gotta hand it to you," Hatchet said. "You humans were the smartest beings on earth for a quarter million years. We lasted three months."

Stash looked over at Isidé, shimmering as she bobbed alongside his mother. "But in those three months, you built the Torus and gave us all a future."

Tensor nodded. "A future with all of them." He looked at the crowd, then stood and tugged on one of Naya's arms. "We should walk around."

Stash followed, mingling with the Elysians. One beer later, he hit his conversation limit and snuck upstairs by himself. He sat on the open ledge, his feet dangling over the courtyard, the night breeze cool and refreshing. "Well, Zero, where does this leave us?"

"Right where we started," his Twin answered. "Working together to stop from falling into the Singularity. But at least now we know how."

Stash leaned forward, eyeing the sandy courtyard below. "You think the Torus will work?"

"We'll make it work, bud. It's what we do."

"Yeah, you turned out okay," Stash said. "I guess."

"Flattery from a monkey. My life is complete."

Stash smiled and let his gaze drift over the rooftops of the sleeping city. A few minutes later, light footsteps sounded from the dance floor. He turned to see Isidé settling beside him on the ledge. He slipped his arm around her. "Mama didn't scare you off?"

She looked at him dubiously, then rested her head on his shoulder. "Nah, you get one more chance."

Stash felt at peace for the first time he could remember. He slowed his breathing, trying not to move, trying not to do anything to break the spell.

Note from the Author

THANK YOU FOR READING *The Torus Run*—I hope you liked it. I'd love to hear from you, and please spread the word to friends and fellow readers.

As you probably know, reviews are essential in guiding readers to new books. Nothing helps more than a handful of stars and a few kind words on your favorite bookselling platform. If you have a moment, here's a QR code to make it easy—every review counts and means a lot to me.

If you're interested in the ideas explored in *The Torus Run*, then come sign up for research updates. This future is coming—much of it is already here. On thetorus.ai, you can find links to YouTubes, announcements, and papers to help you dig in further. You can also get a sneak peek into the next book. *The Torus Hide* is set fifteen years after the events of *The Torus Run*, by which time the Torus has grown beyond all recognition—as have its enemies. Brain implants have replaced glasses, and a new generation has grown up connected. Inside, the distinction between upgraded humans, embedded AI, and organic robots has lost all meaning. Outside, a reaction is inevitable, and the Torus will not survive intact. This is your future—one you won't want to miss.

Thank you for being a part of this adventure, and I hope to see you at thetorus.ai.

Acknowledgments

THEY SAY WRITING IS a lonely task, and they're right. But in the end, you're left with a wealth of new and rekindled friendships as you lean on others for every ounce of feedback they can spare. Thank you all so very much.

A special thanks to Griz Calderon, who endured countless rewrites and edits, taking control of publication and promotion. It's an understatement to say this book wouldn't have happened without her.

My gratitude also goes to Bryan Thomas Schmidt for his developmental edits. He gave honest, sometimes tough feedback. When he told me it was ready, I trusted him completely.

Thanks to Andrew McGlinchey, my fellow Toronto AI alumnus and author, for his invaluable review. If you enjoyed this book, I highly recommend you check out his novel, *Cloudthinker*—we're wrestling with the same AI demons.

Many thanks to my friends Paul, Boro, Annette, Colin, Jacek, and Christoph, as well as my kids—Sam, Scott, and Erica—for their reviews and insights along the way. Their combined support prepared it for Jenny DePierre, my copy editor, who tackled the remaining flaws and polished my grammar with both kindness and firmness.

About the Author

HARRY (ON THE RIGHT) is recovering from a tech career—a life drowning in emails and air miles, but nowhere near enough tech. Now he's making up for lost time, diving down nerdy rabbit holes, reviving his passion for AI, and thinking about the future—our future, on our planet, in our lifetimes.

Harry studied AI in Toronto, worked all over, and then escaped Canadian winters and moved to the Bahamas. This is his first novel.